D0240511

The
SWEETNESS
of
WATER

The
SWEETNESS
of
WATER

NATHAN
HARRIS

TINDER
PRESS

Copyright © 2021 Nathan Harris

The right of Nathan Harris to be identified as the Author of
the Work has been asserted by him in accordance with the
Copyright, Designs and Patents Act 1988.

First published by Little, Brown, USA

First published in Great Britain in 2021 by Tinder Press
An imprint of HEADLINE PUBLISHING GROUP

1

Apart from any use permitted under UK copyright law, this publication may
only be reproduced, stored, or transmitted, in any form, or by any means,
with prior permission in writing of the publishers or, in the case
of reprographic production, in accordance with the terms of licences
issued by the Copyright Licensing Agency.

All characters in this publication are fictitious
and any resemblance to real persons, living or dead,
is purely coincidental.

Cataloguing in Publication Data is available from the British Library

Hardback ISBN 978 1 4722 7437 3
Trade paperback ISBN 978 1 4722 7438 0

Offset in 10.89/15.85 pt RequiemText HTF by Jouve (UK), Milton Keynes

Printed and bound in Great Britain by Clays Ltd, Elcograf S.p.A.

Headline's policy is to use papers that are natural, renewable and recyclable
products and made from wood grown in well-managed forests and other
controlled sources. The logging and manufacturing processes are expected
to conform to the environmental regulations of the country of origin.

HEADLINE PUBLISHING GROUP
An Hachette UK Company
Carmelite House
50 Victoria Embankment
London EC4Y 0DZ

www.tinderpress.co.uk
www.headline.co.uk
www.hachette.co.uk

CHAPTER 1

An entire day had passed since George Walker had spoken to his wife. He'd taken to the woods that very morning, tracking an animal that had eluded him since his childhood, and now night was falling. He'd seen the animal in his mind's eye upon waking, and tracking it carried a sense of adventure so satisfying that all day he could not bear the thought of returning home. This had been the first of such excursions all spring, and tramping through splintered pine needles and mushrooms swollen from the morning rain, he'd come upon a patch of land he'd yet to explore in full. The animal, he was sure, was always one step away from falling into his line of sight.

The land his father had passed down to him was over two hundred acres. The large red oaks and walnut trees that surrounded his home could dim the sun into nothing more than a soft flicker in the sky passing between their branches. Many of them as familiar as signposts, long studied over many years from childhood on.

The brush George encountered was waist-high and coated with burrs that clung to his trousers. He'd developed a hitch over the last few years, had pinned it on a misplaced step as he descended from his cabin to the forest floor, but he knew this was a lie: it had appeared with the persistence and steady progress of old age itself— as natural as the lines on his face, the white in his hair. It slowed him, and by the time he caught his breath and took a moment to assess his surroundings, he realized that silence had overtaken the woods. The sun, above his head only moments before, had faded into nothingness over the far corner of the valley, nearly out of sight.

"I'll be."

He had no idea where he was. His hip ached as though something was nestled there and attempting to escape. Soon the need for water overtook him, the roof of his mouth so dry his tongue clung to it. He took a seat on a small log and waited for total darkness. If the clouds gave out, the stars would appear, which was all he needed to map his way back home. His worst miscalculation would still guide him to Old Ox, and although he loathed the idea of seeing any of those sorry desperate sorts in town, at the very least one of them would offer a horse to return him to his cabin.

For a moment the thought of his wife came to him. By now he was typically arriving home, the candle Isabelle had left on the windowsill guiding his final few steps. She would often forgive these absences of his only after a long, silent hug, the black ink from the trees leaving faint handprints on her dress, irritating her all over again.

The log beneath him yawned and George's rear end sank into the waterlogged mess. Only as he moved to stand, to pat himself dry, did he see them sitting before him. Two Negroes, similar in dress: white cotton shirts unbuttoned, britches as ragged as if they'd fitted their legs into intertwined gunnysacks. They stood stock-still, and if the blanket before them had not swayed in the wind like some flag to signal their presence, they might have disappeared in the foreground entirely.

The closer one spoke up.

"We got lost, sir. Don't mind us. We'll be moving on."

They came into clearer focus, and it was not the words that struck George, but that the young man was precisely the age of his Caleb. That he and his companion were trespassing was beside the point entirely. In the nervous chatter of his voice, the eyes that darted like those of an animal hiding from prey, the young man gained George's sympathy, perhaps the only morsel of it left in an otherwise broken heart.

"Where is it you two come from?"

"We're Mr. Morton's. Well, was."

Ted Morton was a dimwit, a man who, if offered a fiddle, would be as liable to smash it against his own head to hear the noise as put a bow to its strings. His parcel of land bordered George's, and when an issue arose—a runaway most often—the ensuing spectacle, rife with armed overseers and large-snouted dogs, lanterns of such illumination that they kept the entire household awake, was so unpleasant that George often deferred all communications with the family to Isabelle just to avoid the ordeal. But to find Morton's former property on his land now carried with it a welcome irony: Emancipation had made the buffoon helpless to their wanderings, and for all his great shows of might, these two men were now free to be as lost as George was in this very instance.

"Our apologies," said the man in front.

They began to bundle up their blanket, collecting a small knife, a bit of stripped beef, pieces of bread, but stopped once George started in again. His eyes wandered the ground in front of him, as if searching for something lost.

"I've been following a beast of some size," he said. "Black in color, known to stand on two feet but usually found on four. It's been years since I saw the creature with my own two eyes, but I often wake to its image, as if it's trying to alert me to its presence nearby. Sometimes, on my porch, I'll be dozing off, and the memory of it is so strong, so clear, that it travels through my head like an echo, bounding through my dreams. As far as tracking it, I'm afraid to say it's gotten the upper hand."

The two men looked at one another, then back at George.

"That's...well, that's mighty curious," the smaller one said.

In the last remnants of light, George could make out the taller one, a man whose eyes were so placid and displayed so little emotion that he seemed simple. His lower jaw was cracked open wide, revealing a hanging slab of teeth. It was the other one, the smaller one, who continued to do the talking.

George asked them their names.

"This here is my brother, Landry. I'm Prentiss."

"*Prentiss.* Did Ted come up with that?"

Prentiss looked at Landry, as if he might have a better idea.

"I don't know, sir. I was born with that name. It was either him or the missus."

"I imagine it was Ted. I'm George Walker. You wouldn't happen to have some water, would you?"

Prentiss handed over a canteen, and George understood he was expected to ask after them, investigate why they were here on his land, but the issue took up such a small space in his thinking that it felt like a waste of what energy he had left. The movements of other men interested him so little that the indifference was his chief reason for living so far from society. As was so often the case, his mind was elsewhere.

"I get the sense you've been out here some time. You wouldn't— you wouldn't have happened to have seen that animal I spoke of?"

Prentiss studied George for a moment, until George realized the young man's gaze was trained past him, somewhere off in the distance.

"Can't say I have. Mr. Morton had me on some of his hunting trips, I seen all sorts of things, but nothing like you described. Mostly fowl. Those dogs come back with the birds still quivering in their mouths, and he'd have me string 'em up to the others, and carry 'em home on my back. I had so many you couldn't see me through the feathers. Other boys would be jealous I got to go off for the day, but they didn't know the first thing about it. I'd rather be in the field than have that load on my back."

"That's something," George said, considering the image. "That's really something."

Landry pulled apart a chunk of meat and handed it to Prentiss before taking one for himself.

"Don't be rude, now," Prentiss said.

Landry looked over to George and motioned to the meat, but George declined with a shake of his head.

They sat in silence, and George found their aversion to speaking welcome. Other than his wife, they seemed like the only individuals he'd come upon in some time who would rather leave a moment naked than tar it with wasted words.

"This is your land, then," Prentiss finally said.

"My father's land, now mine, one day it was to be my son's…" The words fell away into the night and he began again on a different course. "Now it's got me turned around and I don't even know which way is what, and these damned clouds in the sky."

He sensed the woods themselves taunting him and went to stand as if in protest, only for the pain in his hip to coil itself into a tighter knot; with a yelp he fell back onto the log.

Prentiss stood and walked over to him, concern in his eyes.

"What'd you go and do to yourself? All that yelling and carrying on."

"If you knew what hell this day has been you might yell yourself."

Prentiss was near him now, so close George could smell the sweat on his shirt. Why was he so still? So suddenly unnerving?

"If you wouldn't mind at least being quiet for me, Mr. Walker," he said. "Please."

George recalled the knife that had been beside the half-wit with such urgency it nearly materialized in the darkness; and he realized then that beyond the confines of a household, lost in the woods, he was simply one man in the presence of two, and that he had been a fool to assume his own safety.

"What is this about? My wife will be calling for help any moment, you do know that, don't you?"

But the two men's frozen, desperate gazes were once again not on him, but beyond him. A whipping sound broke out at George's side, and he turned to find a rope and the counterweight of a large rock beside it: the makings of a fine-tuned snare holding the leg of a jackrabbit writhing a few feet along the way. Landry rose up, faster than George might have thought possible, and gave his attention over to the rabbit. Prentiss took a step back and waved off the moment.

"I didn't mean to worry you," he said. "We just. We ain't had something land in that trap yet... We ain't had a proper meal in some time, is all."

"I see," George said, collecting himself. "Then you've been out here longer than I first thought."

Prentiss explained then that they had departed from Mr. Morton's a week ago; had taken what little they could carry on their backs—a sickle left in the fields, a bit of food, the bedrolls from their pallets; and had not made it any farther than where they stood now.

"He said we could take a few things from the cabins," Prentiss said of Morton's minor generosity. "We ain't steal a thing."

"No one said anything about stealing. Not that I would care, he has more than a simpleton like himself could ever make use of. I just wonder why, really. You could go anywhere."

"We plan to. It's just nice."

"What's that?"

Prentis looked at George as if the answer was right before him.

"To be left alone for a time."

Landry, ignoring them, had chopped the loose bits of an oak tree limb into feed for a fire.

"Ain't that why you're out here yourself, Mr. Walker?"

George was shivering now. He began to speak of the animal, how it had led him here, but the sound of Landry's chopping interrupted his train of thought, and he found himself, as had been the case since the preceding day, reflecting on his son. When the boy was younger, they had walked these very woods together, chopping wood and making a play of such things as if a hearth, permanently aflame, was not awaiting them at home. With that memory the others streamed forth, the small moments that had bonded the two—putting him to bed; praying with him at the table, empty gestures with winks passed from one to the other like whispered secrets; wishing him off to the front with a handshake that should have been so much more—until they dissolved in the face of the boy's best friend, August, having come to visit him that very morning with news of Caleb's death.

They'd met in George's small study. August looked very much like his father, the same blond hair, the boyish features and the air of vague regality rooted in little but family folklore. August and Caleb had left Old Ox in their clean butternut grays and polished boots, and George expected his son to return a muddied, threadbare savage; foresaw himself and Isabelle as the dutiful parents who would nurse him back to normalcy. In light of this, something felt indecent about August's evening wear: the frocked shirt, the pressed waistcoat with the gold timepiece hanging freely. It appeared as if he'd already discarded his time at war, and this meant Caleb, too, had become part of the past, long before George had even known his son was gone from him forever.

While August sat across from George's desk, George himself could only bear to stand at the window. August informed him that he'd been injured, a had tumble on patrol that had led to his discharge only a week earlier, the first day of March. He looked perfectly healthy to George, who figured the boy's father had paid to see him to safety as the war in its last throes grew more dangerous. But his suspicions weighed nothing against what it was that had brought them to this moment. To this room. And so August began to speak, and even with his first utterance, George grasped the hollowness of the boy's words, the theatrics of his delivery; could picture him in his runabout, coming to his property, going over each sentence, each syllable, for the greatest possible effect.

He told George that Caleb had served honorably and had welcomed death with honor and courage; that God had willed him a peaceful passing. Caleb had been going off with this boy since they were both so young that neither reached George's midsection. He recalled a time they'd run into the woods to play, only to return with Caleb so mortified, August so filled with glee, that George took the contrast as the result of some competition, an occasion that might lend itself to a moral lesson. *Take your losses like a man, now,* George had said. But later, when Caleb would not sit for dinner, winced even in consideration of doing so, George pulled the boy's trousers down.

Slash marks, some still flush with blood, the others bruised to a deep purple, covered his backside. He told George of the game August had hatched, *Master and the Slave,* and that they had only been assuming their proper roles for the afternoon. The pain was not from the marks, Caleb went on, but from the fact that he could not conceal them and that George might tell August's father. He had to swear to the boy that he would keep it secret.

Standing in his study, George sighed and made it clear to August that he knew he was lying. His son could lay claim to many traits, but bravery was not one of them. This single comment was all it took for the varnish of August's act to peel away; he stumbled over his words, crossed his legs, checked his timepiece, desperate for an exit that George would not provide.

No, no. His son had died. And he deserved to know the truth of what had happened.

George had not seen Landry start the fire before him, but light from the flame overtook their corner of the forest and cast the bigger man in relief; he retrieved the skinned rabbit and spitted the bloody mess on the end of a shaved branch for roasting. The clouds had parted and the sky was full of stars so clear, so magnificent, it was as if they'd been arranged just for the three of them.

"I should be heading home," George said. "My wife will be worried. If you could give me some assistance…I'd make it worth your while."

Prentiss was already standing to help.

"I mean, you two could stay here, if you wished to. For a time."

"Let's not worry about that right yet," Prentiss said.

"And if there is something else I could assist you with, perhaps."

Ignoring George, Prentiss put a hand beneath his arm and lifted him in one swoop, before the pain could set in.

"Just like that," Prentiss said. "Slow-like."

They walked as one through the trees with Landry trailing them. Though George needed the stars for guidance, it was all he could do to keep his sight straight ahead to stop himself from falling over, from giving in to the pain. He placed his head in the nook where Prentiss's chest met his shoulder and allowed the man to balance him.

After some time had passed, he asked if Prentiss knew where they were.

"If this is your land as you say it is, then I've seen your home," Prentiss said. "It's a beautiful place, isn't it? Not far from here. Not far at all."

George realized as they reached the clearing how absolutely exhausted he was. At once, the entire night, which had been suspended in time, unspooled itself before him, and reality presented itself in the form of his log cabin, standing before him and the black outline of what could only be Isabelle carved in shadow against the front window.

"Can you make it?" Prentiss asked. "Best you go it alone from here."

"Might we wait a few moments longer?" George asked.

"You need to rest, Mr. Walker," Prentiss pleaded. "There's nothing for you out here."

"True, but." How unlike him. It must have been the dehydration. Yes, he was disoriented, a bit confused, and the tears were merely a symptom of his predicament. It was only a few of them at that. "I'm not myself. Excuse me."

Prentiss held him. He did not let go.

"I don't—I haven't told her, is all," George said. "I could not bear it."

"Told her what, now?"

And George thought of the image August had left him with that morning of his boy abandoning the trenches he'd helped dig, so gripped with fear as to soil himself, to cower and run toward the Union line as though they might pity his screams of terror, might see him through the glut of smoke and grant his surrender and not shoot him down with the rest. It occurred to him that Caleb might have inherited some flawed trait from his father. For who was the bigger coward, the boy for dying without courage, or George for not being able to tell the boy's own mother that she would never see her son again?

"Nothing," George said. "I've been alone for such long periods, sometimes I speak to myself."

Prentiss nodded, as if some reasoning might be found in his words.

"That animal you spoke of. Mr. Morton taught me some tricks through the years. Tomorrow, perhaps, I can help you track it."

There was pity in his words, and George, sensing the irony of a man living with so little offering him charity, straightened himself up and harnessed what little energy he still possessed to regain his composure.

"That won't be necessary."

He looked Prentiss over once, considering that this might be the last time they ever laid eyes on each other.

"I do appreciate your assistance, Prentiss. You're a good man. Good night, now."

"G'night, Mr. Walker."

George hobbled to the front steps, the cold already slipping away from his bones before the front door had opened and the heat of the fire found him. For the slightest moment, before going inside, he peered back at the forest, silent and void of life in the darkness. Like there was nothing there at all.

CHAPTER 2

George's love of cooking was just one of his many eccentricities. Isabelle had tried early in the marriage to take the role of house cook, but her husband's opinions on the preparation of a ham hock were no different from his thoughts on the hunting of a mushroom, the building of a tree swing: refined, specific, and executed with concision time and time again. Sitting at the table for breakfast, she would watch his routines with a mix of fascination and delight. These were habits he had perfected over time as a bachelor—the cracking of an egg was a one-handed affair, a smooth motion of the thumb, a rather feminine swoop that broke the shell in two; the buttering of a hot pan involved a quarter-inch slab, greased in semicircular motions until it hissed across the surface and disappeared.

He was more satisfied during the cooking than the eating, the latter of which seemed merely a slog to get through. They spoke few words at the table. Yet this morning was different. He'd somehow risen before her, an accomplishment in and of itself, considering how late he'd been out. And when she came downstairs, she found him at the table, staring at a spot on the wall, like the splintered wood might get up and carry on with its day.

"How about some breakfast?" she asked.

His face was expressionless. He'd never been handsome, for the balancing involved in the physiognomy of beauty had escaped him.

His nose was large, his eyes small, and his hair fell in a ring like a well-placed laurel wreath; his belly had the taut rotundity of a pregnant woman and was always safely stowed away in the midsection between his suspenders.

"I could go for some hotcakes," she said.

He finally made notice of her.

"If it's not a bother, sure."

Standing in front of the stove, preparing the batter, she felt she'd forgotten the procedure altogether. She created it from memory, not from her own cooking, of course, but from watching her husband over almost a quarter century now. The cabin was modest—two stories—and stairs cut across the center of the home. From the kitchen, she could make out George sitting in the dining room, but whenever he shifted he disappeared behind the stairwell, only to reappear again.

"Perhaps a bigger stack than usual?" she called over. "You must have built up quite an appetite last night."

This would be her only attempt to draw forth an explanation. It wasn't that he did not tolerate questioning (he was rather indifferent), but that greater investigation rarely led to greater discovery. She had learned to save her words.

"Did you find it?" she asked in conclusion. "The creature. I imagine you were after it again."

"It escaped me," he said. "Very unfortunate."

The cakes sizzled—bubbles opening and closing again like a fish struggling for air above the water's surface. George would turn them now. For the sake of experiment, she let them be.

She brought two plates to the table, returned moments later with two cups of coffee. There was a rhythm to their eating. One would take a bite, and then the other, and it was in these slight recognitions—no different from the way they exchanged deep breaths while falling asleep—that the brushstrokes of their marriage coalesced day after day, night after night, the resulting portrait rewarding but infuriatingly difficult to interpret.

When George had returned home the night before, his face was so flush, his shivering so severe, she did not know whether to wash him down with a rag or slip him under the covers. Under the pain of his hip, he wavered with every step, agonizing his way up the stairs and refusing assistance. He could barely get a sentence out, let alone an explanation for his absence, and he fell asleep so quickly she wondered if he'd already been in a dream state, his body leading him back to where he'd belonged the entire night. She realized that other than the mention of passing interest in tracking a beast of some mystery—the same one he'd sought with his father years ago, an adventure they'd shared in, the same beast she'd never seen with her own two eyes—the man was intent on keeping the secrets of his nights to himself. Which would have been more irritating had she not had a secret of her own.

Not that she wished to. She could scarcely recall keeping anything from George, and the burden of her silence was a weight so heavy it sometimes felt difficult to breathe.

"How was the social?" George asked, his eyes never leaving his plate.

"As tedious as they've all been of late. Katrina left after tea and I joined her. They talk only of who's returned, or rumors of who might return, and I simply can't bear it. They treat their boys being paroled with the self-satisfaction of a victory in hearts. Which was why I stopped playing that game completely. Their winning is fine and all, but it's the possibility that I might lose…"

"One must lose with grace, Isabelle," George said between bites.

"Not in this instance."

On this, his eyebrows rose. "I don't see hearts differently from any other competition."

"Perhaps I'm not speaking of hearts."

He shrugged the comment away as if he hadn't understood a word she'd uttered. Sensing that he was lost in his own mind, she turned to the window, took in the lane leading to the main road toward town. She had no green thumb, but that hadn't stopped her from planting the squat and unpretty shrubs that paved the trail. To the side of it stood the old barn, still housing the farming tools that George's father had stored away which George himself had little interest in. And by its rear, masked from the public eye, stretched the clothesline, naked in this instant, a simple white etching outlined in the morning dew. It was this very place her secret had been born, and just the thought of it brought color to her cheeks.

She dropped her fork onto her plate.

"I don't like this, George," she said. "I don't. How do I say this...I don't believe we've been honest with one another. For you to disappear at odd hours as you have. To let me burn the hotcakes and say nothing."

He looked up from his food, placing his own fork onto his plate.

"Well. It goes without saying you turned them too late."

She shook her head in defiance.

"It's a matter of taste, which is *entirely* beside the point. Whether you wish to tell me why you've been off late at night, I can't go on any longer without sharing the thoughts that fill my mind."

He was about to speak, but she cleared her throat and went on with a declaration that came out so quietly it was nearly a whisper.

"I put our clothes on the line the morning after the rainfall, and that very same night, a man tried to steal your socks."

"Did you say my *socks?*"

"I did. The gray ones I knit for you."

Finally, she had her husband's full attention: "Who would do such a thing?"

She explained some of it then. Going out to fetch the clothes before sundown; the feeling of being in the company of someone else; thinking it was George, smelling him when she was really smelling only the scent of his clothes.

"I nearly screamed, but when I saw him, his fear so far outweighed my own, I felt something else. Sympathy, I suppose."

"And this was yesterday?"

"There were two occasions," she said, and now it was Isabelle staring at her plate, unable to meet George's gaze. "I should have told you right away. The man had been hiding behind the barn. When he stepped forward, to flee, our eyes met. He was tall. A Negro—"

She looked up then, and George was returning her glance with nothing but a look of mild curiosity. Behind his unruffled exterior was a man who had always appreciated the odd bit of gossip, the scandalous and bizarre, and she felt almost dismayed that he wasn't more caught up in her story.

"—And he seemed utterly lost. Not only in the physical sense. It's not something one can describe, exactly. I could tell he wished to be there, in my presence, far less than I might wish to have him, and as quickly as he was there, he was gone."

There were emotions she was withholding. Chiefly, the pure rush of the man's presence upon that first encounter. She could nearly count the number of times that the chance of excitement had entered her life in adulthood, and this was surely the most urgent of them. In that moment she had felt nothing but fear, yet it came upon her like an unexpected gift rather than a threat. The night it first occurred, she thought about it in bed beside George, and it was still on her mind come morning. The image of the man: his lower jaw unhinged like the bottom drawer of a dresser left open, the awkward hunch of his broad-framed shoulders.

She told herself he might be dangerous, that her preoccupation with his possible return was only reasonable considering the prospect of what he might do in the future. So when George was napping on the back porch, or off in the woods, there was nothing odd about the attention she paid to the clothesline. Yet the absence of the trespasser's shadow at night was disappointing instead of comforting. Which only led her to keep watch about the property more closely, awaiting his reappearance as if the mystery surrounding him might reveal some hidden part of her, too. If only he would come back to divulge it.

His return two days later, as if her desire had summoned him, was a shock, something she thought would only ever take place in the workings of her imagination. She saw him before he saw her, as he was lost in his own shadow, his movements so deliberate they seemed like those of a toddler. She observed him from the safety of the house, knowing she could call George any moment from upstairs in his study, and he could come down to deal with the matter. But soon she was nearing the back door, and with the turn of the knob she was on the back porch, watching as the man once again inspected the clothes on the line.

There was little that frightened her. Once, as a child, her brother, Silas, had attempted to scare her with ghost stories, the moonlight drifting into their bedroom, the tendrils of its soft glow cutting through the darkness. These were the stories their father had told him not to share with her, meant only for the men in the family, to be passed on to Silas's own boys in the future. By the midpoint of his tale of gore and death she had reacted so coolly, with such piercing skepticism couched in her silence, that Silas had stuttered and quit the story outright. He was not the last boy to test her courage, and she would not be cowed by this man by the barn who had somehow managed to unnerve her once before.

She held her dress up from the reeds of oat grass and made her way over to him so quickly that he had little time to react. The first thing she could make out, standing there next to him, were the blackened tips of his fingernails lodged with dirt. He reached forward to the clothesline and took one of George's socks, then the other, and turned to face her. Isabelle did not know what to say. He did not run. Did not even move. His eyes expressed little and he clenched the socks as if they were the one possession he owned, already his to keep forever.

"May I ask what you're doing?"

He said nothing.

"Where do you come from?"

There was something frustrating about the condition of his mouth, perpetually open but vacant of any words.

"Say something," she pleaded. "You must."

But if the reason for his first appearance was unclear, his current errand was so obvious it needed no explanation. His clothes were still wet from the downpour the night before, his leather shoes so dark with moisture and so shabby they looked like they'd been put through a kiln and had their charred remains refashioned into the shambles they were now. Surely there was nothing more enticing for a man in such condition than a dry pair of socks.

She let the hem of her dress fall to the grass.

"I see. You must have been caught in the storm."

The simplicity of the fact fell upon her with a wave of embarrassment and now she wondered how she had happened into a position so undignified as to be alone in this man's presence. She could recall a time when her life had the stitching of a well-bound corset—her husband and her son the interwoven laces that held together the ribs of an active social life, the relationships she had cultivated since marrying her husband and moving to Old Ox. Yet in the past year, since Caleb joined the war, it had all come undone, and she felt naked before this stranger, disappointed not by his silence, but by the idiotic expectations she had assigned to him.

"Please," she said. "Just go on your way. You may take them. I don't mind."

He blinked once, peered at the socks, and proceeded to put them back on the line where he'd found them, as if, upon further scrutiny, they had not met his standards.

"Do you not hear me?" she said. "I said to take them."

He stood still, looking at the job he'd done with some satisfaction, and casually turned to walk toward the woods without even glancing in her direction.

"Now where are you going?" she said to his back, voice rising. "It may rain again. Come back, now. You will catch something. Why don't you listen?"

He lumbered on, his shoulders swaying with each step until he had slipped back into the darkness, lost to the trees. Unheard and unseen, Isabelle lingered for a few minutes, stirred only by the wind that crept under her dress. The clothesline bobbed at her side. She was still choking back shame when she returned to the cabin.

Now, at breakfast beside George, the only thing she shared of the entire exchange was the man's actions, his silence, and his sudden departure. "I shooed him off," she said in summary, collecting the plates on the table. "He was gone in an instant. I can't say he won't return. I didn't want to worry you, but I thought it best to share." She hurried to the kitchen, wanting him to say something, anything, that might allow her to move on from the memory.

"I believe I've met the man," George said, wiping his mouth with a napkin. "You say he didn't speak."

"Not a word."

"Then yes. And from what I gather he's perfectly harmless. You need not worry about him."

"Well. Then I won't."

There were questions. There always were questions. But she did not care if George had actually met the man, or how, for his nonchalance acted as an immediate balm. How easily he left the past behind, made light of the worries that plagued her. If ever he lacked warmth—which he often did—his unflagging ability to bring her back to port when she strayed into choppy waters was an asset that made up for it many times over. No one was more reliable, and if that was not the ultimate act of compassion, she did not know what was.

"I'm glad I brought it up," she said, "just so I can let it go now."

Her husband looked unchanged, though, as if he'd taken on her guilt. It was in the stoop of his shoulders, the hollowness of his cheeks. Only then, in that very second, did she see the pain he carried. When he turned to speak to her, it was with a gaze so haunted, so debilitating, it might have paralyzed a lesser man.

"There is something I need to bring up with you, too. And I want to apologize for not saying something yesterday, but I did not know how to say it then. I still don't. Isabelle…" But he faltered.

That tone. She wasn't sure when she'd last heard it. Maybe in the almost tragic shyness with which he'd sought her father's blessing for her hand in marriage, ignorant that she was sitting in the carriage right before them; or perhaps years later, when he peeked his head into their bedroom to ask the midwife whether Caleb had finally been born, as if his cries weren't evidence enough. She realized it was not his distance she had sensed that morning, only his nervousness. And before he uttered another word, she knew she would not forgive him for whatever he'd kept from her. She felt the urge to run, but her legs were stuck in place. By the time he shut his mouth, the plate in her hand had dried itself in the morning air—she managed to put it down, as if her tears were better falling to the floor than sullying something she'd just made clean.

CHAPTER 3

P rentiss held his brother's feet in his lap. He kneaded each of
Landry's toes, then the sole, then the heel, digging his
thumbs so deep into his left foot that he could see it drained
white before the blood brought back its color. Landry lay on the bed
of the forest, his head upon a log. He stared up against the skyline.

"You always tryin' to sneak one by me, ain't you," Prentiss said.

Landry groaned, although it sounded more born of joy than
anything.

"Ate up the last of that rabbit like it was 'bout to take off. Like I'm
too stupid to notice." He hit the groove of his brother's foot, and
Landry looked down, as if to take in his brother's technique, before
casting his gaze back toward the still-rising sun. "Well, we ain't got
no other food, and you might've stole a few scraps but we're not
making it past the afternoon without putting something down."

Landry stayed silent, an act for the man that had nothing to do
with speaking, and more with his senses, the way he existed. He
always took to foot rubs in such a way. Prentiss would sense his
brother's body slow to a state of near-sleep, his breathing stalled, his
shoulders limp—and it was a model of how to take on pleasure, to
lose yourself in feeling.

It was a tradition derived from the cabins, when they were
children, back when Landry was whole. They would sit on their
pallets across from one another, and long after the tallow candle

had been snuffed by their mother, one would still be working the other's feet, preparing for the day ahead in the field. Prentiss could recall Mr. Morton once leading them on with the promise of a pair of gloves to the best producer, a gesture they knew to be empty, but still representative of how little he understood of them—the hands hardened quickly under the pain of picking, while feet, no matter how protected, would always find ways to ache from the hours spent holding up a broken body.

They'd worked Mr. Morton's land together; they'd left behind the only life they'd ever known; and they often thought in unison, as one. So when Prentiss stood up, it was of little surprise his brother was already standing too, even though neither had said a word in doing so.

Landry reached for the rope they'd used to catch the rabbit, but Prentiss placed a hand on his shoulder.

"No more of that. 'Bout time we head to the camps, see our people."

His brother's eyes glanced slowly around their makeshift home.

"It ain't forever," Prentiss reassured him. "We'll get us some food and be back before sundown."

There were places and sounds that brought Landry comfort, and all that fell outside this sphere of the known was met with resistance. Until a week earlier, that had been true of these very woods. Standing before them, the cabins that had always been their home to their rear, the unknown to their front, the few possessions in their name tethered to their back, the brothers faced a quiet, brooding mystery. A single step forward for Landry became an impossibility. His feet were planted, his head shaking no, until finally, after what seemed an entire hour of pleading from Prentiss, he strode ahead on his own command, as though the act of pushing on had taken a precise amount of courage culled only in that very moment.

Prentiss feared the walk to the camps would be no different. He made sure they were far beyond Majesty's Palace before taking to the road, not wanting to see his old master and those who'd elected to stay with him.

Was it really only a week ago? How strange that morning had

been. They'd heard rumblings that Union soldiers were drawing near, whispered rumors not unlike so many that had traveled through the cabins for years, ever since the war began. The notion of true emancipation had always seemed so fantastical that, were it to occur, Prentiss had expected the heralds of a bugle, rows of men in lockstep who would descend upon Majesty's Palace like angels brought down to serve the aims of God himself. In the actual event it was nothing but a few young men in blue uniforms as scraggy as the clothes that Prentiss and Landry had on themselves. They came down the lane and called them from their cabins with Master Morton following in unison, still in his pajamas, exposed in a way Prentiss had never seen him. Morton begged for the soldiers' understanding, insisting his slaves wished to remain in his keep, all while the young men ignored him and announced that each man, woman, and child in bondage was free to go as they pleased.

Master Morton said they were hopeless creatures, and beseeched the soldiers once more to recognize as much, though it was evident to all that he was the hopeless one, carrying on worse than a child who'd lost his mother. Still, none of them moved at first. It was Prentiss himself who stepped off the cabin stoop and toward one of the soldiers, a baby-faced white man perhaps even younger than he was, who clearly cared as little about this farm as he would about the next one, where Prentiss suspected he would soon repeat the same announcement in the same monotone.

"When might we go?" he asked the man, low enough that Morton wouldn't hear, for what if there was more to this arrangement than met the eye, and a punishment lay in wait for even deigning to ask?

He'd never heard such precious words as those that came next from the boy:

"Whenever you feel the urge, I suppose."

Prentiss wheeled around to face Landry without a second thought, for their lives could now begin and it was time to craft them in whatever way they saw fit. The tremble of Landry's jaw, the nod of his head, told him that his brother was in total agreement.

To enter the forest had been an expedition all its own, and now, as they left it behind, its sounds shrank and folded into silence; the odd carriage began to appear before them, quickly passing at their side. They made their unhurried way, step by step, dirt filling the unpatched pits of their shoes. Each home they came across either less or more impressive than Majesty's Palace, but all of them remarkable, all of them white.

"You figure you'd take to that one?" Prentiss said, but Landry kept his eyes on the road. The veranda of the home before them was vast enough to host a large party. Small blue bushes were given comfortable space before each column at its front.

"I don't take to it neither, no more than the rest," Prentiss said. "What, with all that space? How you s'posed to explain to someone that you got lost in your own house? Answer me that."

The question had dawned on him before, but as this was the first time he'd seen any homes beyond Majesty's Palace and its neighbors, he'd not known that whatever plague of excess had befallen his former owner had clearly consumed the town as well.

They carried nothing. They met the eyes of more oxen than men, yet each step felt like it was being watched, as so much of their movement had been in the past. The farther they got, the more real it felt—each step a confirmation of their freedom.

"Look at us," Prentiss said. "World travelers. Sightseers. Ain't that something?"

He gave his brother a prod in the ribs, but his sweet talk took him only so far as they came to the sign that bore the name Old Ox. Landry stopped as if he'd run into a wall. Suddenly there was the whir of noise and sights—the moaning cattle hidden in unseen stables, the shrieks of bickering children, a man spitting his muck juice indiscriminately from his porch. Prentiss experienced it all at once, perceiving it as his brother might, and he knew then the struggle that lay ahead of them.

"It's just a step like any other," he said.

Landry looked at him, eyes stern, in the manner of a statement.

"Okay," Prentiss said. "Okay then."

He wouldn't force his brother to go into town, any more than he had forced him to enter the forest. So much of their lives had been pressed upon them by other men, it felt only right that each decision be prized—their own to make.

"I'd ask you this. Why go through town when you can go around it? Wouldn't you ask the same?"

Landry eyed him again. He swayed a bit, readying himself, the tips of his shoes rising from the ground in preparation for an acceptable compromise, and that was all Prentiss needed to start walking again, to know his brother was at his side.

The town was hugged by the forest, making it easy to maneuver around its rear without drawing attention, not that anyone wished to pay it to them. They stuck to the backside of buildings. Behind one fence they glimpsed a stewing, bubbling basin of hog parts, so huge a man might take a dip if he wished to. The voices of what Prentiss figured to be hungry men trailed from inside the place. Within another yard stood a woman using a brush to clean the arms of a lounge chair, taking great care with each stroke, as if she were applying a coat of paint. Prentiss stopped looking after that. His clothes were damp with sweat, and he realized how quickly he was walking, like something chasing them might take to their trail. Never before had he seen such people without their permission, caught sight of regular folk about their business in private, and it immediately struck him as a dangerous circumstance.

"Not too long now," he said, although he had no idea if that was true, as the rumors of the camps being situated at the opposite end of Old Ox were just that to him. The words were less for Landry and more for himself, a fillip of self-belief, a routine in a life where his only companion had no words, no confidence, to spare.

Prentiss didn't fault his brother for his weaknesses—in his irregularities lay the groundwork of his strength. For if ever his brother was prone to stalling in place, he never wandered. Landry went where he was expected, and there was bravery to be found in someone willing to either go forward or face his fear head-on, unblinkingly, even if it sometimes stopped him right where he stood. It had been a principle mapped onto Landry at birth, no different from his love of food, which only made the day of reckoning that was to come more difficult.

That was way back when, a time when they were not quite grown but not quite children, slight in the chest, long in the limbs; young enough to have their mother on their behinds as much as the overseer but old enough to be expected to pick their full share in a day. They lined up one particular morning before their cabins, which in itself was not odd, as they lined up for a head count every morning, the spots where their feet rested so ingrained upon the ground that the imprint remained overnight. Yet it took no more than a moment to recognize the absence in front of the cabin across from theirs. Where Little James and Esther were supposed to be sat nothing at all. There was a quiet agony in this disruption of routine that Prentiss had never known before. His heart felt enormous in his chest. He was supposed to stare straight ahead, but instinct led him to look everywhere else, hoping they might appear from behind a clothesline or hop down from a willow before Mr. Cooley appeared and assessed the loss.

But just like that, Mr. Cooley had arrived. He came to a stop before their cabin but did not dismount. He simply took his hat off, assessing each person before him, and plainly asked where the two had gone off to. There was no response.

"Y'all stay where you are," he said, turned his horse, and broke off at a gallop back to Majesty's Palace.

"Don't want to hear a word from either of you," their mother had whispered, placing a hand on both of their shoulders, standing between them like a shield.

Nobody dared move when Mr. Cooley returned, Mr. Morton paired at his side. They stood tall in front of the group, and Mr. Morton brushed the hair from his eyes, breathing through his mouth.

"It won't be long," he said, "till that heat is on me. And Mr. Cooley will tell you the heat ain't never took a liking to me."

"It ain't," Mr. Cooley said.

"Why do any of you think I ain't down here in the fields? Y'all think I wouldn't appreciate the company? No, see, I'm just naturally a hot-blooded man, sure as hell ain't looking to get hotter than I already is. When the sun hits, I get a little dizzy. My stomach don't sit right."

"It sure don't."

"Mr. Cooley." Mr. Morton extended his hand to silence him. "So you tell me before I feel that heat on my back where these two went off to, or else I might get a bit moody, and if my day's ruined this early, y'all being such sympathetic creatures, I imagine you might share in my plight."

When there was no response, Mr. Morton continued his speech-ifying. Without Little James and Esther, he said, he would have loss in value in production which would only build upon the loss accrued by losing two slaves. And why should he, a man who did no wrong, a pious, righteous man, be punished for the heedless insubordination of these two individuals he fed and clothed so dutifully? Thus, if no one was willing to tell him where Little James and Esther could be found, he would pick one slave—and that slave, at the end of each month, would bear the whippings for the entire lot of them. Any wrongs done would be tallied, and they would fall solely on his back, and if there was someone willing to be a martyr, to take on that responsibility, he was open to volunteers.

"Come on, now," he said, casting his sight from one to the other. "Any of you will do."

Landry did not step forward. He merely reached for an itch upon his arm. Prentiss was never sure after the fact if Landry knew what he'd done. He could only recall his brother's eyes locked on the cloud of flies before their cabin, his mind wandering, as it was prone to.

"Here stands my man!" Mr. Morton said, to the surprise of even Mr. Cooley, a taskmaster of equal stupidity but only half the cruelty.

Prentiss did not dare turn to his pleading mother, or even to Landry, and he would forever bear the guilt of not stepping forward himself to save the only person he was ever made to protect.

Each month Mr. Morton would watch over the lashings as if they were a special occasion—doled out for Mrs. Etty waking too late, or for Lawson working his row too slowly. After the beating when he broke Landry's jaw, it took only a season for the boy to stop using what few words he had. Their mother would say that Landry had once been full, and then halved, until he was inevitably left in so many bits she could not piece together the boy she'd once called her own.

The only quarter Mr. Morton offered Landry was to avoid taking offense when he failed to utter anything in response to being called forth. "I don't take it as a show of disrespect," Mr. Morton would say, loud enough for the others to hear. "I sometimes wish the others might develop your fondness for silence, Landry. I do. I really do."

The sole pleasure left to the rest of them lay in the abandoned cabin that mocked Mr. Morton whenever he paid them a visit, the indignities of his loss on display for all to see. With each whipping he seemed to believe Little James and Esther might reappear, and it brought Prentiss quiet satisfaction imagining they were so far away, so gone, that they would never hear Landry's cries; never return to give Mr. Morton the peace of mind he so doggedly sought.

———————

Once they were beyond Old Ox, the camps were easy to find, as one needed only to follow the bodies. They accumulated as the road went on, a few covered by the broad leaves of the crab apple trees scattered about, others by discarded rubbish found in town—a collection of men and women sleeping off a lifetime of toil. At some point a makeshift road forked off, a marshy patch of mud etched by the footsteps of those who had come to pass. For a few feet there were dense horsetail reeds all around them. But then, along the creek that ran through town, the road cleared into an expanse of tents with people appearing from nowhere. A town with no buildings, no markings, and no name.

"Looks right," Prentiss said.

They were paid little mind at first. Rows of tents, most made with nothing more than blankets clasped together, sat beside one another. Shoeless children played in the trees while their parents slept or visited with the others.

When the brothers started forward, careworn eyes sought them out but looked them off quickly. There was no hostility to be found, rather a collective meekness that Prentiss recognized, having experienced it himself. This was their new life. Work replaced with aimless sitting or scrounging for food like an animal. The faces were unknown to him. Prentiss thought of calling out some names, but he didn't wish to draw attention.

"What you got?" said a voice from a tent at their side.

Prentiss turned to a group of men and women huddled around a skillet. Charred remains lay crisped and burnt in the pan. Each of them cradled a sheet of newspaper holding bits of potato skins, and Prentiss quickly realized how hungry he was. His eyes were fastened on the ink running off the newspaper wet with lard. He found Landry inching toward the tent himself, just as eager for a taste. The leader inside called out to them once more to gain their attention.

"Either you tryin' to trade something or you pickin' around for some trouble. Which is it?"

Prentiss told the man he was looking for his own from Majesty's Palace.

The man licked his fingers. "Boy," he said. "We from Campton."

"I ain't heard of that house," Prentiss said.

"I tell you, he thinks it's a house."

When Prentiss failed to respond, the man slapped his knee, and asked the others, a second time, if they'd heard what the boy had said.

"Campton, Georgia, son. It's a *town*. Ain't no more than ten miles up the road."

The man took pity on them. Explained that the camp was at the crossing of a number of towns. Many freed slaves had already started north with little more than a day's rations. Some had gone right up the road, where there was a sawmill seeking extra help. Others had gone farther. He mentioned Baltimore, Wilmington, and enough other places that Prentiss couldn't keep up.

"I ain't got no business in Baltimore," Prentiss said.

"None of us ain't got no business nowhere. But that ain't stop nobody."

"Y'all just up and leave?"

The man nodded.

"Now it seems I answered your question, and you ain't answer mine. What you got?"

He wanted their canteen. Prentiss looked it over in his hand, having never considered it of value. Perhaps he was missing something etched in the tin, something signified in the chipped edge of the cork. In return for it he got three potatoes. The man even handed Landry the remains from the skillet, which he ate with the most speed he'd shown all day.

"I bet down the road you might find some room," the man told them.

The sun was higher now. It was so bright outside the tent, so dark inside, Prentiss could barely see the man who'd been speaking. He turned to his brother.

"Give the man the pan."

Landry handed back the skillet and they returned to the road, the smell of the potatoes lingering long after they'd left. Landry grew calm with a little food in his stomach, walking alone up ahead of Prentiss, leading them back to the woods with a meandering gait.

"Keep on the path," Prentiss said.

He was already thinking about when they would leave, how he would inform his brother when the time came. And alongside this decision there was some forfeiture in the thought he found unsettling: that for every pound of weight they'd carried across their backs, for every drop of sweat that had poured off, no inch of this land was theirs. As long as they stayed, they were no better than the others, kept on the borders of town, hidden among the trees just like their brothers and sisters. And it grew clear that the only path to a life worth living would be found elsewhere, where they might not have more but could not possibly have less.

There was a hurried movement before him.

"Landry!" he screamed.

His brother veered off through the brush at the side of the path, and before Prentiss could grab at him, he was being led through the backwoods, ankle-high mud pulling at his shoes, clots of mosquitoes so loud about him that his head felt abuzz. The reeds were higher here. Nettles punctured his pants and stabbed at his legs. He could not see his brother, and for a moment he did not know where to turn, or which way was straight. He closed his eyes to the wall of grass before him and stampeded forward, and only then did he break free, fresh air overtaking him. He would have fallen into the water if it was not for Landry, who was crouched down at his feet, stopping him from hurtling ahead.

"What's gotten into you? Now you answer me—"

He saw it then—a pond, no more than the span of a few men across. The surface was covered with floating lilies, shoots of cattails like digits reaching out toward the sun. At its center sat a small island of sedges. His brother dipped his hand over and over, and lapped at the water. Prentiss watched his brother's hand make contact, submerge, and reappear, glimmering ripples that fanned out and grew still in the heat. The sight was seemingly new to Landry each time.

His enthusiasm brought to mind the cotton fields, where troughs of water were stationed at the end of the rows. The overseers would often let their horses drink as the day wore on, and if a row was picked clean in short order, they'd sometimes let those at work kneel down and drink themselves. Yet the fields were shaped like a horseshoe, and at the end of his row, near the farthest bend, Landry seldom took to the water, but fixed his eyes upon the fountain that lay in front of Majesty's Palace. Prentiss would tell him to drink, but his brother seemed to find the fountain a better source, as if it fit him to wait out his thirst for what lay ahead, water that would never be his own. Here, in some way, he appeared to have found that fountain's equal.

"Feels nice, don't it," Prentiss said, relaxing now.

He sat beside Landry, marveling not at the beauty before him but at the grace of his brother, the hum of curiosity hidden behind his distant stare, the parts of him others failed to notice. His fingers were especially delicate, graceful things, and their mother would often say they were fit for playing an instrument, one of class, an organ being her decided preference. In private, she told Prentiss it was where she looked when they strung Landry up for his whippings. There were parts of you they could touch, she said, and parts they could not, and his hands, even tied to a post, would never lose their beauty even if they broke the rest of him down. If only she knew how strong he'd stand as the days and years wore on, long after she'd been sold, even after the monthly whippings had quit but the threat of the lash was still ever-present.

It was only a few weeks ago that Mr. Morton had approached the slaves who could still stand a hard day's work with the wartime rations and doubled quotas, waking a few who had turned in early. He told a select number of the stronger men that he had a generous offer, born of his patriotism at the behest of President Davis: he'd give them their freedom if they would volunteer to fight for the cause.

"Prentiss," he said, working down the line. "You were always a reliable hand. They need men like you. What do you say?"

Prentiss had looked upon Mr. Morton with as earnest a disposition as he could muster.

"Well, me and Landry here move as one." He then turned to his brother. "Landry, how you feel about fighting for the cause?"

Mr. Morton sat forward on his horse, eager for an answer, but Landry's mouth stayed shut, his head moving with neither a nod nor a shake.

"Don't sound like a yes to me, master," Prentiss told him. "But he don't say much at all. I wouldn't take it as a show of disrespect."

And then the slightest uptick at the corner of Landry's mouth, the start of a smile, too faint for Mr. Morton to catch, but so clear to Prentiss that he could hardly keep from grinning himself.

Their lives had changed so drastically since then that the moment struck him as though it was from the distant past. He wished to feel the joy he'd felt then, but it was gone to him. Nowadays the only memories that got his blood rushing were the ones he so badly wished to be rid of. Perhaps his great fear was that this would always be the case—that the long shadow of the cattails at his rear would always cause him to swallow at the arrival of the overseer's mare; that the shiver of the water's surface would forever take on the spasm of his brother's backside on impact with the master's whip.

He put a hand on his brother's shoulder, slow enough not to startle him.

"That's enough for a day, don't you think?"

And when he stood up to leave, Landry did so too.

CHAPTER 4

O ld Ox had burnt down twice in the last fifty years, and both times it licked its wounds and roared back to life as if it fed on the very flames that had turned it to ash. The place made little sense—you could buy yourself a better haircut at Mr. Rainey's Meats than at the barbershop, and better cuts of meat from a Chickasaw who came through town once a week in a covered wagon than at Mr. Rainey's—but its resilience could not be called into question, for each passing resurrection gave it more life than its past selves could ever claim to have.

It had grown to be a loose grid of connected buildings and homes that George could scarcely make heads or tails of, and he was suspicious of the newer establishments in recognition of the chances that they might not be there the next time he laid eyes on them—if not for a fire then an unpaid debt, if not an unpaid debt then a move to the next opportunity down the road in Selby or Chambersville or Campton. That was why he paid mind to none but the places he frequented, coming in on Saturday mornings for supplies or business only when necessary.

Venturing there from home took him half an hour on the back of his donkey, and he always tied Ridley up to the slumped hitching rail in front of Ray Bittle's home on the farthest edge of town. Ray slept on his porch with a lust for dreaming that George admired, yet the old man often managed a twitch of his hat in acknowledgment whenever passersby stopped before his home. It was the only correspondence George had shared with him in years.

"I won't be long," George said, more to the donkey than to Bittle, then grabbed his saddlebags and made his way to the main thoroughfare.

The walkways of the town were composed of wooden planks, most of them as thin and uneven as coffin lids; it took only the slightest hint of rain for them to overrun, fits of water creeping through the slits like cooked juices seeping from a roast. The main road headed off into alleys that led to new constructions and finally the oldest part of town, the original row of homes that found ways to survive when others languished. The landscape felt expansive, yet the flow of people was suffocating and the surplus unraveled what little thread of decency there'd once been in the place. The walls of Vessey Mercantile were smeared with so much waste, human and otherwise, that the resulting splatters resembled the markings of a child who had put all the colors on his palette into one muddied shade. Between Blossom's Café and the general store were nooks and crannies no wider than a dog's cage, and nearly all of them housed the clustered tents of the homeless—some whites returned from the war still in tattered uniforms, others freedmen, the contrast fit for the pen of an ironist with a low sense of humor.

It was of some relief when he broke free from the crowd and entered Ezra Whitley's shop, taking in the air as if it had been preserved over time, untainted by the outside world.

"Ezra?" George called, placing his saddlebags near the front door and looking around.

Long tables—where Ezra's sons had taken their lessons in the family business before founding their own shops—sat empty. A bookshelf commencing on the far wall wrapped itself around the room, falling just short of a full revolution.

He was about to call out again when a rattle came from the stairs. Ezra, hunched over himself, gingerly made his way down with a sandwich in hand, hailing George as he took a bite.

"Come, come," he said.

"Well, don't you come down if I'm going up," George said.

Ezra by then had reached the foot of the stairs and waved him off.

"The movement is good for my legs. The doctor tells me there's a pustule buildup behind the knees. At rest, they each take on the look of a ripe cantaloupe."

"Good Lord. Is there a cure?"

"The doctor said time, so nothing really short of death. But the stairs bring some relief."

He put a hand on George's shoulder.

"Now follow along."

So George followed Ezra, as he had for nearly all his life. No one had been closer to Benjamin, George's father. Ezra had taken care of the family's finances since George's parents had moved from Nantucket down to Georgia in search of the cheap land that would make their fortune. Although Benjamin was keen on purchasing farmland, Ezra suggested his investments should bleed into Old Ox proper, the result being that Benjamin had for a time become the biggest leasing agent in the town altogether. Ever since, Ezra had kept them abreast of opportunity, monitored their ledgers, and shared rumors of the market that most men weren't so blessed to catch wind of. George, who'd been born on the farm, had barely reached Ezra's thigh when he first started coming around, and held fond memories of the man visiting their home, a salted caramel always in hand to keep him busy as the men talked business.

With the carefulness of the brittle-boned, they mounted the stairs and reached Ezra's office, by which time the old man had finished his sandwich. He instructed George to sit down across from him. A bison pelt that Ezra had no interest in lined the wall behind his desk, for as he'd told George once, other men liked such things, and their comfort was paramount to assuring him their business.

"I hope the ride to town was peaceful?" Ezra asked.

"I suppose. For all the talk of hell descending upon us, it feels no different to me than before the occupation."

"You'd feel differently if you were here every day as am I. Union soldiers patrolling and asking after us as though we might revolt at any moment. Not to speak of the slaves they've freed."

"Is that so."

"It's an abomination. There is one of them in want of charity every way you turn. The lot of them congregated in the town square on Sunday for prayer, and the way they were crying and carrying on I wasn't sure if it was in praise of their freedom or at the plight of what their freedom entails."

"Their hands were only unbound days ago. You can't blame them for still feeling the chafe of the chains."

"Oh, aren't you the pious one," Ezra said. "Painting me as cruel as you retire to your home in the country. While I will go across the road here at day's end and sleep with one eye open."

George yawned.

"Why are we discussing this? Must we?"

Ezra shrugged, not only with his shoulders, which were perpetually hunched, but in the despondency of his gaze.

"We are friends. Friends speak of things that involve one another. This is called polite conversation."

"Well, it bores me."

"Then might I ask why you're here?"

George fiddled with a button on his shirt, and finally told Ezra why he'd come: he wished to keep his holdings.

"So. Sell nothing, then?"

George had, since the passing of his father, elected to forgo work and simply unload parcels of his land as a means to get by. The freedom this had produced was worth more than the bother of tending to acreage he didn't wish to farm. Ezra had been an eager buyer, a man as interested in business as George was in idleness. Where many speculators had stopped purchasing during the war, Ezra had remained committed to acquiring the very land he'd helped Benjamin make his own so many years ago.

Ezra shook his head.

"This doesn't sound like you. Too sudden."

"Men change."

"I'd believe a skunk's scent had come to smell like flowers before I believed you'd changed, George. I know you don't take pride in much, but you don't lose sight of yourself for any man."

"Think as you wish."

"Surely, there must be some reason—"

"My son is dead." He said it very plainly, as though he were reading off the last item from the back page of a newspaper.

Ezra stiffened. He stood up and walked around his desk. George thought he might move to console him somehow, which would make for the first physical contact between them since his father's death, when he was still but a boy. Yet Ezra merely winced, his eye twitching, as if in display of a care more genuine than any words might carry.

"I'm so sorry," he said. "So, so sorry."

George told him of August's visit, of his wife having gone silent from the moment he told her the news until he'd left that same morning to come to town.

"Isabelle will pull through," Ezra said. "Give her time. That is the only remedy."

George stood up, brushing off his shirt like the stains of dirt there had suddenly, after many years, come to bother him.

"I cannot control how she takes such things. But I can control what's mine. That land... I suppose I just wish to hold on to what I have left. Do something with it. Something worthwhile."

Ezra said nothing.

"I should go," George said.

And Ezra, it seemed, used this turn to regain his footing.

"Yes, absolutely! This is no time to discuss business. Go see your wife. Even if she refuses you. Even if she spits at your feet."

"Let us hope she stops short of that."

George could see the seams of age that met at the corner of Ezra's eyes; his day-old whiskers looked like a young boy's.

"You feel free to call upon me if you need anything at all," Ezra said.

"Thank you," George said. "Until then."

It was only once he was out the door, saddlebags in hand, stepping from the shadows of the shop into the sagging sun, that he realized his old friend's sleight of hand—shelving George's decision to keep his land as if it was merely clouded by his emotions, so that a deal might be struck another day. Part of him was amused by Ezra's deceit, for in it he saw the glimmer of respect that had been at the root of their entire relationship. The old man would not change his ways on account of his client's grieving, and George would never have wanted him to.

The town square was actually a traffic circle, and at its center sat the always-blooming flowers tended to by the gardening society. A Union soldier stood idle there now with his rifle at his side, rolling a cigarette, licking the paper as a dog might lick a wound. George put his head down and walked briskly, taking to the road before entering the general store. The door was already open.

Rawlings, the storekeeper, greeted George with little more than a glance and asked what brought him in.

"Just the essentials," George said.

Rawlings rose from the wooden crate where he took his rest and began collecting the few necessities George requested every week: sugar, coffee, bread. In the back, near the equipment, sat Little Rawlings, rag in hand, polishing a scythe so sharp it looked liable to cut right through his hand. It seemed a skill, one learned with little room for error.

"Have your eye on something?" Rawlings asked. "We got new merchandise coming in all the time. Might not know you want it till you see it."

George reflexively shook his head, then reconsidered.

"There is one thing…" he said.

After paying, George was out the door, the image of Ridley at the forefront of his mind. It took only an afternoon to miss the donkey—not really the animal, but the peace it might deliver him to. When he reached Bittle's home, he found Ridley attempting to eat the stray fingers of grass on the ground. George stroked his mane, nodding to Ray, who appeared livelier than usual in his stoic, straight-backed pose of dead sleep as opposed to his usual slump.

"We're off, then," he said to Ridley. A thunderous noise escaped from Bittle, and although there was no way to be sure, George couldn't help reading into the way his hat had fluttered atop his head, tipping forward, as if to bid him farewell.

Summer was yet distant, but already its first licks were upon Old Ox, and there was no greater shelter from the newfound afternoon heat than the evergreens that towered over Stage Road; it seemed like the sun, for all its determination, had never glanced upon the ground those trees protected. Ridley's pace was that of a donkey half his age, and George would intermittently tell him to go easy, to save it for another day when time was more precious.

The fact was, it would have been fine for George if the journey never ended, as his homecoming would mean a reckoning with Isabelle. Of course he wished to tend to her. Of course he wished to help her face the injustices wreaked upon them both. But what they shared had limits. It was a mutual passion for independence that had brought them together in the first place, the ability to go through vast segments of the day in silence, with only a glance, a touch on the back, to affirm their feelings. In doing so the bond between them had strengthened over time, and although it was not prone to bending, its single weak point lay in the quiet embarrassment that it existed in the first place—that two individuals who resolutely dismissed the idea of needing anyone else were now helpless without each other.

"What is a man to do?" he said to the donkey.

While possessed by these grim thoughts, George passed Ted Morton's home. Unlike the other houses this far along in the country, Ted had built his almost directly upon the road, as if the bountiful stretch of acres he owned behind it wouldn't do. This made things difficult when Morton's wife, a woman so severe and translucent in her visage as to seem composed of pure crystal, had instructed him to build a fountain at its front. The resulting creation of cherubs and fairies hugged Stage Road so tightly that its water leaked past the property line and beneath the feet of whoever walked there. This struck George as an act of decadence, an intrusion on public land, and moments like this one—the trickle streaming beneath Ridley's feet, caking dirt into his hooves—brought with them the hum of contempt he routinely felt toward the man.

An emotional response he could have conveniently buried within himself had Morton not been standing before the fountain, staring at it from beneath his sun hat with rapt concentration. His wheat-colored locks fell to the nape of his neck, and he blinked when lost in confusion, bestowing on his usual countenance the look of a man with something regularly caught in his eye.

He turned when Ridley drew near and gave George a half smile.

"George, you old horse thief, how you doin'?"

"Just fine," he lied. "And yourself?"

"We're holding up."

Ted inspected the fountain more closely, and the way his eyes scanned it, George knew he was in for a conversation.

"One of my boys, I paid to have him learnt with the stonemason in town. He kept this thing running, and now he picks up and runs off to God knows where. I put money into that boy and he acts like I ain't never done a damned thing for his scrawny ass."

"A shame," George said.

Ted spit brown on the ground.

"I'd say."

There were usually many hands running around the property, but now the place was ghostly. He'd titled the home—another offense, in George's mind, giving a title to anything not breathing—*Majesty's Palace*. It was large enough to demand constant upkeep, its gilded accents so fragile that they seemed made more for tending to than anything else. And behind the home, George knew, the compound of cabins had been kept padded with enough bodies to rebuild ancient Rome, plenty to keep the home and farm operating smoothly.

"Could be worse, though," Ted went on. "Still got a good fifteen hands that are happy to carry on working. I hear Al Hooks lost the whole lot of his, sixty healthy bodies he fed and bred himself. Can you imagine?"

"I suppose I can't," George said.

Ted gave him the typical look of disgust he employed whenever George's Northerly roots were alluded to. Men like Ted often found him untrustworthy, as if the offense of running away from one's home knew no barriers of color. Nantucket or the plantation, it was all the same.

"They say that General they got in charge now…what's his name…"

George recalled the circular he'd found on his front porch, proclaiming the town of Old Ox an asset of the North, as ordered by President Lincoln and executed by a brigadier general named Arnold Glass. Apparently, Roth's Lumber Mill was the prized possession, from what he'd heard of it. He gave the general's name over to Ted.

"Yeah, Glass," Ted said. "They say he aims to be hands-off, let folks do as they please. But he ain't said how we're supposed to make do without no help. How we're supposed to carry on with nothing. Can't even get a damn fountain fixed."

Pitiful, George thought, as Ted stared at the leaky fountain, help-less to a fissure he had no capacity to fix.

"I can only wish you luck with your repairs, Ted. As with all the rest."

"Yeah. You keep out the heat," Ted said.

George readied his leg to give Ridley a tap, but Ted shot a finger into the air.

"Before you go. You wouldn't mind if I ask a question."

He didn't have time to answer before Ted carried on.

"My boy William, well, he likes to shoot. Been taking his scatter-gun out into the woods recently. Now he's young enough to still think he sees spirits and whatnot on occasion, but he swears up and down he's seen you out there, near our border, walking on your own, out in the distance. I told him you're speaking of a man who keeps to his front porch so much that he probably ain't even left so much as the county in decades. Now tell me that boy ain't seeing right."

George took a moment. He would have to lie again, and it gave him the slightest pang of guilt knowing it was at the cost of the little Morton boy, who had yet to attain his father's nature.

"It's common for boys that age to see things," he said, "whether that be spirits or shadows of nothing. William's imagination has yet to be shot, is all."

Ted shook his head with some satisfaction, as if the steadiness of George's habits was confirmation of the world being right again.

"You take care now, George."

George gave him a tip of his hat and finally relaxed as he led Ridley off at a canter. The afternoon was coming to a close; the sun played upon the trees with the touch of a soft tune, the road narrowing as it broke off toward his cabin.

He parked Ridley back in his stable next to the barn and took a minute to collect himself. The woods were behind him, the cabin to his front. The threadbare hangings Isabelle had woven covered the window of their bedroom. He thought for a moment he could see her figure there, watching him watching her, but the shadow never moved and so he let go of the idea.

The door was waiting for him. Once inside, the familiar steps up the stairs, the creaking hallway to the bedroom, the foot of the bed itself, where he could kneel and put his head upon her thigh, asking forgiveness for wrongs he had not committed. But the words weren't there for him, as much as wished them to be. And there was one more errand for the day that needed to be done.

He put his saddlebags on the ground before the back door, unclasped it, and pulled out the one item he sought: a single pair of socks. He glanced up once more at the figure in the window, the shadow that was not his wife, and turned again, disappearing into the woods to repay a debt.

CHAPTER 5

P rentiss and Landry arrived back to their camp late enough that the shade of the trees brought goose bumps to their skin. Prentiss had no mind to eat, even with the potatoes in his knapsack that he'd got from the man in the tent. He was hungrier for sleep.

"I'll cook you up something," he told his brother. "But I'm saving my half till morning, and that don't mean you get any of it before then, you hear me? Just because it's cooked don't mean it's free to all comers, I know that's how you think of it but you wrong there..."

He stopped when he saw, standing before the remains of one of their old fires, George Walker.

"Hello again," George said, waving at them.

"Sir," Prentiss said. "Mr. Walker."

"Just George. I have something for your brother. My wife tells me he took some interest in our clothesline a few days back, when he was doused from the rain."

He handed over to Landry a pair of socks.

"Landry?" Prentiss said. "I believe she might have the wrong man."

"She was quite particular in her description. He's very...unique in his appearance."

The old man yawned and itched his backside. He had a lassitude greater than anyone Prentiss had never known, white or black. He seemed the sort who might walk the streets without his britches and not pause to consider it odd, let alone a reason to turn back home before his errands were complete. But given that his brother had wandered off a few hours earlier to a pond neither had ever laid eyes on before, Prentiss did not feel in a position to protest the claim further. Perhaps Landry really had strayed to the Walkers' clothesline.

"It's for helping me last night," George said. "Consider us even."

"I'm sure he's very grateful," Prentiss said.

Landry gave George a glance and sat before the fire pit, inspecting the socks.

"You'll be happy to know we're fixin' to leave," Prentiss said. "I think we'll take to the camps up the road. You've been mighty gracious."

"So quick?" George said. "There's no rush, really. Besides, you mentioned hunting that beast with me. If I may remind you."

Prentiss put down the potatoes. Up until that moment he'd forgotten what he'd told George the previous night. He'd been so lost in the old man's suffering he would have told him they were born of the same mother if he thought it would bring him some kernel of peace.

"I ain't forget," he said.

George clasped his hands together behind his back.

"How would you feel about a short expedition now? As I return home."

Prentiss's feet ached from the walk. The coolness of the forest had nearly lulled him to sleep just standing there. Landry meanwhile was scrutinizing the knit of the socks, happy to tend to himself, and his brother's fascination with the gift led Prentiss to consider George in a new light. If the man wanted a stroll in the woods, a stroll he would give him.

"I don't see no reason why not," he said.

George smiled encouragingly.

Prentiss looked back to Landry, content before the fire, then started off with George. He thought he might ask about the animal in question—which, at least according to the description George had given, he had neither heard of nor seen in his life.

But George cut him off before he could begin. The man's eyes grew slant, looking around as if someone might hear what was to follow.

"Are you familiar with peanuts, Prentiss?"

"Peanuts?"

"Cultivating peanuts. Surely you're aware of the plant."

"What you gettin' at?"

The edge of George's mouth flickered in discouragement, but he was not dissuaded.

"I mean to use this land. I have to, if I'm to make enough money to keep it. But I would need some help. I've given it more thought than you might imagine."

Prentiss knew white men liked to hear answers of their choosing, but the problem with George was that his questions were never quite clear enough to hint at the suggested response. Under the spell of hunger and the exhaustion of the day, he found it near impossible to discern how to appease him.

"You, Landry, and I," George said. "We could learn the business together. Would that be amenable to you? If you were to stay?"

What was wrong with this man? The only ailment Prentiss could assign to him was a bout of loneliness, the same affliction that had shadowed him the night before.

"Forgive me, Mr. Walker. George. But I just got rid of one owner. I ain't looking for another. Now, it's been a long day, and we best get on. I do wish you the best," he said, and turned to go.

"Don't be silly. We can get you some lodging. And I'll pay you like any other man. You can get yourself some food, proper clothes."

"I can't be of help," Prentiss said. "But you take care." He started off again, faster this time.

"I'll bring some food by tonight anyhow, we got a stew cooking, I believe—"

"Why can't you take no for an answer, mister?" Prentiss said. He whirled back to face George. "We ain't your help. Now you know I don't mean nothin' by it, but I must be gettin' back to my brother."

The pain in George's face, so immense it might split him two, was momentary, and he managed to disguise it with a grin.

"Of course," he said. "You take care as well, Prentiss."

Prentiss would have apologized, for he'd glimpsed how fragile George was, but the old man had spun too quickly and set off.

"Can you find your way?" Prentiss called out.

No words came back to him, and the woods sat silent in the old man's absence. He turned then to find his brother at his backside, looking on, studiously.

"I ain't mean for it to come out as it did," Prentiss said, walking to meet him. "I made a go at being polite, but they try you. They always tryin' you."

CHAPTER 6

His love had never been gracious, and he had no means to recognize what Isabelle might require of him—the necessities of her grief. There were few times as a grown man he could recall being intimidated, but the door to Caleb's room, where she had locked herself up, was so overwhelming that he had to lean against the hallway wall just to settle his bones. He moved forward, reassured by the sliver of lamplight that reached under the doorframe and lazed over his feet—the only signal that she was within.

"Isabelle." Somehow his voice cracked even on the single word. He stepped back and put his hands on his hips, then stepped forward to try again. "Isabelle," he said, "I've made a stew."

The entire process was undermined, at its root, by the fact that he was not truly capable of consoling Isabelle, as they both knew. This was the man who had spent her father's funeral not at her side, in the chapel, but feeding downed apples to the horses that had carried the coffin; a man who had caused her great anger early in their marriage when, in the dead of a winter's night, after embracing her with the heat of his body, had decided it was too cold after all, made a fire, and happily dozed off sitting before it by himself. His words, however he might form them, would be sincere, but they were bound to be rejected as so misaligned with the man his wife knew that they did not bear serious consideration.

"Won't you eat?" he asked. "May I bring you a bowl?"

He let some time pass, and only when he could no longer with-stand the silence did he walk downstairs to eat alone. He wondered how long she would last in there. An apology might do. But it was unclear if his delay in telling her was even the cause of her seclusion. Perhaps she simply needed time, a night to herself, but the desire to do something for her that might assuage his guilt was so crushing that he could barely sit still. He added kindling to the fire. He paced incessantly, the floorboard creaking where the wood was polished with wear, and no matter how unbearable he found it to wallow in his wife's misery, he knew that it was the better option than making contact with his own grief, that place of darkness he'd ignored ever since August had delivered the unwelcome news. The quiet of the evening pushed up against him. Against the far wall the shadows of tree branches dipped like fingers playing keys on an organ. He withdrew from the evening to his armchair before the fire.

It was not until the following morning that his ponderings reached any sort of conclusion, and by then he was resigned to what lay ahead for him and felt only ridicule for his actions the day before. His foot-steps on the stairwell, his knock on Caleb's door, his invitation to eat: it had all reached her as a disappointment; the boy she wanted to see, the one who might mend her heart, would never appear there again. And if that was so, why had he ever thought she'd open the door at all?

It was three days before the flowers started appearing on the front porch. Some visitors came by foot, others by carriage, and the sound of horses clopping was enough to send him to the back of the house. He would wait out these visits as he'd waited out the temper of his quarreling parents when he was a boy, hidden in the cool shadows of the chicken coop, ignoring whatever noise did not suit him. These were all Isabelle's friends, garrulous women wearing hats as tall as flowerpots.

Isabelle, for her part, refused to answer their calls as well, and he thought perhaps that they had a shared desire to ignore them and their gifts. Yet it took only a trip out to the barn to water Ridley for him to realize things were not entirely as they seemed, when he returned to find a pot of carnations that had been left on the front porch suddenly placed upon the dining table. The next day an arrangement of lilies found their way to the fireplace mantel. The small shelf above the stove was the next to be decorated, bearing enough pots that the room smelled more like a garden—soil and perfume—than a kitchen.

It felt, meanwhile, as if he were living with a ghost. Isabelle had appeared downstairs on occasion, but only as a spirit might, in the hours he was asleep, when her presence might have been no more than a part of his dreams. The couple of times he did awake in his armchair, his attempts to speak to her were scorned, and he was almost afraid to look her in the eye, as if her days of pain and isolation might have brought on some actual ghoulish transformation.

He was preparing a plate of eggs for himself one of those mornings when a rapping on the door would not quit. The eggs hadn't fried through, and the pull of his attention between these two things— the cooking of the food and the aggressive knocking—became so bothersome that he picked the skillet up, went to the front door, and began telling off the visitor who had intruded upon his meal before he saw who it was. Then he looked upon Mildred Foster and knew that any peace the morning had brought him would soon vanish.

"George," Mildred said. She wore slick-shined leather riding boots, and her horse was tied to the front gate of the cabin, where it was now grazing freely.

"Mrs. Foster, I really do not have time for this. We are in mourning."

"I know how much you both loved the boy," she said. "And I'm forever sorry for your loss. I know how fortunate I am that my sons have already returned, and I could not bear the suffering had they not, so I sympathize with your position."

He might have tried to thank her if he didn't know better. When it came to Mildred, a comment meant to prop you up was always followed by one that might very well put you on your back.

"But if I'm supposed to believe that Isabelle is stowed away somewhere in this home of her own accord, I'm going to see for myself and not take the town's word for it, be sure of that, Mr. Walker. Now please call for her, and if she wishes to have me go, I'll hear her say as much."

Her eyes, as usual, were cutting and hostile. She was older than Isabelle, and upon the death of John Foster had assumed the role of father to their four boys, and in turn had become more of a man in widowhood than John himself—who was born sick—had ever managed. She took off her riding gloves, long shoots of black satin, and stood before George as though a boulder could not shake her from her purpose.

"At least let me put the pan down," he said.

The eggs were already ruined. He set the pan on the stove, wiped his hands on his shirt, and called mildly up the stairs:

"Isabelle, Mrs. Foster is here to see you."

Mildred, unimpressed by his effort, stepped forward into their home, and although another man might have protested, he did not have the energy to stop her.

"Isabelle!" she yelled. "Isabelle, it's me. I only want to make sure you're well."

Then, in a businesslike tone, she asked George if Isabelle was eating.

"Some."

"Bathing?"

"That I cannot speak to."

"I see. Isabelle!"

Mildred Foster was one of Isabelle's oldest friends, and it had been clear from the beginning that she did not consider him suitable for Isabelle's hand. Not that anyone was. He could hardly think of a time that Mildred had kind words for any man at all, even her own husband, whom she often described as either lacking in backbone or "limp in nature." Which George found humorous. John, although shy, had been one of the few people he could tolerate over a dinner table, careful with his words, intelligent when he shared them. Mildred decried his condition and recognized the same faults in George, seeking always to display how much closer she was to Isabelle than he was. Little surprise that the silence from the stairwell brought him a tinge of glee now. He was almost happy she had arrived, just to be rebuffed.

"It would appear," he said, "that my wife would rather be left alone. Now if you would"—he nodded at the door—"I have my breakfast to eat."

Her eyes flitted from the stairwell to the front door. He let the moment sit, relishing her uncertainty.

"Get her through this," she said. "You owe her that much, George."

He went to close the door behind her.

"I will let her know you came. Thank you for your call."

At the sound of pattering on the stairwell behind him, he turned around in disbelief. Isabelle was holding up her dress as she descended the stairs. She floated by George and out the door as if he were invisible.

Mildred turned in the yard and embraced Isabelle in a prolonged hug, petting her hair like a horse's mane, cooing into her ear.

"It's okay. Oh, Isabelle. Oh."

George retrieved his eggs and ate them cold from the skillet, surveying the reunion of the two women lost in each other's arms. There were no words for the resentment that claimed him, a jealousy of such magnitude he had half an urge to throw the skillet into the yard and make a show of things. They spoke too softly to hear the words, and after a time he stopped trying to listen. His curiosity shifted to his wife's appearance, which seemed to bear no relation to his earlier fears, the idea that she might have wilted into something awful. Her hair was pulled into a ponytail, gray but with bits of brown glinting like cinnamon in the sunlight; her face was soft and full, as vibrant with life as the day he'd first met her.

For a brief flash, like a glint of light caught in one's eye, he saw before him that young woman he would one day come to marry. He was already in his thirties then, decrepit by the standards foisted upon a bachelor, and yet he hadn't cared a whit that his household belonged to him and him alone. His days involved only what he cared them to, and no woman could help him find contentment, for he already had it in spades. Perhaps it would have remained that way had not a traveling wind band come to Old Ox, an event at the outdoor concert hall that Ezra insisted George attend, if only to be in the company of others for an afternoon. There were no theatrics upon that first sighting. She was with her father, both of them speaking to another young man, and when the boy had walked off, she'd scowled at his back, as though his words alone had been foul, forcing her father to giggle, and in that slight show of play, the willingness to shove modesty aside, George knew he'd found his match. Ezra was quick to inform him of who the young woman was, and, more important, that she had yet to marry. But before Ezra could ask if he'd liked to be introduced, George had already departed, so frightened was he by the prospect of even a conversation.

Isabelle. He could not rid himself of the name, the memory, no matter how many days passed, and soon he was so preoccupied that it became a matter of grave importance that some action be taken. So he carved a figurine, with the flow and shape of a beautiful woman (however much definition might be had in the medium of wood), and had it sent to her by mail. When a week went by, he sent a basket of flowers, all picked on the farm, this time hiring a courier so they would arrive without having wilted. When this, too, garnered no response, he finally found the nerve to take the trip to Chambersville himself. He asked after Isabelle's house and was soon before a brick home, built in the Colonial style, a large lawn out front being tended to by a modest number of Negroes who were currently caught up in a conversation so lively he was afraid of interrupting. When they looked him up and down, he felt himself shrink before them, like he feared his flowers had only a few days earlier. They asked him who he wished to call on.

"I believe her name is Isabelle," he said.

Right inside, they told him.

When the butler informed her of his arrival, and when she came to the door, he was so stunned by being granted another sight of such a beautiful woman that he could hardly utter a word.

"You are the one sending those gifts, aren't you?" she said, the words coming before she had even stepped off the stairs.

A stutter. Some babble. He could not recall the specifics, or if he had even managed to cobble one word to another.

"Really, a simple note would've done. Easier to respond to than a carving. The flowers were nice, but much better presented in person. I figured I'd wait until you showed up yourself to offer my thanks."

The tongue, the wit (not to mention the intimidating presence of her father across the room, watching their every move). He would soon learn all the reasons why so many other suitors had been over-whelmed by Isabelle, not daring even to try to make her theirs. But he wasn't like them. And she wasn't like the other girls.

So it began that afternoon. A life of happiness that transcended George's former independence, one of unity. Two lives merged. Her beauty was secondary to the strength of her character, the fortitude in which she housed her beliefs, her way of life, that same stubborn-ness that he shared himself. It softened a bit as the years passed, as she attempted to assimilate with the women of Old Ox, who were suspicious of her husband, that curious landowner with not a close friend to his name. She grew cordial, then matronly when Caleb was born. But that fierce woman was always present regardless, so perhaps he shouldn't have been so surprised she was holding up quite well in the face of the shock that had now transpired.

His admiration only made him want to speak to her more than ever and share in the conversation that Mildred Foster was now robbing him of. After a few more minutes Isabelle came back inside, passing him with only a cursory glance.

Mildred was putting on her gloves and twice called out, "Rest, honey," yelling past George.

He held the skillet before him on the front porch, inwardly begging for the slightest morsel of information, like a vagrant might appeal to a passerby, tin cup in hand.

Mildred flexed her hands in her gloves. Her skin, like porcelain, shimmered in the morning sun.

"Be patient with her," she said calmly. "She doesn't yet know how much you two will need each other."

Startled by the comment, he watched her for some hint of sarcasm, a hidden note meant to spear him, and by the time he registered her sincerity, it was too late. She was already halfway down the lane. He dropped his fork into the skillet, went back inside, and placed it on the stove. As had been the case the last few days, he felt trapped in the cabin, not by the quarters themselves, but by the memories they exposed, which lay in wait wherever he turned. A long walk, he felt, might put them from his mind.

He plucked his jacket from the back of his kitchen chair, gave a last look up the stairwell, and ambled out the front door and into the morning air. He had no specific trail in mind, but he made sure to avoid the path he'd taken to meet Prentiss and Landry. Only after he'd walked away from them had he realized how crass his request had been. The talking one, Prentiss, had all the right in the world to tell him off. But if he was to keep his land, and to put in any crop at all, he would need help, and there wasn't a hand in Old Ox he trusted enough to lift a finger on his behalf. Other than his privacy he had little left in the world, certainly now more than ever, and he wished to keep it at any cost.

Leaves hissed around him as if they'd been trampled, yet with no wind the trees stood still and there was nothing else to see when he looked about. That was the beauty of nature—it was always a step ahead, privy to a joke he did not know, a riddle with no answer. He sat and leaned back against a wide oak and focused on a point before him that ran on endlessly in swirls of copper-colored bark and blankets of green foliage, the lot of it mixing as one the farther it went along.

He'd stumbled upon part of the land that was familiar, a favorite getaway of his father's. It was perhaps where he'd first instilled the idea of the animal in George's imagination, the idea that something monstrous, even sinister, was roaming the property. His father would grip George's hand with such intensity as they walked that he could feel his blood pulse in time with his heartbeat. Benjamin spoke in tones so low that the act of listening required an effort equal to keeping pace with his father's steps, but George's endurance was always lifted by the sacred importance of the story.

The background of the beast was unclear, but his father had seen it once while walking alone, and could describe it with a startling vividness: a black coat of fur that clung to the shadows, moving fluidly as if it were part of the darkness itself; it appeared upright, but took to all fours upon being seen, disappearing as quickly as it had materialized; its eyes were the greatest giveaway, marbles of milky white, like those of a blind man, so haunting that even Benjamin had raced off in fear (a decision he would come to regret).

Their afternoon hikes were a call to arms to track the animal, however real it was or wasn't, and even a young George figured this time together, more than anything, was simply a chance to be with his father and learn the land that would one day belong to him. That is, until he saw the beast himself one night from his bedroom window, and then many nights thereafter…

His memory was interrupted by a yell. He couldn't be sure, but it sounded like Isabelle calling his name. He bolted up and returned the way he'd come. Nothing had led him to believe this was anything but his mind playing tricks on him, yet when he arrived in the clearing, there she was on the front porch, her hand cupped to her mouth, staring off. He had walked fast enough that his hip was bristling, with pinpricks thrumming the length of his side.

"I'm here," he said when he reached the porch. "I'm right here."

He stood at attention and swept the dirt from his pants. "Was just on a stroll." He peeked past her, wondering if she'd received another visitor, but the house appeared empty.

"I'm sure you were," she said. "I was hoping you might go to town and send a telegram for me. To Silas. He should know the news of his nephew."

"If that's what you want. I'd only remind you his last message made it clear he was only starting back home a week ago. In which case he wouldn't receive it for some time."

"Send it to the house. Lillian will receive it. She should know as well."

"First thing tomorrow."

"Thank you. I don't wish to hold a…hold any ceremony until Silas returns. He'd wish to be here for it."

George had no quibble and said that it should be up to her in any case. They stood there. Now was the moment. It seemed to George that a great decision hung in the balance. Isabelle would either stay down in the parlor or else retreat again upstairs away from him. He felt an overwhelming urge to act, to keep her near, to rectify all that had gone wrong between them.

"Perhaps we could read something together," he said.

She didn't seem disturbed, exactly, or even moved to respond. When she spoke, the words were cold, as if to extinguish his own. "I believe you can read without my assistance, George. I will be upstairs if you need anything."

He went into the kitchen and found that in his absence she had cleaned the egg-caked pan and hung it back above the stove. There was little else to do but tidy up the kitchen further, and so he did this, pondering her actions once again, whether they were due to her suffering or her defiance—the latter directed at him or the former at what they had lost—and he wept standing against the sink, the same place she had when he'd delivered the news, lengthy moans and embarrassing sobs. When the time came he prepared a dinner of eggs, as the chickens had been active in recent weeks and he was the only one who might eat the eggs now and he wished to correct the injury paid to his breakfast.

The only accompaniment for dinner, as darkness descended, was a Dickens novel, one he had read on and off again for some weeks, putting it down when distracted. This time he meant to make significant progress, but at a rustle off in the woods he set it aside. A voice stemming from some distance pleaded in an ever-rising tone. Nothing appeared out the window, not even the moon. Finally, there was a crackling and a pair of rambling shadows broke through the trees and drifted toward the cabin, one in front of the other. The large shadow—Landry, George saw now—advanced beside Prentiss, who walked with his back to the cabin, speaking harshly and attempting to wave Landry off.

"You ain't thinking, you ain't ever thought, I should slap you on the backside like the papa you ain't ever had and watch you crawl back to them woods."

The two men had reached the house now, and George rose charily and opened the front door with caution, as to make no noise. The air was cool outside and the hair on his skin rose and his body stiffened as he met the brothers in the lane.

"What is this about?" he said.

"Mr. Walker," Prentiss said. "George."

"Keep your voices down, Isabelle is resting. I thought you two had gone."

"I've been trying to be gone," Prentiss hissed, looking at his brother.

Landry stared back at him with severe concentration. They were both sweating, Prentiss more so, his hair glistening even in the darkness as if it were sprinkled with frost.

"Start from the beginning," George said.

"Ain't no *beginning*. This fool"—he pointed at his brother—"he won't go. You got this idea of this stew in his head all those days back and he ain't quit talking about it."

"*Talking* about it?" George said.

"Yes, that stew of yours."

"Right, the stew I understand," George said impatiently. "It's the speaking I don't get."

Prentiss returned his impatience. "I mean I saw his face when you said you got that stew made up. Since then he's been sneaking this way every night, and he ain't moving out of them woods, not for me or no one else. Only reason I can imagine—other than him being stubborner than a gimp's foot—is that you got that idea in his head and he can't shake it."

"Well, I can assure you," George said to Landry, "that I ate the stew some time ago. And if I had any left, I would not give it you, not because I'd go against my word, but because it'd be fouled by now."

"Which I tried to tell him," Prentiss said. "His hunger just got him acting crazy."

The party calmed and George grew aware of the sound of bullfrogs, louder now than the brothers' labored breathing. The two men did not look well. Landry, his frame lankier than when George had last seen him, was clearly underfed, which meant that Prentiss, too proud to say as much, likely was as well.

"I have a store of eggs," he said. "It's not a stew, but there are more than I or Isabelle could manage on our own."

Whether he had only his brother's interest in mind, Prentiss did not object.

"If you'd wait here," George said, "I could prepare them for you."

"What about the missus?" Prentiss said.

"She's retired for the night. For the foreseeable future."

Landry moved past his brother and took root on the porch steps, his back to the house.

"I guess if them eggs are going to go to waste anyway," Prentiss said.

George returned inside. He cooked eagerly, as he always did for guests. He'd always been of the opinion that what he lacked in personality, or charm, was embodied in his dishes, even one as simple as this: in the perfect accent of salt and pepper, the bit of cheese melted upon the scramble in a blanket so threadbare one wondered how it stayed intact. It was his favorite act of goodwill. The brothers seemed surprised when he returned with their plates, followed by the slices of bread, and finally cups of water.

"Mighty grateful," Prentiss said, and his brother nodded. "If I had a dollar to my name."

George ignored him. They ate slowly, even Landry, both of them savoring each bite. When Landry finished, Prentiss gave him what remained of his eggs, handing over his plate without a second thought. George stood behind them on the porch all the while and said nothing.

It was Prentiss who spoke first. "The land you wish to clear. Am I looking at it?"

George stepped forward and pointed at the woods beyond the barn, off to the right of the cabin. He was thinking of clearing that area, he said, farther from the house and down the hill, still in sight but beyond the first line of trees.

Prentiss took a sip of water.

"You'll need all the sunlight you can get, and them trees ain't going to help your cause."

"I don't know the first thing," George admitted.

"We still aim to head north," Prentiss said. "But we need some funds if we're going to make it. We can't be helping you for free, is what I'm saying."

A jolt traveled through George at the thought of this prospect renewed. His money was tied up in the land, he said, but he would speak to someone about that. It wouldn't be a problem to pay them.

"Will it be fair? You tell me now, 'cause if it ain't, I'd rather cut this boy at the knees and force him off your land than work a day for so little we won't ever make it gone from here."

"Within reason. The same I'd pay any other man for the same job."

"A white man?"

"I've never cheated a man," George bristled, "color be damned."

There was no shake, or any further acknowledgment of the

59

conversation. Prentiss collected both plates, stood, and handed them to George.

"I'll take the cost of the eggs out of your first installment," George said. "Only right, I imagine." When Prentiss cocked his head, as if these were the words of a different tongue, George reassured him that it was a joke, a little one, something to conclude their bargain.

Prentiss said nothing and his features did not soften.

"I didn't mean anything by it," George tried again.

"Good night, then," Prentiss finally said.

"Boys," he said.

He watched them off, Landry's size shrouding Prentiss as they disappeared into the dark.

"Now you're following me, after all that nonsense," he heard Prentiss say. "Waddling on like an overstuffed hen."

It was late for George. The upstairs was unlit, the drapes closed, the house silent. He decided to sleep on the armchair again, knowing that the activity of the night, of the last few days, would keep him wide-awake, and that he'd rise early, ready to act on everything that now occupied his thinking. It seemed only wise to leave Isabelle undisturbed, and with the freedom to roam her portion of the house however she saw fit.

CHAPTER 7

Ge   eorge wasn't the first in the house to rise the following
            morning—it was Isabelle's voice that startled him awake.
            The fire had died. The room was awash in sunshine.

"George. You have visitors."

He followed Isabelle out to the porch. Prentiss and Landry stood
before the house, each holding a bundle of their belongings. Until
now he had seen them only in the shadows of the trees or the
darkness of the night. In the early light there was a magnification of
all they'd endured, the hollow of their cheeks, the splintered cracks
of their lips, the shirts so thin they might crumble like burnt toast if
given a rub.

"That is the one," Isabelle said to him, as if they might not hear.
"The one I spoke of at the clothesline."

"My apologies for my brother," Prentiss said. "He ain't never been
much of a wanderer but he's taken an interest in your property. I know
he wasn't meaning to scare you or steal a thing, just got a little curious."

Isabelle turned to George. There was a luster still about her from
her morning rituals, her hair combed to a full sheen, her cheeks
plumped and colored by the application of a hot rag. Still, George
recognized her irritation in the prim pursing of her lips, perhaps
an impression on her part that on the heels of his withholding the
news of Caleb, there was yet another secret he was only now getting
around to sharing with her.

"I can explain this," he said. "It's not at all bad. I have a project in mind."

"George," she said flatly.

She went inside and George motioned for the brothers to wait a moment, then chased after her.

Coffee was already brewing. He poured himself a cup and joined her at the dining room table.

"I want to *have* something, Isabelle. I've been made to feel so helpless, at such a loss. I don't want to lose this land, too. What we've been through has changed me. Not *all* of me, but a part. Just as it's changed you. And those boys, well, they're fresh off Mr. Morton's land, and eager for a change, too. To make a respectable wage doing what they know in the manner of any other men."

She sipped her coffee and appeared to be deep in thought as she gazed out the window.

"I want to use this land for what it's intended for," he said. "I want to plant, and toil. Do something tangible, something…*real*. I want this land to be my legacy, just like it was for my father. Tell me that is okay. If you could say that little bit, it would mean everything."

Only at that moment did she deign to look in his direction.

"How is this different from anything else? You'll do as you will, and I will do as I will, and we will tolerate whatever comes of it."

He had, a moment ago, felt himself grow tall as he'd shared his feelings, but a part of him was punctured under the weight of her coldness, and he immediately resumed his usual mode of being—one of slouched withdrawal.

"Will you still find a moment to send the telegram?" she asked.

"Oh. Yes."

"You said first thing this morning."

"Then I should get going."

He stood and collected some cups from the cabinet and poured some coffee he thought the brothers might enjoy. He stopped himself before stepping back outside.

"Isabelle. Are you feeling better today?"

She took a deep inhale through her nose, sipped her coffee, and finally gave George a rather friendly shrug of the shoulders.

"It is a nice morning."

———————

George got them started in the storage shed before he went to town. When he returned they held two axes they'd fished from the deep maws of the place, in a corner littered with mouse droppings. It had taken them longer to locate a sharpening stone, but they'd managed this as well and had brought both axes to a point that George found almost intimidating to behold.

Prentiss, who had already surveyed the land they wished to clear, explained to George the dimensions they might accomplish as a unit of three, an estimate figured by mapping out over time the toil of three men on Morton's plantation.

"Well, there is no rush," George said. "Efficiency is important, but we don't want to exhaust ourselves."

Prentiss stared at him blankly—a look that was becoming a regular occurrence— ready to carry on with his plan.

There was no mention of George's trip to town. He'd gotten the telegram off to Silas's home. The man himself was on the way back from yet another venture to sell goods for high premiums in locales others wished not to sojourn, most recently positioned outside a surrendered Confederate fort in the Everglades, where George imagined him lazily sipping whiskey before a swamp in the same fashion he lazily sipped whiskey at his farm back in Chambersville.

He had kept the telegram brief and to the point: *Caleb killed in action. Few details. Your sister grieves.* For a moment he'd considered the wording, as to whether his own grieving was notable (*We grieve*; or, *We mourn his loss*), but it was none of Silas's business how George felt, and he'd left it written as it was.

He had then walked across the street and spent ten minutes with Ezra, interrupting a meeting with his request for a small loan, which

Ezra gave him with little curiosity and without requesting any papers be signed. The only confusion to Ezra was George's wish to be given the amount half in coins and half in small notes—Ezra muttered that he wasn't a bank, then obliged. And George was home with almost a full day of sunlight to spare, yet he did not wish to begin working, although both Prentiss and Landry—for what little Landry betrayed, standing stoically against the barn—were more than willing to start the job.

Prentiss trained an appraising eye upon him now.

"I seen you struggle with that leg. Got yourself a hard enough time just getting off that donkey."

But this was one point on which George would not budge. The job, if done by others, would not permit him the purpose, the distraction, of the whole campaign. He did not wish to admit how little he wanted to be in his own home, and how little else there was in the world that interested him. He simply insisted it was vital he join them, side by side, so that when they left, he would know how to continue on his own.

"You claim you itching to get started, Mr. Walker, but from what I seen I'd hazard you ain't worked a day in your life."

"As I've said, *George* is fine. I'm not my father. And until now I always considered a successful day to be defined by a lack of work, so I cannot say you're far off with that estimation."

Prentiss stood at attention. "Well, you about to make up for lost time, I'ma see to that."

"Who is in charge here, exactly?" George said.

Prentiss smiled then, knowing, perhaps, what was to come in a manner that George himself did not.

That day was the first of many together. The three men would take turns with the axes, George chopping meekly when he could manage, passing it off and wiping the sweat from his brow when he could not. Each tree's fall was startling, the later ones no less than the first. The very act had a meaning that fueled him, the bark splintering on contact, the groan of the tree and the felling and the strike of the impact cascading through the forest like a whoosh of wind, sudden and ominous and wholly arresting.

George was far from capable of the effort the brothers expended. When the day grew long, and he took one swing too many—his hip burning, his arms sore—Landry would lean forward and put a hand on his shoulder, as if to tell him he'd done enough, and wrest the ax from his hands. George exclaimed that he was only getting started, yet Landry, ignoring him, assumed his place, slashing at the tree with guttural thuds so violent they quieted George.

He was dutiful in paying them—a dollar a day each—enough that in time they would be able to save an amount sufficient to afford not only railroad tickets but also extra clothes and some lodging and meals until they landed on their feet. For lunch George usually fetched a bit of salted pork from the storeroom, some hard bread from the previous night's leftovers, and cobbled together two meals apiece to get them through the day.

On occasion there were the afternoons when they left the work behind and simply walked, or rested, though George noticed this seemed to make Prentiss antsy. Nevertheless he would listen attentively to George's stories, tales of an old man's past. George understood that, as with his own lackluster participation in cutting down the trees, this listening of Prentiss's was nothing but a courtesy paid to him. He relished it all the same.

One day, when they'd finished early and were sitting on a felled tree soon to be chopped into smaller logs that they would stack on the sled for Ridley to haul, George told them again of the beast. Prentiss entertained the idea, seeming to recognize the manifestation of such things being birthed in the dark—creatures that existed on the border of reality and legend.

George told them, too, of a mental exercise his father had hatched: that each day of each year, a man might imagine a tree in his mind.

The tree, upon doing good in the world, could grow strong and thick, but with every poor decision, rot would start to sprout—gnarled roots at its base, limp branches that snapped with the lightest touch. At the end of any given period—a month, a year—it was wise to consider the growth of one's tree, and the decisions you had made that led it there. It was yours to let grow or die.

"I rather like that," Prentiss said.

"Count yourself as one of the few to lend it credence," George said. "I take little heed of it. My father himself failed to follow the instruction and he invented the whole damn thing. Hell, my own son scoffed at it when he was half your age. But it sounds nice, doesn't it?"

Prentiss looked at him and it took George a moment to realize that he'd invoked Caleb—whom he'd studiously avoided mentioning in the brothers' presence—for perhaps the first time since the night he'd met them. Prentiss asked him, directly but with a note of tenderness, what had become of his son.

George thought for a moment to deflect but then he told him.

"That's a shame," said Prentiss, who seemed inclined to add something more but stopped there.

"It's indescribable," George said. "I wouldn't wish it on my own enemy. I hope you never experience such a thing."

Landry, who until now had sat motionlessly beside them holding an ax beneath its blade as if it were a child's plaything, picked up a loose branch and began sharpening it to a point with the ax.

"I lost my oldest cousin to a sale when I was thirteen," Prentiss said. "That was after the crop caught ablaze. Mr. Morton sold our mama a couple years later. Had her inside the house weaving on the loom when she stopped picking her share, but her hands took to shaking so he got rid of her. My father died when my mama was pregnant with Landry. I wasn't old enough to know him."

George squinted under the gaze of the sun. He did not know what to say for quite a long time and came to wish he had trusted his instinct and refrained from speaking about Caleb.

"I suppose no one owns a claim on suffering," he said at last.

"S'pose not."

They returned to the cabin as the day cooled. He had been allowing Prentiss and Landry to stay in the barn as a way to escape the woods. Isabelle was on the porch, as she had been since that morning when he left, and they quieted when they saw her. She had taken visitors once or twice since Mildred Foster had been to the house but still said very little to George, all in all. On this day, Mildred was to have paid her another visit, but George—to his great relief—had been in the woods long enough to miss the occasion. He imagined that he and the brothers appeared as a group of schoolboys, sweating and talking loudly and suddenly hushing in her presence. Landry, fidgeting awkwardly with his shirt, stepped behind his brother, though the move to obscure himself was all but pointless, given his size.

George asked after her day.

"Fine. Mildred says hello."

"Oh, well, that's nice of her."

"She's a strong woman. Helpful in times like these."

He had hoped that Mildred might lift his wife's spirits, but she was clearly morose. She stood and disappeared inside, then reappeared bearing a pitcher of lemonade and a ring of cups, her index finger threaded through each of their handles. She came down the stairs and handed each of them a cup and poured. Her gaze was fixed on the ground, as if she'd been commanded to perform an action that rankled her. Prentiss thanked her, more than once, and George, though lost in his confusion, finally managed to utter a thanks himself as she retreated to the porch, where she poured her own cup. Up to this very moment she had ignored the brothers, so that the act seemed to indicate some kind of truce, not with them but with George, and with the circumstances surrounding their employ.

"We should leave her alone," he said quietly.

"She seems fine there," Prentiss said, sipping the lemonade. "I don't think she minds us much."

But they walked to the barn in silence, as a unit, their feet crunching the grass.

"You think she's done with you," Prentiss said.

"I did not say that," George said.

"You act like it."

This felt like an opening, an invitation, but George, recalling the conversation in the woods about Caleb, elected not to take it.

"Let me see what we decide to eat and I will bring what I can," he said.

Landry went inside the barn. He took off his shirt. There was a basin no bigger than a sink but they could fill it and wash there. George left them to it.

He would wash up himself, and to do this he would have to retrieve a fresh pair of clothes from the bedroom. The night was looming, the house was quiet, his least favorite moment of every day. His study was the first room up the stairs, their bedroom the last, and Caleb's sat between the two, where the narrowness of the hallway became most apparent. The door to Caleb's room, slightly ajar, teased George, beckoning him, but he could not bear the temptation. Even the simplest glance could uncork an endless stream of memories: the sight of the boy sneaking into his study as if George didn't see him there, or, worse yet, the image of young Caleb reading at the lip of his bed, facing the window, and turning to see his father as he passed, with a smile so broad it took over the width of his boyish face.

If he did not open the door it felt as if Caleb was still there, reading indefinitely, and the realization that he could not face the truth, and would rather heed some childish sense of denial, pained him as much as the boy's death. He might not have been a man of strength, or great resolve, but he had always thought he could look within himself with an honesty few others could lay claim to. Except here. Except before his son's door.

He retrieved a shirt from the bedroom and hurried back downstairs.

———

For the first time since he had delivered the fatal news, Isabelle ate beside him that night. And in the days ahead, she began to return to active life, though as this new variation of herself—transformed into a cold fixture on the porch who was willing to take care of the home, to cook and garden, to entertain visitors for an afternoon, but without any of the cheer that had once rounded out her demeanor.

Still they slept apart. Each day George woke in his armchair with a doubt that the brothers would appear again. He had a strong belief that they might take what little money he'd given them thus far and disappear. But each morning they emerged from the barn and approached the steps of the house, and George, seated on the porch, itched his backside and rose gratefully to greet them. They would lean against the barn drinking coffee, discussing what was to come in the day, and then act upon it, finishing in the calm glow of the approaching evening in a race to clear the trees in time to begin tilling the ground in preparation for the eventual seeding.

Although he spoke freely with them, he kept to himself the single lie he'd told, which was that his father's allegory bore no importance for him. In fact, in his mind's eye he conjured his life as a languishing oak, throttled by the elements, with branches so tortured that they sprouted at impossible angles, its bark flecked with yellow fungus and its leaves burnt through by the sun. The decline only furthered as the years passed, but George felt the tree had been born rotten, as if he knew he had begun on poor ground, with an unsteady and shifting sense of morality, and that there would be no improvement.

On a morning that was awfully windy and, for the early spring, uncommonly cold, they came upon a dying tree that was an uncanny replica of the one in his mind. George demanded he cut this one on his own, and although it took nearly an hour, he exulted in the labor. It was as if, in excising from the property this tree—so puny compared with the rest—he might somehow also cut the disappointing past from his very being. And so he swung the ax with abandon, with a childlike belief in reversing years of inaction, of squandered land and squandered relationships. He felt a great release, the opening of a space within him that might allow for something new to sprout—something good, something worth living for.

The meager tree made little sound when it fell, which meant that the noise finding his ears had to have been borne from somewhere else. Long howls like those of a child reached him, and together with Prentiss and Landry, George followed the sound, at first plodding, then jogging toward the cabin with a great apprehension filling his chest. When they emerged into the clearing, his worst fears were realized, and then dropped immediately away.

It was Isabelle, moaning and overtaken by the occasion. He could hardly believe what he saw next: the long blanket of blond hair, snapping in the wind like a flag before his son's face. Caleb tried to turn, but his mother held him so tightly that his features stayed hidden. When George drew close enough for their eyes to meet, they were strangers to each other. Isabelle released Caleb for a moment, but both father and son stood frozen, some distance apart, as if in need of an introduction.

"Well then," was all George could say. "Well."

His voice caught, and he struggled to subdue the swelling wave that had been stored away for so long. He could not run to meet him, his legs would not move, but there was time now. At last he approached, cautiously, and could finally make out the markers of his face, the same ones he saw in his mind's eye, night after night, when he pictured the boy reading on the lip of his bed, beckoning to him. As with any moment of unbridled emotion, he did not know how to react, or what he was expected to say, and could only think of how he was supposed to appear, how another man, a better man, might act in his position.

He put a hand on Caleb's cheek to make sure it was real.

"I heard your mother, but never did I think." Then he slid both hands into his pockets. "Why don't we go inside."

CHAPTER 8

Caleb had not quite managed to kill his father, but he had certainly aged him. The old man looked pained when he walked, and the lines of his face appeared as cracks upon glass that had flourished with time. His mother, at first glance, was more of a comfort. He'd missed her as the other soldiers missed their mothers, knowing that his home was not so much the cabin but the place where she existed, waiting for him to return, waiting to embrace him. When they hugged, when he held the shape of her against him, he felt like a boy again, and wished he could draw upon that feeling on command for the rest of his time alive.

Now, at the dining room table, she caressed his face and ran her hand along the scar of his cheek, the new shape of his nose, and demanded to know whether his health was intact.

"Shall we call a doctor?" she said. "I think we should. It's decided, then."

"I'm all healed," he said. "It's done. It's all over."

After his long absence the house presented itself as a dreamscape, and he was inclined to inspect every room, to confirm the particularities of each in relation to the whole. And there were simpler urges: to see Ridley, whom, in an unforeseen turn, he had missed deeply; to bathe; to sleep in his own bed.

His mother set him up with a plate of white cheese and bread and promised him an apple pie—her one true specialty—once she'd

71

procured the necessary ingredients. She spoke of the pie at length, overwhelmed at the excitement of his arrival to such an extent that her mind had narrowed to this single track of thought—the coring of fruit and the retrieval of some cider to spruce up the innards and the readying of the flour for the crust and so on.

"If you carry on like this," his father said, "I fear what we'll have to endure when you get to talking of dinner."

He was in the big room, seated in his old beaten-down chair. Caleb could not hold back a bit of laughter.

"Don't set her off," he said.

"It's too late for that, clearly," his father said.

His mother, ignoring their banter, took a breath and grabbed Caleb's forearm, rubbing it with enough vigor to kindle a fire.

"A mother has a right to be worked up. My child is back! Now tell us what came of you. August was here. He gave us the gravest news. That, well…"

"That you'd been killed," his father said.

Not quite, Caleb said. He'd been made prisoner. Exchanged. Then paroled. As had so many others. Given a parchment describing how he was to yield to the law of the Union and return home. This condensation of the events felt like the first step in letting them slip away into the past. Unlikely, but he had to make a go of it.

"So August is home," he said, betraying no feeling.

"He suffered an injury himself," his father said, "although I could not make sight of it at all. A bad fall, apparently."

Caleb shifted and dried mud sloughed off his pants and landed beneath his chair. His mother, for all her excitement, could not refrain from looking at the carpet as if an animal had just released its droppings.

His father asked him how far he'd come.

"The Carolinas."

"You walked all that way?"

There had been a few ambulances with room for him, and the occasional farmer with space in his wagon had shown sympathy, but before he could explain as much, his mother interrupted.

"What did they do to your face? How bad was it? You must tell us everything and leave out nothing."

"I'm afraid there's not much of a story. Happened before I was captured. Just the boys fooling around. A late night and we'd had a few too many. Nothing exciting."

He bit into the bread and after a second finished off the cheese. His parents seemed to be waiting for him to speak, and the expectation that he might somehow lead the interrogation they'd started was worse than their prodding.

"Has all been well here?" he asked.

His mother again looked at the floor near his chair.

"Other than my untimely death," he said, in an effort to lighten things.

"These are difficult times for everyone," his father said. "I think your mother would agree."

It was then that he noticed the vastness of the space between his parents· the way they had yet to make eye contact, or draw near each other, or even exchange words. He had come so far to return to what little he knew, and all at once it appeared that it might no longer exist. While his parents had been waiting, interminably, for him to find his way home, they had changed, and now all three of them were altered but in the same place they'd occupied for so many years.

He was having trouble sitting still, his knee bouncing and his foot chattering against the floorboard.

"Perhaps we could continue this later on," he said. "If I could just get a little rest I think it might do wonders."

His mother stood up.

"Of course. Your bed is made. Everything is tidied up. Fresh towels on your dresser."

She squeezed him so hard it robbed him of breath. Then her hand slipped to his side and alighted on the leather of his holster. They'd been made to turn their guns over to the Union, yet he'd managed to hide the sidearm, knowing what might befall him on the journey home, the dangers that found men alone on the open road. His mother pulled back and stared at the weapon.

His father stood, too, and eyed the pistol with caution.

"No need for that anymore," he said. "I'll put it with your grandfather's rifles in the cellar."

It was best to oblige them, Caleb knew—to return, as thoroughly as possible, to the edition of himself they'd once known: a boy who would never lay a hand on something so vulgar. He unholstered the pistol and passed it to his father.

Upstairs, his room, as clean as his mother had described, exuded an element of the macabre—the miniature walking sticks of his youth, leaning against the wall, had been dusted and polished; his hats, stacked in a column, were spotless, unmarred by so much as a speck of dust. How long would she have kept this up? Months? Years? His death something best laundered away on a washboard, swept up with a broom.

He removed his boots and then his trousers and fell onto his bed in a heap. He slept peacefully but was greatly confused upon waking, not knowing where he was or how he'd gotten there, as had been the case for so many days preceding this one. The difference this time was that, reaching to the side of the bed, he could not find his trousers. A bleary glance out the window revealed his mother dipping his pants into the boiling water of the copper washing kettle. She slapped at them with the dipping spoon, hard enough to get a life's worth of grime from the rags. He thought he would have to go pant-less about his home, until he remembered the drawer full of clothes across the room, a bounty to a man who had held on so dearly, to so little, for so long.

───────────

His father had killed a hen for supper the night before but Caleb hadn't woken up to eat it. In the morning he tore at it, and his mother, seated with him at the table, watched him as if it was a performance, an animal picking at scraps. When he finished he informed her he wished to head into town, and her disappointment was almost enough to make him change his mind.

"You act like I'm a prisoner *here*, too," he said.

"Don't say that, don't *ever* say that. I just wish to spend time with you."

"We'll have a world's worth of time. Won't be a thing to do but sit around here together. No reason to rush it." He leaned over and kissed her on the forehead and pushed his chair back. "Where's the old man?"

His mother nodded to the barn, from which his father was now returning. Caleb went onto the porch and his father gingerly made his way over to him and asked how he was feeling.

"Top-grade," Caleb said.

Wisps of steam rose off his father's cup of coffee, and it brought to mind the last march under the colors of the enemy, when the flatlands had yielded to a punishing cold front. The boys put in charge of him were his age, rowdy and prone to thieving from farmers and townsfolk when they could get away with it. They'd stolen overcoats to fend off the weather, but when the sun reemerged one day, they chose to cast them aside, yet saw no reason to leave them in the woods where they'd be of no use. A skinny lieutenant mentioned how often Caleb had whined of being too far from the fire, and the rest decided he would be the best choice to inherit the excess coats, which they packed onto his shoulders until the weight buckled his knees. The heat was so great as the day wore on that the sweat collected in small puddles at the cuffs of his sleeves and pants.

He grew damp behind the ears just thinking about it and was happy when the memory passed. It was then he saw the two men leaving the barn. One was remarkably large, with an unmistakable current of muscle at his shoulders, his body broad enough to dwarf the other man.

"Are you going to explain that?" he asked his father.

The two were brothers, he said, giving him some assistance with a peanut farm he was setting up down below the hill. "If you want I can show you the progress."

"A peanut farm. You?"

"Is that so difficult to believe?"

"You could barely be made to help Mother with the roses she put in. Said she only had them because Mrs. Foster did and there was no pride in spending your life matching wits with others lost in vapid hobbies. If I recall correctly."

"You do," his father said, taking a sip of his coffee. "But this is different."

"Always different when you do it, isn't it?" Caleb said, thinking of how his father's short-lived foray into making moonshine was deemed to be unrivaled compared with other enthusiasts, as his eye for quality whiskey was unmatched; or then there was his spontaneous wish to construct a cabinet, a process he thought valid only until he realized he hadn't the slightest skills, at which point the entire field of cabinetmaking suddenly became trivial, so unworthy of time that he shook his head when passing the woodworkers in town for years after.

Caleb spat over the railing and commented that the men had been with his father the day before, when he arrived.

Yes, his father said, their names were Prentiss and Landry, and he explained how they'd come to the woods. They were staying in the barn for now.

"You have Mr. Morton's Negroes in your keep, then."

"I wouldn't call that a fair interpretation. They've elected to stay here."

"Yes, well, I suppose having Negroes is different when you do it, too."

His father sipped his coffee, swallowed hard.

"I feel that you're being stubborn for no reason at all. And it's a bit much this early in the morning."

It wasn't the first time his father had made a claim about his stubbornness, and such words had lost their power over time. In this instance, with his mood lightened by his return home, he chose to ignore them. The birdsong was picking up a rhythm, and he recognized the same tunes he'd heard since childhood.

"I told them they could do what they wished today," his father said, "as I aimed to spend some time with you."

"Actually, I was meaning to ask if I might borrow Ridley. I'm thinking of heading to town."

"Already bored with us, then."

"Now you sound like Mother. There's just other folks to see. I'll be back before nightfall. We can finish off that hen together."

"You're grown now," George said. "You'll do as you will."

Caleb stood before him, motionless.

"You don't need my permission to ride Ridley. If you want the saddle it should be beside the feed bag."

Caleb left his father at the porch and retrieved Ridley from the stable. So little had changed with the donkey—the twitching rabbit's ears, the mane spiked like a jagged mountain range which took to his hand but still shivered at the touch—that the reunion felt diminished by the animal's familiarity. To the donkey, it seemed, Caleb had not been gone at all. There was little ceremony to the brushing and haltering, and afterward he led Ridley out of the stable and past the house, waving goodbye to his mother and catching another glimpse of his father as he finished his coffee on the porch.

"Tell August I say hello," his father called. "And when you get back I'd like to hear what really happened to that face of yours. About that horseplay."

Caleb said nothing and continued down the lane, the sound of the birds still mingling in the melody of the air, the naked spring sun just bright enough to cast a golden glow onto the lane like some premonition of encouragement from above, as if to suggest that the day ahead of him might just go his way.

They had opened his face with the butt of a rifle. He'd cupped his face with both hands, but no amount of dabbing at the wound could prevent the blood from slipping through his fingers and wetting the ground. That night he'd cried, not from the pain but from the fear of deformity, the image of himself as another mangled relic of the war, a curiosity for children, fit for a circus. Later, as if it might cheer him up, they said the blow was more for the desertion than for anything else—even if it wasn't from their side, the action itself was worthy of punishment, regardless of the colors of his uniform.

He had simply been relieved they hadn't shot him the second he jutted his head out from the trenches where he and the others had taken cover. The pull of August's father was strong enough to keep them from the front lines—or danger in general, really—and until they came upon that string of muzzles bursting so hot the smoke assumed the look of a forest fire, he'd yet to see a bullet fly. He was certain they'd encountered a full-scale attack, the sort that would make for lore when they were back home, the stuff to tell one's grandchildren. But later the blue-clads would slap his face playfully, laughing as they polished their rifles with ash from the fire and stuffed tobacco into the bow of their lips. "That," they told him, "is what we call a skirmish."

He hadn't found any shame in his desertion—to him it was merely pragmatic, with survival in mind—but he knew how it would be perceived by others. His only regret was that he had abandoned August. There was solace, though, in the fact that August was the only other soldier from back home to witness his cowardice. Again with Mr. Webler to thank, they'd been assigned to a company wholly separate from the one the other boys from Old Ox had ended up in. Where so many were losing life and limb, he and August had been kept to guarding the railways, off in the distance, spending their nights with little worry, wrapped up in childish pranks and games of draughts, such that the whole enterprise had the air of a tour.

Until the company took to the woods and got themselves lost. That had been the irretrievable mistake, a refrain he repeated to his escorts as the days passed. The entire business was terribly wrong, he said, he wasn't supposed to be there with them at all. But if he imagined they might release him, it was nothing but wishful thinking. His only good fortune was that when they got sick of his complaining, they aimed for his groin and let his face go on healing.

Ridley carried him along now, and the first sight that greeted him in Old Ox was an aging whore revealing herself on the walkway to a gang of horsemen. She slipped on a streak of mud, gathered herself, and returned to the brothel from which she'd come, laughing all the way. The town had grown in his absence and there were few faces out that assured him it was even the same place from the year before. One or two folks took notice of him but their stares quickly went from his face to the ground, and he could not be sure whether it was his battered features or the fact that he had come back from the grave that brought him attention.

The Union soldiers had occupied a number of storefronts, and from their posts out front they eyed him suspiciously, more with weariness than disgust. The schoolhouse near the roundabout appeared to be their headquarters. One woman seemed on the verge of a fistfight with a soldier over rations he did not have, and Caleb could not help wondering which punishment was worse: his own, for having been made a captive after proving himself a coward; or that of these poor souls who were stationed so far from home, surrounded by so many who despised them.

He turned off with Ridley where the traffic began to slow and the lean-tos were replaced by real, sturdy homes—the sort that might survive a rainfall or two—refined dwellings with slanted rooftops and swings hanging from the trees in their yards. The tilted sun cast its favor on two girls beside their home playing battledore and shuttle-cock, one hand on their rackets and the other on their bonnets. A smaller boy sat on the lap of his mother near them, struggling against her grip to be let into the game. The other homes were empty, their front doors shut with families going on with their business as if this day were like any other, which for them, Caleb understood, it was.

Where it seemed the town might up and end altogether, the land came into its own and expanded, with great swaths of fresh grass giving way to larger estates tucked in before the start of more woods beyond. Counted together there were no more than ten in all, and the townsfolk called this bundle of homes Mayor's Row.

The Webler home was the last one—a sloping mansard roof, three stories of living quarters, and tightly groomed shrubs forming a hedge just high enough to allow privacy but not so much to deter a welcome visitor. From the street Caleb peered up at August's room, wondering if, as had been the case for so many visits that had preceded this one, the boy might be waiting there for him. Back then, after gazing down and waving, August would vanish, only to reappear on the front porch to lead him inside. But the bedroom was dark. He turned, as if what lay behind him might signal some command of what he should do next, but saw only shrubs. Caleb had considered this moment since he'd been released by the Union soldiers and set off for home. Yet here he was stalled on an ass, lacquered in sweat, as frightful as the day of his desertion.

The voice at the front door calling his name was startling enough to bring both him and Ridley to attention. They looked up together, although the donkey returned to grazing while Caleb was forced to think of something to offer in response. Not that this was new. He had always struggled to speak up in the presence of Wade Webler.

"Howdy!" was all he said, to his great dismay.

"Caleb Walker, as I live and breathe. August told me—well hell, he told me you went and got yourself killed. But that don't look to be the case. You get over here. Looking like you're halfway to melting and that sun's giving us a perfectly polite start of an afternoon. You got way too much of your father in you, I swear. Not a Southern bone in your body."

Caleb tied down Ridley and walked over to the veranda. Mr. Webler had on an assemblage of formal wear—well-cut trousers, a jacket with tail—yet his silk shirt exposed his pigeon chest, with great cumulus puffs of hair poking out. Caleb had never quite seen the man so exposed and was not sure if he should offer his hand for a shake or let him return inside to tidy up.

"What a sight," Mr. Webler said. "*What. A. Sight.*"

They shook, and already his body was tensing up so tight with nerves that part of him wished he might trade spots out front with Ridley and spend the rest of the day eating grass in solitude.

"Are you well? Have you seen your parents? They must be ecstatic."

"They're quite happy, sir."

"Well, it's a shame you made your return only today. You missed my gala last night, a rousing success, if I do say so myself."

Mr. Webler motioned inside and Caleb followed him to find Negroes on their knees cleaning the floor and little boys and girls on their rear ends reaching behind cabinets and couches with rags where their elders could not; glasses were still being collected onto trays and although he only glimpsed the dining room as the door closed he caught sight of a tablecloth blotted over with wine. After being led into the parlor Caleb was forced to sit beside a grandfather clock that complained at timed intervals he could not make sense of. Mr. Webler held forth, speaking as if Caleb had come here to see him, and Caleb could discern no means of wriggling out of the interaction without appearing rude.

"I thought it wise to put on something of a fundraiser for the cause. We collected an amount I'm quite proud of that will go toward doing some fine work for this great county. The people here, even in times of emergency, are still as Christian as they come, and you could station all of Grant's army in this town and we would still preserve our values, our heritage..."

They called the man the freight train, for when the words gained steam he kept his engine stoked with so much liquor and tobacco he could entertain late into the night without a stop to rest. He had never run for office, but often spoke like a pol, and lorded over the town as if he were the mayor. There was talk of a seafood stew, of women dancing as their husbands fell asleep. Indeed, the whole affair harked back to a time when the world was right, and made them wonder if Old Ox might yet escape from the Union's embrace altogether.

"It's sounds like quite the ball, sir."

"Not a *ball*, Caleb. A gala."

"I'm not sure I know the difference."

Mr. Webler grunted and Caleb realized, for the first time, that he was still drunk from the night before. He paused to collect himself, enough to pretend at some greater interest in Caleb.

"Put it aside," he said. "I'd rather hear of your time. I only know that you got separated from August. Beyond that things are… unclear."

This was exactly the kind of statement for which Caleb should've been prepared. On his way home, after he'd been released by the Union, whenever he was asked by strangers about his service—the battles seen, the toils endured—Caleb had often delivered a line of grand vagueness that tended to silence whoever had posed the question: *I don't wish to brag of the triggers I've pulled or the places in which I did so.* (Which omitted the fact that he had not pulled any triggers at all.) Yet Mr. Webler would so easily parry his routine that he knew it was wise to avoid it from the start.

"I imagine August told you everything there was to share."

Mr. Webler looked upon him with a stinging sense of either disgust or remorse. His mustache bristled like a tickled caterpillar. He reached to the cellarette at his back and produced a tumbler and an uncorked, half-empty decanter.

"Let me tell you something, son."

He began to pour himself a drink so carefully that the stream kept up with his story, the smell of the whiskey so potent and the tang of his words so biting that the resultant mixture of the two felt combustible in the air.

"I fought down in Mexico," he said, "when August was but a babe. There was an expedition in Puebla, before we saw any gunplay. By the time we set foot into the city they were already raising our flag, so I spent the night carousing with the boys, the usual business. But one of those Mexicans stumbles into our camp, starting trouble, probably as drunk as I was, and I see the threat and I know I got to earn my stripes somehow. So I call him out, get him to square up with me, and I have him on the ground before you could say your own name.

The boys are hollering and that bug juice has me feeling invincible and I'm not about to let up."

Mr. Webler leaned back and sighed as if he had just unearthed a new interpretation of the story that had previously eluded him, and Caleb listened to the performance as a spectator grasping for an appropriate reaction—to applaud or laugh or cry—unsure of where the man was taking it but waiting patiently for it to end.

"I get a nice little angle, press my fingers into his eyes, and squeeze to hell and back, and those things leak out so soft and easy you would've thought they were two slugs under my thumbs. And when I get up I'm smiling, and I don't realize in the moment, in all that exercise, that I went and pissed myself. So of course I tell them it was all that effort I put in, fess up just to get on with things. But wouldn't you know it, before I went to sleep that night I turned over in my tent, had a little cry, *and pissed myself again.* They never knew about that one, though. That one I kept close to the vest."

The women and children, all of them mute, were still cleaning around the two men ceaselessly and the place had the feel of a prison, with Caleb being forced, along with the inmates, to endure a speech by a warden displaying his power over those in his charge. He pitied these people who had put up with Mr. Webler for so long, working now for what must be pennies after years of bondage, and wondered, if a domestic uprising were to take place, whether anyone other than the man's wife and son would bemoan his skull being smashed in.

"I believe I regret that day," he carried on. "Not the pissing. I wasn't the first boy in uniform to piss myself. But only that that Mexican did nothing to earn my violence. It's not as if he deserted his own. He was still in Puebla. Still looking for a fight. There's honor in that."

Caleb, for some time, could not conjure a word. The clock sang out once again.

"Sounds like quite the mess, sir," he finally managed.

Mr. Webler downed his whiskey in one pull and offered Caleb the slightest grin.

"I'm sure you can imagine."

Just then the light above the staircase was interrupted by the opening of a door that shuttered out the sun. The parlor went so dark, and then so bright as the door closed once more, that even Mr. Webler paused, although the scrubbing of the floor continued unabated.

Caleb could not help standing.

"Ah. There he is," Mr. Webler said.

As footsteps started down the stairs, Mr. Webler stood and excused himself.

"I suppose I'll leave both of you to it."

August invited Caleb to ride with him to their favorite hideaway, the place where they'd spent great swaths of their youth. On the way, August apologized for his father's behavior. (He'd been up, as Caleb had guessed, since the party the night before, and apparently the Union occupation of Old Ox had brought him to seek counsel in drink almost every night.) But neither of the friends seemed willing to speak in anything other than circles of small talk.

Caleb asked August about the rest of his time in the field.

"Boring for long stretches, really. Faced off against a few bluebelly stragglers, got to point my Colt at them."

"I bet you liked that."

"For a time."

Footsteps on grass. That familiar crunch.

"Might I ask what brought you home?" Caleb said.

August was silent, a flicker of a smile forming at the corner of his lips. Near the end, he said, they'd gotten orders to head toward Fort Myers, down in Florida. At last a real battle. Unfortunately, en route, he took a little spill down a hillside while on patrol and nearly broke his leg. He spent a week in the infirmary and was then sent home.

Like his father, Caleb could find nothing wrong with his friend's leg upon examination. He looked no different than he had the day they'd left Old Ox together—if anything he seemed sprier now. Caleb knew, of course, that August would never have seen a battle-field. His father wouldn't have allowed it. But he wasn't about to acknowledge this fact.

"Not even a hobble," he observed.

"No. I'm lucky in that way."

Rather than lob his own volley of questions, August told Caleb how he'd been working for his father in the weeks since returning home, learning about lumber and construction and the properties they might own and sell. There had always been the sense that his father's work was not exciting enough for him, but his talk hinted that he might have had his share of adventure, no matter how brief and pampered, and was ready to investigate the doldrums of every-day living.

When the town was at their rear they slowed to a stop and tied off both Ridley and August's horse to a naked tree. They searched for a large stone they'd marked as children with a white stroke of paint, and did so with such great intensity that it felt like another opportunity to keep away from each other, from even sharing a glance that might shorten the distance between them. The stone appeared smaller than it had when they were children, but Caleb picked out the faded slash mark and they walked beyond it, breaking through the trees and into the high brush. The whip and crackle of the weeds underfoot were the only noises. At last the pond revealed itself, the lilies and the chickweed spread along the borders of the crystalline water.

"No different," August said.

Time had forgotten the place. They'd never seen another soul here. Once, they'd spotted a solitary duck, drifting in place, but it had never returned, and the memory felt fuzzy to both of them, lost somewhere between the real and the imaginary. Caleb sat before the water and August did the same, and it took only a moment for them to turn and face one another in earnest.

This, Caleb thought. This is what he'd been waiting for. August's eyes were so boyish, so blue with innocence and charm, that he'd withstood scrutiny from even the cruelest superiors; his pink lips, hardly there, suggested a false shyness that had no bearing on his real feelings at any given moment. The sight of him was greatly relieving, and by the time Caleb had drunk his fill it was too late to consider his own appearance. He glanced away as bashfully as a girl might.

"What'd they do to you?" August asked coldly.

"That bad?"

"It's not like that."

Caleb said he'd been clubbed.

August itched his neck and glanced back at him sharply before turning away again.

"Did they break your spirit?"

"I suppose so. But the guilt at leaving you was worse. Or just as bad."

August said nothing after that, and Caleb's heartbeat quickened at his friend's reticence. He had always been more comfortable being given direction, and from the day he and August had met, as boys, Caleb had found in August someone he could follow, someone whose hobbies he could adopt, whose thoughts he could make his own. It was the simplest path to pleasure. But if the arrangement offered him a ready-made structure and purpose, it was also a weakness that, in this instance—when instruction about what he ought to do or think was being withheld—was used against him. August was spooling out their conversation so slowly that Caleb felt it as a great anguish, and also as a fear, for if August never gave him a chance to confront his actions, they might never reconcile, and if they did not reconcile…

"I'm sorry," Caleb said. "At my deepest core. What I did, I've thought about it every day since and will think of it every day that's to come. I went there to be at your side, and even that I could not see through. I wouldn't lose a wink of sleep at the thought of another man calling me a traitor, but I cannot bear for you to think such a thing. Forgive me. Please. That's all I ask."

He could not cry. Not at this juncture, with everything said. But he could feel the tears—lying in wait.

August had curled his legs up to his chest and his posture reminded
Caleb of the old August, the child August; recalled the nights they'd
come to this place and lain on their backs and dotted the stars with
their fingers, trusting that their gaze had brought them to the same
ones. They were moments that felt as timeless as the place itself.

But that was then.

There was a touch on his face, and suddenly a hand gripping his
jaw. August brought Caleb so close to him that their noses nearly
touched; their eyes were locked as one, and soon they were studying
each other's faces so closely that Caleb felt himself being given over
to his friend, as if awaiting a commandment. And then August struck
him so hard with an open hand that he lost sight. Bright sparks spotted his vision. After a blink the world returned, the look of August,
his lips pursed, his cheeks red with fury.

"After everything," he said. "To leave my side."

"You don't have to tell me! I know. If I could take it back…" Caleb
sighed in frustration. He could not coax forgiveness from others like
August could; he was no charmer. "Would it be so hard? To just say
the words? To let it go?"

"*Let it go?*"

August drew his hand back again, but before he could bring it
forward, Caleb tackled him. It was not an act of defense but rather
the eruption of everything he'd carried on those long days spent returning home, the bottled-up ponderings and the haunting torment
of his regret. As he mounted August and held him down, his friend
bucked against him to no avail. Caleb kept repeating the words, *forgive
me, forgive me,* which became so pathetic that after a time August's
body unclenched and went limp, his anger replaced with what could
only be pity. But when Caleb let up, August slipped out from under
him, reversed their positions, and, with a vacant stare, pinned him to
the grass, his weight heavy and final.

He put a hand against Caleb's throat.

"Are you done?" he said.

The grip grew firmer, and Caleb held out for only a moment

before nodding. August released him, collapsing to the grass beside his friend, both of them too spent to do anything but breathe, their chests falling and rising, the mosquitoes hovering in the wake of their commotion. It was the same way they had dealt with such matters as children, and it felt right to begin patching up their differences by turning back to their past selves, to fists and slaps and grunts—base punishment, the most ancient of remedies.

"You told your father, didn't you?" Caleb said, still gathering his breath. "About what I did."

"I thought you were dead."

"I wish you hadn't." Caleb raised himself on his elbows. "And my father?"

"Just that you went down. Honorably."

August, lying on his back, stared into the sky, his blond locks just long enough to conceal his eyes.

With this confirmed, to his relief, Caleb scanned the catalog of thoughts he wished to speak on, but his brain was too scattered to put them in order. Nothing new in that. Even in school, years ago, there had scarcely been a night during which he hadn't shored up an endless string of topics to share with August, the long hours made restless by not only the distance separating them but also the anxiety over what he might forget. The following morning they would meet in class and Caleb would be forced to play calm, to conceal the irresistible stream of conversation that awaited his friend's approval or condemnation, excitement or uninterest. Yet the greatest pleasure came whenever August turned to him first. *I was thinking of something last night,* he would say, with such aplomb that Caleb, knowing the torment he'd put himself through in wanting to say the same words, grew jealous—an emotion which nevertheless failed to match his happiness that they'd both been thinking of each other, and that each was the other's first outlet for all that came to mind. Lying there next to the pond, Caleb thought it best, now as then, not to appear overzealous; he would discuss the simple things and build slowly, casually.

But it was August who spoke first.

"I don't imagine my father told you. When he was dressing you down."

In the pause that followed, Caleb felt something coming that he did not wish to hear.

"Why he held the gala, I mean. Why he was so happy."

"He raised money," Caleb said. "That usually seems to bring him happiness."

"Well, yes, but only partially," August said. It was true his father had been given the contracts for the rebuilding work, and the money raised would go toward that cause, but that wasn't why he was celebrating.

"I'm listening," Caleb said.

"It was an announcement. He wanted to share the news with the whole town so I couldn't squirm out of it. A rather mean ploy, really."

"August."

"They chose for me that Natasha girl. The Beddenfelds' daughter."

August was smirking with some detached amusement, like a joke was being played.

"And what?" Caleb said, incredulous. "You...?"

"She's fine. A bit dull, but it will make life easier. It had to be someone, I suppose. I've come around on it."

Caleb's back arched, his body tensing against his will. He had no right, of course: to consider this a betrayal; to think that his friend was somehow getting revenge upon him for his transgression. He raised his hand as if he were holding a champagne glass and feigned a smile.

"To you and the new Mrs. Webler."

August had not stopped smirking. "You're mad."

"Please. I've just given you my blessing."

"You don't have to pretend."

But that was what he had done for the entirety of their relationship, whenever it was asked of him. At every juncture that August had gifted him a gesture of love, it served only as the precursor for the detachment, the chilliness, that was bound to follow, and Caleb would be left to pretend the kiss, the touch, had never taken place at all. Each erasure was like a bruise, and each pained him equally. It was why when they had finally consummated their feelings, at this very pond, only weeks before August enlisted, Caleb had decided to join up with his friend. He thought, in the foolish part of his brain which had made him love August in the first place, that it would bring them closer. Perhaps more importantly—and even more foolishly—he feared what would happen if August was left in the presence of other soldiers without him. To imagine him building bonds that might very well discount their own was an impossibility. No, he had to go. He had to follow his love. It was hardly a surprise when August cozied up to the other boys, building friendships and ignoring Caleb like he was his little brother, best left in the tent while the others went out for a smoke, or to talk of the girls back home. Nor was it a surprise now to hear he was to wed Natasha Beddenfeld. The only thing he could do was play nice. Pretend, as he always had when it came to August's cruelty, that his world wasn't coming apart at the seams. That his heart wasn't broken.

Caleb sat up. The trees, only a short while ago still burnished with gold from the sun, had dulled, their sheen stamped out by the onrushing night sky.

"Perhaps we should go," he said. "I told my father I'd have supper with him."

They stood together. The scenery was motionless, the pond before them a dark pool of ink. They brushed the grass off themselves, the specks of mud.

"You needn't worry," August said. "This won't change anything."

He once again put his hand on Caleb's jawline, his thumb on his bottom lip. This time he did not squeeze his face. There was a tenderness. He said nothing more, simply let go and started back home.

CHAPTER 9

S he was on her own. That was what it was. The conclusion
came slowly to Isabelle, cropped up as a fear, the trailing vapors of an idea that lingered after Caleb's death. Her first
thought, upon her son's return, was that these inclinations would
vanish. Instead they had strengthened over time, and now she was
privy to a perspective on life that might once have overwhelmed her:
an existence of uncompromised freedom.

The understanding stole into her consciousness as a kind of awak-
ening, a spiritual outpouring, then assumed a physical manifestation,
in the parts of herself she discarded. The widow's blacks had been
the first to go—even before she knew Caleb had in fact survived—
relegated to the back of her closet without a second thought. Next
came her projects, those obligations of little significance: a purple
merino cap she'd been knitting suddenly felt like a waste of fabric
and time, and her workbox went missing under the bed, not to be
seen since; she left her roses untended mid-bloom, forgetting some
weeks even to water them, until their petals wilted and drooped,
corpses in plain sight of all who came down the lane.

Early on, this inactivity was a pulsing shame. She sensed her
old self, the dutiful and productive self, knocking at her conscience,
begging to be let back into her life. But this feeling passed, and what
took its place was something akin to bliss. Sitting on the porch with
Mildred was not a respite from another task but a way to spend

the day. Cleaning the kitchen could wait until tomorrow; dusting George's study could wait a lifetime. There were stretches where she did not even bathe. A life without motion, without expectations—it was the secret she kept from the outside world, for no one else comprehended the great joy in abandonment, in giving up and starting over with a blank page, a page that might never be filled.

Truthfully, she had George to thank. He'd ventured off first, altering the order of their home, and shored up his grief in the two boys who lived now in their barn, the land they worked together. After that she'd had to face life by herself, to brave it anew each morning upon waking, and to continue without knowing where the journey might lead her, if anywhere at all.

There were still moments of doubt. When Silas had returned, galloping up on horseback in a veil of dust, the disturbance in his countenance on beholding her disheveled appearance and the unkempt environs around the cabin was matched only by his confusion an instant later at the sight of Caleb.

"I suppose you got the telegram," she said. "Fortunately, Caleb is alive and well."

"That much is clear." He was huffing. "A second telegram proclaiming as much would have been appreciated."

Aside from his complexion, transformed by the Florida sun to a muddied bronze, he was all but a duplicate of the brother Isabelle had known all her life—the boy with yellow hair and loose pants who used to keep her company on those long days growing up. He'd kept their father's land after his passing, worked it, and started off on new projects in more recent years, with little time to pay her any mind.

He dismounted and joined her on the porch, declining her offer of tea and giving a stern once-over to Caleb, who stood awkwardly before the door, his hands in his pockets.

"You're well, then?"

"As well as can be," Caleb said.

"Your nose?"

"Just a scrape."

"From what little I saw, there were plenty of those to go around."

Caleb left her alone with Silas at the first opportunity, and there was so much to cover that it was difficult to begin. Robbed as they were of Caleb's death to discuss, it seemed that no one trivial matter was more worthy of inspiring conversation than another. The silence grew into something tangible and was alleviated only when she asked after his wife, Lillian.

"Oh. She is perfectly fine."

"The boys?"

"Quite well. I believe they'll make something of themselves one day. Both fond of school. Quincy likes steamboats. I can picture him as an engineer."

Although Silas had never cared for George, a rift that had only grown deeper over the years, with Isabelle he had always exhibited a jubilant nature that allowed for lively chatter. Yet it had been more than a year since she'd seen him, and he seemed in that time to have lost this bearing, so much so that her brother, her closest relative, now appeared to be a total stranger.

She asked him if he wished to stay for supper, but he stood and demurred, telling her that he shouldn't. If all was well he would be on his way. He spun the brim of his hat in his hand, flicking it and catching it, just as their father had done in times of nervousness. The action gave her pause: here was the boy who had inherited another man's entire constitution—all while she was attempting to reinvent herself with no guidepost or assistance. How easy Silas had it. Yet she was proud of her brother, even comforted by his surety.

She reached out before he left and put a hand on his shoulder.

"Silas. I might call on you one day."

His face pinched together in concern.

It hadn't been her intent to worry him. She confessed that she wasn't sure what she meant.

"It's just—well, you never know these days."

"I'm only a day's ride away," he said. "If you need anything, you come find me."

Satisfied, she let go of his shoulder and watched him off, pondering, once more, how far two siblings might grow apart without ever losing the bond that united them. She thought to call out and thank him for coming but realized, catching herself, that with a brother like hers, such a show of gratitude would never be necessary. He'd simply carry on, ignoring her words altogether.

———————————

The days that followed were quiet. True to his word, Caleb was often around the house and would eat or sit with her. Like his uncle, though, he seemed to have molted part of himself, and tended to keep his distance, aloof in the way most men, in her experience, were inclined to be. His mangled face weakened her if she looked at him too long. His skin had been raw and pale from birth—his nose, eyes, and mouth all too delicate for a man—and when he had departed the previous year, she was sure that his body, too soft and fragile for the climate of war, would leave him more prone to hurt than the other boys. His scar traced a line between his cheek and his nose, separating them as if two compartments, and the nose itself hooked right like it was chasing a scent it could not capture.

Reminders. These constant reminders. Of time lost, relations frayed. She was resigned to it all but refused to let her son dwell in the center of that pain. In those moments he grew distant she nudged him, certain that some activity, any activity, was better than none at all.

"Your father could use all the help he can get," she suggested.

"He's got help."

"I'm sure he'd be happy to have more, is what I mean."

Caleb would retrieve eggs from the nest boxes in the coop, or wash down Ridley, lingering with a faraway look at the field down the way. George was not sensitive to his son, any more than he was sensitive to anyone else. His life now was one that excluded his family, which was fine as far as she was concerned, but such treatment could not extend to Caleb. This she would make sure of.

94

"He could pay you," she said. "You could work at your own leisure."

They were sitting at the dining room table, alternately talking and, when the mood to converse left them, reading. It was early April, mild weather, patches of mugginess tempered by soothing winds, and yet the length of the days, perhaps owing to the lackadaisical approach her life had taken on, felt laborious.

"And you suggest I go ask?" Caleb said.

"Would that be so terrible?"

"I would consider it if the request came from him. And not until then. I don't wish to discuss it further."

He fanned the newspaper at himself theatrically and disappeared upstairs.

That night, as George readied for bed, Isabelle told him to ask Caleb for assistance in the fields.

"I thought he was still convalescing," George said, removing his boots.

She said he was not and that it would be good for him to have some structure.

George inquired with him early the following morning.

Caleb looked at his father, then at his mother, knowingly, and shrugged his assent.

"If you need the help."

"Well, we are doing fine, but—"

Isabelle's glare cut him off.

"Yes," he said. "I suppose we do."

Not once had Isabelle herself visited the land that had been cleared for the farm, mostly out of uninterest, but now that Caleb was reporting there each morning she began to develop a curiosity. It had been another week with no visitors—not so much as a letter from Mildred—when she put on her boots and walked out the back door. The sun touched her right away and she moved briskly, as if to outpace it. Although the expanse, bare land where once there'd been a forest, was visible enough, the sun cast a flowing cape of gold upon the field, and at first she could discern no sign of human life. She shaded her eyes with a hand, to give them a moment to adjust, and the farm appeared in the distance suddenly, with the awe of a miracle. It wasn't the scope of the operation—Old Ox had many farms that were double, if not triple, the size—but the fact that this one had been born from nothing. Its mere existence was akin to a wonder of the world materializing in her own backyard.

Furrows, like the carefully drawn lines of a fountain pen, ran at length toward the edge of the forest. They were fertile, coffee-brown in color, and lush in comparison to the soil at her feet. She could see the four men now. Each of them clutched a hoe, with a furrow to till on his own, and none spoke, the work taking precedence. They were not beneath her, but somehow they seemed to be, as if the land was tucked into a valley under the shade of two parallel hills, safe and at arm's length from the rest of the world.

She could make out George, could take in the long strokes of his hoe, the gentle means by which he brought the tool down and lifted it again, taking precautions to upturn every bit of soil, each swing delicate but true. The wind struck her then, and she shivered like a plucked harp string, her toes clenching in her boots against the momentary chill. She could not shake the feeling that she was witnessing something intimate. This was, she realized, no place for an observer; no place for her. She started back to the cabin and decided that she would not return to the field.

This promise was kept for only a day, though Isabelle was not herself the cause of its undoing. The following afternoon, as she lay in front of the house on a blanket, enjoying a temperate sun, visitors on horseback appeared in the distance. It was Ted Morton and his hand, Gail Cooley, both slowing as they drew near. They did not dismount until the shadows of the horses crept over her and the sun vanished at their backs.

"Mrs. Walker," Ted said.

She pushed herself up to a seated position and greeted the men.

"I'm looking for your husband," Ted said. "It's urgent."

Knowing George, and knowing his views on Ted Morton, she found it difficult to imagine that the two men might share a single concern, let alone one of urgency. But she was well aware of the one entanglement that bound them together and could surmise what had brought her neighbor here.

"He's very busy today," she said. "Why don't I let him know you came by?"

"Oh, I know he's busy. I can show myself the way."

"Ted."

Ted put his horse to a slow trot and Gail trailed him out beyond the cabin. Isabelle followed, trying without success to persuade them to turn around. When they arrived at the field, all four men were shirtless, even George, who was rotund in the innocent manner of a child, his gut bouncing about with each thwack of his hoe. He seemed as confused by the sight of Isabelle as he was by Ted and Gail. He stopped working as they dismounted, and Caleb and the brothers did the same.

"George!" Ted proclaimed. "I believe you have some explaining to do."

He looked at Prentiss and Landry, then back at George.

"What is this about?" George said.

"You ain't earned the right to play dumb, George."

There was another stroke of silence and this was to be the last indignity Ted could weather.

"You quit it now. We both know these boys are my property!"

The proclamation was loud enough to cause a scurrying in the woods at the edge of the field.

"Deceiving me right under my nose. Not more than a few miles from my own home, from where I raised these boys from the cradle. We might not get along but you're better than this. My God, do you know these two stole from me? Not just these two, all of them.

The kettles and linens and every other damn thing I provided them. Whole stock rooms gone overnight."

The brothers averted their eyes and George stepped forward.

"Settle down, Ted."

"I won't!"

He was red from his outburst and huffing as though he'd been struck and was trying to hold back tears.

"Your charity ain't no different from mine. I treated them best I knew how. You could talk your way up the Mississippi with that tongue of yours but that don't make you better than the rest of us. What little I have I made on my own, and you swoop in and take what's mine just like your pa swooped in and took whatever he liked around this whole damn town. This is my livelihood we're talking about. I might not be up to your standard, but I'm good people. So's Gail."

George, leaning his belly against the handle of his hoe, looked worn under the gaze of the sun, but still tranquil.

"These are men, not boys. And they are their own men. If you were to ask them to come back, I would not stand in their way."

Ted wiped the spittle from his mouth. He appeared pained to face Prentiss and Landry, and at first could only point a finger in their direction. Finally he turned and met their eyes with his own.

"I put a roof over y'all heads. Fed you, clothed you. It's just shameful, how you done carried on."

Landry, shoulders above the others, yawned, unmoved.

The field was silent.

"Bones," Prentiss said. "You fed us bones. And the roof leaked every rain. We might as well have slept outside. And ain't a soul on that land raised in a cradle, except your kin. My mama raised me in her hands. Same as Landry."

Ted looked at George, then Caleb, as if expecting them to punish Prentiss for this outburst, this insolence. There was something unbound in him, Isabelle thought, the anguish of someone spurned.

"Why don't we save it for another day?" Gail said. "They ain't going nowhere."

"Yes, listen to Mr. Cooley," Isabelle said with a careful tenderness, thinking, perhaps, that a woman's softness, however false, could stamp out his anger. "This is nothing that can't be dealt with in the future. No one needs to be hurt today. You wouldn't want me to witness something like that, would you?"

Ted's nostrils flared like a spent animal's might. He whirled and mounted his horse. Gail did likewise.

"Since we're being honest," Ted said to George, "you should know this is all wrong. I ain't a peanut farmer but even I know you want to plant in a bed raised at least double what you got here, not down near the furrow. If I was to take a guess, your seed won't make a thing."

George poked at the ground with his foot.

"Well, that's appreciated. But Ted, and don't take this the wrong way, I'd appreciate it even more if you did not return unannounced like this. It's not neighborly."

There was a thundering taking place in Ted, and Isabelle was surprised he did not break into pieces right before their eyes. He managed to steady himself.

"Y'all be well," he said.

They shot off at a gallop and left great clods of soil upturned in their wake. A dust cloud gathered and slowly settled back to the ground.

When they were gone, George turned to Prentiss, his tone light.

"Is that true? I never would've thought of such a thing. To raise the beds."

Prentiss was still watching the men off. He could not muster a response.

"They'll come back," Caleb said.

"We cannot mind Ted," George said dismissively. "I've long speculated he suffers from some aberration of the brain and this only proves the point. Waving his arms about like he's leading an orchestra. It really does not suit him to get so riled up."

"He will," Caleb said. "You watch."

Ignoring his son, George turned to Isabelle.

"I hope they did not alarm you, too."

"No. Not me."

"Good, good. What do you think of the farm?"

"I don't know, George," she said. "It's impressive."

Satisfied with this, he thanked her and raised his hoe, brought it down again.

"For what it's worth, I believe Ted is wrong. You show these plants some love, feed them properly, they will grow in just fine."

He did not seem to notice he was the only one working. The rest of them stood quietly in place, as though frozen by what had transpired.

———————————

Was it bravery George had shown? Or just his typical naïveté? Isabelle did not have the answer, which in itself provided yet another glimpse at one of the greater questions of her life: whether she knew the workings of her husband at all. Consciously or not, in front of his family he had stood up to those men without even the slightest show of fear or hesitation, his voice as confident as when he described a recipe to her, or shared one of his favorite jokes. He had not been impassioned, but it was the closest she'd seen him approach the concept, and it fascinated her.

She twiddled a gilt button on her dress. She was wearing her Sunday best, although it was Wednesday, and had recruited Caleb to escort her to the Beddenfelds' home by carriage. Mildred had passed along an invitation to an evening gathering, a celebration of Sarah's daughter Natasha, who was to be wed to August Webler. This would be her first social occasion since before she and George had thought Caleb dead, the first appearance in town where she would have to pretend at cheerfulness and play nice.

It was not by chance the invitation had reached her. Back during the height of the war, the Beddenfelds had housed a Confederate general, one of Sarah's relatives, and his presence at their dinner table demanded some show of luxury. The Beddenfelds, it turned out, had sold their finest silverware, the price of maintaining appearances otherwise. And who better than Isabelle—off in the woods, removed from polite society, a woman of little gossip and littler interest in spreading it—to borrow china from? She had obliged the Beddenfelds, and since then, as though in some effort at a fair transaction, Sarah wished to include Isabelle in every event that took place at her home, including this one.

"You look nervous," Caleb said.

He was holding the reins, his gaze trained not on her but on the road. They'd been together much less since he'd joined his father in the field, and she cherished their moments together all the more. She still often remembered the letters he would send her during his time in the war. Small notes, really. *I am well—Caleb.* Or, *Still at it—your son.* This was like him, to perform his duties as her child but with minimum effort. She had relished the letters, though, kept them in her dresser and read them whenever the pang of his absence struck. Now, with him back, each conversation felt like one of those cards, to be cherished and stored away within her. Even their most trivial exchange brought her happiness.

"Hardly," she told him. "It's all old hat by now."

"The clucking hens," he said. This was her term for the pedigreed women in town, and he'd adopted it as well from an early age.

"Yes, squawking about in the henhouse, pecking at one another."

He smiled and continued to look ahead rather than at her.

"Father speaks of you often, you know. When we're in the field."

"I get on just fine, as you've seen."

"It's the same as with the books he reads—he overthinks every last word with you, finding symbols where there are none."

"As is his nature."

"Precisely. He thought you were disturbed by Ted."

"Ted still holds your father to task for not being his friend. The man would bow at his feet if he would only give him the slightest show of respect. He should be more worried for Prentiss. He looked ready to flee."

"I worry he had reason to. I've never seen that sort of anger crop up in Ted."

"There was something desperate about him," Isabelle agreed.

They were approaching Old Ox. She stiffened, preparing herself for what lay in wait at the party. Lee had surrendered only a week earlier, and the timing could not have been worse for a celebration; and yet if the hens were skilled at anything it was turning a blind eye to reality, existing in a collective reverie where weddings and romance were the only things worthy of discussion. Virginia was a world away, and why should General Lee's decision hold up Natasha's special day?

Caleb leaned back into his seat.

"To be quite honest, I'm not sure why Father has made such a strong stand. His loyalty to those two. They're perfectly fine help, but I'm not sure it's worth the grief. No other man in the county is willing to pay the wages he does, and some don't pay at all. It's becoming the talk of the town. Folks say cruel things behind his back."

Her dress felt tight, the stitching coarse at her backside. She'd been gone no more than half an hour and already missed her rocking chair on the front porch and the solitude of the cabin, the distance from the world, that space all her own. In this, along with so much else, she and George were alike, even if they weren't always willing to recognize it in each other.

"It's rare for your father to find fellow travelers. Those two boys are outsiders. They understand him. And he them."

"I'm not sure understanding means much," Caleb said.

"I don't follow you."

"*You* understand Father like no one else might. Yet you two speak less than bickering schoolchildren. It's vexing."

"Yes. Well…"

She closed her eyes, ignored the whine of a caged hog, the ring of hammer meeting anvil. Sounds of excess, vice not of the religious order but of the human order, the noises of society fending off despair with routine.

"Consider that it's not as simple as you might have it. Your father and I—we made sacrifices, not for each other, but for the kind of life we sought. In the face of the alternative. What's all around us."

The dappled shadows of the town blighted her eyelids until the noise ceased and they'd gone beyond it all. Time unspooled in lock-step with the patter of Ridley's footsteps, and neither disturbed the spell cast by their silence. When at last they arrived at the Bedden-felds', she let herself out of the carriage with only a brief goodbye.

The flowers around the home appeared to have been placed indis-criminately, their presence explained not by any sense of taste but by a general preference for extravagance. Gaudy carpet stamped with designs like illegible handwriting snaked through the entrance hall. The women, six in all, were seated in the parlor. At least Mildred was among them. They stood at her arrival, mothers every one, dragging the length of their dresses as they came to say hello, each of them other than Mildred fawning over her as if she were a puppy brought in from the cold.

"Oh, I thought you would never show!" Sarah Beddenfeld said.

"You look simply stunning," Margaret Webler said, stroking Isa-belle's dress, the same model she'd most likely discarded years ago. The skin at her cheeks looked thinned by years of grinning, and her eyebrows, the same crimson hue of her hair, had been drawn on so recently that Isabelle suspected they would smear at the touch.

"My apologies if I'm late," Isabelle said. "The ride took longer than I'd expected."

This was a lie, the first of many to come. They sat at the dining table of polished wood, a lace runner spilling from either end, with a bowl at its center so overflowing with fruit that the table seemed to have been set for a Roman feast, or a still life. Isabelle lied about the beauty of the décor, and then about the salad in which flaccid lettuce had been drowned in a surplus of vinegar.

"You are the envy of the town," Martha Bloom said to Sarah, seated at the head of the table. "Who with a daughter would not wish for such a betrothal? August Webler is destined for great things, just like his father. That I'm sure of. Quite sure."

"Have you noticed," Katrina said in a hush, "how sometimes even the gentlemen in town grow quiet when he appears?"

Natasha's sister, Anne, who'd failed to touch her plate, nodded along vigorously. The nodding, Isabelle ventured, was a symptom of being the youngest present, the sign of a need for approval from her elders, but the frequency of the nods had increased to the point that she had developed a dew of sweat at the hollow of her neck, and it remained to be seen whether she would last the evening without her head lolling over at the strain and falling face-first into her plate.

"The poor girl needs to relax before she faints."

It was Mildred speaking into Isabelle's ear. Thank heavens her friend had been seated immediately to her right.

"Yes!" Isabelle said, at a lower register, grateful to have her darker observations shared. "They'll need to bring the wine early just to ease her nerves."

"Oh, did you not have some yourself before arriving? It's etiquette to steady yourself with a glass—or two—before any appearance in such company."

Isabelle laughed heartily and the rest of the women at the table turned their expectant gazes upon her. It was a regrettable outburst. She dabbed her mouth with her napkin and took up the mantle of conversation that had been placed before her.

"Well, Natasha is certainly lucky to have August's hand," she said, "but let's not forget the qualities of Natasha herself. Caleb would be lucky to find a young woman so delightful."

"You flatter!" Sarah said. "She can be charming, but we know how fortunate she is and couldn't be more excited. Caleb is friends with August, no?"

"The best of friends, I'd say," Mildred added.

Isabelle said it was true, and was backed up by August's mother, who was quick to confirm the strength of their bond.

"Well then, I would not be surprised if he has a role as grooms-man," Sarah said. "How marvelous that would be."

"It would be an honor for him, I'm sure," Isabelle said.

"I can promise that you will not be far from the ceremony," Sarah said. "So you can see your son up close as he stands beside August."

"I'm quite sure I will be pleased wherever you seat me."

From the corner of her eye, Isabelle caught the slightest gleam in Mildred's expression, as if her friend recognized the act, the false notes that rang true to all but her. But this ability to reach inward and extract the spare bits of her old self that had yet to be disas-sembled was more dispiriting to Isabelle now than it had been in the past. Perhaps these women had the same feelings she did but were stronger at heart, able to store away the thoughts that were useless and continue on as if they did not exist. Or perhaps they were simply as hollow as they appeared to be.

An onion soup was served, a film of broth bubbling along the surface. She recognized her china immediately: the flowing willow pattern, the swirls of blue continuing onto the brim of the bowls and spilling their way onto the saucers beneath.

"And I will hope George makes an appearance as well," Sarah said. "He is a pleasure of a...unique sort."

Isabelle caught every glance exchanged across the table.

"For such an occasion," she said, "I'm sure he'd put aside the time."

"You must tell us," Sarah said casually, "if what people say is true. Has George really started some sort of plantation of his own out there? Some means of circumvention in keeping slaves? He has always gone against the tide, it would be so like him."

"That's not what I've heard at all," Margaret said. "Although what I've heard bears no repeating."

Martha, from the corner, lost in her ignorance, seemed flummoxed.

"This is news to me. *Slaves?* I'm certainly no authority to speak on commodities, but such property in this climate...well, it does seem like a poor investment."

It played as a joke, to Martha's own confusion, and a round of giggles sounded off around the table.

Isabelle opened her mouth but her voice caught. She turned to Mildred, seeking assistance, yet her ally was busy looking out the window in a show of neutrality. Katrina would be of no help. Although they were friendly, they were not friends.

"He's simply started farming," Isabelle said at last.

"Is that all?" Sarah said. "I don't see how the rumors began, then. With so much news being bandied about, I swear the oddest speculation has cropped up in this town. Most of it false. Let's say no more of it."

Isabelle reeled—then sat up squarely. So this was it. An unexpected reckoning. For in the passing words there had been a declaration, however fleeting, against George's name—against her household. No matter what she thought of George, of his decisions, she would not cower before them as her husband's character went judged.

"He has boys helping him," she said. "Let me make that clear. Or *men*, I should say. Freedmen. Yes."

It was silent enough to hear the help in the kitchen.

Then Margaret straightened her dress and put her spoon down.

"So it is true what they say. Cohabitating with them? Treating them like his own kin. My."

One of her eyebrows lurched upward. She gathered a spoonful of soup, but the spoon paused before her lips when Isabelle stood up.

"I believe I must be excused," Isabelle said. "My apologies, Sarah."

"Is something wrong?"

"No. Nothing is wrong."

Sarah stood in turn, the legs of her chair bunching up the carpet behind her.

"Oh, I shouldn't have said a word. I just meant to involve you in conversation, Isabelle. But it did not come off as such. I see that now. Forgive me for misspeaking. Margaret as well."

"I forgive no one," Isabelle said.

A ripple charged through the room. There were so many eyes fixed to the table that it appeared every woman present was suspended in prayer.

"I do not appreciate anyone," Isabelle continued, "who pays mind to cruel rumors and outright lies. Or those who speak behind the backs of others. Now hear me say this. My husband is a kind man. A decent man. And he has done nothing, since the day he entered my life, but follow his passions, no matter how remote, no matter how odd, and often in the face of those who might think him different. But nothing he's done has ever had ill intent. Such trifles of character are beneath him. Can any of you say the same of yourselves? I surely cannot. But I admire those, like him, who can. Now, if you would excuse me."

Of all the women present, Anne, her lip quivering, decided it was her place to speak up.

"You cannot mean what you say, Mrs. Walker."

"Anne, you are a child. Nothing I've said involves you. But I swear to every word of it."

She smoothed her dress and pushed in her chair, readying to go, then stopped herself. She picked up the saucer beneath her soup and turned again to Sarah, wielding it as a preacher might wield a Bible.

"And this *my* china. I would like it returned to me, the full set, at your earliest convenience."

She held the saucer to her chest like a form of protection and carried it with her to the front door, where she declined the help of a butler and retrieved her overcoat from the closet.

"I can show myself out," she said.

Night was already falling on Old Ox and the shadows of the trees were long enough to creep over the path forebodingly. The rush she'd felt at her departure began to diminish in relation to how chilly it had grown and how alone she felt. She'd advanced only a few paces beyond Mayor's Row when the steady clop of a horse, the creak of carriage wheels, fell in line behind her. She did not look, fearing some stranger shrouded in the dark, but the voice brought her gaze upward.

"Climb in. We must get you home before you do more damage tonight."

Mildred Foster, reins in hand.

"You left the party for me."

"I thought it best to come fetch you."

Isabelle thanked her, but there was little else she could muster. Although she still believed every word she'd unleashed on the party, she knew the occurrence at the house would fuel the flames of Old Ox gossip for years to come. For now, silence seemed the best option. To let things rest.

They were about halfway back to the cabin when Mildred let out the slightest noise, the start of a laugh. Isabelle shook her head and carried the laugh along, giggling herself. Before long it was an uproar, both of them gasping for air, enough laughter that they seemed to spook the horse.

"My God, the looks on their faces!" Mildred said.

"What have I done?" Isabelle said, wiping the tears from her eyes.

"Darling, you put on a wonderful show. Though I can't imagine you'll be receiving that invitation to the wedding now."

"It was worth it. Every second."

"On that we agree."

It took nearly the entire ride home for them to regain their composure. By then it was full dark. Smoke poured from the chimney, and the sight of the cabin, and all that came with it, was enough to bring Isabelle back to the edge of tears.

"Thank you, Mildred. It goes without saying, but I did not have you in mind during my rant. I cherish our friendship. More than any I have."

"Of course you do. Now go. Get some rest, dear," Mildred said.

She gripped Isabelle's hand and guided her down from the carriage.

"A word of advice, from someone who knows," she said. "Do not make them hate you all at once. Take it slow. By the time your prejudice is laid bare, they will be so acclimated to your distaste they'll be loath to say anything."

"Perhaps it's too late for me," Isabelle said, "but as with all of your wisdom, I will keep it in my thoughts. Good night, Mildred."

She had never been happier to be home. She stepped into the cabin and the crisp scent of fresh logs in the firebox was soothing enough to put her to sleep. But any thoughts of slumber were stalled when she saw the eyes fixed upon her. George, wearing an apron, with skillet in hand, was placing food onto a plate held out by Caleb. Beside Caleb sat Prentiss and Landry, both already having been served.

"Isabelle," George said. "I thought you would be gone for some time."

"Yes, well, things ended early."

"Hello, Mother," Caleb said, without taking his eyes off his food.

"It was getting a bit chilly outside," George said. "I thought I'd invite Prentiss and Landry in for supper."

"It's no harm if you'd like us to leave," Prentiss offered.

Isabelle walked to the table but said nothing. Caleb had already begun to eat. There was a time when they would all pray together. There was a time when ceremony mattered. It dawned on her that those days were behind the Walkers. The dinner table was now an assortment of damaged bodies collected together to gain sustenance. This no longer bothered her, an awareness that in itself would once have troubled her but now did not.

"Is there another chair?" she asked.

Prentiss stood up and motioned toward his own.

"Sit," Isabelle said. "I thank you, really, but I'm in no mood for good manners. Not at this moment. If you could just treat me as you treat George and Caleb. As if I was no different. Now, Caleb, why don't you go get the chair from your father's study."

Caleb put his fork down and did as requested while Prentiss reclaimed his seat.

"I had Caleb stop by the butcher on his way home," George said. "I've roasted veal, made a nice side of fried onions. They aren't your favorite, I know. I would have changed the courses had I known you'd be back."

"It looks excellent," she said. "Beyond anything I might ask for."

After serving himself and Isabelle, George sat down. Everyone ate ravenously, with few words exchanged.

Her husband appeared to be as worried about his standing with her as Caleb had suggested; Caleb himself was stifled by the silence of his parents; and the brothers, well, she had heard them speak so rarely that she did not expect a word. Which made for a surprise when it was Prentiss who initiated conversation.

"George told us about that party," he said. "I hope you had yourself a good time."

She looked up. She had sat so quickly she'd forgotten to take off her overcoat. She untied it, let it fall upon the rail of her chair. With a moment to breathe, she realized she was full. Satisfyingly so.

"It's not worth recounting," she said. "I'll only say that the company here is more enjoyable. Much more enjoyable."

CHAPTER 10

A spider's web of lightning and the sudden crush of thunder set off a heavy rain that lasted on and off for days. Then the sun returned, mopping up the moisture of the fields. Soon the empty roads were repopulated with men donning overcoats, steering horses around puddles and stopping intermittently to free their wagons from the viselike mud. George thought little of the weather. He embarked for Old Ox prepared to brave whatever might come his way with nothing more than his soft felt hat and overalls, cuffs tucked into his boots to keep them clean.

He intended to meet Ezra, whose invitation he would most likely have declined had he not been cooped up inside for so many days, bored with the familiarity of his home, without even the chance to walk the forest. He'd tried to spend time with his son, yet Caleb no longer felt bound to him, and if they were not in the field the boy spent his time with his mother or stowed away in his room; during the rain he could stay up there for hours, locked up doing God knew what, great monastic acts of solitude that could carry on for hours.

When the downpour turned ugly, George had gone to the barn to check on Prentiss and Landry, but the roof was patched and as sturdy as the day his father had built it. They had their own food now, too, purchased in town or bagged in the woods. When he came back a second time, and a third, they eyed him as they would an intruder, their voices stilling as they glanced up from the pallets where they played cards, or from the lantern where they shared their secrets. The barn was no longer his, but theirs, and he sensed himself unwanted.

He often had this same feeling in his own home, facing Isabelle: that the space, although shared, had been cordoned off, with invisible lines demarcating who belonged where. They spoke more than they had before, since the night she'd joined him at the table with Caleb and the brothers, but the cold front holding them apart was taking its time in dissipating, and meanwhile he walked around her like a child tiptoeing at night so as not to wake his mother.

These were the thoughts weighing on him as he begrudgingly set out to meet Ezra in Old Ox late one night. The roads were still a slough, and he trod the soft mud as if it were quicksand pulling him under—yet the foliage was bold enough to pass for art, and the woods exuded the pleasant smell of wet leaves, such that the entire walk felt so refreshing he would've considered his arrival in town enough activity to turn around and go home if he'd had no obligations to attend to.

The few visible homeless folks were miserable, as wet as if the rain had never ended, and given that he didn't spot any of the tents that had been so prominent on recent visits, George could only figure the others had found refuge somewhere dry, or else returned to the farms they'd come from, resigned to what little work they could find. The tannery across from the Palace Tavern had put up a sign weeks ago that read, NO SQUATTERS, LOITERERS, OR BEGGARS IN FRONT OF THE STORE, which had, since George's last trip to town, been given an addendum, a slip of paper under the original:...OR BEHIND THE STORE, OR TO ITS SIDES. Yet under its eaves, along the far side of the building, the shadows of bodies shifted and sounded off, forlorn noises that might as well have been the final utterances of the dying.

He was not oblivious to the squalor that lay a few steps from the public square, half hidden behind buildings that townsfolk frequented every day, yet he wished to face this reality as much as the rest of his fellow citizens did, which was not at all, and so it was that shame pummeled him as he walked through the doors of the Palace Tavern—at which point there was some relief in being overwhelmed by the sight of so many rowdy young men, the acrid smell of drink and the stench of sweat, the clanging of the piano.

That so many of the boys were home (many still in their grays and clearly ready to celebrate their freedom, notwithstanding their defeat) surprised him, but the true shock was the collection of Union soldiers clustered near the door, not a single drink in hand, ignored entirely by all the others. George had hardly processed the image when a hand was on his shoulder. He turned to face a squat man who was quick to introduce himself with a hand so slack it nearly slipped from George's grip.

"Brigadier General Arnold Glass," the man said. "And you are George Walker. A pleasure."

The man had sparse, oily hair parted down the center and that particular style of wiry, unkempt mustache that reached so far from his face it seemed liable to attack passersby. He appeared to be George's age, and equally weathered by time, although more graceful in his movement.

"Our dear leader," George said. "An honor to make your acquaintance."

"You do have that dry humor I was promised," Glass said with a smile.

"I'd say you must have your own peculiar brand of it, coming to this bar knowing you're amongst men who must be…less than fond of you."

Glass's smile failed to dissipate, and George recognized it as that of a statesman, unnerving in its perpetuation, guarding something calculated.

"I can't say I share your concerns," the general said. "I have given their mothers rations, clothed their younger siblings, and tonight I wish only to show them my goodwill by buying them a round of drinks."

He raised an eyebrow, like a young rascal withholding a secret.

"Of course, it doesn't hurt that in doing so I am allowed the opportunity to record who might be the *rowdier* individuals being re-absorbed by the community. Should trouble arise at a later date."

"How wily," George said. "I can only hope you have your rifles on hand once those drinks take effect."

"I was actually on my way out," Glass said, with apparent appreciation for George's retort. "But since we've come upon one another, I'd love to ask you a favor in person. One that will save me a telegram."

"I do have plans, but if you make it quick."

Glass straightened, and George couldn't help looking down to see if the man had tried to claim more height by standing on the tips of his toes (he had not). The general informed George that he was hoping to start a city council of sorts and had spoken of the matter to Wade Webler on numerous occasions.

"Allow me to stop you there," George said. "I want nothing to do with that man. Gussying up with his cronies for a ball as others can't afford so much as a sack of flour? What a hideous display."

"I believe it was a gala, to be fair."

"What would be the difference?"

"I—well—he assured me there was one. Although it does not make any difference. By all accounts the man has done right by Old Ox, raising money for this town. More importantly, he believes deeply in the rebuilding efforts."

"I'm confused, General. Do you not know what side he stands for?"

Glass's assignment, he said, was to maintain the peace. If necessary, politics had to be put aside for that cause. In his view, a council comprising the most esteemed individuals of Old Ox, united as one, would facilitate a clear charter that could help the town preserve its unanimity and renew its grandeur.

As the general spoke, a stream of ale snaked under George's foot like a creek might take to the woods.

"Grandeur?" he said. "There are freedmen littered about the countryside having to beg, borrow, and steal, while you dole out rations to those who would spit on each and every one of them if given the chance."

No, there was no grandeur in this town, he said, no unanimity of purpose. At least not with the Union. It was all just the same divisiveness that had brought the place, along with the rest of the South, to ruin.

"Mr. Walker, those men you speak of were freed by my hand. And the cost is restitution to those in this community who have lost their entire way of life. That is not unfair. Actually, on reflection, it's quite just."

"Given the same information, General, you and I have reached opposite conclusions."

Glass, in a show of mild exasperation, whispered to George in an inflection altogether different from his previous tone—as though to speak in confidence might exert a charming effect.

"I was under the impression that half this town was once under your father's ownership. Surely you would wish to do well by his legacy, no? Let's work together. Let's help those less fortunate than we are."

George would've stepped back had he not already been up against the bar.

"Whatever my father accomplished does not require that I work with the likes of Wade Webler," he said. "He has taken you for a fool if you think he has any other wish than to capitalize on this town's decline."

"I see. Well, if you might reconsider—"

"Let me make this clear. I would rather lay down in a pigpen and let the beasts have at me than participate in your council. Besides, I have enough on my hands on my farm. Now I must be going."

But it was Glass who made to leave. The smile, somehow, had not left his face, and he simply extended his hand once more.

"We have no further business, then," he said, with unfailing warmth. "A very good night to you, Mr. Walker."

"And to you," George said.

The Union soldiers followed their leader out the door, and

George, rather than departing, ordered a glass of whiskey to calm his senses. Only when he had downed that one and was holding a second did he turn to find Ezra, seated on the second floor at his usual table, the only one with any charm, a substantial oak plank dulled to a slippery glaze by years of wear and spilt drink. No one bothered him unless invited to do so, and he appeared lost in his own world until George approached. He was dressed in his business wear, his derby still donned. Before him lay a feast: a leg of mutton sweating out its juices, a single stewed peach, and puny asparagus points with the look, taken together, of a bony child's fingers.

George asked if he was enjoying himself.

"There is excellent entertainment to be found here for any passionate spectator of humanity."

"Your favorite pastime," George said, taking a seat.

"If not my only pastime. I saw you had an introduction to Arnold Glass."

"Sadly. He wants me to join some ludicrous committee."

"I heard as much."

"Well, I declined, with some prejudice, no less."

"As did I, though perhaps for different reasons. If I'm to be honest, I've grown numb to those looking for favors."

Ezra picked up the mutton leg, inspecting it like a diamond in need of a grade.

"There is not a soul in this town, General Glass included, who hasn't petitioned me for this or that. Just look at these sorry sorts. Home from the front and already pleading for a loan, begging on street corners, only to squander what little they have here each night by poisoning themselves with swill. Telling their vapid war stories to anyone who might listen and complaining of the Negro who has somehow stolen their jobs. As if they would work for a Negro's wage. As if they would work at all. A whole town wallowing in its own sadness. Pathetic."

His fleshy jowls rippled as he swallowed, his lips shimmering with lamb fat.

"You know," George said, "when I look in the mirror in the morning I see a miserable old bastard looking back at me. Yet when I see you, I take great comfort, knowing how much progress I have left to make on that same path."

Ezra laughed up a bit of food, then caught himself, his smile disappearing.

"You think I delight in sharing my bleak thoughts on humanity." He licked his fingers to the knuckle and dried them with his napkin. "But for someone acclimated to loss, someone who accepts its inevitability, the only recourse is to seek out joy in the darkest corridors of life, even when the calamity is befalling others. There's a word for that. The joy of sorrow. Another man's sorrow."

"I'm not sure I wish to know it," George said, and sipped his whiskey.

"All the better. I didn't ask you here to discuss such weightless things."

"Did you not? I thought we were here to have a good time. To be merry."

"Perhaps there are other topics worthy of our conversation."

"Allow me to guess," George said. "You wish to ask after more of my land, or have me repay my debts to you. I'd venture further to say both tasks are intertwined."

"God, no. But can't we keep each other company without the need to prattle forth on trivial nonsense? To accuse me of grabbing after your land at every opportunity, I find it offensive, really."

Ezra put back half his beer.

"I was only joking," George muttered.

"My only aim, if you must know, is battling a bout of loneliness."

Now Ezra must be joking, George thought, but his friend continued in a soft, serious tone.

"My wife is so familiar she often fades into the makings of our home. A lamp might draw as much attention in a passing day. And the boys are gone."

"But you're well-regarded, Ezra. You field visitors all day, I see them in your office whenever I'm in town."

"That is business. Before you came here, I was alone. And when you leave I will be alone again. Letting time pass before I retire for the night."

George didn't realize what had become of his father's old friend, for he seemed no different than he had since his childhood. Yet part of Ezra, at least in drink, had softened into something infirm, something weak. It took George a moment to gather that the weakness might simply be age. He saw then what would become of the old man, his jowls loosening further until they were no different from the flaps of a dog, even as his excess weight peeled away. Soon he would find himself removed to a bed, in the far corner of his home on Mayor's Row, and he would go the way of Benjamin, George's own father, and not many years hence, George feared, he himself would take Ezra's place across the table, eating with the gluttony of a man who knows it may be his last supper.

"You cannot run from it," Ezra said, as if reading George's mind. "It is just how things advance. We age. And we must be honest in the face of this truth."

"If you're suggesting death worries me more than the next man, I'd say you're wrong." George sank back into his chair.

"I'm not so sure I am."

Neither of them spoke as Ezra ate. The ruckus near the bar had abated, and in the relative quiet, cards being shuffled at the tables below sounded like the ruffled flutter of birds taking flight.

Finally the sheep bone lay bare and Ezra relaxed.

"The Negroes," he said. "Let them go."

So, then. There had been a point to the invitation all along. George felt the need for another whiskey.

"Not you, too," he said.

"The George I knew had not a care in the world for another man, let alone freed slaves. I can only gather that old age has led you to philanthropy. To make right whatever wrongs your heart holds in. But you are exposing yourself to the public in an ugly way."

"I thought you did not wish to *prattle forth on trivial nonsense.*"

Ezra leaned forward.

"Do not mistake the presence of those soldiers for some beacon of safety. This town is not as quiet as it seems. These men have been humiliated at war, and now they're restless. Only growing more so in the face of your indiscretions."

"I'm restless sitting here with you."

"George, there are men who could use those wages. Back from the war, with little more than a few wounds to their name. Men just like Caleb."

"Do not bring my son into this. I have made no statement by my decisions. The brothers work hard, they cause no issue, they are good fellows and good labor."

Ezra's face hardened.

"You simply cannot have those two boys coming into town haggling for new clothes, their pockets lined with bills while they pass white men begging for a few coins. At least cut back their pay. The other landowners have created perfectly reasonable guidelines on how to deal with such circumstances."

"Stop there. I will not run up a debt on honest folk and make them earn back their wages as if they are slaves again. I am not saying they deserve a hog over a spittle every night for supper, but a little decency, Ezra."

Ezra paused, as if gathering himself.

"It's plain that I will have to say this more directly, because you are as stubborn as your father. Do you not see that although some voices have been suppressed in Old Ox, they have not been vanquished altogether? There are certain individuals, those less inclined toward friendly conversation than you or I, who have made it clear—in the back of their stores, in the alleyways at night, even in this very bar—that they will not stand for what you're doing. Frustrated men. Which makes for rash men. I cannot express how troublesome this could become not just for your farm, but for your well-being. Your family's well-being."

He put a hand on the table before George and laid out his palm, as if to gesture at the scene beneath them. And now George wasn't sure how he could've missed an undercurrent so obvious. The cursory glances. The scowls of men he did not know, flitting up before returning to their empty glasses.

"You did not bring me here for company," George said. "You had me here to warn me."

It was only a few minutes ago that Ezra had appeared burdened by age, ground down by time. But he had not grown weak at all, George saw. In fact it was the opposite: George was the one wilting in the very manner he had inwardly attributed to Ezra.

"I had you here from a place of kindness," Ezra said. "To let you know yours has run amok."

"Enough," George said. "I'm leaving now."

He pushed his chair back and stood, then put his fingertips on the table in a moment of dizziness, feeling the punch of the drink after a sober spell.

"Was that true about your loneliness? Or was that part of your ploy?"

Ezra held his tongue for a moment, sitting before his empty plate.

"I don't know a happy man who comes here alone," he said.

That was it. All he needed to hear.

"Please take care of yourself, Ezra. Trust that I will do the same for me and mine. I'll come by and see you at the office in a few days. Not out of pity, or to see that you're well, but simply because I like you. Until then."

George wheeled away from his friend with the sense that he had managed to avoid a trap. The floor of the bar was still so crowded he had to move sideways to slide past the bodies. He pushed his way through without a word, minding each step, hiding beneath the boom of the chatter, lost in the heat of flesh packed together. He could not tell if eyes were upon him, yet he was sweating now and he longed to reach the tavern door, to escape this place and not return.

It was not to be.

"You're George Walker, ain't you?"

He would have kept going had the voice not come from so

nearby, close enough for it to seem as though the words themselves had reached out and grabbed him. He turned to face a young man surrounded by other compatriots his age.

"I am."

"Ain't that the sweetest thing. You Caleb's daddy."

He was caught off guard at a name he had not expected to hear.

"Do you know him?"

"I sure do. Pass a message to the feller, ha?"

The boy looked among his friends and then thrust a loaded fist at George.

"Tell him this is what traitors git around here. And you can go ahead and spread a li'l around for them niggers of yours, too. 'Cause you such kind, sharing folks up at that farm of yours, ain't you?"

The boy raised his fist and George shrank back, retreating with his hands held over his face in surrender.

"Don't!" he shrieked.

"Look at the fear on him!" the boy said. "I guess it runs in the family, ha?"

They were laughing. He was nothing more than a scared child. His impulse was to peer back at Ezra, though his humiliation could hardly be worse even if the old man was bearing witness to his belittlement.

The boy grabbed him by the collar and pulled him forward.

"Now take your whippings like a man," he said, and brought his fist down.

Yet it was caught in the air by another—belonging to a man twice the width of the boy—who spun the would-be assailant around and gripped his wrist as if it were no more than a stalk of celery, something to snap in half. It was Mildred Foster's son, though George had no idea which one, for they all looked the same.

"My mama gets on with Mrs. Walker," he said. "I don't think she'd be pleased to hear you'd put a hand on her friend's husband."

He dropped the boy's wrist and the boy fell backward, cursing under his breath.

"I ain't mean nothing, Charlie," he said.

Charlie nodded at George without a hint of a smile and moved out of the way.

"Charlie," George said. "The rest of you gentlemen. Enjoy your evening." And he escaped out the door and into the night.

Even his Nantucket father had help. A child, Taffy, whom he bought for a price that George had long wished to know but had failed to locate in the pile of ledgers gathering dust in the cellar. She was a year older than the eleven-year-old George, and arrived ashen, unwilling to make eye contact.

When she came inside, his mother sniffed her across the scalp and said, in an even tone, that she didn't warrant a bath.

"A bath is a luxury," she said. "A wet towel should do. The friction of the air will dry you. It is no different than washing dishes, which I may have you prove out once we have you clean."

This was Taffy's first lesson. Many more would come. Bedmaking was an involved process—with the creasing of pillows, the proper turning of a mattress—and it would take long stretches of the afternoon for Taffy to finish the steps correctly. Yet not all was physical, and Taffy excelled even in the domestic mental exercises, memorizing containers (*the necessities of a kitchen: tinware; basket ware; a box for darning needle, thread, and twine; etc.*) with the same thoroughness in which she de-lumped the soil for the flower seeds in season. George never asked why Taffy had come, when his mother seemed perfectly happy to clean and tend to the house herself. And not until Taffy was gone, a few months after his father's death, did it occur to him that, more than anything, his mother had simply wished for someone else to pass her duties onto, knowing so well the eccentricities of her son: his steadfast wish for privacy, his lack of interest in others, the little care he showed in keeping even his own room in order. Perhaps she thought he might never have a woman of his own, and Taffy was being made to fulfill the role.

He gained from Taffy in many ways. When he was outside alone—
his usual place in the world—she would meet him after completing
her own work, a piece of fruit in hand, delivered at the request of his
mother, and ask if he might wish to have her along. He always said yes.
They would carve spears together with his hatchet, then fling them
into the woods and pretend they'd felled the dark beast his father
spoke of so often. She could throw farther and climb higher than he
could, but never put her amusement above his own. He knew this
was the task assigned her, but he did not let this knowledge affect his
inviolable belief that she cared deeply for him, and understood him
in ways others did not. He told her once that he loved her, although
he did not know the meaning of it beyond the fondness he felt for his
parents. When his mother lost sense after his father's death and sold
Taffy, George took refuge in the idea that it had not been love, but
something more distant, which allowed him to forget the makings of
her face; the thudding joy in his heart when her shadow crept over
him on the front porch; the soft wind upon his shoulder when she
overtook him in a sprint and the sight of her back as she disappeared
before him, all of it stamped out until now, in his middle age, he
remembered her as nothing more than something forgotten.

George carried on past the tavern. Puddles in the mud reflected
the glare of the moon, and with those shards of light he knew where
not to step. He'd meant to go home, but now another stop felt
necessary, one he had told himself he would not make when setting
off that night. He took the side road before him toward the old
section of town. It was silent, and the pathway narrowed as he went,
so much so that even the moonlight was blocked from view. He'd
peered over his shoulder more than once but he was not followed.

He came upon the whorehouse. The windows were the only ones
alight on the row, and the sounds from inside were rowdy, although
he hadn't ventured through the front door in ages and had little
interest in what he might find there. Rather, he went around the
back and up the winding steps to the second floor. He did not know
if she would answer, but the door swung open on the second rap.

He shared only a glance with Clementine, in whose face he'd always detected Taffy's, before following her inside and sitting at the end of her bed. Was it a bad time? he asked. He'd figured he might catch her before her night began.

"You always have my ear, George. Tell me how you've been."

This was all he asked of Clementine: to listen. Which wasn't to say he'd gleaned nothing of her from his time in her company. He knew she had a child—had seen her walking with the girl one morning, before their first encounter, which was when he'd tasked himself with tracking her down, unable to shake Clementine's resemblance to Taffy. Her family, he discovered, were mulattoes from Louisiana. Against her will her husband had swept her off to Georgia to live as his property. She had escaped his bondage with the child to fend for herself, and had earned enough to make do on her own. If few men were fooled by the white wax and paint she applied to her face, they were more than willing to indulge themselves on a lonely night— regardless of her tawny complexion, the rumors of her past, her heritage—eager to experience the revelation that was her presence. Given how few spoke ill of her, they apparently did not regret their time. Society made exceptions in matters of great beauty.

It had been the winter, in the midst of Caleb's deployment, since he'd last seen Clementine, and he told her everything now, as he was apt to do: spoke first of Caleb's supposed death and then his shocking return, of Isabelle, and of the brothers, whom she was well aware of, for she knew of most happenings in Old Ox. She did not look at George while he regaled her with the details of his life. Instead she spent the time cleaning the space of her vanity desk, prepping her gown for the evening, dressing her hair. Yet each time they were disturbed by a knock on the door, which was often, she made it clear to the house attendant that she was busy, and encouraged him to carry on.

"You say you're struggling."

He could hear the sounds of other men in other rooms—a rocking against the wall—along with the goading moans of women that went unstifled. The smell of the liquor whose stains here and there had rotted the wood of the floor outstripped even the aroma of perfume.

"In a manner of speaking," he said.

"You have more words in your head than I've heard in my whole life, George. Say more about it so I know what you mean."

She said he should relax and take his time, although he knew she had none to spare. He could see, in his mind's eye, the regulars in the parlor, their steady glances at the stairwell, waiting impatiently for her to appear. They would have to wait, for it was his turn to have the room, to occupy her bed.

He used her. This did not escape him. How he laid her bare, opened her up bit by bit, filling her with his old memories, or the great worries that plagued him (his wife's chilliness, his son's shame); how he asked her— as if she could possibly know, as if she were more than a scarred vessel forced to sit there beside him and brave the winds of his words—to whom the cries he heard at night belonged, for they were not his, but perhaps they came from the barn, from the brothers, or from his wife, yes, was it Isabelle, who had lost him and whom he had lost, or maybe that beast in the forest, waiting for him to find it, just as his father had, or perhaps the cries carried all the way from town, the men and women and children alongside the creek in their mud-spattered tents, searching for new land at home and finding there was none, that this was it, that for so many life went no farther than Old Ox.

Clementine was standing beside him, the room dark, a tallow candle flickering beside them like the wings of a bird. She lifted her soft hand, which had been resting on his shoulder, and felt his cheek, filling it with her warmth. This was the only touch he asked of her— that of a caregiver, as if she were a mother tending to a sick child.

"Tell me what more I can do," she said.

"This is it. No more."

The usual shame washed over him, for revealing himself, for expressing such darkness, and there was still more yet. One last admission he could not let pass. The real truth was selfish, he told her. For while his wife and son were tethered to him and must endure him, Prentiss and Landry were not. What had he used them for but entertainment? What had he paid them for but to keep him company? To keep some facet of himself alive? Look at him—a man so afraid of the unknown that he'd never even been out of the county. His land was his only escape, the only place a man with such a narrowed existence might find a sense of adventure. So he kept the brothers around to keep that part of him alive. Yet where would he stand on the night when the men in town carried torches to his property and demanded payment on the misshapen justice they sought? He would not pay with his life. He couldn't say the same for Prentiss and Landry.

"I fear I would no sooner walk down the road with your hand in mine," he told her, "than I would stand beside those two in the face of this town's need for revenge. And this is the truth that breaks my heart, perhaps more than any other."

He began to suspect, without any evidence, that the grime on the floor was not spilt liquor, but the sweat of others that had gone uncleaned; he heard the sound of water sloshing onto the ground in another room, the moan of a man, and knew he was not lost in any act except the one of entering a bath. Curious, George thought, how different it sounded from that of those in congress down the hall— less pernicious, wholesome in its way.

"I should go," he said. "Let the others have their time."

"There are no others. I told you we have as long as you wish."

"Is that what you say? Do men believe that?"

He put money down on the vanity table. It was the rest of what he'd brought to town with him. She had remained sitting on the bed all the while, legs crossed, alert. He'd watched her make a bun of her hair, strike a feather down its core to keep it in place as an arrow might pierce a heart.

"Men think as they wish," she said. "The next up the stairs might believe he's my only customer, just as you believe you're the only one hearing these cries at night, like other people don't suffer. I can't say who is more right."

He thanked her and took his leave. It was worth far more than three dollars to have the blessing of her compassion bestowed on him—so real in his heart, in every light step he took down the stairs of the whorehouse, that he cared little if such feelings were born naturally, from Clementine's bosom, or merely from the sight of the money placed upon her desk.

It was not just that Clementine had revived his spirit, but that she had illuminated the path he must take, the decisions that must follow. He knew, now, what Ezra had meant in the tavern, but the cry of the town was not his burden to bear. No, it was he, George, who was the burden: a burden on his family, a burden on Prentiss and Landry.

Once more Taffy came to mind, the manner in which she had disappeared from his life, as though she had done him a service, only to be disposed of by his mother when that was accomplished. It did not matter that he had cared for her like a sister and treated her with a goodness he'd reserved for so few people in his life. What did his gratitude mean if his mother had sent her off with only a signature, a fluttering motion of her hand, as if to say, *Be gone?* He recalled that moment now, too, however much it pained him. He'd been beside his mother at her desk, Taffy at the door, the man's hand—for it was a man, of course, heavy, tall, stone-faced—on the girl's shoulder, as if she was already his. George had said nothing. No hug, no goodbye. He was stunned by what was happening, but he was only fourteen, still mournful and adrift after the death of his father. In his shock he had no way to recognize this other child's feelings. The grip of a stranger's hand on her shoulder. Her wracking fear of whatever might come next. George could look away—and did. But she would live with that fear forever, the knowledge that she would have to obey whatever order came out of that man's mouth. Just as she had done with his own parents…

But while it was too late to save Taffy, the plight of the brothers, at least, could be settled. If he had any courage at all, he could help those two. One way or another, he would secure their safe passage out of Old Ox for good.

CHAPTER 11

Landry roamed the countryside as he pleased. The desire to do so, the fascination with it, had once been a fear: whenever he'd stood before the forest with Prentiss in the flitting sunlight, the darkness in its farthest reaches had always felt like a monster lying in wait, one who had taken down his name long ago, eager to stake its claim on him. That was the dread Prentiss was blind to and that Landry could not describe: that these were two different worlds. That this new one might consume them as it had consumed their mother, and Little James and Esther, and then what?

But it turned out that each step did not bring danger. The unknown led only to more clearings, more sunlight on the other end, and so it dawned on him that there was less to fear than he'd once imagined, which was maybe a truth he'd long wished to believe—that all danger carried the faint trace of comfort, all wrongs the hint of what may be right. How else to explain a world of cruelty that had also carried in it the great joy of watching his mother at the mercy of Little James's fiddle on a Sunday afternoon, the miracle of a fresh tick mattress, the sweetness of water after a day spent picking in the fields?

He always sought out pleasure in silence, usually on his own. Given a free Sunday, the one day of the week he and Prentiss did not work with George, Landry would wake there in the barn before the rest of the world had stirred and boil a kettle of cornmeal. He'd eat alone and leave half the pot behind. His brother, still in bed, would turn away. Prentiss was awake, Landry knew, but they didn't speak to each other on these Sunday mornings. He'd head off with nothing and start for the woods, seeking life, any life, as long as it was different from his own.

There were days where he encountered nothing more than a doe with her fawn, or an owl hooting from a tree branch, and if this was all he was given by the proceedings, he still walked home content. But there was also the time he came to the creek and found women. They were with children, infants, washing them in the water and soothing their cries with a chorus of humming, soft songs of reassurance. Landry was fixed there for hours, watching the women towel down the children, the mothers themselves patted dry by the sun.

He went far enough one day to run across a plantation, one he'd never known about. There, a field of women: heads wrapped in cloth to hide from the sun, wearing men's trousers cut into pantalets and oversize shirts, turning the soil endlessly. He counted the rows, saw how few of them had been picked clean, and knew the output would not satisfy the bosses. Sure enough, when he returned the next week the place had received a string of hardened, bitter men, convicts who worked alongside the women while still in their chains. He did not return to the place.

Another night he wandered so great a distance that he was buried deep in the woods with little means of finding his way home save intuition. It was dark enough that the forest merged with the blackness of the sky and the world had no beginning or end, as if he might sleep upon the ground and wake up staring down from the stars. But then somewhere in the distant tree line a corona of light flared. He tracked after it, and just as it disappeared it was followed by another.

It was two men, he saw now, as he drew closer to the flame. One of the men extinguished his torch as the pair began to climb a tree together in silence. Then, moments later, one of them sparked his torch anew and the groggy birds lining the limb sat startled in the great blast of light, too stunned to take flight. The other man clubbed them mercilessly and they dropped to the forest floor. The flame died, and Landry could only hear their rustlings as they climbed back down. The crinkle of leaves upon the ground was displaced by more silence.

He could feel eyes on him but could not see them in the total blackness. He figured they were part of the forest in a manner he was not—had learned to live in the darkness so well, to exist in the farthest folds of the wild so long, that they could vanish in the shadows of the night yet still see everything around them. Suddenly his hand was wet. Something had been placed there: a pigeon, its feathers blood-slick, its body limp. There was a small crepitation of leaves again, and the footsteps receded, although the sound of their going rang in his ears all the way home.

He had the bird in hand when he made it back to the barn. He placed it on the small table between the pallets. Prentiss, not yet asleep, stood in the back of the barn, a swirl of moths flickering about his head. The cornmeal Landry had left for him that morning was untouched.

Prentiss walked over to Landry, inspected him, and eyed the pigeon.

"How'd you go and do that?"

Landry made no gesture to reply and Prentiss sat on his pallet.

"George came by," he said. "Tells me he's given it a lot of thought and talked to other folk. Thinks it's best we find our way now."

Landry looked over at Prentiss, and his brother stood up again restlessly and began to pace around the barn.

"You know what I said back? I said, 'George, how you gonna tell me what's right for me without even knowing how I think on it? Spend your days toiling next to me, talking my ear off, but you got the nerve to say you've talked to everyone about me but *me*? That all y'all know what's best, but then what do I know? I ain't ever got a clue, except when it comes to those peanuts? Is that what you sayin'?'"

Prentiss stopped himself for a moment.

"I said *us*, you know. I told him he can't speak for us."

He carried on pacing.

"I showed him what we've saved, pulled out the rag and fanned out those dollars, and I asked after that railcar. I told him at the camps they say there's a car that takes you on the rail up and around to wherever you wish. Just say the word. But we aim to make enough to last us once we're there, too, that we fixin' to be here into the fall, to see the end of peanut season, and if he has a problem with that then he can see us off but we ain't doing it by choice, don't care how many people he talk to. And then he said he won't stand in no man's way to do as he pleases, that we're welcome here. But he still got that look on his face. I ain't ever seen George worried that way."

Landry stopped listening. There was no child in Prentiss anymore. He was no different from their mother now—all his energy devoted to making sure they had full plates at every meal, enough spare clothes for the journey north, enough money saved to last a while when they got there. An unremitting focus on survival at the loss of all else. But it was also that Prentiss looked so much like their mother. Those brows that arched so delicately around soft eyes were hers. The worry in the purse of the lips. The worry of a mother. He could see her standing against the far wall of their cabin, her shoulders fixed up, the hem of her sleeping gown brushing the floor.

The particular memory his mind had drawn upon, replacing the image of Prentiss with his mother, was one he often wished to forget. He was still a boy then, unwounded by anything but the blisters born of the field, and the searing band of pain brought on by the endless picking. It was not long after he'd first seen the fountain of Majesty's Palace from his row, glistening there in the summer heat, each jet of water cresting and falling, gushing with such beauty that Landry thought the water must hold some special property. He requested the furrows nearest the fountain to pick, just so he might glance upon it. Once, Master Morton's wife even took their infant boy there. She dipped him into the water, laughing all along, the sounds carrying down the furrow like a stream of water, although if they were real or something of his own mind, he could not say.

When night fell the moon cast an exclamation upon Majesty's Palace, shafts of lunar light touching its windows and bending to the earth beneath them with such illumination that the house appeared to be alive. Landry could see as much from the hollow window of their cabin, and when he turned and found his mother and Prentiss asleep, he walked himself to the door and opened it.

He did not yet have his fear of rambling, and his feet moved of their own accord. He wore no pants, only his shirt, the night cool upon him. It was just as he imagined once he arrived up the lane: the fountain ran endlessly, as if fueled not by the workings of a man but by some greater power. The water was so white against the glow of the moon that it seemed like streaks of ice spouting into the air. He kept his clothes on. There was no tiptoeing, no slow procession. He leaped into the water as only a child might, a child who had waited a lifetime for this act, plunging belly-first and scraping the fountain's bottom while the water carried over him, through him, and he gasped at the chill, but then laughed, as he had not known play like this, had not thought such a thing possible.

He splashed about wildly. He ran back and forth, pretending Prentiss was chasing him, then dived back under. Holding his breath, he imagined the water might go down and down forever: after all, it had to go somewhere, and there was no reason he couldn't follow it for a while, and then return for his mother and brother, and bring them along with him.

He rose up soaking. The next sound was not his own. He looked up and could not say who it was in the distance. The front door to Majesty's Palace was ajar, and a figure stood in the frame, watching on in silence. Landry tripped over the basin and caught himself, then broke into a sprint, the dirt stamping his feet.

There was a moment, as he paused breathless before the cabins, when he thought it wise to continue on: beyond Majesty's Palace, beyond Old Ox, to find a place yet unknown where the claimed might be set free, where wrongs might be forgotten. But if he was still a child, he was not dumb—not enough to think such a place existed.

Inside their cabin his mother was silhouetted against the far wall, pacing in her gown. She always slept deeply, soundly, and with a workday ahead he'd had no reason to believe she would flinch from her dreams to notice his absence. Now she surged forward as if to whip his behind. "Boy," she said, holding the side of his face before retrieving a rag. When she stripped his drenched shirt and washed him down he began to cry silently.

"They gonna come, ain't they?" he said.

"Who, child?" She spoke softly, trying not to wake Prentiss. "Where in God's earth did you run off to? You're soaking wet."

But that was all he could say: *They gonna come.*

She did not press him any further. She simply put him to bed and sat beside him, continued drying the tears from his eyes.

"You've been asleep all night, child. You've been right here in bed. Not a soul knows different."

He whimpered on for a time, and in an instant a great darkness cratered in on him, and when he woke again, his mother was dressed for the fields, telling him to hurry up—as if it all, in fact, had been a dream.

He did not know how many days passed between that night and the whippings that would follow, the breaking of his jaw, but it was some years, distant enough in time for him to imagine that each lash of the cowhide, each blow to his body, amounted to a day's passing since his sublime trespass upon the fountain, yet near enough for him to believe that he was hardly a random victim sacrificed for the runaways and was instead guilty of a crime, that of a child wishing to play in a world that did not belong to him. If such were the case, every drop of amusement he had gathered that night in the fountain would be drained from him in the weight of blood.

After each beating, his mother set him out like a fallen tombstone on the cabin floor and plastered his wounds with brine. It wasn't that he lost the ability to think then, but rather that whenever he went to speak, the words got lodged in his throat. He might manage the M in *Mama,* but he would seize up in the middle of the word and fail to produce the end. If they asked him what he meant, he might start again, but the words would only swell up further within him.

In time, even upon his healing, even when his jaw allowed it, even when the rivers on his back shored up and no longer pulsed alongside the beating of his heart, he could not bring the words forth in whole units and began to wonder why he would wish to do so in the first place, considering how little the act of speaking had ever done for him. In the months to come, his mother would be placed in Majesty's Palace. In a few more, she would be sold. His brother cried nightly until the seasons changed, but all of Landry's tears had been used up already. Besides, he thought, there was more freedom in silence.

Early June and the peanuts were flowering. Even with their tiny, scattered yellow blooms, they were not as pretty as cotton, those long stretches of purity out of which Mr. Morton made poetics, but in these fields lay the sense of imperfection, the swelling ground cover of green bunches protruding at their leisure. The randomness felt unbridled, more in line with a world that seemed to go on with no rhyme or reason.

There was little work to be done now. The crop needed time before harvest. Still, George had them split up, each of the four starting at a corner of the field and examining the health of the plants. Landry inspected a few, all of which looked hardy, then sat beneath the shade of a walnut tree. He put his hat upon his head and readied himself to doze. He often stole such moments, relishing the desultory enjoyment of napping when more was expected of him. But he was interrupted by a voice greeting him with a hello.

He lifted his hat off his head, peeking out from the shadows at Isabelle, who stood in the sun, beyond the penumbra of shade, her hands clasped at her waist.

"I was hoping we might speak," she said.

He still remembered their encounter at the clothesline, the moment she materialized and made herself known; those socks she wished to give him, her confusion, that glimpse of hurt when he walked off. She was an uneasy person, but an observer of things, and in this he knew they shared common ground. She had likely played through their meeting many times in her mind. It was no surprise, then, that she wished to speak with him again, however unwelcome it was in this instance.

"For someone who lives on my property, who has visited it often—well, I feel that I ought to have been better about making your acquaintance."

She wrung her hands and started again.

"That didn't sound right. As if I'm owed something, or wish to place some responsibility on you due to your sleeping in the barn. That is not at all what I meant. Only that we spoke that one time, and didn't speak again, and I want to remove any sense that I might have been disapproving of you, or might still be."

He nodded to her and smiled, something he did on only the rarest of occasions, owing to his jaw, and hoped this might be enough to satisfy her. Yet she remained.

"I know," she stammered, "I know you don't speak. I asked your brother about this, but all he would say is that your jaw doesn't prohibit you. Nor do you have some social deficit, which I gathered on my own. Yet you choose to remain silent. I sometimes feel that way myself. How often I have said the wrong thing or wished to take back my words."

He wondered whom she was speaking to. It was not him. The Isabelles of the world might view him, but they did not *see* him. They certainly did not want to hear his voice. Although he would admit that on occasion, in recent times, he more often had the urge to be heard. But this was not the place for such a thing. Isabelle was more interested in herself. Her own needs.

"You have helped George immensely," she went on. "And Caleb, too. I believe he still suffers, at times. He doesn't know his place in the world. But then neither do I, or even George, maybe. Is it possible to grow more lost as one gets older? I wouldn't have thought so before the war. Yet here we are. All of us. Which is to say that, well, you and Prentiss have been a calming force…"

Landry stood up. If once his strength had been a rock whose ridges were too sharp to touch, confessions like these, and the burden they visited upon him, had polished him down to a dull stone. Isabelle peered up at him. Her blouse was the color of flowers he'd seen in the wild, flowers so gorgeous that the names George gave them, as proper as they might be, only reduced their beauty.

"Oh," Isabelle said. "You must be returning to work."

He wasn't. Not yet at least. He was simply leaving her to her thoughts and taking his own somewhere to be pondered in private. As he preferred.

What went unspoken was the burden of freedom. Not that Landry missed Mr. Morton's ownership—far from it. No, it was rather that he and his brother had been tethered to each other then. The chains that held them down also held them together. In their new life, Prentiss traveled in his own way: his appreciation for trips to town with George to gather supplies; his cheery banter with Caleb, who'd seemed to grow closer to Prentiss since he'd stared working alongside them. The idea of simple chatter, of finding friendship, appealed to his brother in a manner Landry had no interest in. And his own silence, which had once been obscured by the shadows of their bondage, and was a calming peace that gave Prentiss time to think for them both, now laid bare a space that expanded between them. They'd become their own selves.

Still, Landry knew they would never be separated. That Prentiss would always be there, no matter what, waiting in the barn, or keeping watch over his shoulder as they worked the field. And Landry, for his part, always returned to the barn to show he was not gone for good, always returned his brother's glances to assure him that he, too, was keeping watch.

The next Sunday he woke early, eager to take to the woods, only to find Prentiss already sitting up. Leftovers from the night before were boiling in the kettle, cabbage stumps and turnip, cotton seeds and some ham George had given them. His brother looked uneasy, playing with a kink in his hair, sucking air through his teeth.

"Morning," Prentiss said.

Landry wiped the sleep from his eyes. The stick of sweat from the previous day was upon him. He would take to the water when the sun rose, he thought. He would bathe beside the fish, hide himself beneath the surface and go unseen.

"I was wondering," Prentiss said, as if reading his mind, "if maybe I could come along. I know you like your time alone, but you got me so curious when you're out I sometimes can't look at a damned thing but your cot, wondering where you is. I thought I might tag along. Maybe see what you see."

Landry had never considered that his brother might have the slightest interest in joining him.

"You can tell me," Prentiss said. "If you feel like tryin', I'll wait for the words to come."

He wasn't unwilling to stammer in front of Prentiss. He'd done so before, although only rarely, for even Prentiss grew impatient with the excruciating unfurling of each word, until he began guessing at the end of a sentence that Landry had worked so hard to unspool. But even if he wished to convey his feelings on it, there was something inexpressible about his time away. He shared a life with his brother, the barn they occupied, all the worldly goods between them, but these mornings were his. To put it into words would not make his brother impatient. But he feared they might hurt him.

Landry approached his brother, who watched him warily, as if Landry might spring upon him as he had when they were children, forcing him into a scrap. But he only put a hand upon Prentiss's head, held him to his chest.

"What's this?" Prentiss said.

Landry hoped this would be enough, this touch. Perhaps his

brother might even come to relish it more than a Sunday walk. Then Landry turned and started for the door.

"That's it?" Prentiss said. "Just gon' up and leave? I'm up early getting this food ready and you ain't even gonna eat? You ain't right sometimes, you know that? Probably out there spying on folks from the trees and making a fool of yourself. I ain't even *wanna* go, so how's that?"

But by now Landry was beyond the barn door, and if Prentiss said anything further it didn't reach him. Though the days had all been hot, this morning was cool. As he walked, his brother's playful words, the bark in his voice, echoed in Landry's mind, pleasing him. Of course Prentiss wasn't really upset. He knew Landry too well— respected his idle Sunday mornings, had come to understand them in the same way he understood everything about his brother. They were always only a few paces apart. Prentiss had probably returned to his pallet to sleep away the morning, and Landry was even now keeping him company in his dreams.

––––––––––––

That first hour, he did not go far. George had once shown him a spot of copper bunchgrass that claimed a slice of the forest; they had been seeking a certain plant that, according to George, was an exceptional addition to a particular stew. But sometime later Landry spotted the little outpost of seclusion on his own, and it had become a favorite of his haunts.

His things were hidden there, beneath the bed of greenery, and he sought them by running his hand upon the soil until it brushed against the cold of the knitting needles, the doughy embrace of the yarn. He'd bought them from an aged woman at the tent camps whose legs were entangled in a crush of children vying for her attention. She would feed them for a day or two with the money. In return, he rediscovered a lost pastime.

It was true that their mother had been moved into Majesty's

Palace, working the loom and going over designs with Mr. Morton's wife, but she wasn't selected by chance, as Prentiss thought. His brother, Landry figured, had forgotten how skilled she was with her hands. After the whippings, when Landry remained in the cabin, recovering, afraid to go back outside and risk the chance of further punishment, their mother would stay with him, and he would watch her as she worked, her fingers guiding the knitting needles as if playing a fine-tuned violin, knuckles pointed and taut, knots of yarn forming and collecting upon one another in careful bunches.

"Come, child," she said once, and when he pulled up alongside her, there was a set of needles for him to work as well. He hadn't known that his hands were allowed to be delicate like hers—hadn't known they were capable of such creation.

The knitting ended when the picking snatched away the magic of her fingers, and by the time she was brought to Majesty's Palace, she could not live up to her reputation. That was the last they saw of her. Her vanishing happened that fast. Their cabin was quiet then, and they spent many sleepless nights staring at her empty bed until the dawn edged in, hoping she might appear.

He never stitched in all the years of her absence, not until he found freedom. The first item he made was a shawl, which was of no quality, and he hid it in the barn so as to not let it be found. The second, a pair of gloves that appeared to be made for someone with three fingers, achieved the same result. Yet there in the bunchgrass he was regaining his loss at the third attempt, a pair of socks, working at them tirelessly, ignoring the saliva that escaped his mouth, the numbness that colonized his legs— crossed upon the grass—as he toiled. Not until this very day had he felt satisfied with the final product. Now he put his tools beneath a cloudy bed of chickweed blossoms and, for only a moment, returned home.

He avoided the barn. Prentiss was either still at rest or off with George, lending his ear. The cabin appeared unoccupied, but he watched for a time to make sure of it. When there was no movement in the kitchen, no shadows on the second floor, he stole to the backyard. On that first encounter with Isabelle, he had come only to see the socks on the clothesline—to ascertain a job well done, a model that might guide him—and he had found, in addition, a woman begging to be heard, a woman who herself had gone unseen. He knew this pain. He was not one to let it go unacknowledged. A gesture—the socks—might do. There were no clothes on the line. It hung limp in the summer heat. The socks were a bit bigger than the size of a child's foot, which he hoped would be proper for a woman. He looked at them in appreciation of his own craft. Took a clothespin and hung them proudly.

Another sweat was coming on. He slipped off into the woods and followed alongside the road to town, veering off toward the meadowland when it suited him. There was a lightness to his step, and he made quick time. The pond was just as he'd left it—the lilies upon the water unified like a carefully drawn illustration; the water reflecting his image, made beautiful if only by the beauty that surrounded him. He loved the silence, so totally encompassing that his thoughts arrived as if he were speaking, the sentences full and alive, the sort a preacher might thunder to an audience who would respond with whoops and wild *amens*. Here, things were different. For the sliver of time he was allowed, the pond was his.

He removed his clothes and waded into the water slowly. Each step was a clap of cold and he let it spread until he felt himself dissolving, his whole body going numb. When his senses returned it was like he'd pieced himself back together part by part, everything broken and then mended. The pond always filled him with whimsical thoughts. He wasn't sure who owned it, but perhaps, he imagined, a home could be perched beside it. Why not? Perhaps George would enjoy a new project. Perhaps Prentiss would let go of his determination to leave Old Ox if only he dipped a toe into the water that Landry now floated in, if only he could accept the comfort, the belief that this was where they belonged. That finally a place might be theirs. Landry had even brought it up to him. Would do so again in due time.

But he knew the prospect of staying beyond the peanut harvest was unlikely. Prentiss spoke of leaving once they had sufficient savings. Landry himself was content here, with a pallet all his own and so much open land outside the door that it seemed like all the freedom a man might need in one life. But Prentiss would keep them up at night with talks of far-off locales. Maybe they'd hop from town to town, city to city, until they found the one that fit them just right, a place with more work than you could ever hope for, a place where men spent dollars like pennies and thought nothing of it. Or they'd ride on the railcar, not even asking where it might lead to, and disembark wherever the scenery called out to them, find a little bit of land where the weather was cool and no one knew their names, where they could sip lemonade on their own front porch and never be bothered again.

But though these fantasies involved just the two of them, their mother was always present in the back of their minds. Prentiss would ask him what means he thought they might employ to find her when the time came. Landry would get that sinking feeling in his gut, try to think himself away from the barn like he used to think himself away from the plantation, like he used to think himself away from his own body when the whip was meeting his back. His brother talked of going door to door, through the whole state of Georgia, inquiring of their mother's whereabouts. Went so far as to consider asking Mr. Morton, knowing full well he would never tell them, for they'd tried that before, only to be mocked by his laughter, to be told that she wasn't even worth recording in his ledger of transactions. A lie, yes, but as hurtful as anything anyone had ever uttered to them. Best for Landry, then, to take leave of such thoughts, to disappear from those conversations altogether and leave them for his brother to spin around in his own mind.

The slime at the bottom of the pond grazed his toes now when he let it. Small guppies flitted before him, darting about like children at play. He took a deep breath and dunked his head. Silence consumed him. He was entombed in tranquility, in the boundlessness of his floating, his weightlessness. How to capture this feeling. How to make it last forever.

He heard them only as he rose up for air. He kept his body hidden beneath the water, and the marshy mound of plants at the center of the pond concealed him from the other side. But he could glimpse them. Caleb was beneath the other one, the bigger one. Both of them were faced away from him. Landry had never seen a white man naked, so pale beneath the sun. In the fields, Caleb was a man in his own right, or at least on the cusp of being one, but he appeared now as a boy, emitting childish moans as the other boy choked him, took hold of his hair, and delivered heavy blows to his backside.

At first it didn't enter Landry's mind to leave the water, to hide himself. The pond, as he thought of it, was rightfully his. So far and free did his imagination roam here that he thought he might somehow have conjured the scene, for unknown reasons. But the possibility evaporated as the boy's moans grew louder. Yes, that was surely Caleb, George's son, Isabelle's treasure, and no matter how many times Landry had come to this place, no matter how he thought of it, the presence of these two meant that it was theirs entirely—it was he who was trespassing. Perhaps he could dive down, suspend himself in silence, wait for them to depart, and find himself a new refuge. He and Prentiss could leave for the railcar. They could search for another place like this one.

Their bodies were contorted, with Caleb on his stomach and the other boy mounted upon him. Landry drifted backward, water dripping from his chest and hair as he emerged from the pond, shivering despite the heat. They did not turn as he collected his pants, his shirt and boots. Nor as he slipped them on. He could disappear. Yet he knew this would be his last glimpse of the pond, the last time he would ever have this image so clear in his mind. He breathed it in and let it go.

It was then that the other boy whipped about. Landry did not freeze out of fear. More so at the oddness of it all: that after so many years unseen, he would be taken notice of by a boy such as this, and from a great distance. He started back to the barn. First at a walk. Faster when he heard the footsteps upon him.

CHAPTER 12

The world pressed upon their secret. Caleb could feel as much, deeper than the heat of August's breath upon his neck, the cutting strokes of each blade of grass against his naked body, which was pinned to the ground. But prudence meant nothing. His worries were carried off in the slickness of his sweat, in the curling of his toes and the clenching of his teeth as waves of joy coursed through him. It was as if a bell beneath his ribcage had lain at rest since the last time his friend had claimed him, at this very pond, a year ago, and now August penetrated him so deeply, with such force, that the pealing of that bell shook his entire being, great jolts of delight quaking through him, one after the other. They were so intense that he craved a moment of reprieve, all while fearing the bliss of the afternoon might end, might never return to him, if his wish were granted.

It was August who stopped. He pulled off Caleb, his body running with sweat, and turned, war-ready.

"Someone's there," he said.

But Caleb had no words to respond. He was spent, and even though he knew the fear and threat that August's words should inspire in him, he could not summon the power to care.

"Get up," August said.

Caleb's body was red with the exquisite torment of the afternoon, his every muscle cramped, the soreness hitting him as he came to. He'd never seduced another person—August had been the aggressor both times—and on each occasion of being taken he was shocked at how lost he'd become in his emotions, the violent whirlwind of his submission: one moment you are lucid, lost in the quotidian, and the next you are transported to another world altogether, with your pants at your ankles and mulch slathered up your damp thighs.

Aside from their lone previous tryst, in this same spot, back before the war, their behavior together had always been tamer. (Caleb was fine with only the friction of August's body against his own, or a kiss that kept his mind in a tizzy for the rest of the day.) But he didn't harbor the slightest regret. Nor was he upset at being seen. Let the truth of their bond be set free upon Old Ox, upon the world entire. But he knew that for August, the chosen one, this trespass upon them was a threat, and would only confirm that Caleb was a problem, best kept at arm's length, if not forgotten altogether. Perhaps it was this realization that finally sobered him. He pulled his pants up and listened to his friend.

"Collect your things before he gets away," August said, already moving toward the woods.

There was nothing to do but obey, and as they strode, soon picking up speed to a frantic crash through the trees, he tried to lock in his mind the particulars of this fine afternoon: the ringing of each thrust still rolling through his ears; the place at the edge of the pond where his body had made an imprint in the grass; the matching depressions in the mud where August had placed his knees and mounted him. Even if the world learned their secret, and even if the punishment was severe, he would always have access to these memories. They were his alone to be hoarded—protected from the outside world in even the darkest of times.

For weeks before seeing August he'd spent his days working the fields, awaiting the blooms on the peanut plants. He did not care for his father's new hobby, or for farming in general, really. He found the work tedious but drifted to it every morning for lack of a greater purpose, and also to satisfy his mother's wish that he stay close to his father. And they *were* close. He would pull the same stunts he had as a boy, threatening to slap Ridley's behind and send him galloping as his father rode atop the donkey and protested wildly, "Don't you dare, don't you dare." And when his father swung his hoe down with such force that he pitched forward, face-first into the dirt, so that Caleb had to race alongside the brothers to help him up as tears of amusement ran down their faces, the incident fueled dinner conversations for many nights to come. He and his father touched on matters more serious, too: a plan to use new ground for the next planting cycle, perhaps even seed another crop by fall. Cucumbers grew fast enough in the heat that they could mature before the first frost, and while it was a bit late for rice, there might even be time for that if they hurried, though the irrigation work necessary might prohibit it this year.

When discussions fell on business, they were often in the field, and they talked like men talk. Standing and spitting, filling the silence with grunts. Caleb wondered if these were the only two modes they might exist in: either conversing on practical matters or evoking their shared history, overlaying the present moment with the nostalgia of times long gone to them. It wasn't vexing, exactly—just an awareness that his father had his limits, and that there were hallways of thought, of emotion, which would always remain behind closed doors.

What they shared was nothing like what Caleb shared with August. Yet it was a great source of misery that his friend hadn't called on him since their day at the pond, now many weeks ago. On the two occasions Caleb had gone to his home, August's mother had told him—in an icy tone, barely meeting his gaze—that her son was at work. It did not take much to gather the reason for this snubbing. If his father's farm had directed the ire of every man in Old Ox against his family, then his mother's outburst at the Beddenfelds' had done the same with the women. On the orders of her husband, Mrs. Webler informed him, neither he nor August was to be disturbed. When Caleb asked, on the second visit, when August might be free, she said she was far too busy arranging her son's wedding to be of further use.

Going into Old Ox proper was an equally cold proposition. Wade Webler, or someone he was involved with, had spread word of his cowardice, and his welcome among the townsfolk had become even chillier than the one Mrs. Webler had given him. The saloon bartender had a way of looking him off when he raised his hand for a beer. When he sought the services of Jan and Albert Stoutly, who had started fitting harnesses and carts (the sort that might ease Ridley's load a bit), they told him new orders would be fulfilled by the following year, yet the man outside the store was delighted with how fast they'd produced his and apparently promising him more for the rest of his stable in the coming weeks. Even something as simple as buying feed had grown troublesome with all the stares. The prospect of a haircut was out of the question; he'd sat in the waiting chair at the barber's for so long that he'd heard the same stories repeated to three different customers, all of whom had come in after him.

So he passed his time at home. The days were infuriatingly slow, and the distraction of August in town followed him about like the shadow of the sun creeping over the fields. He would often go off to a patch of dirt alone and turn the soil mindlessly, hating the effort of his longing, the pathetic nature of his being. His father, battling his own unknown demons, paid his aloofness no mind, but Caleb was surprised to hear from him one night that Prentiss and Landry thought they had caused some offense and were shunning him.

"Do you hold something against them?" his father asked. "Some notion from the war?"

"Father, please. It's nothing like that."

"Well then, try to be civil. It's not like you have anyone else to keep you company."

Caleb made an effort. One Sunday evening before supper he walked to the barn to say hello and found Prentiss alone, washing his pants in a basin of hot water. Only a few weeks earlier he'd informed Caleb and his father that he'd purchased new pants for himself and Landry. The brothers had arrived in the fields with some newfound pride, strutting like the boys who'd paraded through town in their freshly starched grays before the war. Now the trousers were streaked with large smears of color, and the water was doing nothing to clean them.

"What took to them?" Caleb asked in lieu of a hello.

Prentiss seemed surprised to see him. He patted his hands dry on his shirt and looked at the basin in contemplation.

"Some paint is all."

"I see. Your brother around?"

"He's off."

"Where to?"

"That's his business," Prentiss said.

He pulled the pants from the basin, set them on the ground, and began scrubbing them with a brush, working at them for some time.

Caleb imagined his father watching from the house. Some period of time should pass—but how long?—before it would be appropriate for him to return inside. He thought he might simply wait it out in silence, for there was no way he could ever express the truth to Prentiss: that he envied him and what he shared with his brother; that he had always desperately wished to have his own; that when he'd lain in bed as a child and felt the rumpled sheets beside him, he'd wished it were another, and that each morning, when he woke, he'd pretended to get dressed alongside this boy who didn't exist, helping him tie his shoes, comb his hair. He could never describe how distressing it was when his mother arrived at the bedroom door in the morning and the boy disappeared. He would go silent, looking at his mother as if he wished her dead, as if her mere presence had made the boy disappear. Or, even worse, had denied him that brother in reality.

"What you got goin' on?" Prentiss asked.

"I was just floating about the house mindlessly. I get restless sometimes when it's just my parents."

"Well, you're always welcome here. Hell, it's your barn, ain't it?"

Caleb thought he knew much of Prentiss, but sometimes, he realized, it was nothing at all.

He recalled the time he and his father had been discussing which plants might thrive in the fields, and Caleb had mentioned how well cotton grew. Prentiss, who until that point had been silent, said, "I best long be gone if y'all start in on that. I ain't touching that plant again. I ain't even standing near enough to see the white of the bolls." His father didn't reply and the matter was dropped.

Or there was the night Caleb had tried to help him clean the skillet, only for Prentiss to pull it away as a child might withhold a toy, informing him that there was a technique to cleaning, that you used your palm and the side of your hand to catch the burnt bits in the crevices and on the bottom that wouldn't otherwise be freed. These could be cooked up for a whole separate meal. He'd be happy to teach him, Prentiss had said, just as his mother had taught him, but he wasn't about to see the job done poorly.

The hidden fury. The pride, withered and wounded at times, but always there. He had a part of him that Caleb did not have. If they'd been brothers, it would be Prentiss instructing him on how to tie his shoes, Prentiss the one who showed him how the world worked. And perhaps that was why Caleb could barely utter a word to him beyond a simple greeting. To do so would require that he expose his vulnerabilities to another man, and he did not know how to reveal himself in such a way. It was a form of confrontation, the very idea he cowered from. He would never pull the kettle back from a man grabbing for it. He had never been taught such things.

"What were you painting?" Caleb asked, helpless for anything else to say.

Prentiss was still slapping at his pants with the brush.

"I ain't paint a damn thing. I seen a fella in the camps with some calendars for sale, and I gone that way to pick one up so I could count the days till harvest. I'm minding my business, passing the chapel in town, and a bunch a fools are there painting a fresh coat on it. What would you know, one of 'em drops a bucket of paint right down on me. The whole pack of his boys is laughing, and he's saying, 'Whoops,' like he ain't mean to do it. They had me seeing red. What'd I do to them…"

He waited a moment, then shook his head, dismissing the comment.

"Not that I'd do nothing, really. I just mean he had me roiled up inside a bit. Nothing time won't mend."

Prentiss didn't trust him, Caleb thought. If only he knew those same boys would most likely flip that bucket of paint onto Caleb's head, too, if given the chance. He let the story pass unremarked and asked instead whether Prentiss had gotten his calendar.

"They say the man with the calendars went north," Prentiss said. "I missed him by a day."

Caleb sneezed, and he realized there was something that collected in the barn, some manner of dust. It struck him as odd, for the first time, that someone would live here, among strewn-about farming equipment, skittering mice, and owls that hooted throughout the night and released droppings upon the floor to be stepped in later. *How had it not crossed his mind before?* he wondered. Of course there would be a man with calendars. Anyone who lived in such conditions would count the days in anticipation, marking off the time until that moment in the future when they could move on. For the man with the calendars, that day had come.

He braved town late one weekday afternoon, determined not to be turned back this time. Darkness was still hours distant, but many were already inside for the evening. He tied Ridley off before Ray Bittle's house. The old man's hat was very low on his forehead, his face hidden, his body so sunken in his rocking chair that he seemed melded to the wood. The image was troubling. Perhaps his sleep might be read in the manner one studies a palm: that in the peculiarity of such tremendous slouching, in the purposeful concealment of his features, he was passing on some message of a buried truth he could not bear to face in his waking life. Caleb was taken by the sight, but not enough to linger. He had only so long before August returned home, and he meant to catch him at work, as far away from Mrs. Webler as possible.

August and his father worked out of an astonishingly modest building, a little redbrick house of two stories; few passersby ever acknowledged its presence, innocent of the fact that whatever other building they were going to, or coming from, was probably leased by the men inside this one. To its left sat a hotel, and to its right a furniture depot, both of which received far more traffic. Caleb dawdled on the walkway, then took one measured breath and walked to the front door, banishing from his mind any further hesitation.

He found a clerk sitting behind a counter, looking at papers. Caleb had imagined the foyer would be empty and he would charge upstairs and interrupt a meeting, or storm the library at the building's rear, where clients were being entertained, yet whatever storming was to take place was promptly dashed by the presence of the boy who was now staring at him quizzically.

"Can I help you?" he said. He was no more than a reed, a string of a body, a feather that might get carried off in the wind.

"I'm looking for August Webler."

"Mr. Webler is in a meeting."

Mr. Webler. Was that what August was now? So be it: Caleb would not be made to wait to see even a *Mr. Webler.*

"It will only take a moment," he said.

"Sir—"

Caleb made for the stairs and did not slow down as the boy called out to him. There was an undeniable rush to the way he climbed to the second floor. He had no idea what he might find there, but knew that August, if he still had any care for him at all, would welcome the imposition. How else might he respond to someone so willing to fight for a friendship, someone who might put all social boundaries aside to risk the chance to say hello?

The main room upstairs was empty. Two offices flanking it both bore the nameplate MR. WEBLER. Caleb had no idea which one might be August's. The last thing he wished to do was barge in on Wade Webler, but seeing as he had forced his way this far, a precautionary knock felt incongruous with the spirit of his endeavor.

A spasm of panic rippled through him. The day's heat, having collected on the second floor, fell upon him like a heavy quilt. Finally, he heard murmurs seeping from beneath the door on the right. He followed the sound, and despite his resolution of a moment ago, he knocked. The gruff voice of Wade Webler, without asking who it was, called for him to enter. Only by his initial struggle to grip the doorknob did Caleb realize just how much he was sweating. With effort he managed to turn the knob and show himself in.

"What is this?" Wade Webler was seated behind his large oak desk, leaning back in his chair with an expression of bewilderment.

Beside him, August sat with a pad of paper, a pencil in hand. Caleb knew the man across the desk from the flyers posted around town. This was Brigadier General Glass, standing so upright that he appeared to be in the midst of a presentation.

"Caleb?" August said.

Mr. Webler did not give him any time to respond.

"How did you get up here?" He leaned over the desk. "Jeffrey!" he yelled, which triggered a slight coughing fit, leading Mr. Webler to drink a finger of whiskey from the tumbler at his side before resuming his yelling.

Stiff reports echoed from the stairwell, like knocks upon a door, and in a moment the boy arrived in the office, sweating profusely himself.

"I am so sorry, sir," he said, "but he went and passed me even after I told him not to."

Shocked by the exhaustion on the boy's face, Caleb looked down and registered his wooden leg.

"For Christ's sake, Caleb," Mr. Webler said. "I know you struggled to follow orders as a subordinate, but is it too much to ask for you to take proper instructions from my secretary?"

For a second Caleb pondered the question quite soberly, and wondered, with a calculated rationale, if he might serve the moment better by excusing himself and jumping out the window.

"What on earth is so important for you to evade a hop-legged man and steal your way up the stairs?"

"I didn't know he was lame," Caleb mumbled.

"I should excuse myself," General Glass said.

"Absolutely not," Mr. Webler said. "You have an appointment to speak here today. Men with *appointments,* who obligate themselves to decorum, must not be made to bow to those who are so selfish as to defy procedures of civility. An esteemed soldier such as yourself knows as much."

"I'll go," Caleb said, in the meek voice of a chastised schoolboy, as though he was best put in a corner facing the wall.

"But apparently only after ignoring the pleadings of a young man who is merely working to save for a prosthetic leg? For a soldier who had his face mangled, one would think you'd have understood the plight of a fellow cripple."

Caleb's hand spontaneously reached for the scars on his face.

"And then you go and interrupt the right honorable General Glass," Mr. Webler said. "This man, an army man, who has entered our community to serve even those he fought against, simply wishes to procure a loan for his ailing mother, in need of emergency surgery. Imagine what it must've taken for him to humble himself into coming here today. Only for you to interrupt just as he's making his request."

The only sound now was the boy, Jeffrey, huffing in fatigue, and Caleb could see General Glass staring upon the ground in some private humiliation and Mr. Webler's depraved glee. And then there was August. Caleb sought desperately to detect a hint of sympathy in his gaze—the sort he might offer him when they lay beside each other. Or at least, the very least, he hoped to find August looking away, to know his friend shared in his embarrassment.

But Mr. Webler, in his command of the room, would not let

them share so much as a glance. He turned to his son and drew his attention at once.

"Would you mind telling your friend to heed his own advice and leave us in peace?"

August put his pen down on the table. There was the start of a long breath, as if he was pained, and that was enough for Caleb. A sign of his anguish. Or perhaps Caleb was so broken that he could interpret his friend taking a breath to mean the world.

"We have a lot of work to do," August said, businesslike. "It's best you go."

Caleb didn't need to be told twice.

———————

He had a recurring dream that took place among Wade Webler's stables. He knew why it was set there: once Mr. Webler had held a party when Caleb was a child, and he and a group of boys had gone to the stables to play in the hay. He remembered well the heat of the place, warmed only by the bevy of bodies running about, as well as the horses, so many of them, leaning their heads over the gates as if to supervise the boys' roughhousing. But in the dream, Caleb is grown, and the other boys are grown, and they are watching him from each stall, having replaced the horses altogether.

He is slung sideways over the saddle, stomach first, his body fit smoothly upon the leather, his back arched at its groove. The stirrups are chained to two posts at his rear, his legs in turn tied to the stirrups. He cannot go free. Beside him there is a growing warmth, a crackle, akin to the sound of stepped-upon leaves: a basket of coals in line with his ear. The others have their eyes on him and him alone.

It's August who appears at his back. Caleb can crook his neck and make out the fall of his blond hair, the slow bounce to his walk. His friend plucks the branding iron from the coals, hoists it for the others to see, then menaces Caleb's face with it.

"A *T*, fit for a traitor," August says, and the other boys howl.

The iron glows so hot that he can sense it over his entire body. Not a searing pain, but like a drop of wax, slowly spread wide by a single finger until it covers him whole. Caleb feels August pull his shirt up, his hands brushing against his back, and he can only grit his teeth as the iron descends upon him, and it is then, right then, he wakes up, so bothered, so perversely excited, that he has no option but to evacuate the energy within him in the most repugnant of manners, the remnants of the dream sloughed away as they're drained from his being. He must go and retrieve a rag from downstairs. Clean himself of his embarrassment. Which was how he felt now, as he walked back toward Ray Bittle's: repulsed by his own actions, by ever thinking it had been a good idea to come find August, or to come home from the war in the first place, for that matter. Perhaps Prentiss and Landry had the proper idea. Go north. Escape Old Ox for good. Ridley was in sight now, and he had half a mind to ride away on him and leave town forever.

A familiar voice called out his name. He carried on toward Ridley as if he'd heard nothing but the cawing crows settled on Ray Bittle's home. But he couldn't ignore the pull on his shoulder, the fingernails digging into his shirt.

Caleb recoiled at the touch. He spun around and caught August off guard.

"Don't," Caleb said. "Leave it alone."

He had reached the donkey and began to untie the reins but August would not budge from beside him.

"He ribs you seeking this very reaction," August said.

"Well, he should consider himself successful. You can write that down on your little notepad and report back to him."

August stretched out his hand and grabbed the reins from Caleb.

"Do you think I enjoy such things?" August said. "To see you suffer like that?"

"Considering I haven't heard a word from you in weeks, I'd imagine you're indifferent to how I feel."

"You cannot seriously be this sensitive. This has little to do with you. It's that the wedding is next Tuesday and the planning of it goes on from the moment I'm relieved of work until the sun goes down."

"Please. As if anything ever stopped you before. We both know your father is behind this. Just as he was no doubt behind the decision to uninvite me and my family from the wedding."

And wasn't it so much like the Weblers to plan a wedding for a Tuesday, to rob the town of a good day's work and force them to come and pay their respects to the prince and his new princess bride?

Their backs were to town, with Ridley shielding them from the main thoroughfare, and before them sat Ray Bittle, still fast asleep on his porch. They were very much alone. It was difficult to bear August's gaze, for the blue of his eyes was as piercing and as suddenly felt as the center of a lit match before one's face.

"You have no idea," August said. "I must live with him, Caleb. Endure him. At least until I get my own home, which I don't look forward to. My God, the prospect of living with Natasha. When I see her it's with the same boredom I feel when I read the reports on my desk every morning. It is a troublesome affair, weddings and women and work, and I had far more clarity in the war than I do here. I mean that, too. I'd much rather dig graves in the most hardened ground than marry Natasha and work for my father and listen to a Union general debase himself for a few dollars."

"You think I don't feel that way? I work in the field all day, playing with soil, and at night my father has me reading books on agriculture. As if I have the slightest interest in knowing whether grass clippings or straw work better than mulch. The only reprieve would be our times together, which you've denied us for no reason I can tell."

"Must I make it plain to you?" said August, struggling to keep his voice down. "Because I will. If that's what you need."

Caleb shrugged with deliberate nonchalance, yet his heart beat so rapidly that he felt it reverberating beneath his feet like a ground tremor.

"He knows," August said. "He has always known. How we feel for one another. He makes it his goal to ridicule. He calls you the little girl, and any mention I make of you is met with derision at your being a coward. Even at socials he cites you as an example of every-thing wrong with the Southern cause, the lack of spirit that allowed us to lose so much."

Caleb tried to reclaim the reins from his friend's hands, but August would not relinquish them—would not stop talking.

"And don't even get me started on your parents. Your mother's outrageous behavior at the Beddenfelds', acting like some sort of lunatic—"

"She was offended; she was only protecting her family."

"—or your father with his Negroes. The gall to let them live in his home—"

"They don't live in our home. It's a silly rumor that will not cease." Caleb stopped himself. "And what if they did?"

"Caleb," August said. "You know there's no one I would rather spend time with than you, but it can't be."

"Yet you said nothing would change. Your exact words."

"*You* changed. All of you Walkers changed."

"We *lost*, August. The *world* has changed. Can't you see that? Or are you as dim as your father?"

"Keep it down," August hissed. He looked around, but the road was empty and even Ray Bittle had yet to stir.

Caleb shook his head and finally yanked the reins so hard they slid through August's grip. He mounted Ridley and addressed his friend once more:

"I recently overheard Prentiss, one of those Negroes your father hates so dearly, tell my father how he'd seen a fellow he knew as a boy, another slave, begging in the camps outside town. Prentiss didn't spare him a cent. *Was that a crime?* he wanted to know. To be so cold to someone he'd grown up beside? What if this distance happened between him and his own brother? He seemed to have a fear somewhere in him that they were growing apart. My father told him not to be silly. That two people so close would never let such a thing happen. What bound them was too strong. I thought my father had provided him sage advice. I wonder now if he misspoke."

August's jaw was locked tight in rage. There was no remedy for this occasion, and Caleb knew how this had to have jolted him—what it meant to lose control of the relationship August had steered with such command that Caleb's obedience had never been questioned. And now, it seemed, their old ways were over.

"Take care, August. Give Natasha my kindest regards. Also, you can let your father know I consider him an insufferable prick."

He took Ridley off at a saunter, and by the time he was home, he had made his own decision to leave Old Ox, for once and ever. It was only a matter of where to go. Somewhere more temperate, maybe—certainly someplace no one would know him, a town, or even a city, where a man with a curious face and a quiet disposition might go unnoticed in a crowd.

These thoughts occupied him until late the following morning, when he was washing up at the water pump beside the fields during a break in his work and his mother appeared with a paper in hand.

"A message from town."

"From who?" he said, drying his hands on his pants.

"He didn't care to say."

There were only two words, written in pencil: *Pond. Sunday.*

He knew by the lumbering gait, the colossus of the shoulders, the sheer immensity of the man, that it could be no one but Landry fleeing them through the woods, as there was no one like him in all of Old Ox. It seemed at first that because Landry was of one world and August the other, some force, some greater balance of things, would keep them separate. The belief persisted in Caleb even when August grabbed a solid castoff branch, thick as an arm, and carried it upon his shoulder like a carbine rifle; even when they emerged from the end of the woods to the beginnings of his father's farm, the distant cabin in sight, and found Landry fallen in the dirt, clutching an ankle.

August stood before him, and Caleb, at last understanding the moment, cried out for him to stop. He had never before heard Landry make any sound at all, but now Prentiss's brother issued dreadful moans, so pitiful and high-pitched as to bring to mind a wounded child.

Yet August appeared oblivious to everything but the source of darkness within him that had brought him so much pleasure in the war. He asked Caleb why he was protesting, for this was simply a nigger, one that didn't know its place. Caleb explained their relation and August smiled. He told Caleb he was doing him a favor. That this would be good for his family.

Landry attempted to stand but August put his boot against his chest and that was all it took to hold him still. Where was Landry's strength? Caleb wondered. He'd never seen a man more vicious with an ax, yet Landry now whimpered under the sole of a boot. His eyes searched around in fright, and his jaw, that loose appendage, trembled under the weight of his own cries.

Caleb was on the ground. He had no idea how he'd gotten there, sitting in mud and slick leaves, with his hands covering his eyes. If he could only rise up he could stop August himself. He could right things. But he was so terrified he could not bear the sight, let alone think of moving. He watched through his fingers as August coolly took the branch from his shoulders with both hands. Then, at what seemed the last moment, Caleb shouted to August that Landry could not speak. The man had no words in him at all. He would never tell a soul what he had seen.

Caleb let his hands fall to his side, and for a moment August wavered. Landry stared up at this assailant so intensely, so resolute in his gaze, that Caleb thought he might have found some source of strength. And he had. Only in a way Caleb could not have foreseen.

"I c-c-c," Landry stammered endlessly, refusing to let rest whatever statement he was forming, insistent that his voice be heard. It brought him to a sweat. Every ounce of his being was poured into creating the words. "I c-c-c can speak. Ain't no different from you."

August turned to Caleb with a knowing grin, and he knew then that his friend was gone to him.

The first blow landed upon Landry's head. The man's cries stopped immediately, and the forest went so quiet that the second blow echoed with a sickening crack, like a tree split by lightning. A trickle of blood ran from his head where a seam had opened. His head lolled forward, backward, then fell with the torpor of a bird shot from the sky.

Caleb squeezed his eyes shut and covered his ears from the sound of vicious thuds. He could not move. His throat was too dry to emit noise. He sat clutching himself, waiting hopelessly for the barbarity to end.

He might have lain there until nightfall had he not felt the hand on his head, the familiarity of the fingers rubbing his scalp to comfort him. August told him it was off-putting for him to act so sensitive. Caleb could not help now but to glance at Landry, to take in the mangled face, the eye sockets pooled with blood. He wondered if his friend would do the same to him. The branch was still in August's hand, like a child's toy, and anything felt possible. It was just then that two figures appeared in sun haze at the far side of the field.

"Find yourself an excuse," August told him. "I was not here."

The long shadow that had fallen over him lifted away. August was gone.

CHAPTER 13

George had risen early and brewed a strong cup of coffee. The first sip alone was so gratifying that he might as well have been a dog loosed from a kennel and given over to the smell of a fresh-cut lawn, such was the rush he felt. He let it sink into him and thought of nothing else for a time, but soon took to the front porch, where he sat alone in his wife's rocking chair with no greater goal than observing the sunrise that began to grace the bottom of the valley. Sundays were the lone day of rest that he and Caleb and the brothers permitted themselves. Last night he had gone to speak with Clementine again, to hear of her daughter and to inform her of his life since his previous visit. The walk back had been miserable on his bones, and although Isabelle made no mention of his absence, she was quick to comment on how lame he had looked in the past few days. His only response was to ask her, good-naturedly, to stop drawing attention to his decrepitude. Many a thinker had devoted himself to questions of aging and death, yet the thinkers died at the same rate as the idiots, and so George had grown quite content with the idea of ignoring the process altogether. Still, after these recent months on the farm—first clearing the trees and then working the peanut field—he was swelled with pain by the end of each afternoon, and in the morning his joints were rigid, as if needing to thaw. The hot cup of coffee coating his insides was the only fit remedy he'd found.

As the morning progressed, its only peculiarity was that Isabelle went to church, taking the carriage. This was odd, seeing as neither of them had attended in some time, but he did not question her reasons. Landry disappeared into the woods, as was his usual inclination. Prentiss did not appear from the barn. And Caleb was asleep. That was what would afflict George when he considered that day long after it was done: how there had been no rupture in its usual chronology, nothing to suggest the horrors that lay in store. He'd even observed Landry later that morning, sitting in a clearing in the woods, his back to him, wholly relaxed. And so it was all the more shocking to discover his bludgeoned body hours later—his legs bent at the joints, curled in response to the blows; his face so mangled as to be indistinct. No life left in him at all.

George had been having a conversation with Prentiss on the nature of livestock, the productivity of a slaughtered cow in its weight of meat versus a coop of chickens liable to lay eggs indefinitely, when the cries ripped through the forest.

His first glimpse of the body was from enough distance that he did not recognize what lay before him. He thought it was the beast of the forest, caught and killed, and the idea (although vindicating) was anathema to his wish to see it alive, the majesty of it wandering the woods. But Prentiss rushed to the body so quickly that George's mind rearranged its thinking and he knew then. He felt the urge to vomit. He stood there blankly, his hand over his mouth, until he saw the cowed creature sitting in the mud at the edge of the woods, and hurried to meet his son.

Caleb's face was so red as to appear burnt, and when he tried to speak, strings of saliva formed at the corners of his mouth. He couldn't manage a single word.

"You must tell us what happened," George said.

Prentiss had his head above the mess of blood and grime on his brother's chest, pleading maniacally with the lifeless body.

"Now we got plans, Landry, we got good plans, solid plans, so you get yourself up now. You ain't the lazy one, I'm the lazy one, you get yourself up."

He moaned, and grabbed at Landry's chest like an infant might grab at a mother's breast.

"Look at your new pants," he said. "How you gonna dirty your pants right after you got on me about mine? Where do you get off?" he asked, and kept on asking. "Where do you get off?"

Soon his anger was such that he was slamming his brother's chest and demanding he respond, his pain so outsize that it seemed it might expand to take up the entire forest, the entire world.

All the while, Caleb would not answer George, would only stare ahead as if whatever had happened had rendered him mute. George shook him repeatedly and said he knew he was not capable of this, begging that he acknowledge having no part, until finally Caleb wagged his head back and forth, an agreement that he hadn't done it.

"Then who?" George demanded, overcome. "Who would possibly do this?"

Caleb still would not speak. He looked through the forest, as if beyond the trees, and there was only one place that rested there. George had no idea why his son had been in the woods—that part he would get to later—but he knew where his son's eyes were leading him: directly toward the lone man who might have motivation to commit an act so heinous, for he had caused so much grief in Landry's life before.

He left Caleb and Prentiss behind with Landry's body and set off for Ted Morton's property at a pace he had seldom known. He did not go around Morton's rail fence, but climbed it, miserably, and slid down the other side, giving himself a moment to recover from the effort. He was exhausted by the time he'd walked through the cotton fields, but his blood still flowed with rage no matter where it led him. If it was necessary, if it was just, he would bring Ted Morton to the same end that had befallen Landry.

The stalks were a foot high around him and a scattering of men and women scraped at the topsoil, perhaps for the last time before bloom. They looked up at him with some confusion before returning to work, a few giving him nods—smiles even—which he did not return, considering the nature of his visit. He was before the old slave cabins when Gail Cooley appeared, almost unrecognizable with the flecks of mud on his face, his pants rolled up to his shanks, and the wide-brimmed hat shading his eyes.

It was odd to see him without Ted Morton leading him this way and that upon a horse, and it appeared to give Gail great consternation to start the discussion on his own.

"Mr. Walker," he said. "I seen you walking through the fields."

"Where is Ted?"

"In the fields himself."

"On a Sunday?"

"We don't got the hands to take many days off. He says next Sunday, maybe, if we get all that cotton scraped."

"Take me to him."

Gail balled up his face, seeming to negotiate whether to accept direction from George. But he acquiesced and told George to follow him. They came upon Ted in one of the furrows, cutting grass on the topsoil alongside his son, William. Ted was as battered as Gail appeared. The work seemed to have shrunk him, yet he still was huffing out orders as if he owned the workers before him. When he made out George, he stopped for a moment, and the people around him did the same. He and George sized each other up.

"I will give you this one chance to confess to what you did," George said. "You claim to be an honest man. A good man. Then you will admit to your crime."

Ted unbuttoned the top of his shirt and fanned himself with his hat.

"George, I ain't got the slightest clue what you're talking about. But I got half a mind to shove this hoe right up your ass."

"Always voicing one threat or another."

"I'd be right glad to turn it into a reality for you. I'll lay you out on my knee and stick the handle of this hoe so far up your behind you'll be able to turn your soil with a squat and a shuffle."

It was an infuriation built up over a lifetime, but still, the sudden rage in George was a surprise to everyone. He rushed Ted with a ferocious howl. Ted's eyes went bright for a split second. He grabbed George by the shoulder, stepped out of the way, and let the old man's momentum carry him to the ground.

"Have you lost your mind?" Ted yelled.

The plantation was at a standstill. William, the boy, laughed like a yipping dog, and Gail rallied himself next to Ted in some show of solidarity.

George stood up slowly, minding his hip, and brushed the dirt off his front.

"Admit what you've done," he said.

"Admit to what? Goddamn it, George, I'm out here breaking my back for pennies day after day, working like a slave to make a decent wage. Whatever you think I done, unless it involves a hoe or a plow, it just ain't happened."

"You killed him. You killed Landry. And you will confess to it. Before me. Before your God. And before the law."

Ted looked at him in confusion. Then, suddenly, recognition broke across his face.

"You talking about that nigger of mine you stole? He's dead?"

George made to rush Ted again.

"Hold on now," Ted said. "I told you, I ain't got *no idea* what you're jawing on about. It's as I said, I been here working, and at night I got my wife screaming my ear off because I don't even have the time to give her a nod hello. And you think I'm out killing niggers in my spare time? My own niggers at that." He laughed at this.

"You did not own him," George said. "And that's precisely why you killed him."

"When did this happen, might I ask?"

George was still simmering, but it was the first time he'd been made to consider the sum of the circumstances, and he answered so as to think through the issue himself.

"I saw him earlier. So it would have been sometime this afternoon."

"And I got a good dozen men who can attest to me breaking my back since dawn."

George felt his temper dropping. He could still smell the dank soil in his nostrils from his fall, wet clay with a hint of manure.

"Lord in prayer," Ted said, "I did not lay a hand on that boy. Not in some years, at least. I mean I nearly skinned him alive, but that was some time ago. Even then I had the smarts not to kill him. And you know, I rather liked his brother, the one who spoke. He had a knack for picking."

Gail nodded along in agreement. "Ain't that the truth."

Ted went on. "Now, if you feel the need to get the law out here, and you think you got some case, well, I'll be happy to have another break in my day to make a fool out of you. But if this is all over, I'd give you the same advice you gave me a while back—get the hell off my property. Pardon me for not having them pretty words to make it sound as nice as you did."

It was clear that Ted hadn't done it. Between him and Gail, the two had barely enough wit to mount a horse without falling off its backside, let alone murder a man, form an alibi, and defend it so vigorously. There was no choice but to apologize, turn from Majesty's Palace, and walk back to the woods with an anger he could no longer point toward Ted. Or anyone else for that matter. It wasn't anger anymore. By the time he climbed the rail fence again, it was sadness that injured him—rang through him with the same tone of Prentiss's cries, shook him like the trembling hands of his son.

CHAPTER 14

Prentiss had learned from Landry that the language of grief was often nothing more than silence. He'd felt it himself on occasion, but never with his brother's fervor. Until now. Until this very moment. There was a strange way of his hurt he could not grasp. For so long Landry had been the focus of his dreams, his world, and Prentiss felt there was a selfishness in his brother's sudden absence, as though rather than truly dying, Landry had been set free, only to leave Prentiss in the horror of living without the very person who had made doing so worthwhile.

There was no word for what lay before him. He could not say *body*. Could not say *corpse*. It was a desecration. Something unholy. The feet leading to the legs, the legs to the torso, the torso to…

When he'd gathered himself, he stood and refused to look back down. His eyes landed on Caleb, the boy so pathetic, so loaded up with his own fright, that it took every fiber of Prentiss's being not to put his hands on him right then and there. Caleb rose, his eyes bulging, animal-like, staring about as if lost in his own delirium.

"Sit back down," he said.

"I need to go to the house," Caleb said. "I need to clean this grime off of me. Need to get away from this."

Prentiss told him he wasn't going anywhere. Neither of them were.

"I can barely breathe. My heart, I can't stay here."

Prentiss knew not to touch the boy. Knew, with what had already taken place, with his position in this circumstance, how even the slightest mistake would mean more ruin. But he blocked Caleb's way with a menacing stance, his shoulders wide, mouth curled, emanating every ounce of anger he had in the hope of keeping the boy in place. Caleb cowered once more to the ground and covered his face with his hands. No blood on those hands, Prentiss noticed. Just more mud.

The boy was blabbering now, muttering about a twitch, a movement of the body, a chance to bring Landry back to life. Prentiss, fighting back the tears that threatened to overwhelm his anger, told him not to speak again. Not a word.

The forest was still, the only sound that of Caleb's foot jerking in place, the mud beneath his shoe squelching in rhythm, as if the ground itself wanted to bear witness but couldn't get out the words.

"We gonna figure this out," Prentiss said. "And we gonna need your help. Can you pull yourself together and be of some use? Can you do that for me?"

It was as though Caleb reverted entirely to a child, his words coming in between sobs.

"Mother!" he yelled. "I need to speak with my mother. Let me go. She'll know what to do. She can help get me balanced, and then I can speak on this, all of this, but I'm begging you to let me be gone from here."

Prentiss went numb, and once more he felt the consuming silence that had stifled his brother for so many years, as though Landry's pain had left his body upon his death, entered the air in that awful smell (of iron, of blood, of a body opened and laid bare), and entered Prentiss's own soul. For the first time he felt a pang of sympathy for the boy before him. Because Prentiss desperately longed for his own mother. He could not blame Caleb for calling for his; for wishing he could hear her say his name and give him the measure of comfort he wanted more than anything else in the world.

And the boy's father was always one remove away. Even now George was already out seeking answers, already finding ways to rectify his son's wrongs. What Prentiss wouldn't give for his own saviors. His mother, beneath the courage, beneath the firm hand she used to keep him and Landry in line, had been as scared as they were. It went unspoken but he could sense it hidden behind the false smiles she gave Mr. Morton at every opportunity, desperate to keep her children from harm; the grimaces she displayed when her sons acted out, knowing they could spell their own end with the slightest wrong move. For hadn't she already seen the result of Landry simply reaching out to touch a fly in the air? A mother's love didn't seem quite so full when she couldn't offer even a glimmer of security that the following day would bring the contentment that they sought. That they deserved.

Even still, he wished to call her name, to sit beside Caleb and wallow in the mud. To feel anything but the pain. To hope, to pray, that someone might come and make things better. He'd even prayed for a father back then, during the time it felt all right believing the man was somewhere nearby, just waiting to make himself known, to come inside their cabin and hold their mother with one hand and Prentiss in the other (for his arms were wide, all-encompassing, of this Prentiss was certain). Soon he would hold Landry as well, all of them together, and inform his family, finally, that he had made a life for himself beyond Old Ox, and they were now fit to join him. It had even been a game, of sorts. To work hard enough in the fields, to complain so little, that Papa would return and make things right.

He'd let the notion slip once to another boy around his age as they were cleaning the grime off their feet on a Saturday afternoon. The water from the well was so cold that they'd run to the cabin porch to dry their feet in the sun, and as they'd recounted the morning's work, Prentiss had said his own father might just be so proud he would come right back home to swoop him away. Wouldn't that be something? he asked. Maybe, he said to the boy, his papa would have room for him, too. The boy didn't even blink before relating what his own mother had told him on the matter. That Landry and Prentiss's father had dropped dead when the sun was going low after a day in the field. He'd been working hard to maybe earn a little extra ration for Prentiss's mother and had started yelling out about a dizzy spell, screaming for some water, but no one answered. They said his heart gave out so fast nobody saw the body drop. He was found in the row, the cotton from his open bag covering his face like fresh linens blowing in the wind. Even the boy, hearing himself tell the last part, grew quiet at the eeriness brought to life. It didn't take him long to recognize that Prentiss hadn't ever heard a word of what he'd just shared. Later Prentiss would realize his mother had to have been carrying Landry at the time. That of the two brothers only Prentiss had been alive, a baby seen and felt by his father, before the man passed on and became something imaginary.

The boy left then, and Prentiss, marooned on the porch, had been stricken with the same numbness that Landry's death now occasioned in him. Back then, evading the pain wrought by the image of a man he'd thought of as invincible alone in the fields, hand on his chest, cotton flittering into his mouth before the wind shooed it off, Prentiss's mind had focused only on the positive: that his father had really been there, working the same rows his son would come to work himself. If he blocked the hurt, there was a thrill to that single fact. In the days to come, he would wonder what other similarities might exist between his father and him and Landry. He knew it irked his mother, knew she had no interest in revisiting the past, but Prentiss couldn't help peppering her with questions. Was their father ungainly and careful, like Landry? Or did he run with the speed that made all the other children envious of Prentiss? Which of them had their father's smile? His eyes?

He no longer remembered her answers to those questions. Not a one. Rather he recalled her row with the mother of the boy who'd shared the truth of his father's death. She reprimanded the woman for putting into her son's head awful things he didn't need to know, much less tell her boys about. Prentiss watched her from the side of the cabin, her voice booming with fury. It was her secret to tell when she saw fit, his mother shrieked. *Her* husband's death, *her* hurt to share with the man's boys.

At the time Prentiss couldn't imagine what she found so terrible that she'd made the entire plantation swear an oath to keep the information guarded for so many years. But turning back to face what was left of his brother, he perceived what must have come to her mind anytime he mentioned his father at all: that body in the field, the torture of the loss. And he realized what image would come to his own mind, from that point on, whenever his brother was brought up. The horror was so unimaginable that he wanted to collapse, but when Caleb moved again to try to leave the site for home, Prentiss once more stood tall, stood strong.

"I can make this right," Caleb said. "I just need—"

Prentiss put a hand on Caleb's shoulder. Did not grip it. Just a touch. And then whispered into his ear, "There ain't gonna be no going back, Caleb. You can't make none of this right. We gonna wait right here. Just like I said."

Out of the corner of his eye he recognized, wrongly, the shadow that he had come to intuit as his brother, forever one step to the side, out of sight but always present. Rather it was George, holding his hip and hobbling toward them, covered in mud. George would speak now and take control and that was all right. For however long Prentiss had sought to steer his own way in the world, this was one occasion where he wished to relinquish that drive and to live without feeling, without thinking, to sit in the dark and consider nothing but the blackness of the inside of his eyelids, or the darkness of the world itself, as he had on so many sleepless nights in his youth, after his mother was sold away.

"Thank God!" Caleb said, enlivened by the sight of his father, his protector. "Now we'll really fix this, Prentiss. I vow to you."

It was knee-jerk for Prentiss, thinking that the boy was trying to run off again. To step to him once more. This time Caleb did not startle, but stood there eyeing Prentiss, for Prentiss had no power now that they were not alone. He and Landry had played a game like this as boys. One would move forward, like a taunt, a threat, testing whether the other would flinch. Then Landry would give chase, his eyes wide, the two of them running in circles until Landry caught his older brother and slung him over his shoulder, then tossed him into a pile of leaves, or hay in the horses' stable, with a flick of his arms.

There would be no chasing here. Prentiss retreated, turned away from George's approach, and glanced again at Landry's corpse (for that's what it was, he'd settled on it, and the word must be said). The eyes that had once been as wide as could be were now shielded in blood and would see Prentiss no more. The sight brought him to his knees. Brought him, for one last time, to grab hold of the brother he'd lost.

CHAPTER 15

P rentiss refused to move from his brother's side. George left
him there and deposited Caleb at the cabin with his mother,
who had returned home from church. She had no idea what
had taken place but already sat beside him on the couch. He would
not let her touch him, but only shifted back in his seat whenever she
drew too close. He brushed away her hand. Looked beyond her when
she sought out his gaze.

"There's been a murder," George said. "Landry."

"A murder. What on earth?"

She had as many questions as George, and he could only tell her it
was not Ted, whom he'd already accosted, and that Prentiss was still
in the woods.

"I need to get word to the sheriff," he said. "You keep him calm."

She was trembling now. "And Caleb? What's happened to Caleb?"

"You know as well as I do."

"Heavens," she said. "Oh, good God. Go."

George fetched Ridley from his stable. He rode to the house of
Henry Pershing, his nearest neighbor toward town, yet even though
he could hear voices inside, not a soul came to greet him.

"Henry! Show yourself!" George shouted. "Your horses are stabled,
I know you're home."

No answer arrived. The same was the case with Robert Cord.
Blair Duncan peeked out the door but had no interest in his cause,

owing to the conflict with the Beddenfelds' supper party, and soon, to George's dismay, it was apparent there was no one who would lift a finger in any pursuit he had authored, and that once-helpful neighbors—peers from grade school, neighbors his entire life—saw him as unworthy of so much as a favor.

He was nearly to town when he came upon a barefoot man who, upon closer inspection, was nothing more than a tall boy. He looked a bit like Landry, in fact. It was the first moment George felt overcome by the recent loss, and he could not muster any words.

The boy stared back in confusion.

"Sir?" he said, after an uncomfortable moment. "Can I help you?

George collected himself. He pulled a dollar from his pocket.

"I need a job done. I don't care how long it takes, long as you see it through."

Whether his plan would accomplish anything was uncertain, but the authorities must be summoned—that much was sure. The sheriff for the county, one Osborne Clay, was a rare sight. When he was around it was often to investigate the brothel in town— operations that lasted long into the night. But other than his nocturnal proclivities, he was known to be a decent man, and if there was any chance to discover more information about Landry's death, they would have to hope that Osborne might live up to his reputation.

George hurried back to the farm but did not return to the cabin. He let Ridley carry him straight through the fields, to the edge of the forest.

Prentiss was no longer crying. He lay facing upward, with the back of his head on his brother's chest, gazing at the sky, his eyes so red with grief that he looked possessed. His hands were interlocked upon his own chest.

George gingerly dismounted and rubbed his hip, clearing a clot of pain. He walked to Prentiss and told him he'd called for the sheriff: "I don't know him well, but he is a good man, I'm told. He can help make this right."

A small theater of flies circled the air above the brothers' heads. Prentiss sniffed loudly and rubbed his nose with the back of his hand.

"Imagine the maggots will show up soon," he said. "How long we got, you figure? Few hours?"

George thought it best to remain silent.

"Why ain't you talking?" Prentiss said. "Of all the times for your mouth to run dry it's gonna be right now?"

George conceded that he didn't know what to say. His hope was that the sheriff might show and they could begin to piece the crime together.

"You think a sheriff's gonna help."

"If he doesn't then we will find other means of recourse. We will work through this intelligently. Review the particulars. Prepare a timeline of events."

Prentiss stood up so quickly that George stopped speaking. They stared at each other. Prentiss's entire face was swollen with grief. His cheeks had the puff of a newborn. His hair was matted with the filth of his brother's death.

"Prentiss, please."

Prentiss raised his fist and George cowered from the pending blow, but Prentiss merely splashed a finger across his cheek. A smear of blood. George touched his cheek, instinctively ran the wetness between his fingers and thumb.

"You got all this," Prentiss said, waving his hand about.

"And what is that?"

Prentiss stepped aside, and George's gaze fell upon Landry: the bloodied cavity that had once been his cheek, the muddied swamp of blood that held his eyes.

"How's that for *particulars,* George?"

As much as he wished to speak, George knew his words would offer Prentiss nothing. That to give an apology would be a vulgarity. The only compassionate act was to face the moment with nothing more than a pose of sympathy—to provide his friend the ministry of his company. They stood together for some time, neither uttering a word until Prentiss returned from his depths.

"Where is your boy?" Prentiss asked George.

"Inside."

"I'd like a word with him."

"He did not do it. I'm not sure he could even if he wanted to."

"He ain't do it, that's true. But I think he knows who did."

George could not disagree. "Perhaps it's best I speak with him first. He's more likely to tell his father what he knows."

Prentiss breathed and let the idea settle.

"But we need to get"—George paused—"this body to the barn. We can't wait for the sheriff for that. Like you said. The elements and whatnot."

"I can carry him," Prentiss said. "I've carried him my whole life. You deal with your boy."

"At least get Ridley and the sleigh. No need to make this harder than it already is."

"You just worry about getting some answers. By the end of the day, I'd like to know who I gotta kill."

George walked back to the cabin through the peanut fields, still blooming magnificently with their radiant rows of greenery and their yellow flowers. He could only guess at the bounty under the soil. He knew, passing by these plants, that he might never work the field again. But even so their beauty was radiant, peaceful even, and he deemed the months of labor worthwhile, even necessary, if it worked to offset the slightest fragment of horror that had passed in that one single day.

———————

How long had George been gone—almost to town and back, and then out to see Prentiss—and Caleb was still staring listlessly out the window when he came into the cabin. His mother was surveying him closely, taking stock of his every movement. The boy wouldn't say a word, wouldn't make eye contact with Isabelle or himself. As a child, George remembered, Caleb had often hid his head inside the folds of her dress when he was distraught, and Isabelle would walk around the house as if she'd sprouted these pale little legs overnight. Now, like George, Caleb had learned to hide within the folds of his own mind.

His wife and son looked up at him, and he went to Caleb and pulled him up by the shoulder.

"My study," George said.

"Give him some time," Isabelle said.

"We don't have time."

Isabelle stood and watched as George took Caleb by the hand and led him upstairs, through the hallway, and into the study.

"Sit," George said.

Caleb obeyed.

George went to the other side of his desk and sat as well, feeling like the doughy mound of flesh and bones that he was, seemingly on the cusp of coming apart, a culmination of so many years sagging and creaking. The fatigue had come on the second he stepped inside the study. His body was so eager to give up on the day that he had to squint to keep himself alert. He considered calling down to Isabelle for some coffee but thought better of it, assessing that he had just enough energy left for this single conversation before he collapsed.

"Why were you in the woods, son?"

Caleb, who had been hanging his head, raised his eyes.

"I'm okay," he said. "If you're wondering. If the thought of my well-being entered your mind."

"I see that. I see that you're healthy, that you're safe inside your own home, that your mother is waiting on you, hand and foot. Why were you in the woods?"

"God forbid you might *ask* how I am. No, that would not do. Because nothing escapes the almighty George. Because you *see* I am well and it is impossible, simply impossible, that I might feel differently. That it might stand to ask me, instead of telling me, how I feel."

"Why were you in the woods?"

"I was only ever another project of yours. Like your cabinets. Like your moonshine. Like your garden. Like Prentiss and Landry."

"Caleb, I will ask you once more."

"I know I was a lost cause. Just like the others. And I have come to terms with that. But how bitter must you be? To know you're the one standing behind every single failure that has come through your life, and in the face of so little success."

The ground was shaking, as if some tremor were claiming the cabin, and it took George a moment of panic, of thinking to rush outside, before he realized the feeling had been born within his chest, some fissure in his heart. He pulled himself out of his chair. The blinds were drawn against the ebbing sun and there was no candle-light. The shadows of the books cast a blackness upon the room. George could not remember hugging his son since he'd returned from the war. He walked around the desk and stood behind him, then leaned down and crossed an arm around Caleb's chest. The boy began to cry like a child.

George asked the question once more. At last Caleb told him what August had done.

CHAPTER 16

As night fell, George heated water for a bath. He asked Isabelle to let him know if Prentiss left the barn, if Caleb emerged from his room (where he had been since their conversation concluded), or if the sheriff arrived. She sat in the dining room, following his wishes. She knew Caleb would not come downstairs, seeing as he had refused to open his door for over an hour. It was deathly quiet. Every creak of the house or whine of the wind brought her to attention, but not a soul appeared. She was growing restless when George called out her name from the bathroom.

"Yes?" she said, walking over.

"Could you come closer to the door, so we might speak?"

She retrieved a chair from the kitchen table and put it beside the door.

"Are you there?" he asked.

"I'm here. But I cannot see outside from my seat, George."

He let it pass unremarked.

"I suppose everyone is asleep," she said. "It's quite late."

There was no light except the candle on the windowsill. She found the shadows of the house, each specific slant of darkness, intensely familiar: they fell upon the living room like patterned echoes of the furniture, as if the night, in conversation with her designs, was offering its own interpretation.

"We will need a coffin," George said.

She opened the door slightly. A candle was lit there, too, yet the room was still lost to the steam of the bath. She could make out only the sodden strands of George's hair and the slope of his shoulders before his body merged with the lip of the tub.

"It should be sweet birch," she said. "It has a hint of wintergreen but…stronger notes. Bolder. I think of peppermint."

"Peppermint?" George said.

She turned away from him, back toward the shadows.

"I know it sounds silly. But my uncle was buried in a birch casket. They delivered it while he was still alive. Seems odd, doesn't it? But my aunt was nothing if not prepared. She had it stored in the cellar while he was expiring upstairs. Silas and I went down there to see it, and it had the most delightful smell. Bear in mind the cellar was perhaps the most odious place on their entire property. I recall having Silas take the top off so I could lie in it. It was roomy, all in all. He objected to putting the top on while I was still inside, but eventually he did, and I lay there in silence, alone with myself. It was peculiar. The inside smelled like nothing. As if they had somehow managed to keep the scent on the outside of the coffin. Which I don't find possible."

"You were grieving," George said after a time. "Perhaps there was no smell at all. Inside or out."

His voice was muffled by the door and so she entered the bathroom. The room swirled with the steam of the bath, great clouds of heat. She placed her chair a few feet behind him and then came forward, grabbed George's towel, and dabbed her face before dropping it back on the stool at his side. After a pause she grabbed it once more, refolded it properly, and placed it there again.

"Will you tell Prentiss?" she asked.

George sank lower into the tub. He'd told her what Caleb had confessed. There were so many horrific elements to the tale that she had trouble separating her emotions: those toward her son, and those toward Prentiss for what had befallen Landry. Not to mention her hatred of the Weblers, long suppressed but now overpowering.

"What do you think?" George asked. "What should we do?"

She could not recall a time in recent memory when he had asked her opinion on anything of such significance. The shallowest part of her took it as a weakness—as if her husband, in his increasing frailty, now had to look to his wife for help in ways he never had before. Yet the truest part of her relished his need for her.

"You must tell him," she said. "Any omission of truth would only injure him further."

"Yet if he was to seek revenge…"

"We must do our best to deter him from any such inclination. Perhaps you wait a time to tell him. Let the anger subside."

"No more than a day."

"Any longer would be wrong," she agreed. "And what of the sheriff?"

George said he believed that Osborne, who had a spine, unlike most everyone else in the county, was levelheaded enough to take this seriously. He wanted to do all he could to avoid involving the army, given that the town hated them enough already without them proclaiming their allegiance to the other side once and for all.

He relaxed a bit farther into the tub. The last thing she wished to do was burden him, but a final, awkward question pressed on her mind.

"George, what was our son doing out there with August? What is between them?"

He took a long breath.

"What is between anyone?" George asked her. "I couldn't say. Trust. Suffering. Some element of love, to be sure. How often did we see Caleb come home in tears, cursing his friend, only to keep his eye on the window all throughout supper, hoping he might appear once more? They had a bond. Why inspect it any closer?"

"Perhaps it's easier for you," she said. "I just don't know any-more. This business with August—it was a relief, I believe. The idea that someone else might carry the responsibility for how he's turned out. But I go back and look at Caleb's letters, searching for some semblance of the boy we raised, yet they're so empty. So hollow. I fear it was always in him. That blank space. And we missed it."

George appeared to be at a loss for words, but when he finally spoke it was with a confident tone of finality.

"Every time he fell, we were there. That is all that could be asked of either of us."

He looked so helpless, so at rest. She moved her chair closer to the tub, so close she might see the grime of the water, the ripples of George's belly descending into the depths of the bath.

"Hello," he said.

"Hello," she said. She put out a hand and stroked his cheek, rolled her finger down the length of his chin.

"If Prentiss agrees," he said, "I think sweet birch will do."

Isabelle made a small noise of agreement. "It's the finest option," she said. "Appropriate for the occasion."

And with this, exhausted, she stood up to leave. It was time she got some rest.

When she rose in the morning George was fast asleep. Once dressed, she thought to knock on Caleb's door, but figured him to be asleep as well, and went downstairs instead. Outside, in the early-morning dim, the grass was tinged with dew. She started out the back door to feed the chickens, and in doing so glimpsed the outline of Prentiss, with only the clothes on his back and a bucket in hand, walking off toward the fields. A part of her wished not to intrude upon his morning, yet another part felt deeply that in times of grieving the hospitality of others was paramount to overcoming loss. When her friends had brought flowers upon learning what had turned out to be the rumor of Caleb's death, it had been a source of comfort. No one, she knew, would be bringing Prentiss anything at all. She slipped on George's boots, as they were the only ones sitting out back, and made her way after him.

The farm was still edged in dark, the plants dappled in the morning shadows. For a moment she simply watched Prentiss. He was hand-weeding one of the furrows—pulling ryegrass out by the root and dropping it into the bucket, carefully working around each plant.

As she drew closer she called his name and waved. He offered her a glance before continuing. She was beside him now but might as well have been invisible.

"Should you be working?" she asked. "I'm certain George is not expecting you to. Not with all that's happened."

"I don't mind," he said.

"Is there any way I get you to quit?"

"No, ma'am."

"I was about to make myself some toast. I could brew some coffee as well. Why don't you join me inside?"

He shook his head resolutely.

"Ain't nothing for me in that house."

"Coffee does not interest you, then."

"Ain't what I mean."

"What do you mean?"

The bucket hung limp in his hand. He stared at her, his eyes sparked with anger.

"I mean what I said. This ain't complicated, Mrs. Walker. I'm right where I want to be. With these plants. See 'em? They *thriving*. I made 'em that way. Me and my brother. And I'ma keep 'em thriving, keep 'em strong, 'cause there ain't nothing else I—"

He could not finish. He rubbed his hand from his forehead to his mouth, then from cheek to cheek, as if doing so might scour his pain.

Though hers had abated with Caleb's miraculous return, Isabelle knew the feeling: the utter helplessness, the all-consuming pain. She could only say what was on her mind. What came to her naturally.

"He left me a pair of socks. It could not have been anyone else. Right on the clothesline, the same place where I first met him. They're the color of the sky, soft blue, and they fit so snugly you would have thought he'd taken the measurements of my foot. It was perhaps the nicest gesture I've known. We hardly shared a word, but his kindness was unrivaled. There was a purity to him I can't even begin to express. I'm not sure I understand it myself."

Prentiss stared at her vacantly.

"You can have the socks if you wish," she said. "A way to remember him."

He shook his head.

"If he went and knitted you some socks, then they belong to you."

He reached down to retrieve the bucket and continued weeding.

Isabelle stood for a time, wondering if they might continue talking, until she realized the moment was gone.

"Perhaps it's best I go back inside. Feel free to join us if you wish. Our home is open to you."

"He told me once about a field," Prentiss said, stopping her. "It took him just about a whole morning to get the words out his mouth, but he told me. Said he went out in the woods and found a field of dandelions, so many together that the ground was white as snow, and he sat there for a time thinking, and in the time it takes your heart to beat, a gust of wind poured through that field and every single seed shot up into the air, ain't a single one left on the ground, and the whole sky was bright with their travels, and then they were gone."

Isabelle stood there frozen, contemplating the image.

"My brother seen more in the past few weeks in them woods than a common man might see in a lifetime."

His eyes sought her own and he looked at her with a curiosity she'd never seen in him before.

"Do you know it?" he asked. "That's where I'd like to have him rest. I think he'd like that."

She didn't know it, she said, but she would ask George. A plaintive smile flickered on Prentiss's face and disappeared, and he turned his attention back to his weeding There was nothing further she could do, or say, to comfort him. What had passed was all there was.

She walked back to the house, which was still at peace, and sat alone in the parlor with her knitting. It was a pleasant surprise when George appeared and asked what she'd like for breakfast, a mild shock that was exceeded when she heard galloping upon the lane. She opened the door to a halo of dust rolling toward them. The sheriff's horse burst through it with his deputy in tow.

George had her brew some more coffee as he went to get dressed, and both were prepared when the knock sounded upon the door and the two men came inside. Although her husband was familiar with Osborne Clay, she had seen him only once, from a distance in town, walking off-duty with a gang of other men. For this reason, it took her a moment to realize how large he had become, and still she gleaned nothing more from his appearance than the star on his chest before she retrieved his coffee from the kitchen. Only when George followed her over and whispered into her ear did she learn that Osborne Clay hadn't gotten any larger. No, The man before them wasn't Osborne Clay at all.

CHAPTER 17

The news regarding Sheriff Clay was unexpected. He'd come home one night after a meeting with one of his consorts, a woman of uncertain reputation, only to find his wife with a pistol in hand. She shot straight through his gut and watched him bleed out until his screams and profanations turned to apologies—at which point she called for a doctor. Clay managed to hang on for several days, but his body gave in by the end. His handpicked successor, Lamar Hackstedde, now sat at the kitchen table, sipping coffee and regaling George and Isabelle with the story.

As to Mrs. Clay's freedom, Hackstedde explained that the former sheriff demanded that no charges be pressed against his wife.

"He made it quite clear that his crime of philandering, and the extraordinary number of counts committed, was enough to warrant his punishment. His wife dabbed his forehead as he expired, and he seemed to depart this world on the best of terms with her."

George stirred his coffee.

"And you have replaced him."

Hackstedde pointed at the star upon his shirt.

"You see the bronze," he said. "Rightly anointed by Osborne the day before he passed. He wasn't willing to pass the job on to Tim, him being thickheaded and what have you."

Tim, his deputy, either oblivious or indifferent, was guarding the door as they spoke, watching the desolate lane as if a horde of barbarians might stampede toward them at any moment.

"Now you sent word you have a dead body on your hands."

George could only nod.

"Then we have some work to do. What I'm about to say is in strict confidence, and ma'am"—he eyed Isabelle, who stood behind George—"this does stay at the table, don't go running off and gossiping with your lady friends." He cut his eyes back at George. "I got a telegram from a colleague upstate to the effect that government officials will be arriving in a week's time. Now Arnold Glass been on good behavior, keeping his nose out of folks' business, mine included, but these boys coming, well, they aim to lay down the law. I hear they put a nigger in command of the police force out in Cooksville when they seen the officers in charge weren't up to their standard. I can't even imagine. Look at that! Hairs standing up on my arm just at the thought. So I made myself a vow that this county won't be reaching that same end. We'll show them we keep things peaceful around these parts. So we get this matter settled quickly."

Hackstedde was perhaps a decade George's junior, a robust man with a cluster of hairy moles adorning his chin like a pile of raccoon droppings in miniature. He had a manner of clenching and unclenching his jaw, and filled the room with a general air of anxiety.

Everything was already quite against the plan George had envisioned: Osborne would arrive. They would go meet Prentiss and then examine the body. Caleb—currently locked in his room upstairs—would give his testimony (or George would offer it in his absence, if he refused to appear). Osborne would take this information and make the appropriate decisions.

But Hackstedde was no Osborne Clay. As known to everyone in Old Ox, the man had made his name as a slave patroller—a rather inept one—and to conceive of him as anything but an inept sheriff, in turn, was an impossibility. An even greater impossibility was that he might care whatsoever about a dead freedman. Hackstedde would not leave now that a murder was reported, but there would be no justice for Landry if it was up to this man. Not if Caleb's story were true. The town was already hostile toward George. Without the aid of the sheriff, and with an accusation so galling directed at the likes of August Webler, he was sure he hadn't seen even an inkling of the backlash that would strike their farm if the case was pursued.

"How about we see this body," said Hackstedde, who had begun to roll a cigarette upon the kitchen table. "I'll have you show the way."

———————————

Prentiss was waiting in the barn. He sat on his pallet beside Landry's body, which they'd wrapped in cloth so tightly, so many times around, that its shape was barely discernible. George had offered to put the body in the stable, perhaps on ice, but Prentiss had refused him— he wished to wake up to his brother at his side. Who was George to tell him no?

Hackstedde put a handkerchief to his nose against the noticeable odor and pointed at Prentiss. "This would be?"

"He is in my employ," George said.

"Right," Hackstedde said. "Suppose I've heard talk of this arrangement."

"He's my brother," Prentiss said. "He's been killed. Ain't no two ways about it."

"We don't know that, exactly," George said, his eyes so wide he might as well have been waving his arms at Prentiss.

"How are you so sure?" Hackstedde asked Prentiss.

"Ask me that after you've seen his face," Prentiss said.

"Tim," Hackstedde said. He made a twirling motion with his finger, and his deputy came forward and crouched down by the body.

"I wouldn't wish for Prentiss to relive the sight," George said to Hackstedde. "The two of them being brothers and all."

Hackstedde did not demur as George put a hand on Prentiss's shoulder and led him outside the barn. His words were hurried, and he whispered to Prentiss under the thrum of the squawking chickens and the weather vane on the roof creaking like a rusty door hinge.

"That man was once a patroller," George said. "I swear we will give Landry the burial he deserves. He will rest at peace. But we cannot say another word to this man. It will only cause trouble. I'm sure of it."

Prentiss showed no expression at all. There was a shadow cast over him, and George saw the darkness as such resignation, as such total defeat, that no further words were needed. He did not have to tell Prentiss to surrender to these men. He already had.

"When they're gone," George said, "we must speak again about your leaving here. I think we can both see by now it's what's best."

Their time together appeared to expire in that moment outside the barn. The silence between them was something vast, and both seemed to be wading through it for an answer, a means to explain this sudden rift that now felt permanent. George knew the feeling well. How often in his youth he had tried to forge a friendship, only to see it rupture when he voiced an unwanted opinion or behaved in some manner the other party found strange but seemed perfectly normal to George. There would be no contempt in this instance, no anger. Too much had transpired between him and Prentiss in the months since their meeting. There was no fault on either side, but all of it was irrevocable.

"You will keep those peanuts alive, won't you?" Prentiss said.

"What? We don't need to worry about that."

"George, you listen. I'll leave from here. I promise I will. S'pose...s'pose I'll go look for my mama somewhere. Lord knows that's just my dream, to find her somewhere safe and see her again. And if it ain't come true, I could at least do with the hope that you gonna tend to these here plants. Doing right by them is doing right by me and Landry. I ain't wanna see 'em die, George."

Voices rose from the barn and soon Hackstedde and Tim reappeared.

Hackstedde spoke as he removed his gloves. "You know," he said, "my daughter had a beau who fought out in Long Point. He got a spray of grapeshot to the face from a cannon and died faster than you could trip over a word. We never saw him again. Just got a telegram saying as much. But when I see that dead Negro in there I can't help but think of that boy. Probably got his face blasted open just like that big fella. A sorry business. A real sorry business."

"What's that sorry business?" Prentiss said, his voice so low it was barely audible. "Her beau or my brother?"

Hackstedde put his gloves in his back pocket.

"A real sorry business," he repeated to George, shaking his head. "But I see no reason to think there was any foul play here. Boy that big, going through them woods…well, a bad fall is not out of the question."

A fall. The sheer lunacy of the conclusion—or the lie—was enough to make George laugh in the man's face. Could he not at least be more creative? Was his imagination so stunted?

"With all that's going on in this town," Hackstedde continued, "the worries of a fallen Negro, alone out here, I just can't see putting our resources toward what looks to be an accident."

He glanced at George with a steady gaze and George merely nodded in response. This could end here, he thought, with Prentiss safe and the farm spared. It was as Hackstedde said: no one cared about a dead Negro.

"I suppose that makes the most sense," George said. "We might consider the issue closed."

Hackstedde's eyes, two little black bullets, lit up, and he patted George on the back.

"Good, then," he said. "So, I'll be on my way. Tim."

His deputy went to the fetch the horses and Hackstedde spoke with the vigor, the enthusiasm, of a job well done. "Those woods ain't safe. Some boys just aren't bred with any sense of caution. Maybe a bear got to him. You got bears out here, don't you?"

Sensing that Prentiss was at his breaking point, George placed a hand on his shoulder to steady him, to signal that they had nearly made it through. It was best to ignore the sheriff's incompetence, the rank idiocy, with a patience that would pay off once Hackstedde had finally ridden away. But when he heard the voice behind him, he knew the day would take a different turn altogether.

"Wait! Wait right there!"

Caleb had barreled out the front door in his one-piece pajamas. He was pallid, eyes sunken, as if he hadn't seen the light for days. He hardly resembled his son at all.

"Who's this?" Hackstedde said. "What's the boy saying?"

George introduced Caleb, then shook his head vehemently, urging his son to quit. But Caleb was so stirred to action, so resolute in his demeanor, that there was no deterring him.

"I'd like to make a confession," he declared.

"Caleb, no—" George said.

But the boy waved him off, tears welling and spilling down his cheeks.

"No more lies," he said. "I'll let the truth be known."

George lowered his head. Just as his son had told him about August's crime, it was now all, in one stream, given over to Hackstedde.

A day had passed since Landry's murder. The stench of the body had intensified, though not a word was spoken about it, and Prentiss continued to walk around the barn as if there was no smell at all. He was packing a small duffel that George had given him, and George himself was standing at the entrance to the barn, watching on while keeping his distance. If Prentiss bore him any resentment over his son's inaction, he kept it concealed.

"I should be back with the coffin shortly," he said. "There's a furniture maker in town who has a roomful of coffins in the back. Had a racket going all through the war. He should have exactly what we're looking for. We can hold the ceremony later today if that sounds right to you."

"It does."

"Good. Good."

"You want help?" Prentiss asked.

George shook his head. "I can manage with Ridley. You keep packing."

The donkey was lethargic in the heat, but George harnessed him with his cart and took him to the main road at a slow clop. The day was not friendly. The screech of a mockingbird struck him like the clapper of an alarm. Exhaustion plagued him. He had slept fitfully last night, a problem so common recently that he'd begun to wonder if a good dream, or the fine mood that follows a true slumber, might ever find him again.

The morning had been weighed down by the chaos of Caleb's confession, which soon led to the emotional unraveling of the entire home. Isabelle was quick to take responsibility for Caleb's actions, having gone upstairs and pleaded with him to come clean with the sheriff, not knowing how dubious Hackstedde's title of sheriff might be. After it was over, Caleb paced endlessly about the parlor, walking to the bookshelf, back toward the kitchen, telling them repeatedly of how he only wished to do right. That was all there was for him now. A lifetime of wrong that must be made right.

"You are barely grown," George told him. "If you only knew the many wrongs awaiting you."

This one was different, Caleb said. His reticence, his fear, had led to Landry's death. It was entirely his responsibility.

With that, Prentiss stood up from the dining room table and addressed them all. "My brother's laying out there!" he exclaimed, and the room fell silent. "Like a bled-out pig. If y'all don't plan on helping me get him in the ground I'll do that bit myself."

The words rang in George's mind now as he reached the edge of town. There was some relief in the activity of Old Ox. The bodies, the voices, the noises all drowned out the emotions of the last twenty-four hours, and George appreciated the distraction. He left Ridley at his usual post and went on alone. No one bothered him, although a moment of disorientation left him dizzy. It appeared that the town was no longer laid out as he'd once known it to be. Each building was at once familiar and foreign, and he stopped a moment under the awning of an empty merchant's shop to steady himself. What he needed was rest. With the protection of his father's wealth, his whole life had maintained the air of an extended tour, and yet now he felt the need for a real one. Time away from it all. But there was so much to do. He needed to focus; he needed to get that coffin.

He neared the square but pulled up at the sight of two stallions tied off in front of Webler's little brick workhouse. The same horses that had just been at his home. Hackstedde and his deputy. It was not a shock. After all, Hackstedde had stood there, stone-faced, with a perfunctory promise to investigate the veracity of Caleb's claims. But George found it difficult to imagine a Webler exiting the front door in handcuffs.

He had the urge to go in. He did not know what he would say, or do, but he perceived what little power he had left in town slipping from him. Hands were being dealt in this very building, but he was absent from the table. It would not do. The furniture depot was immediately up ahead, but he turned and walked straight through the roundabout, avoiding the gardening society's colorful arrangements, and made his way directly toward the very schoolhouse where he had once learned letters and which now acted as the headquarters for the Union Army's outpost.

"General Glass," he called out as he neared the door. It did not cross his mind to acknowledge the line of men and women standing beside the building, papers or hats in hand, all of them waiting their turn—something George was not wont to do.

A drab-faced soldier blocked the door before George could proceed. "Visitors are met with in the order they arrive," he said.

"This is a matter of some urgency," he said. "Glass! It's George Walker. I need a word."

Pointing with a finger, the soldier told him to step back.

In response George put his own finger against the door itself. "You must let me in. What I have to deliver warrants urgent attention."

To George's relief (and perhaps to the soldier's as well), General

Glass emerged from the door, trailed by a young man struggling to balance a tall stack of papers in both hands. A minor uproar traveled down the line of people as Glass slipped away. George was on the general's trail from the moment he started down the main thoroughfare.

"Mr. Walker," Glass said, making no effort to mask his irritation, "did you not see the line? I'll return shortly to speak with those in need of my attention, yourself included."

"This is no trivial matter, General."

"No? You mean it extends beyond food rations for starving children and updates on the status of wounded relatives?"

Suddenly George was swallowed in a stream of oncoming traffic and stumbled against a woman carrying luggage. He almost lost track of Glass before hustling back to his side like a lost child returning to his mother.

"How does this squire keep up with you whilst holding those papers?" George said. "He might well double as a circus acrobat."

"This man is hardly a squire," Glass said. "He is my aide."

"What's that, now?"

They'd just arrived at the lumberyard as Glass stopped, wheeling around so quickly as to shock George into a standstill.

"Brigadier generals have aides, not squires. Address my men with respect, please."

A soldier approached with a paper, which Glass signed without a second glance.

George apologized and nodded to the aide, then turned back to Glass.

"I'd like you to know I've decided to join that council of yours," he said. "I would be more than happy to, actually. I will arrive early, and smile, and do your bidding. In return, might you allow me five minutes of your time—"

"The council has carried on in perfect concord without your presence."

"So be it. Might I still have a moment? What I have to say will be of no imposition on your day. I could have been kinder to you perhaps, but I have not been cruel, either. Grant me this one favor. Just a few minutes. I am begging."

Glass's face seemed to condense itself to a single point, his eyes collecting themselves in deep contemplation and his nose scrunching up to meet them. He exhaled deeply and scooped half the papers from the arms of his aide and handed them to George, who nearly toppled over from the sudden weight.

"Make yourself useful and lighten my aide's load," Glass said, "and I'll give you two minutes."

"As fine a deal as any," George said, gritting his teeth.

They entered the lumber depot and George was struck by the presiding aroma of the place. He knew the smell of walnut trees, of freshly dug dirt, black and bitter, but in the close quarters of the tentlike depot the elements were noxious enough to bring tears to his eyes. Beyond the depot, soldiers were occupied in loading onto wagons the rows and rows of planks cut to size.

"I'm listening," Glass said.

George followed him into his makeshift office, a desk shadowed by several soldiers and littered with blueprints and telegrams, and began to explain what had happened to Landry; that not only the town but also his own neighbors had abandoned him. How, with nowhere else to turn, he needed to know there was at least one honorable man he could count on as an ally. One individual who would help him seek the justice that Landry deserved.

Glass had seated himself as George was talking, and was now jotting a note, his aide a resolute statue at his side. Only at the sight of the boy empty-handed did George realize he himself was still holding his half of the stack of papers. He put them down on the desk. Having concluded his monologue, he stood quietly, feeling incredibly small in the whirlwind of movement around him—a whole universe of activity he hadn't even known existed before this afternoon.

"I've spoken with Mr. Webler already," Glass said. "The issue will be delegated solely to Sheriff Hackstedde. He is more than capable of investigating this incident with impartiality."

George was stunned. "But did you not hear a word I said? Hack-stedde is a fool, and to seek the counsel of Webler, the father of the accused, is as foolish as anything the sheriff might manage himself. This is dereliction of duty through and through."

This, more than any previous statement, captured Glass's attention. He folded his hands upon the table and delivered George a look so stern that he wanted to hide himself behind the stack of papers he'd just laid down.

"My duty?" Glass said, incredulous. "I doubt you have the faintest clue what my duty is. The very definition of the word is beyond you, as it is for so many men who come from so much and need so little from those around them. Allow me to explain it clearly so as to remove any confusion. My duty is to my country. In this case, my superiors have seen fit to assign that duty to a single task of little esteem but great importance, which is operating a lumberyard in a sorry country town filled with individuals who despise me. This duty also requires me to keep the peace amongst the very people who wish to see me, and all these soldiers surrounding me, gone from their home. That is my lot. And I have done it, and will continue to do it, until I am relieved of doing so."

"I did not wish to offend you—"

"Which is the *problem*. Your selfishness knows no bounds. You don't see past your own person. God forbid you consider that those folks waiting in line all morning outside that old schoolhouse might take priority over your own needs."

"I have presented my case poorly," George said, backtracking however far he could. "I am not perfect—that I will grant you with zero reservation. But that does not change the fact that there is a dead man, a man who was good to all he met, who deserves better than to have his murder treated as a matter of no consequence. Quite frankly I'm flabbergasted you've fallen under Webler's spell. For someone so attuned to the wiles of men seeking favors, you have aligned yourself with the worst of them."

"Wade Webler is exactly as selfish, and as callous, as you, or I, or any man or woman who desires this or that from me. Yet he was the first to greet me when I entered this town. The first to tell me who might help me with our common aims. I might add that in a moment of great personal need, when I needed money for a relative in dire straits, he assisted me without question. His generosity has been unmatched, Mr. Walker."

"You're in his pocket," George muttered, but Glass went on as if he hadn't said a word.

"Not until today, in these past few months, has Mr. Webler ever asked of me anything in return. And the one thing he has now requested is that I recuse myself from this business with one dead freed Negro, lest there be grave trouble riled up. If that is the lone requirement to maintain peace amongst the citizenry of this god-forsaken town, to keep my superiors happy, and to aid a man who has helped me dearly, well, I will happily turn a blind eye."

At this, Glass returned his attention to the papers on his desk and did not deign to acknowledge George.

"I've strived for this town to be a model for others in the state," he continued, "and when the Freedmen's Bureau arrives, I believe they will see it as such. This sorry fellow will help make that possible. If you ask me, his is a sacrifice with more resonance than many who died on the battlefield. Be content knowing that. However sad it is."

George had failed to notice the soldiers standing at attention, waiting for their superior's ear—for George's own departure. There was something in their eyes, neutral and dispassionate, that translated as belittlement. This pitiful stranger flailing wildly before them, denied all he sought. He'd embarrassed himself.

"I suppose it's as you said at the saloon, then," George said. "We have no further business between us."

Glass looked up, confused, it seemed, that George was still in his presence.

"General Glass," George said, already turning to take his leave.

He thought of visiting Ezra but couldn't muster the energy to weather any kind of reprimand; instead he took himself to the furniture warehouse, still in a sour mood. He had to slip past a toilet—a rusty tin can beneath a splintered wooden stool—and a baby carriage just to reach the front door, and inside it was mostly just a collection of more unwanted goods. The path to the register was defined less by any clear direction than by the absence of obstacles barricading the walkway. At one point, George turned and ran straight into a globe the size of his waist and followed this by nearly tripping onto a feather bed, which at the time felt like an acceptable end to his afternoon.

By then the proprietor, a man in a white shirt and black vest who reeked of tobacco, had found him. When George stated his purpose, he led him to the back of the store where the coffins were housed.

"They don't tend to put customers in a spending mood if we keep them out front," the man explained.

Having spoken with Prentiss and gained his approval, George requested a birch coffin.

"I got walnut trees out behind my house," the man said. "So I sell walnut coffins."

There would be no gain in protesting.

"Lined, trimmed, and raised," the man said. "All for the price you'd pay for a decent cask of sherry. It might not be birch, but it's a steal."

George eyed him, but the man only returned the look, and so he simply paid and asked for assistance in carrying it to where Ridley was tied up.

"It can be arranged," the man said. "But I'm afraid the labor is extra."

"It's only a hundred yards through town."

A long silence hung between them, and in the small bends of light that reached the back room the ancient dust of the place milled in the air. The man lit a cigar and stood there idly.

"Oh, good Lord," George said. He pulled out all the bills he had left and put them on the table. "Just grab an end and help me already."

"Jessup!" the man yelled.

From the back door appeared a boy dressed identically to the man—white shirt, black vest upon it, a ghoulish look transposed upon him by his surroundings.

"Yes?" the boy said.

The man pointed his cigar toward George. "Help this man carry his coffin."

It was heavy for one but tolerable for two. They walked outside with it and down the steps, but George told the boy he needed a moment and they set the coffin down. Hackstedde's horse was gone now, along with Tim's—Webler's as well. No life stirred behind the curtained windows of the brick building.

The boy grew restless. "I ain't got all day, mister."

When the coffin was at last on the cart hitched to Ridley, the boy lingered.

George wagged his finger. "You will not receive a penny from me. Skedaddle."

The boy rolled his eyes as though George had ended his world and spasms were coursing through him, then turned and was gone in a blink.

George collected himself and climbed upon Ridley. How was it, he wondered, that he might accomplish one single errand yet already be so done with the day? He could make it a task to sit in bed for ten hours straight, without moving a single toe, yet he would still somehow exhaust himself by the work. It was unbelievable, yet it was so.

"Git," he said to Ridley with a nudge of his boot.

The donkey made no move.

"Go on," he said.

Still nothing. Ridley flicked his ears about as if bouncing the commands away. George gave him a kick for good measure. This, too, produced no effect.

"Move your fat ass!" George cried. "Go, go, go! Goddamn it."

Ridley did not stir in the slightest. He was looking off—at the long road, at the great stretch of forest in the distance, perhaps at an oblivion only he could see.

George leaned down to the donkey's ear, his voice furious.

"There is nothing there," he hissed. "That road goes to another town just like this one, and then to another, and there is nothing in any of them but the same thing repeated, different yet identical, the same stores with different fronts, the same simpletons with different faces, and absolutely none of it should interest you at all because you are a goddamned brainless donkey who has ruined my day."

George slid off Ridley in a fit of rage, ready to come to blows with the creature, but the moment his feet touched the ground Ridley began trotting forward.

"I see," George said, huffing. "Very well." They walked beside each other then. He concealed himself in Ridley's shadow and his mood was one of conciliation. "If the load was too much you only needed to say so," he whispered. "You can't just sit there in silence."

As if the donkey might speak. Still—it was the only apology George could manage. He put his hand upon the base of Ridley's mane and it gave him comfort just to feel the beast, to be in the presence of another warm-blooded animal with no greater wants than to take the step that followed the last one toward home.

———————

There had been little time to prepare for the burial, but Isabelle had collected roses from the garden, the few of any quality, and tied them together in a bouquet. Prentiss, George, and Caleb carried the coffin, Prentiss at the front and George and Caleb side by side together at the rear. George told them of a clearing in the woods, one he'd shown Landry some time ago, and where he'd seen him on numerous occasions since. He guessed it to be his favorite place in the woods, untouched by human life except for him—and what better place for a burial.

"Do you want any words said?" George asked Prentiss. "I know a few verses by heart."

Prentiss was focused on the coffin so intently that George thought he'd gone unheard, but then Prentiss looked up at him and said, "Let him go as he lived."

So they dug in silence, the three of them taking turns, Isabelle standing alongside. It took nearly an hour to make the hole large enough.

When the coffin was interred, Caleb turned to Prentiss and spoke for the first time. "If you don't want me here for this…"

Prentiss once again kept his eyes on the coffin.

"You ain't killed my brother," he said. "I won't stop you from saying your goodbyes."

All four of them stood silent beneath the canopy of sunlight that had begun to close like a lid, encircled by the limbs of the trees reaching toward one another in the slanting wind.

"Isabelle," George said.

She stepped forward and from the bag at her side retrieved a wooden stake, no taller than the leg of a child, and stuck it into the ground at the head of the coffin. She then pulled forth another item from the bag, a sock, the same blue as the one Landry had knitted her, yet large enough for a grown man—for Landry himself.

"I knew if you two went north," she said to Prentiss, "eventually the weather would be chilly, and seeing as your brother was so kind as to knit some socks for me, I thought I might return the favor. At the very least it might commemorate his kindness, to mark where he found some peace after all."

She hooded the top of the stake with the sock and fastened it with a length of twine. When the sunlight touched it, the blue was intensely bright amid the expanse of green grass, such that it could be glimpsed from any angle at the edge of the entire forest.

"I'd like you to have the other," Isabelle said.

She pulled the sock's twin from the bag and handed it to Prentiss. He rubbed the fabric with his fingers, placed the sock against his chest, and thanked her.

She opened her arms for a hug and when they embraced she made one last point clear, her voice hardly louder than a whisper:

"Don't think for a moment I forgot you. Your pair is back at the house. I'll finish soon."

He could not hold back a bit of laughter.

"Looking out for me like your own," he said. "I won't be forgetting your kindness, Mrs. Walker."

They stood for a while longer, none of them wishing to hurry the proceedings, until Prentiss faced them all as one.

"If y'all don't mind," he said, "like to be alone with my brother for a while."

"I'd like to help you fill in that grave. I imagine it will take you some time—"

"George," Isabelle said.

"I can manage," Prentiss said. "Can manage that all on my own."

They returned to the cabin. Supper was short, and when it was over, George cleaned up alongside Isabelle and Caleb, putting dishes away in silence as they wiped off the dining-room table. When Caleb went upstairs, George found himself drifting toward the window, staring at the starless night, the miles of nothingness, the last breath of the lantern dying within the barn to which Prentiss had returned.

"What is on that mind of yours?" said Isabelle, who had crept up behind him.

"Oh," he said. "Nothing worth mentioning."

"Everything is worth mentioning to you, George."

She was now standing beside him. Her hair, though elegant, seemed to have picked up some added gray, and there were wrinkles he hadn't noticed before, constellations as beautiful as those in the sky on a late-night walk.

"Do you remember my father's help? Taffy?"

"You've spoken of her."

"We were so close," he said. "Yet I can recall so little of her. A shadow of her stayed with me after she was sold. I cannot describe it other than to say I would still feel her running beside me as I played alone. Or hear her washing clothes outside when I woke up."

"I had the same when my father died," she said. "Silas and me. We'd hear him yelling up to us. A memory speaking out."

"Isn't it eerie?"

"You were the one who told me I'd imagined the smell of my uncle's coffin. I suppose what you're talking about is no different. Children bear things however they can manage."

George sat down at the kitchen table once more. Isabelle stayed by the window, looking out toward the barn.

"Well, it felt real to me," George said, "and it upset me more than I can speak to. I railed at my mother for days. She was not well, but I couldn't help myself. She would only tell me that such relationships must be severed quickly. That it was best to focus on the memories of our play, and our time together, rather than her departure. But Taffy's absence was far more acute than any memories of fonder times." George was tapping the table now as the thoughts racked against one another in his mind. "Isabelle, Prentiss must go. And go now. For his good and for ours."

She put a hand upon George's shoulder. "Let him finish packing," she said. "Let him mourn tonight. And at first light…"

"First light," George said.

It could not come soon enough.

CHAPTER 18

It was his last night on the farm and Prentiss could hardly shut his eyes, let alone fall asleep. His pallet felt like a solid slab of rock and he tossed and turned endlessly. On his side, he faced the place where Landry had once lain. The fact was one he would confess to no one, but it had given him great comfort to be there with the body. Left with either nothing or the body, he would happily take the body—gaze upon it, speak to it, and love it like Landry himself. He'd thought of broaching the idea with George, refusing the funeral. So much had been taken from him—must the ground claim the body, too? Still, the funeral had been right. He wondered if it was the same field his brother had spoken of, the one with the dandelions, but he hadn't seen any and didn't dare ask George, since he'd rather have the hope that it was than learn otherwise.

His thoughts swam, and he flipped onto his stomach just to steady himself. He had money for lodging and food that would last a month at least. George had told him to go north until the sights suited him; to find a job, a wife, a home. Easy to imagine, he told George, but difficult to accomplish. Especially if he was to be alone.

"You are not alone," George had said. "You're never alone."

Which was a lie. His isolation was numbing. He was no longer a brother; no longer one of the many who populated Morton's land; and more likely than not, he was no longer a son, at least not in any way that mattered. For all he knew, his mother no longer walked the earth. And what did it matter if she did? His odds of ever finding her seemed about as good as the odds of bringing Landry back to life. The idea he'd long cherished—that of his mother living elsewhere, perhaps even in the North—rang true only to the side of him that still entertained fanciful notions. He would see her walking up ahead on a dusty trail, a woman with black hair like a nest upon her head, her primrose dress alight in the eye of the sun; or imagine her in the woman getting water from the pump on a dusty road, her delicate fingers cupping water to her child's mouth. Yet he always knew it was the work of his mind. He figured Landry had known as well, that it was a secret they withheld from each other so as to keep the truth untrue, to keep their story, and her being, forever alive.

Now he faced reality. That it was him. Alone. The thought was a bolt of fear, but he knew that he would come to know this new life as he'd learned to know all those that had come before—for every step in life had been an obstacle, yet here he was, still standing day after day, ready for whatever might happen next. The shred of hope felt like salvation, and it drew him toward a deep slumber.

He awoke to an orchestra of horse hooves. He rushed to the door of the barn and peeked his head out, taking in the party coming up the lane. Several men on horseback led the charge. Behind them plodded a black carriage.

Prentiss yelled for George and walked toward the cabin. He did not wait for a response but went straight through the back door and nearly slipped into the stove top in his haste. The parlor sat empty. The house was asleep.

"George!" he yelled upstairs. "Best you get up!"

Outside the horses were pulling up to the roundabout, the carriage settling in a cloud of dust. The men reined the horses in, although the beasts still pranced in the throes of their energy. The two in the lead had been at the house the day before, and the others, near the back, were none other than Ted Morton and Gail. Prentiss thought to go upstairs and knock, but as he stepped forward, the bedroom door opened.

George appeared in a nightgown.

"What's the racket about?" he said, eyes squinted.

"Out front," Prentiss said. "It's that sheriff. And he ain't alone. I seen Morton as well. It's a gang of 'em."

George's eyes snapped open.

"Don't go outside," he said. "Let me put some pants on." He returned to his room.

In the roundabout the coachman opened the door of the carriage and out strode a man in evening wear, prim as any Prentiss had ever seen. A second man, about his own age, came next, and the two stood beside the carriage, saying little. The older one spoke to the younger one, then adjusted his tie and took a few steps toward the house. What followed was almost in lockstep: George's bedroom door opened, and so did Caleb's, and one after the other father and son descended the stairs.

"Saw them coming through the window," Caleb said. "August is with them."

"What nerve," George said. "To come here unannounced. If they dare try anything."

"George! Is that you in there?" It was the older one in the suit, whom Prentiss presumed to be the father of the boy, his brother's killer. "Why don't you come out so I don't need to go in."

"You set foot through this door and I'll put a pan to your head, Wade. Trust to it." George went onto the porch, hobbling all the way.

The man in the suit waved him off, his face pinched in disgust.

"Threats do not suit you, George. You're better than to say such things."

Hackstedde and his deputy were still on horseback, along with Morton and Gail, while the man called Wade and his son stood before their carriage on foot. Prentiss hadn't seen the boy before, although he was as Caleb had described him—reserved in demeanor but with something wild in his eye. He wanted to have at him there. He wasn't one for fighting, but he'd make an exception, take those blond locks in a fist and guide his face toward the ground, repeat those steps until the boy quit trying to get up.

"I'm not looking to have a conversation this early in the morning," George said as he and Prentiss stepped outside, "so you better bring this to a point quickly. None of that jabbering on you're about."

"*Jabbering on,*" Wade said merrily. Suddenly his face set and he grew stern. "Today, as you may or may not know, is a very special occasion. August is to be wed. And yet yesterday, in the midst of our preparations, we were met with what can only be considered nefarious allegations, leveled at August by your son. You can imagine how distressing this was to my boy. Isn't that right?"

Wade grabbed the shoulder of his son, who remained as stone-faced as his father. Prentiss tracked the boy's gaze to Caleb, who had joined his father on the porch and was looking right back at him, eyes still caked with sleep.

"I would not deign to repeat the perverse accusations," Wade said. "But I thought it wise we come see you in person, just so August might stress how innocent he is of these charges."

August broke in, speaking as if reading off the page, in one tone, a rapid stream of words.

"I fear Caleb has experienced severe trauma from the war, and that his condition has caused him to invent a fiction about our time together that did not take place."

"Oh quit it," Caleb said. "Just quit. My God. You were never good, but I thought you were honest, or at least tried at it. I mean, your lying about being injured in the war was one thing, but this is beyond the pale. Had I known you were just a sicker version of your father, and equally heartless—"

"Do not speak on what happened at war—"

But Wade was quick to step on his son's words.

"Suffice to say Caleb's impairments are currently on display," he muttered.

It was at this point Isabelle appeared in her nightgown, hair still wrapped in a bun.

"You know better than to speak ill of a son in front of his mother, Wade Webler. You'll not do it here."

"Isabelle! Good morning to you." Wade raised his hat. "Not to worry. I will say no more. The sheriff can take it from here."

Hackstedde came out of a deep slouch and straightened upon his horse. He appeared to have had no sleep, his eyes sunken in their sockets, the bags under them so swollen it was as if his face had folded in on itself.

"Right," he said. "I'm afraid there's nothing to these rumors your son's hatched, George. I interviewed Ted here, says he had at least a dozen men in his fields and not a one saw anything out of the ordinary in those woods or heard a peep."

"He said it better than I could," Morton allowed.

Hackstedde carried on. "August denies the charges and has a fine alibi. Him and his father were working at the office when this all took place. So, that's all there is to say. The case is closed."

George's chest was rising and falling so quickly Prentiss feared the old man's heart might give out. Yet they all intuited that it must be the plan, as before, to remain silent and let the result play out. And so George did his part.

"Very well," he said.

"If you wish," Wade said, "for the sake of goodwill and for the loss y'all have incurred, I have a few horses I am willing to donate to your enterprise. I know you only have that ass, and I loathe to see you struggle on that thing every time you come through town, looking like a sad Mexican weaving his way through a canyon trail."

Morton and Gail snickered, both of them putting a hand to their mouths as though they were twins privy to the other's movements.

"I am very happy with Ridley," George seethed. "If I wanted a horse, or three, I would get them myself. But your kindness is very much appreciated."

"So be it," Wade said. "We'll be on our way. I have to pick up my mother. I tried to send her a driver, but oh no, I must fetch her myself."

This man was an individual, Prentiss now saw, entirely different from himself. It wasn't his cunning, or the evil coursing through him, but his confidence—the surfeit of knowledge in his broad smile, which indicated that although his son had been accused of a cold-blooded murder, everything in the world was aligned to ease his livelihood, no matter who, or what, got in the way.

"Might I also offer my apologies," Wade said, "for not extending an invitation to the wedding? What can I say? We decided in the end to make it an intimate affair." He turned from a deal well done and began to return to his carriage with his son.

"A man died," Caleb said, his voice squeaking with emotion, as it was prone to do. "Setting aside who did it, or how little I think of that person for the rest of time, does the fact itself mean nothing to you? That a life was lost?"

It was the smallest comfort that these goons had no response. Wade and his son paused and turned back, seemingly roused by the slightest discomfort.

"His name was Landry," Prentiss said. "He wasn't just any man, but my brother. Best person I ever known. Best person I ever *will* know. And there ain't no number of horses that could make up for him being gone."

"That's enough from you," Morton said. "Best learn what little you might from that brother of yours and keep your mouth shut."

George stepped up, tucking his shirt into his pants, eyes alight.

"You are a callous fool, Ted," he said. "You have no right to speak a word in polite society, or any society for that matter."

"If you're aiming to start something again," Ted said, "I'll finish it again."

"Now everyone calm down," Hackstedde said, raising his voice.

"I saw him put paws on Mr. Morton once," Gail said, "and I ain't about to let it happen again."

The horses tensed and whinnied, and the whole yard, still awash in the breezy morning light, had the feeling of boiling over. Voices trampled one another now but Prentiss was quiet amid the uproar. Although Morton was a pathetic creature, lower than he was, he could not shake the hold of Wade Webler: the grandeur of his costume, the smugness of his countenance, the self-assurance in his total command of the situation. He stood leaning against the carriage whispering to his son, grinning once more. In the face of his strength Prentiss felt a sudden shyness, as if he were a boy again, hiding in fear behind his mother's gown. He could not have it—could not be made small anymore. The insults continued in waves and the energy carried him forward. He was halfway to the carriage before the sheriff noticed the body moving toward his party.

"Stop where you are," Hackstedde said.

"Prentiss!" George said. "Get back here."

But he did not take orders or commands. No longer.

"What *is* this boy up to?" said Wade, still lounging against the carriage as Prentiss approached.

The sheriff and the others all turned their horses to face the carriage. Behind him Prentiss could hear the scuffing of George's hobbled steps on the dusty road.

"Prentiss! Please."

Still Wade's eyes were sanguine, a mellow brown, his lips plump like a woman's, his chin jutted out. But at last the power in those eyes dissolved before Prentiss, who was close enough to the man to smell his cigar mouth. This was primal. Wade could not maintain his ease at such close, bare-knuckled quarters.

"George," he said. "Call your dog off me."

Prentiss took a deep breath. When he exhaled, it felt like a lifetime of grief pouring out of him, exorcised and offered back to the world as a righteous rebuke. The sensation was so pleasant, so transporting, that he would have been content knowing that single breath had been his last—indeed, it was so rapturous that he did not think much of what came forth with it: the ball of phlegm that rocketed from his mouth like cannon fodder into Wade's face.

Wade stood stock-still, his eyes unflinching, as the mucus dripped off his nose. Time stopped then. The yard was silent. The world itself stuttered to a pause. When it commenced to moving, it was impossibly slow, laid out like a tune written note by note in real time. Prentiss's gaze fell upon the upholstery of the carriage, blisteringly white; he then looked onward: out the back window, at the blanket-sea of green, the grass whipsawed in the wind, and he saw the breeze before he felt it upon his neck, perhaps the last of the morning before the heat swept through.

The blow of the rifle butt followed the wind. It slammed into his ribcage and was chased by a second at the dent of his leg behind his knee. He felt himself begin to fall but grabbed the side of the carriage and turned to face Hackstedde as the butt of the sheriff's rifle came down upon him again. Prentiss dodged and was caught upon the shoulder.

"On your knees!" Hackstedde screamed.

By then his deputy had dismounted as well. As he came forward Prentiss felt a grip about his neck—Wade Webler locking him in a choke hold.

"Enough!" George yelled, drawing near.

The air was going out of him and Hackstedde pulled back for a fatal strike just as George stepped between them and waved the sheriff off.

"Put that goddamn gun down, Lamar. Wade—" George's eyes darted toward Prentiss's own with a look of terror. "That's enough now," he said calmly.

Prentiss's heart beat so hard he felt it in his head. He could not free himself from this bear of a man and had begun to panic, squirming toward his own unconsciousness. There was a circle about them now: Isabelle and Caleb pleaded while the others remained silent, their eyes steady on Prentiss and Wade. The pressure on his neck was relentless.

George held his hands up in an attempt to pacify Wade.

"You know as well as I do those agents are coming to town. His brother's death was cause enough for alarm. You go and kill this man right here, right now, what do you think will happen?"

Wade spat his response practically into Prentiss's ear: "Do I look like a man who cares?"

Prentiss was lifted nearly off the ground. He could not believe the strength of the man, whose arm was wrapped so tightly around his neck that his tongue writhed in his throat against his will.

"Consider the very real chance," George said, "that they decide to make an example out of you. Glass might be an ally, but these fellows coming don't give a hoot how many buildings you own, or how much money you have. These bastards on their way have it out for men just like you. They will relish the chance to punish the most powerful they can. Think about it. For the sake of your business. For August."

Prentiss figured George's words might well be pure inventions, but they did the job. Wade released him, his body unclenched, and he fell to the ground in a heap, gasping for air. Before he could gather himself Hackstedde was at his back, placing irons upon his wrists. He grabbed Prentiss by the hair at the back of his head and yanked him up. His head was still ringing—the world still dizzy.

Wade took a deep breath and wiped the spittle from his face. His son looked on with such hatred that Prentiss thought he might come for him just as his father had. Yet he said not a word.

"Put that boy in a goddamn hole in the ground," Wade said. "I want a judge sent for. By tomorrow."

"Only judge they got circulating is Ambrose," Hackstedde said. "He was hearing cases in Chambersville last I caught wind."

"If I pay, how quickly can I get him here?"

"I imagine as soon as the money touches his palm."

"Get word to him. I'll cover the expenses. I want this boy charged and I want it done by the law. Anything less than a hanging would be a travesty. Make sure Judge Ambrose hears I said as much."

Prentiss exchanged a glance with George, and in the hollow of the old man's cheeks, the strain in his face, he found a look of disappointment so profound he had to turn away.

Wade fixed his collar, and as if this was a signal, the coachman came forth and opened the door for him and August.

"Now we have a wedding to attend, if you do not mind."

Morton, still atop his horse, faced Wade with remorse in his eyes, his hat in his hand.

"Before you go off," he said, "might I just lend you my apologies for that boy's spitting? I take responsibility seeing as he's the issue of my land. The Lord himself can attest to the fact that he ain't never committed such a unholy act before, not toward me nor anyone in my home."

Under the spell of his anger, Wade's entire body appeared engorged, and his head, equally swollen with rage, the color of a tomato, swiveled to face Morton atop his horse.

"I imagine he was waiting for someone worth the effort. Good afternoon."

And with a single whip from the coachman, the Weblers were off.

It was an uncomfortable moment before Morton nodded at Gail to follow him down the lane.

"Me and Mr. Webler get along rightly," he said, fixing to leave. "He's just in a bad mood is all." He directed a terse command at his horse, and the two departed themselves.

This left the sheriff and his deputy. Hackstedde pulled a length of rope from his saddlebag, tied one end to the horn of his saddle and the other to Prentiss's already shackled wrists.

George could only shake his head at Prentiss in a show of defeat.

"You were so close to being gone," he said. "Why?"

There was no means sufficient to explain the pleasure: how fantastic it had been to gather the courage, to step forward, to give in for the first time ever to a forbidden act of protest. The joy of standing before Wade as if he had power—just for that one second— was ineffable.

"It felt good," he told George. "That's all I know."

The tug of the rope, yanking him toward the horse, produced a piercing stab at his side where he'd been struck. He had the urge to vomit, but he would stay upright, no matter the pain, until he reached wherever they meant to take him. The horse settled as Hackstedde mounted him.

"We'll figure something out," George said.

"Let it be," Prentiss said. "Let your family rest."

George opened his mouth to speak but stopped himself. Perhaps he realized there were no words.

Isabelle bade Prentiss goodbye.

"Ma'am," Prentiss said, nodding. "Caleb."

"Prentiss," Caleb said.

"He'll be in the county jail," Hackstedde said. "No visitors."

Prentiss looked up and wondered at the clouds, soft as feathers pinned to a harsh sky. There was a second tug and they started off down the lane.

CHAPTER 19

John Foster had built his home along the unnamed creek that wound its way through all of Old Ox. The stream met at a pinch, and the levels were so low that there was hardly a current to speak of; on quiet days, if one listened close from the rear portico, that infinite trickle of water could be heard upstream, so distant it sounded as though it was sourced from the pit of a seashell. Yet it went unheard almost always, as John's children were hellions, and rained terror upon the home until his dying day, after which his wife, Mildred, brought discipline down upon the house with a force so swift that the water was often heard not only from the back of the home but by all those who passed before it. Even still, her sons, now grown, were not often on their best behavior, and Mildred was always eager to inform Isabelle of the ongoing trials of her parenting that sometimes failed—but the general accomplishment was still enough to bring a sense of satisfaction over Mildred, and although it was not the heroism one might read of in a novel, its place in the annals of domestic triumphs was secure as far as the women of Old Ox were concerned.

Isabelle had heard the creek quite well this early afternoon as she walked through the gate before the clapboard home. Mildred had set two chairs out upon the veranda, a serving table between them. A vase of sunflowers rested upon the railing, and the gleaming sunlight fell under the roof, glittering a yellow so bright it seemed to be drawn from the petals themselves. Mildred, a finger in the air to note some forgotten article, went back inside and returned with a bucket she dropped in front of the empty seat beside Isabelle. Against her chest she held a bowl of potatoes.

Isabelle apologized for her tardiness, explaining that she'd had to go to Selby to see Prentiss.

"They took him to the jail there, as I'm sure you know by now. That imbecile Hackstedde leading the charge."

At first Mildred was silent, occupied with her peeling. The creek was audible again—like the hollow hiss of a snake. Ridley stood motionless before the road, as stoic as ever, the carriage at his rear.

"It was nearly the only topic of conversation at the wedding," she said, finally. "Wade wasn't shy on the matter, even when it pertained to the allegations against August. Horrific allegations, I should say. It was as though the whole thing was a joke to him."

"I cringe contemplating another moment in that man's presence. And it would only be reliving what took place yesterday."

"I can only imagine," Mildred said. "How was your journey?"

"Not entirely successful. Hackstedde said there would be no visitors, but I brought along some fruit, perhaps to entice him, however stupid that sounds." She picked up a peach and dropped it back into the basket. "I argued with him about how long I'd traveled, and he backed his statement down to allowing family to visit, as those were the rules in general. It was hardly a concession. He knows full well what has happened to the only family Prentiss had."

"A fine gesture to make the trip, at least," Mildred said.

"Something had to be done. Far be it from George to go to Selby himself. He thinks nothing will be accomplished by paying a visit, but I believe it's simply his fear of travel that holds him back. Yet he talks incessantly of Prentiss. It grew so exhausting I felt the urge to set aside the pair of socks I was knitting him and go and see the man myself."

"So you did." Mildred put the peeler down and rubbed her palm, kneading out the kinks. "And Caleb? How does he fare?"

"Where to begin? He eats crumbs and says nothing. This morning he appeared from the shadows like some ghoul. I don't know if he'll ever be the same."

Isabelle removed her bonnet and placed it on the railing. She considered doing the same with her shoes but thought better of it.

"After what Wade described," Mildred said, "well, if it's all true, and I don't doubt your son..."

She shook her head and picked up the peeler, holding it before an unscathed potato.

"He's seen evil, Isabelle."

Then she put the peeler down once more and stood up, suddenly charged by the conversation and raising her voice as if a tornado had gathered in her chest.

"And perhaps you shouldn't be denouncing him for acting as he does. My boys—good God. The day they got back from the war I prepared them a turkey dinner, and they spoke almost exclusively of the horrors they'd doled out to other soldiers. The conversation wasn't a celebration of their staying alive, but of the deaths they'd wrought. I couldn't see the slightest morsel of sensitivity at that table. Which is to say, perhaps there's some good to Caleb's transformation. In light of the alternative."

The story unfolded so quickly as to be dismissed as a harmless anecdote, but Isabelle had never heard her friend speak of her sons in such stark terms. That they might be a cause for shame was startling.

"Mildred," she said.

"I've weathered worse than my sons' behavior," Mildred said.

"Yes, but you don't have to do it alone. It's why we have each other."

Mildred was staring down the road, her apron crumpled against the railing. Her face was angular and the firmness of her disposition almost ensured that her features would never soften—would remain as they were for the rest of time.

"I don't hold it against you," she said, "but please don't tell me how to manage my demons. I don't judge you for bringing fruit to prisoners to ease the pain of your home. Let me deal with my emotions as I see fit."

Isabelle stiffened against the back of her chair. After a time, Mildred returned to her seat. Both women seemed uncomfortable enough that they might sit there bolted permanently to the veranda before either would speak a word to the other again. The landscape before them was a vast stillness, which only brought more attention to this rare disharmony between them.

"I should apologize," Mildred said at last.

"You're *wrong*," Isabelle said, and put her hand in the air. "There's nothing to apologize for because you're simply wrong in your accusation. You don't have a clue how I feel. *You* might stifle your hurt, but that doesn't reflect why I went to Selby. Any pain I have is not to be hidden. It's a point of strength. And I will do good with it. A goal so esteemed as to help an innocent man wrongly accused—well, your apology would only tarnish the undertaking."

Mildred looked over at her as if assessing a stranger, and her gaze did soften, minutely but perceptibly. She nodded as though the act carried a hint of encouragement.

"Much of what you've done recently is…let me put it this way: Your demeanor isn't what it once was. And that can be confusing. But it would be narrow-minded to write you off like all the others." Mildred bestowed a deep, comforting smile upon her friend. "You're immensely courageous," she said. "I didn't speak ill of your trip to Selby out of any distaste for it. I think I was more so speaking to myself. To my own weaknesses."

"Your own weaknesses?" Isabelle exclaimed. "I learned to carry myself by watching you. Any courage I might have is mere performance compared with yours."

"What bravery is there in sitting on my porch twiddling my thumbs? It is a gaping lack of purpose, and it haunts me. Has *always* haunted me."

Isabelle leaned forward. "Is it John?" she asked. "Do you miss him?"

Mildred scrunched up her face like a raisin.

"The feeling was as present when he was alive as it is with him in the grave. The problem is that I can't locate what it is. Which doesn't make the lack any easier to bear. If anything, the pain is only greater because of the stubborn mystery of it."

Her friend's countenance slowly crumbled, her jaw trembling, her almond eyes gone watery, and when her hand began to shake Isabelle reached over and took it in her own, lacing each of their fingers together, telling her it was fine—that everything was fine. The clammy warmth of the afternoon was like a sealant upon their palms, and it felt as though nothing could bring them apart, nothing could undo their bond. As far as Isabelle was concerned, they could sit here for the rest of the afternoon. She had nowhere to go.

"It's okay," she said. "It's okay to *feel*, Mildred."

"It's not just that. Not right now, anyway."

Isabelle leaned forward. "Then what?"

Mildred sighed. "I am loath to bring it up, but God, if I can introduce another topic, no matter how tawdry, to divert us from this one, it would be the greatest favor for you to allow it."

"Anything at all," Isabelle said.

"Even if it regards you?"

"Say what is on your mind."

Mildred held Isabelle's hand firmly. "Some at the wedding spoke with the utmost confidence of a certain woman. A woman of the night."

"I can assure you I hold no employment beyond the duties of my home."

Mildred didn't laugh.

"Another woman. One George has apparently been seeing quite often. For some time. It may be the charge is just meant to slander your family further. I couldn't say."

Isabelle pulled her hand from Mildred's, almost involuntarily. She quavered, unsteady, and then recovered herself, for even this—in all its dark suggestions—could not unravel her constitution totally. She stood up and began to pace, and the sunshine felt like a spotlight on the uncertainty welling up inside her.

"I overheard it at the reception party," Mildred said, "and thought I should tell you myself rather than risk having it passed on to you by someone who would do it out of malice."

Isabelle paused before the vase of sunflowers. "You know who she is, then?"

"I do," Mildred said. "In certain circles she is not a secret."

"Then you need not say more. Just tell me where I might find her."

The place was known to Isabelle; she'd walked by it before: a small sloping home of tin, not quite a shanty, not quite a house. It had taken on the color of mud and was so undistinguished that Isabelle never in her life would have paid it a second thought. Until now.

This was not the first time she'd confronted the specter of George's infidelity. There were those long nights in his absence, and she was not naïve. He blamed them on his evening hikes, but there was no explanation as to why the walk sometimes required his evening jacket, his finer boots. He would have told her—he did not lie to her—yet she never asked. If indeed he had sampled other fruit, then he was returning home to what he liked best. He would immediately slide into bed beside her, sighing in comfort, and with his body near her own, she felt a renewal of his devotion. Besides, the instances were rare enough—and so fleeting—that they acted to her as confirmation of their bond.

But the randomness did not correlate to the report Mildred had given her. If there was one particular woman, then what he had was a lover, no matter if he paid for her time. The thought hurt Isabelle, yes, but not for its suggestion of adultery alone; there was also a resentment that someone else had solved the only puzzle she'd laid claim to her entire adult life: the understanding of her husband's inner workings. She wished to meet the woman who had managed the same feat.

She'd parked Ridley and the carriage in the center of town and walked the rest of the way. When she reached the home, it stood as she recalled it, tucked between two others in the poorer side of Old Ox. The roof comprised no more than rotted branches bound beside one another, and a pipe jutted out above it, coughing up smoke. She asked a man outside the neighboring home if anyone was in. He looked at her from under two thick eyebrows, grumbled something, and finally cocked his head yes. She was still carrying her fruit basket, which she lowered to knock on the door.

After a moment, it opened slightly. The eyes of the woman there were animal-like, as though she sensed a threat.

"Can I help you?" she asked.

"I was hoping we might speak," Isabelle said.

"Is this about your husband?"

"How would you know—"

"Ma'am, I often get confused for another woman similar in looks. But I have no business with any men. Good day."

"Wait," Isabelle said, yet the door was already shut and latched.

She peered through the window, a single panel covered by a thick curtain. Then she knocked once more.

"I have no qualms with you," she called out. "None at all. I would just like some answers." She waited.

"I told you, you have me confused," the woman's voice called back. "I don't know any man."

"You must know *some* man," Isabelle said.

"Not yours."

The door was hardly more than a sheet that might blow away in the wind. Isabelle had the urge to push through it. She felt desperate, almost naked, lingering in the wake of this woman's rejection.

"I swear to you," she pleaded. "We'll speak civilly. My husband..." She took a breath. "George Walker. That is his name. And if you do not know him, truly do not know him, I will walk away from here and not return."

The clank of silverware was followed by the thud of footsteps. Yet no voices. No movement. And yet, just then, the door opened a slant.

"Really?" the woman said. "His wife?"

"I'm Isabelle. Isabelle Walker."

"And you're not about to bring trouble into my home? Because I have a daughter. This is a place of peace."

"I will respect your home," Isabelle said. "You have my word."

The woman seemed to contemplate her decision once more, then opened the door the rest of the way.

Save for its size, the home was curiously elegant, bearing almost no relation to its external trappings. Numerous lamps brought a dim luster to the place. The chairs at the dining room table were carved of mahogany, upholstered, the backs of them crest-shaped and ornate in design; the bed along the opposite side of the room was raised and well-kept, and tucked against the wall next to it was a mirrored dresser fit for royalty.

"I receive many gifts," the woman said, as if sensing Isabelle's surprise at the decor.

It was irrepressibly hot. Before the hearth a glazed roast was speared on a spit, jeweled droplets of fat dripping onto the pan beneath it. Isabelle could see why the woman was wearing only a nightgown, for anything more might well cause one to melt.

"Wish there was a little more space to prepare supper," the woman said. "But we do with what we have for now."

"It's no bother," Isabelle said, and turned from her inspection of the quarters to face the woman, who introduced herself as Clementine and offered a gentle handshake. "I know your name," Isabelle said.

The many corridors of the woman's beauty were apparent. Her cheeks registered like two well-fashioned slopes falling toward a smooth, rounded chin, and the tracing of all these points was so fine that Isabelle felt the desire to reach out the back of her hand and run her fingers down the length of her face. Her loose hair lingered upon her shoulders in a bramble, and her disregard for its provocative dishevelment made Isabelle burn with self-doubt for keeping her own confined within her bonnet.

"And this is Elsy," Clementine said.

How had she missed the child at the woman's feet? The girl was quiet, no more than two or three, and stared up at Isabelle with a captivating innocence, all eyes—her mother's eyes.

"Hello, Elsy," Isabelle said, waving.

The child looked back cautiously, holding to her mother's leg, and said "Hi" in a small voice.

"She's just about to nap," Clementine said.

"I'm sorry to intrude as I have. This shouldn't take long."

"You're here, now."

They sat down at the dining-room table, and Clementine clasped her hands together, still wary.

"Mama, mama," the child said.

Her mother grabbed a toy from the ground, handed it to the child, and led her to a space near the bed, then returned to Isabelle.

"What can I do for you, Mrs. Walker?"

Of all the times to lose one's train of thought. Yet Isabelle could not figure where to begin. Their only commonality was such a vulgar one, and her wish to be polite was so overwhelming, that she felt reluctant to mention her reason for stopping in. She sat there staring at the table, as though studying the basket of fruit she'd placed there, and was immensely relieved when Clementine spoke first.

"George talks of you," she said. "Whenever he stops by."

There it was. His name from her mouth. This by itself was gratifying, since to hear her say that one word was an admission. But although the honesty—the confirmation—was strangely comforting, the mention of George by someone who was so familiar with him, and yet so distant to Isabelle, unsettled her further.

"He has great respect for you," Clementine went on. "A deep fondness."

It did not sound ironic, but it was difficult to take it any other way.

"My husband harbors little sentiment," Isabelle said. "But it's nice to know he makes his love clear when he is with you, at least."

Clementine lowered her head, the light of the lamps softening her features.

"What I said sounded wrong," she said. "This is…new ground. I have had wives come see me before, but never have I entertained them."

"Yet you let me in."

"I have an affinity for George. He's a kind man. Caring."

Isabelle sneered. "I'm sure you say that in regard to all the men you see."

"Mrs. Walker—" Clementine raised her hand from the table and placed it back down. "I'm not working right now, and I have no incentive to comfort you. What I'm doing you is a favor. My time is valuable. The only thing I ask is that you respect me by taking me at my word."

The roast was hissing, the room at a boil, and Clementine seemed awfully cooler than Isabelle in the moment.

"I apologize for my tone," Isabelle said, taking a breath to calm herself.

"It's understandable. But you must get to the point now."

There was another pause. Then Isabelle's voice came out low, empty, and quick.

"What does he ask of you?"

"Here we are," Clementine said, as though she'd been waiting for those exact words. "George and I have never done anything untoward. Physical touch…it does not seem to interest him."

Isabelle was able to look up then. She lingered on Clementine's gaze, her careful charm, the quiet in her eyes, and finally saw behind her beauty the guarded reserve of magnetism that lay hidden within her. It was surely what made them come to her, and then, in the days afterward, come back again.

"George is more a friend than anything. He likes to sit bedside and talk. Of you and your son. Those two brothers he works with. His past. He's very chatty if given an opening."

"Now that does sound like George."

"He *can* go on. Yet he always respects my time. Although he pays like the others, he's always asking after Elsy, and requests I put it toward her upbringing. Which is where all my money goes anyway."

The child was playing on the ground with a music box, a small ballerina twirling endlessly on a wooden platform. The box must've been broken, as no song accompanied the twirling, but she seemed unbothered by it.

Isabelle was encouraged by Clementine's boldness, her utter transparency, for it represented a detachment that spoke not of love, but a simple fondness, a professional sort no less. Yet it did not dispel all of her concerns—did not explain the foremost question on her mind.

"I do wonder…" She glanced at Clementine uncertainly. Her voice trembled. She felt like a dog—asking a stranger of the intimacies of her husband, as though she knew him not at all. The embarrassment burned her insides, and she had a craving to get up and go. "Is George…unguarded with you? Is he open in that way?"

It was the first time Isabelle saw emotion in Clementine's expression, and it gave her the answer she sought without a single word uttered. Clementine responded almost under her breath, her eyes sympathetic as they met Isabelle's.

"It's what he pays for. It has little to do with me."

"What exactly does he do?" Isabelle asked. "Hug you? Does George want a hug?"

It sounded like a joke, but she could not have been more serious.

"Sometimes, maybe, yes."

"Is it more than that? Does he cry for you?"

Clementine looked at the ground, her lips tight, eyes veiled.

"I see." Isabelle stood up quickly, grabbing the basket of fruit as she readied to leave.

"It could be any girl," Clementine said.

"But he's chosen you."

The room was suffocating in its heat and Isabelle felt desperate to breathe fresh air. She'd reached the door when she felt the hand clasp her wrist and she pulled away with all her might, turning to catch Clementine breathing heavily, with an intensity that rivaled Isabelle's own state.

"He hasn't chosen me," Clementine said. "He's chosen *you*."

She spoke as a boss might to an underling, directives that stung Isabelle.

"He fears you. And he would have nothing if he was to lose your trust in him. So he can't cry for you. *Because* he loves you. That's how he operates—yes, it's flawed, but it's George. You can be angry at me if it helps you in some way, but if it's because you think I've taken something from your marriage, you'd be mistaken. For George, at least, I'm helping keep it strong."

Isabelle opened the door and stepped out. The heat from inside the home had been so staggering that the sunlight was like a cool breeze. She stood along the railing of the home, peering out toward the street, where a man led a meandering tow horse down the way. By the time they were beyond her, she had calmed, and when she wheeled around, Clementine was leaning against the doorjamb, her head cocked in concern.

"I have given up so much for that man," Isabelle said. "Twenty-two years. And I hardly know him."

There was nothing for Clementine to say. Isabelle knew this, and was content to receive no response, only a look of understanding—the same, she was sure, that Clementine gave the men who paid her.

Isabelle faced her fully, pressed out the wrinkles of her dress with her free hand, and stood straight.

"Thank you for your time," she said. "You were very accommodating."

"If you need anything further," Clementine said, her concern still apparent, "don't be afraid to ask. I do feel for you. Being George's wife—that's not an easy obligation."

She nodded and stepped back into her home.

Isabelle collected herself and tried to put on a smile for anyone familiar she might meet as she reentered traffic. After only a few paces, her mind ventured off. Not having eaten all day, she was ravenous. She might devour all the fruit in her basket and still have room for more upon returning home. She imagined the juices staining her dress, the sticky remains of the peach crusting her lips. Perhaps she'd return to the cabin like a heathen having fled the wild. The thought nearly made her laugh.

Near the square she stopped at Blossom's Café. She'd never dined there but it felt like a perfectly worthwhile place to sit and ruminate. She leaned against the side of one of the barrels out front, put her basket down, and snatched a peach. She was halfway toward taking a bite when she caught sight of a few men inside the establishment, playing dominoes, sliding the pieces across the table, linking them to others. Her brother had a set as a child. There would be days when their father would be at work, their mother entertaining, and Silas and the other neighbor boys would be occupied by the tiles for hours. They did not play the actual game, but the child's version—setting the pieces up in a row to fall. Her brother and his friends would line the dominoes up in as exotic a locale as possible: over books, under the bed. She would watch but was not allowed to play herself. Because she had never been included, she was left mostly to think of how little there was for her to do. Now, on this day, she pondered the opposite: not how little there was to do, but how much had been done—a trip to Selby, to Mildred's, to Clementine's—with so little accomplished. She was eating a peach. Watching men play dominoes. Thinking about how much life was like her brother's games, each day a tile falling toward the next, leading to nothing but the end of the line.

A boy appeared from the shop, youthful, his hair so fair it was clear it would darken as he got older and it drew color from the world. He could've been her son. He told her she would need to buy something if she was going sit in front of the store. She was still eating her peach. She took another one from the basket and gave it to the boy without uttering a single word. He didn't pretend to decline, and instead put it to his mouth immediately.

"Do you play?" she asked, and pointed at the dominoes inside.

"No, ma'am," he said, his mouth full.

"Smart," she said, picking up her basket. "That's smart."

She left then but did not go home. Instead, she turned back and found her way, after a moment's hesitation, to Clementine's house. This time she knocked rapidly.

When Clementine came to the door, Isabelle said, "There is something. A favor. I'm not beneath asking it of you."

"Well, be quiet about it," Clementine said. "My girl's asleep."

"You're better with your words than I am. Far better. And the job I have in mind requires that skill." Isabelle propped up her basket of fruit.

Clementine looked back inside, checking on her child.

"Let's take a little walk," she said. "And discuss whatever you're on about."

"It's a good cause," Isabelle said. "A worthy one. I promise you that."

CHAPTER 20

The world was visible to Prentiss only as it passed him by. Through the front door down the hall from his cell he caught a glimpse of patches of light, a blurry stream of bodies, the clipped colors of clothes. He heard the booming and fading of voices But not a single soul stopped in to visit the man who would soon be hanged.

There were other cells, all of them empty, as they had been since he'd arrived the day before. The only person who paid Prentiss any mind at all was Hackstedde himself, who sat at a desk, alternately throwing darts or rolling cigarettes, whistling and playing with his timepiece. He was, somehow, more restless than Prentiss, and after their first few hours together he could not help making conversation, which for Prentiss was far worse than the pain of silence. The sheriff seemed to believe that Prentiss was interested in his previous work as a patroller. He said he'd earned the nickname *Bloodhound,* though Prentiss could divine no reason for its bestowal, since not a single story ended with Hackstedde finding the slave he sought.

"There was that boy on Aldridge's land," Hackstedde said. "We had him cornered in the woods when I got myself stung by a whole swarm of bees. Now, listen—I was so swollen from head to toe that I had to leave the Negro behind and get the rest of the gang to carry me back to town. I was on bed rest for a month of Sundays."

There was a waste bucket in the cell, half-filled by the last prisoner. No bed. Just an empty space. A pen hardly fit for a pig.

"Another time," Hackstedde said, "they sent me over to Pawnee, and I get to the front door of the plantation house and who owns the place but a Negro. Yeah, you heard me right, they had in there a *Negro* who went on and bought himself some *other* Negroes. I could hardly figure such an arrangement. And this Negro tries to tell me it's not so uncommon. That might be the case in Pawnee, I tell him, but it's not exactly a natural occurrence up in Old Ox. But anyway, his property was long gone, we didn't even get a sniff of the boy. Probably in Canada by now."

Prentiss never responded, and eventually Hackstedde took offense, pausing to cast a wandering glance over the empty jail cells and tempting Prentiss to fill the silent lull. When he didn't, the sheriff scowled at him.

"Ain't too long now," he said balefully. "Tim should be back with that judge by dawn. Good Southern gentleman. He'll take Webler's word on things, sure enough. Promise you that much."

Prentiss retreated into himself. He knew how to live in his head. He'd made a similar journey every day in the fields, wandering in his mind's eye to a place he'd never been, a place that was equal parts destination and idea. *Elsewhere* was the only name it carried. The barn beside George's cabin was elsewhere; a patch of free ground up north was elsewhere; his mother was elsewhere; salvation was elsewhere; all those lives that passed outside the jail existed elsewhere (praise be to their good fortune); and a fate, any fate, other than the one that lay before him would be a perfectly fine road to elsewhere. The map, with all its many variations, was in his head, yet he knew quite well he would never make the journey.

"Tim gets a bad reputation," Hackstedde said, reclaiming his good cheer. "He is stupid, that I grant you, but the boy is a veteran, fought that first year before he was gutshot, and if you show your mettle on the battlefield, who am I to say you can't be a county deputy? The least I can do is give him some time to show his grit. Besides, I spoke to the doctor, who said the boy is 'battle weary.' That's what they're calling it. He can hear a footstep and think he's got his flank compromised, eyes all big, sweating and carrying on. Doc says he'll get better, though. A matter of time."

For no other reason than boredom, Prentiss had begun to tabulate the many symptoms that Hackstedde's girth inspired. The man's mouth closed only when he needed to swallow; he was unsteady in his chair, prone to falling over but never quite doing Prentiss the favor; his skin was blotchy; and when he breathed, especially after one of his monologues, it sounded like the airy whine of a child nearing the end of a tantrum, so labored that the flame of the candle atop his desk would often flicker.

His daughter, a young woman, had brought him lunch wrapped in paper—from the tavern next door, Prentiss guessed. It had been too hot to eat, but after a few minutes Hackstedde stuck his finger in the mashed potatoes, judged the temperature, and commenced. In contrast to what one might expect, given his slovenly appearance, he ate daintily, quietly, and with a solemn devotion to the task, as if it were an act of prayer.

The silence didn't last.

"You know," Hackstedde said, working through a chicken thigh, "you had yourself a visitor this morning while you were napping."

Prentiss propped himself up against the wall.

Hackstedde waved the bone at his face.

"That got your attention, didn't it?" He laughed and clanged the chicken bone down. "Mrs. Walker came by. Drove that donkey all the way over here to make sure you'd made it in one piece. Tried to bribe me with a basket of fruit to see you. I told her, 'Now, Mrs. Walker, do I look like someone who gets stirred up by the sight of a peach?'"

"You ain't let her in?"

"I did you a service, boy. You needed that rest."

Prentiss could still feel the chafing imprint of the irons upon his wrists, though that wasn't the worst of the punishments he'd faced on the journey to Selby: when they'd reached Stage Road, Hackstedde had shortened the leash, and Prentiss was bound so close to the horse that he could not avoid its droppings when they fell at his feet. The smell, ripe and putrid, was still on him. He couldn't help thinking, much as it pained him, that it was better Isabelle had stayed outside.

The sheriff took up the drumstick once more.

"Don't think I'm all bad because I showed her out. It's just the rules: *family only*. And even that's a privilege."

He stood and continued eating. The rest of the mashed potatoes, seasoned generously and dolloped with butter, disappeared in a few bites.

"You know, the whole patrolling business, I didn't have a passion for it. But you needed patrollers just like you need boys putting down railroad track, driving drays, tending bar—you get the idea." He walked over to Prentiss's cell, sniffed with displeasure, then snorted and spat toward the bucket of piss on the other side of the bars. "Same with sheriffing. See, you smell like a horse's behind but I'm still over here feeding you like any other prisoner. It's a job. I don't play favorites."

"Maybe 'cause there ain't no one else to pick out," Prentiss muttered under his breath.

Hackstedde leaned down, eyes glued on Prentiss, and slid the plate sideways between the bars. Chicken bones fell onto the floor of the cell.

"Those are good leftovers," he said, and returned to his chair. "You let that food go cold, it's on you."

It was garbage, but Prentiss was so ravenous he couldn't take his eyes off it. A remnant streak of the potatoes, snow white, had skittered across the floor of the cell a few inches beyond the plate; the remains of the chicken still gave off a drift of steam that tempted him. Hackstedde spectated with a single-minded intensity. Prentiss felt his eyes on him, could sense, deep within the man, a dire urge to see his prisoner capitulate.

Prentiss put his nose up, assuming an air of disappointment.

"Went and dropped your trash, sheriff. Best get a broom and clean it up."

"I'd say it's up to you to keep your own cell in order, son."

"I'm fixin' to die," Prentiss said. "You can't make me do a damn thing. So you can pick up that trash yourself. Or if you feelin' lazy, which you seem prone to, you could wait for that deputy of yours to do it. I hear he'll be back soon enough."

The sheriff's face flashed a brilliant shade of red; his mouth flicked downward, and his double chin began to quiver. Then, like a river undammed, he burst forth, not in anger but in laughter, his whole upper half roiling in delight until he wobbled the legs of his chair. He slammed the table in relief, lit himself a cigarette with a last giggle, and shook his head in satisfaction.

"You are *delightfully* mouthy," he said. "There's nothing quite like a nigger clever with his words." He took a long drag. "Right and ready for the noose. Yes you are."

Prentiss sank against the back of his cell. It was darker there and he turned himself so that his face was to the wall and shut his eyes once more.

"There was a fellow who worked alongside me when I was a boy," Hackstedde said. "He was just like you. His name was Goodwin."

"I wouldn't mind some quiet," Prentiss said. "If you'd do me that much. And it really ain't much, sheriff."

"No, now, this is a good tale. I thought ol' Goodwin was the funniest fellow I'd ever met, black or white, red or yellow. Hell, the boy was so fair-skinned he was almost light as I am. Always had this grin painted on his face. God bless him, he could find the sunny side of a shadow…"

If he focused, Prentiss could hear his brother's footsteps. A soft patter behind him, like fat raindrops falling slowly from the leaves of a tree. That was all the noise he needed in a day. Not the utterance of a single word. Just the assurance that those footsteps were following his own. He tried to stay with them, but each moment they grew more distant, and he worried what would fill the void when they were gone for good.

"…You can imagine my shock when they told us that fool had run off. 'We got a deserter'—those were the boss's words. You could say that was the first time I ever hunted another man. The boss had me tag along with the dogs, and it took all night. I for one was certain he was long gone, was about to tell them as much, but then, in the light of the lantern, you see the folds over those dogs' eyes lift for a moment, see their eyes spark, and suddenly they're all barking at the same tree…"

"Sheriff, if I clean up that food will you give me some peace?"

"…Now I'm the only nimble one in the group, still a boy at the time, and seeing as I'd climbed my fair share of trees, they send me shimmying up myself. When I get to the first branch, and they give me a little light, I see Goodwin crouched there, naked as the day. Nearly wet my pants. He smelled so foul I almost vomit. His face was beaming, teeth white as ivory, and I noticed something off. Took me a minute to see it. But around his lips, and on his forehead, and all across his body, he'd gone and smeared himself with shit. Whether it was human or animal shit, I couldn't tell, but it was smooth, like he'd taken his time, with a butter knife, maybe. Just about the color of the bark, too, so he almost disappeared into the tree…"

Prentiss tried to listen past Hackstedde, to listen for his brother's footsteps, but the sheriff had roped him in. He could think only of the rituals. Not his own people's, but those he'd heard of on other plantations. Men and women gathering when certain stars aligned and heating clay, smearing themselves whole, dancing naked, first in unison but then alone, twirling endlessly, as though if they twirled fast enough they might spin themselves right into the ground and return to the earth.

"…And right then he puts his finger up to his mouth, with the widest grin I ever seen him give, like we're in on a joke together. Only when I look close, his eyes are gone red, and there's a steady little trickle of tears coming down his face."

Hackstedde took a long drag, and Prentiss could smell the smoke as the sheriff exhaled.

"I jumped down that tree and told them there wasn't nothing up there but a bird's nest."

Prentiss opened one eye and turned away from the wall to look back at Hackstedde.

"I could never shake the thought they knew I was lying," the sheriff said. "I still wonder about that. Like I let them down. But hell, I was just a boy. And I liked the fellow. Tomorrow ain't too far away, though. I got you to fix my conscience. Make things right."

Prentiss didn't linger on the sheriff's words. He shut his eyes once more, thinking the judge would arrive and have his say and he would awaken to the sigh of the iron door swinging ajar, after which he would have a reckoning with a noose—his own return to the earth.

It felt like the fabric of a dream when a woman's voice called his name. When he came to, he was so startled to see the figure before him that he nearly jumped. But she said his name once more in a soothing tone.

"You thought you wouldn't ever see your cousin again, didn't you?"

The woman winked, and Prentiss nodded along, as he would have done to any string of words coming from her mouth. It was night already—yet even in the dark her beauty was immense: her eyes like flowers in bloom, the lashes the petals. She wore a flowing blue dress with tassels at the bottom that looked like catkins hanging from a tree. His life had always been a loaded coil held taut by the discipline of hard work, the allegiance to the duties of each day, yet he could sense how the very sight of a woman like this could spring it loose and scatter a lifetime of order.

She reached through the bars with a peach, which he clutched dumbly, and assured him, in a whisper, that she'd come to see a certain Prentiss. "Haven't you missed me?" she asked him, more an instruction than a question.

He hadn't considered that he might need to respond. It seemed almost too great a task.

"Yes," he managed. "Dearly."

Her face came to a rest—his answer had satisfied her—and she settled back in her chair on the other side of the bars. Hackstedde was watching them intently from his desk.

The woman looked back at the sheriff and then turned to Prentiss again, whispering once more.

"You must be hungry, you poor thing. Eat."

He looked at the peach in his hand, having already forgotten it was there. He hadn't eaten in two days, since the evening of Landry's burial, but although his hunger was wolfish, he took only a slow bite, keeping his eyes on this heaven-sent woman whose business with him he still did not know.

The woman explained her encounter with Isabelle and the mission to visit Prentiss that she had accepted.

"My name is Clementine," she said.

"Pleasure," Prentiss said.

"Mrs. Walker sends her regards."

Hackstedde's chair squeaked as he shifted forward.

"What's all that whispering about?" he yelled.

"Just being polite, sheriff," the woman said. "Minding you your space."

She could inflect her voice with the softest of tones and Hackstedde fell under the spell of her words. He grunted and said no more.

"Are you well in here?" Clementine asked.

"It ain't exactly paradise," he said. "Apologies for the smell. He had me walking through filth before we made it to Selby. I don't have no way to clean up."

He could hardly look at her, but she returned his gaze so generously, so kindly, that his shame was expunged.

"You should see my home," she said. "Oh, does it get filthy sometimes. Nothing shameful about a mess."

He took another bite, thought to speak, but had to have another before going on.

"You know Isabelle?" he asked quietly.

"Somewhat," she said with hesitation. "We're better acquainted now. In fact, she's watching my daughter as we speak. But I knew George first. He would come by my workplace on occasion."

"What do you do?"

"I'm a whore, mostly." She said it as though she were a seamstress.

He kept chewing, contemplating the image of George even standing next to a woman this beautiful, let alone being so close to her. He would never have thought George had so much as talked to a woman other than Isabelle until this very instant.

"It has its perks," she went on. "It's possible the sheriff is falling for this ruse of us being related, but it probably has more to do with my promise that he could have a few free visits, girl of his choice. I'll owe someone back at the house a favor— a rather large one, considering." She appraised Hackstedde again. "But life is all about compromises."

"For me."

"For you and yours. The Walkers are good people. If they say there's a man in need, to bring him a basket of fruit is not too much to ask. But I ramble. Tell me about yourself, Prentiss. I'd be curious to know the man who's caught the Walkers' fancy."

No one had ever uttered such words to him—even George hadn't been especially curious about him—and he was at a loss to speak of himself, even to know where to begin. He told her about Morton's plantation, about the sorrow he'd found there, and she was quick to cut him off.

"We don't need that," she said. "Not now. Not here." She slapped her knee and put her fist under her chin, grinning mischievously. "Tell me a secret. Something you haven't ever told a soul."

He had to think hard about what to share, all the more difficult with Clementine's eyes locked on him.

"Well, there was a girl once," he said, and looked down bashfully.

"Do tell," she said.

"I feel silly saying it."

"I bet you haven't got your fill of silly your whole life, and a man's entitled to some. Make up for lost time."

So he told her. First of his brother, for the story started there. Never had he seen a man so obsessed as Landry was with the Mortons' fountain, and it made him curious every time he saw his brother stare. He told her of Landry's love of water and how he'd never understood how one could have such an intense fascination with any one thing until a certain afternoon, when he got his own obsession.

"And just like that," he said, "I start thinking about girls like I ain't never done before. Just that age, I s'pose."

There was one in particular, he said, name of Delpha.

"She had eyes like yours, you lock in on 'em and they wouldn't let you go for a whole afternoon. Thin as a branch, couldn't pick to save her life. She was too small to take a beating, but the overseer would make her life hell, just like the rest of us, and one day I couldn't take it. All day I been watching her and I knew her sack was only half full, and it was nigh on weighing time. I had to do something to help her out."

He laughed on recollection, and the sudden joy on his face brought another smile to Clementine's, too.

"Oh, you played her savior."

"You go on embarrassing me I won't be able to finish out the story. But I tried, yes I did. I spy the overseer, name of Gail, big fella, dumb as a cow, halfway 'cross the field, minding another boy, so I make a run for her row."

"You don't."

"And I'm reaching into my sack, already pulling out handfuls of cotton, ready to cram it into her own, to show her just how far I'ma go for love."

Clementine had her hand over her mouth.

"Now I'm three, maybe four rows away, calling her name, 'Delpha, Delpha, turn around,' and right as she does, I trip over myself, fall

forward, and land right square on a cotton stalk. I broke it off at the
root, and what's left of me slides down the other side. I got scratches
all on my face, burrs in my hair, and the next thing I see is the hooves
of Gail's horse pounding my way, and I know I got a bad night in
front of me."

They laughed together, so hard that Hackstedde told them to
quiet down.

"But you were *courageous*," Clementine whispered. "Women are
always swooned by bravery."

"There weren't no bravery when I took that whipping, I'll tell you
that much. You feel that skin peel off and…" The flicker of unease
in her eyes told him to stop. He tried to laugh again, to rekindle the
joy of the previous moment, but it was gone.

"Mrs. Walker told me what you did," Clementine said. "To Wade
Webler. That's courage, Prentiss. Maybe not smart. You're behind
these bars—let's not pass *that* over."

He laughed again, though the no-nonsense warmth of her humor
nearly broke his heart.

"But there are some things we're called to do," she said. "Being a
woman, and an authority on such things, I can tell you that I for one
am swooned, and I'm sure Delpha was, too."

These precious and unexpected minutes had passed swiftly, and
the night was growing long. Hackstedde would make her leave soon,
Prentiss knew, and he was fearful of being robbed of her presence, of
losing her to the shadows and facing the dark alone. He knew what
would follow the darkness, the end that would find him when they
carried him from his cell. He shuddered and swept the thought from
his mind once more.

"Tell me of you," he said.

She asked if he'd heard of New Orleans. It was where she was
from. In New Orleans, she said, the men wore clothes more garish
than the women, and there were parties every night. Drinks flowed
endlessly. Faces were hidden by masks. The port was built to hold
hundreds of ships, schooners, and steamers, and those who were of

the disposition to do so could travel all over the world. And there was a market the size of Old Ox itself, haggling so loud you couldn't hear your own voice.

"You take yourself to a horse race," she said, "and you'll see Negroes, mulattoes, white men, Frenchmen, all packed together."

Prentiss had never heard of a place so peculiar, and he could only imagine how distant it must be from Old Ox. How stupid he must look to her in his shock.

She laughed at him, a little teasingly.

"You have to see it to believe it, I know."

"And you came here? From there?"

"That's a longer story," she said. "One I fear I don't have time to tell."

Every minute with Clementine was so spontaneous, so freeing, that he didn't think he could bear to watch her go.

"What if I was free? Would you meet me?"

"The men I meet"—she rolled her eyes—"you don't want the association, believe me."

Not at her workplace, he said. New Orleans. Baltimore. Anywhere else might do.

"Ah, we would run away! But what of my daughter? My Elsy? I don't think you'd want the extra worry."

They were playing with each other. Yet he couldn't help believing in the imaginary world they were conjuring together. What else was there for him to hold on to?

"I lost a lot," he said. "Ain't got to tell you that. But my heart's grown with all that pain, I like to think. Always making room for what might come. A daughter would fit that bill real nice. Maybe more than one, even."

Perhaps he was fooling himself, but Clementine appeared to be enjoying the game as much as he was.

"That is the sweetest thing a man has said to me," she told him.

"I got more like that one stored up," he said. "Ain't never had no girl to speak 'em to."

"Except Delpha."

"We saw how that worked out."

She grew oddly stern, her eyes narrow and searching.

"Have you touched a woman before, Prentiss?"

He seized up, pulled into himself, shook his head.

"Just my mama," he said. "Isabelle for a hug."

She looked back at Hackstedde, who was pretending to read his paper a mere few yards from them, yet in that moment the man felt to Prentiss an ocean away. Clementine reached between the bars. She nodded at Prentiss, and he reached forward and curled up her fingers, sealing her hand within his own. It was the softest thing he'd ever felt—nothing compared.

She leaned forward. Her voice was so close it rattled the inside of his head.

"I would go with you," she whispered.

There was a snap, like the sound of a whip striking its target. Hackstedde was folding his paper.

"I'm just overjoyed you two got to reunite," he said. "But visiting hours are over. Time to say your goodbyes."

When Clementine did not move, Hackstedde stared at her unyieldingly. Finally she rose, and the sudden movement pulled Prentiss to his feet as though they were tethered to the same rope.

"You tell the Walkers I'm getting on," he said. "That I'm more than fine."

"I will," she said, then paused a beat, giving him a once-over. "Don't give up hope, you hear? Find your strength and protect it."

"I'm standing here, ain't I?"

She gifted him one last smile.

"Goodbye, Prentiss."

Then she walked to Hackstedde and placed the fruit basket on the table.

"If we're to keep our deal, my cousin is to get any of this fruit whenever he wishes."

"Now we both know that wasn't part of our deal," the sheriff said.

"Then consider it changed."

Hackstedde laced his hands behind his head and leaned back, entertained by the negotiation.

"Tack on a visit. I get four. My choice of girl."

Clementine looked at Prentiss a final time, not in shame, but as if to say: *This is what I will do for you.*

"So be it."

"Good, good." Hackstedde gestured at the door. "You get home safely now. I'm sure there are many men awaiting your arrival."

She went into the night without turning back. Hackstedde spoke more—he always did—but Prentiss heard none of it. He was strangely at peace. He journeyed his way back toward sleep. He thought there was a chance, however slim, that he might wake to Clementine's voice once more. And if that wish was too much to grant, perhaps he might find her in his dreams. But as it happened, he got little rest. With Clementine gone, the reality of his predicament wended its way like a slow freight train toward his cell. And when the next person came through the door of the jail, it was Hackstedde's deputy.

The sheriff reacted like a father proud of a son who had accomplished a task above his station. Tim, quite proud himself, informed him that Judge Ambrose had been delivered to Selby and was lodging across the street. The proceedings could take place first thing in the morning.

"Well!" Hackstedde said, taking off his hat. "If the office had medals, I'd award you one. Quite rightly so."

Tim beamed, and Prentiss was galled that in accomplishing their petty objectives, all rendered to bring about his death, these two men, until recently strangers to each other, had located such a profound sense of achievement.

Hackstedde said he would get some rest and ride to fetch Webler with the good news come morning.

"You stay here," he commanded Tim. "Watch our prisoner for me."

Prentiss shut his eyes once more, and this time exhaustion claimed him. When he came out of his doze, Tim was the only man in the jail. He'd pulled a chair up to Prentiss's cell. The candle on the desk behind the deputy had burned itself down to a nubbin. Gripping a peach from Clementine's basket, he monitored Prentiss with a rapt fervor, his eyes sharp, as though Prentiss might take flight at any second. He took a bite of the peach, and juices oozed from the open wound.

Here, here was a simple man, Prentiss thought. *Did he not see the bars? Why watch over him so intently?* But when he considered what was to come, it seemed not so odd. In all the ways that counted but one, the noose was already tightened fast around Prentiss's neck. A man waiting to die was a show by itself. Tim had just arrived early.

CHAPTER 21

C aleb found his army pistol down in the cellar, wrapped in a quilt, left to languish in the company of his grandfather's hunting rifles. The house was pitched with an enveloping blackness. It was neither night nor morning but rather that long lull of hours between the two, a period of nothingness—one Caleb knew too well. He'd awakened to it often as a boy, half-asleep, transfixed by the way the thudding of his own heartbeat penetrated his thoughts, consumed by the terrible sensation that the rest of the world lay dormant, at peace, while he alone could gain no rest. He'd have done anything to avoid that pit of despair. Tonight he welcomed it.

He left the cellar and moved into the darkness outside. By the time his eyes had adjusted, the cabin was already some distance behind him. Each step felt bound to nothing. Old Ox was no longer home. None of this was. Even the cabin had the air of the unfamiliar. He'd swear to his room being smaller, and the passageway leading to the stairs tighter. It was as though the space, in his absence, had begun to shape itself to the contours of his parents, having forgotten the child who'd wandered off. In his heart, though, he knew the house hadn't shrunk. He'd simply learned how immense the world was. Probably any man who returned to his boyhood would discover the exact same phenomenon.

He was in the fields now. His father's plants were still unassuming, and the fact that they had spent so much time tending to them, with so little to show, was a lesson in perversity. Caleb reached down, felt under the topsoil beneath one of the plants, clasped its winding roots, and gave a tug. He didn't haul them up. That was months away yet. He simply wanted to make contact—to see how far down they descended, and how far up they would have to travel to see the light of day. Anyone could tell you he hadn't been raised a farmer, but the feat astounded him. Small miracles stowed away.

He pulled his hand out of the dirt and sat with his knees bunched to his chest. The pistol was in his waistband, the edge of the hammer pinching his side. With a squint and a bit of imagination, he could discern the cabin. Locus of those night terrors of his childhood. Why had he been forced to cross the gulf between the bedrooms in the dark to wake his parents? Why hadn't his mother, in her celestial understanding, come to *him*? Why hadn't she known the loneliness washing over him in those empty hours? It was selfishness to ask this, he knew, and yet the feeling had never left him. Even now he hoped his mother would walk out to find him in the field and guide him back to his bed. What kind of man felt this way? This cowardice was what had permitted Landry's death. The truth was that there was nothing in him worth saving. He was a disgrace.

He touched the soil again, knowing he would not be present when its bounty was revealed, knowing he would not see the look of subtle delight on his father's face, apparent only in the intensity of his gaze upon the plants, an expression radiant with that distant love he dispensed with such parsimony. After a silence, he would pronounce the peanuts puny, unlikely to be purchased by anyone, before back-tracking and declaring: *They will do.* It was his father's quintessential move: embracing his failures to maintain a sense of ambition. But this life—quiet, respectable, replete with meager rewards—would not be Caleb's. No. His own journey, he was determined, would take him elsewhere, to whatever paltry salvation he might find beyond this place.

He started toward home. The darkness was still almost impenetrable, but he felt one with it, as though he were wading weightlessly through water, and it struck him that his time spent alone, all those long hours in his room with the blinds closed, had conditioned him for this very moment. He entered the cabin and placed his foot on a familiar floorboard, stepping on it like the sole key to a piano, relishing the noise one last time.

Without another pause he went back down to the cellar. He could locate the trunk by scent alone, the wafts of cleaning grease that lingered in the air from decades past, before he was even born. The rifles lay waiting. He slung one over his shoulder, not even certain of if it still shot. His recklessness was of a piece with his frame of mind. What was most important was to keep moving—to follow the urge that had woken him and brought him this far.

The stars were out, small bright chasms that scarred the darkness, yet he did not need them to find his way. Stage Road would do just fine, for he could see the path in his mind already: carrying him through Old Ox, past the quiet square, empty but for a few drunken vagrants; spitting him out at Mayor's Row, right before Wade Webler's mansion. It was not where he meant to end his journey, but it was where he would begin it.

———————

He knew, without knowing, that the Weblers slept soundly. This was another long-held notion of his—born of nothing more than the narrative he'd hatched, years earlier, of what it would be like to sleep beside August for a night, under a white sheet, basking with him in the lambency of the moon; to wriggle an arm free from under his pillow and fasten it, as if guided by a dream, around August's torso, pulling him close, both of them granted permission for their bodies to do as they pleased until morning.

The frame of the dream had never extended beyond August's bedroom. But Caleb had to assume that Wade and Margaret slept with the same peace of mind that possessed their son. He could envision Wade moored to his side of the bed, unstirred by the day that had passed, or the day that would come tomorrow, given over to his rest like a newborn in its crib. And perhaps that was the great ill of the world, that those prone to evil were left untouched by guilt to a degree so vast that they might sleep through a storm, while better men, conscience-stained men, lay awake as though that very storm persisted unyieldingly in the furthest reaches of their soul.

He paused before the mansion, a few feet removed from the hedges, still in sight of August's window. Habit was strong. Yet the urgency of the moment wicked it off him now like a sweat. He forced himself to move through the gate and walked around the side of the home, winding his way past the cistern and on to the stables.

The aisle there was pitch-black. He hadn't been inside the stables for years, and the misremembered place was nothing like his dreams, where candles projected onto the walls the lurid shadows of the horses and the other boys, specters bent on cheering his humiliation. Against that brutal romance, the heightened sense of wonder with which his fantasies were imbued, there was nothing special here. If anything, it was smaller than he recalled, and any majesty it held was obscured by the pungent smell of manure. How flawed his imagination had been in creating so much out of so little! He felt himself being freed from the delusion.

The horses were asleep, save one. He saw it not by its form, which was shrouded by the night, but by the sparkle of its eyes, an incandescence beaming in the darkness. The horse crowded the door of its stall when Caleb drew near, as though expecting him to toss over some feed, or, even better, open the door. He offered his hand and the animal did not shy. Some dimension had been lost as he'd approached, and its eyes were now cloaked rather than alight. The horse was not spooked, to his great relief, though he would expect no less from a Webler horse. Wade's footman was known to break them himself.

Caleb went to the tack room and retrieved a bridle and saddle, then claimed a saddlebag for good measure. He crept into the stall and the horse did not try to bolt, but stood still, flicking its neck as if to say hello. When he placed a hand on its mane a tremor ran through the horse, a skittering wave upon its back, which reminded Caleb of Ridley, and he let his hand rest on the beast for a spell, to ease his way with it, before blowing into its nostrils.

"I need a horse that's gonna move for me," he whispered. "Can you fly?"

It was a buckskin mare, beautiful, although he was not sure it had the talent to lead a pack. There was no way to know until he sat upon her. She was well mannered, and he had her tacked up before he'd even paused to make sure he was still alone. He was nearly ready to lead the mare to the aisleway when footsteps sounded on the floor. He peered out, too frightened to reach for his pistol. But it was merely another horse, resettling itself in the humid air.

"You ready, then?" he whispered.

The escape would need to be clean. He'd have to pull himself up and take off at a clip. He had prepared for disaster—certain that, with his luck, a party of Webler's men would descend upon him the second he approached the stables. Yet here he was: for once, some-how, executing a plan of his own design. The night was before him. He mounted, and the mare huffed loud enough to raise the attention of the other horses. A few rose from their sleep, and he could feel their eyes on his back as he gave the mare a start. They were quiet, though, and soon enough his horse was cantering down the road.

He was halfway to Selby before he realized he would never see the Webler home again. Even with all that had been irreparably damaged in the last several days, he couldn't help imagining—almost hoping—that August might have been at the window, curtains pulled, watching his escape. Likely his disbelief would be too great to lend the sight any credence. He'd tousle his hair, return to bed, and in the morning shake his head at the dream that had felt so real.

———————

The mare gained speed until they were gliding, then outright flying. The road was empty at this forsaken hour, and it wasn't long before he arrived in Selby. The town was smaller and quieter than Old Ox. He was familiar with the design, having traveled through before, and easily spotted the jail, buttressed on one side by the tavern and on the other by a little boxed-off dirt cemetery absent any markings. With the candle inside the jail dimmed and contorted by the windowpane, the place was a fit of shadows—none of them moving, all of them still. He had no idea how many men were inside. A lone horse was tied up out front. As Caleb stepped onto the stoop, a voice called out.

"Sheriff? That you?"

In a spontaneous show of theatrics, Caleb kicked the door open, pulled his pistol from his waistband, and took aim at the first body that appeared at the other end of the sight. It was Tim, the deputy, so shocked and wobbly that he nearly fell over.

"Where's Prentiss?" Caleb asked.

Tim fell back against his desk, squinting in bewilderment.

"You're George's boy?"

"I'll give you one more chance," Caleb said, and, as if in a trance, cocked the hammer on the pistol.

"I ain't but a few feet from you," said a voice.

Turning toward the sound, Caleb caught sight of Prentiss sitting in the dimness of the nearest cell with his legs crossed, as if untroubled by the commotion.

"Keys," Caleb said to Tim. "Now."

Tim reached for his waist and Caleb knew immediately that he was gone if the deputy retrieved a gun, for though he had cocked the hammer, he couldn't bring himself to shoot or even to return fire. His finger went soft on the trigger, and he was surprised to discover that he felt inclined to *welcome* such a resolution. To meet death head-on, in a fit of adventure, of great daring—well, *that* was something worth-while. He would still die with his accomplishments tallying nothing more than being a horse thief, but at least others might hear the rumors of his courage, and in the most selfish of ways, this was enough to deliver a solemn peace to an otherwise fraught moment that had nearly caused him to wet himself for the second time as a man.

But it appeared Tim had other ideas than to open fire. After slapping frantically about his waist, he skipped right past his pistol and went for his pockets, though he failed to furnish anything but air.

"I swear they're around here," he said, a little breathless.

Caleb began to realize that, hard as it was to believe, he might've found a man more nervous than he was.

The deputy's eyes were bulging and a sheet of sweat had formed on his forehead.

"I'm begging you," he said, and raised a trembling finger telling Caleb to pause.

Caleb looked toward Prentiss for some guidance, but confusion dominated his face as well.

"I think the sheriff took them," Tim said, stepping forward. "Please!"

He was writhing, waving Caleb off in a show of defeat, bent over so far in supplication that he was nearly crouching.

"Do as you wish, but no guns," he pleaded. "I can't do guns no more. Please. No more. No more."

Prentiss nodded at Caleb as though it were a directive and Caleb put his gun back in his waistband. He was far more rattled now by the deputy's collapse than by the chance of meeting gunfire and could only pity the man.

"I think you might be in the wrong line of work," Caleb said.

The deputy collected himself enough to stand.

"I loved it back when. I did. But I can't do those guns. The doc said it would go back to normal. But it ain't. It just ain't."

The two men were looking at each other. Tim was still shivering as he wiped his nose with his sleeve. They were about the same age, although Caleb guessed that whatever complications in life he had withstood paled in comparison to Tim's. With the guns removed, the feeling in the room was difficult to decipher. A certain intensity remained. An almost inspired nakedness of emotion. Was he supposed to embrace the deputy now?

"The table," Prentiss said, pointing. "The keys are on the table."

Tim turned, grabbed the keys, and held them out to Caleb, who declined them, gesturing toward the cell.

"You get him," he commanded.

Tim slunk over to the cell and guided the key into the lock. The door yawned under its own iron weight and slowly swung open, and out walked Prentiss.

"The sheriff is bringing Webler back this way at first light. They ain't gonna be pleased when they see this cell empty."

"You tell them I just about put a bullet through your skull," Caleb said, retrieving his pistol from his waistband, "and I'm sure they'll understand why you let him go."

Tim shook his head solemnly, like he'd just heard the saddest of stories.

"Sheriff's got a pony that can ride eight hours and still outpace a thoroughbred in the ninth. It ain't me I'm worried about. It's you."

Prentiss was already at the front door, eager.

Caleb motioned toward the desk with his pistol.

"Go sit down now, Tim. You peek out that door, I promise it's the last thing you'll see in this life."

He walked out, back first, facing the deputy, his gun trained on him once more, and when he closed the door he couldn't help smirking with satisfaction at having delivered such an effortless performance.

"You put the fear of God in that boy," Prentiss said.

"Hopefully it's enough to keep him at that desk."

Caleb stopped at the mare. He looked Prentiss over and took the rifle off his shoulder and put it in his hands. The man had not held one before, that much was clear. He handled it like an ancient scroll, as if a careless touch might crumble it to dust.

"Put that strap on your shoulder," Caleb told him. "I know damn well the last thing either of us wants to do is shoot these things. But if you must, you pull that trigger."

"I know how they work," Prentiss muttered.

Caleb mounted the mare and extended a hand down to pull Prentiss aboard.

"You been on a horse?" he said.

"No," Prentiss said, situating himself on the pillion behind Caleb. "And it'd be just my luck to get out of jail and go and break my neck falling off the thing."

"You can trust me," Caleb said, taking the reins. He meant it as much as he could, enough to turn back and repeat it. "You can, Prentiss. Just hold on to me and don't let go."

Prentiss looked skeptical, but he placed his hands around Caleb's waist and squeezed. They set off fast enough that their voices were silenced by the wind and they were quiet for a spell. In time they adjusted to it, and Prentiss's grip on Caleb loosened as he gave himself over to the cadence of the horse's gait, the rhythm of the gallop.

"Where we headed?" he called out from behind.

"North," Caleb said. "Pass by the farm first. Don't worry, we'll take the back trails."

"Where to then?"

"Wherever we want."

The shadows of the trees and the bushes appeared and disappeared like apparitions in their wake. The sun finally began to rise, and the road was floodlit with its first seeping glow, the essence of something otherworldly, as if the earth itself was dissolving into glittering fragments of light. They didn't see a single soul the entire journey. Not until they reached the cabin, where a candle was lit, illuminating his mother and father at the dining-room table in the twilit dawn, still in their nightwear. Waiting, he liked to think, for his return.

His mother engulfed Prentiss in a hug, letting go only to inspect her son, perhaps unsure if either of them was real, and absolutely bewildered as to how they'd ended up back home.

"I went and got him," Caleb said. Apparent, but somehow necessary to affirm in words.

"I hope you have a better explanation than that," his father said. "Is that your grandfather's rifle Prentiss has?"

Caleb eased his way past his father and made toward the kitchen. There was no time to explain, he said. What was important was that the plan had been successful, at least so far. They just needed some provisions and would be on their way once again.

His mother was following him.

"If you two don't explain yourselves I will lock that door and I assure you no one will be going anywhere."

"Go and do that and you'll only be leading me to the gallows right alongside Prentiss."

Caleb searched the shelf of canned fruit, taking the jars he pleased and placing them on the counter. His mother looked to Prentiss for an answer instead.

"Ma'am, all I know is he came in and told off that deputy and got me out. Says we're going north."

"This is madness," his father said. "Storming off in the night on a suicide mission. I thought you'd lost your mind before, but you have outdone yourself. I applaud your stupidity."

Caleb had found a sack and began stuffing the cans into it.

"I didn't think you'd wake up, to be honest. I thought I might leave a note."

His father rolled his eyes.

"As if there's ever been a single night you snuck out that we didn't keep an eye on you. Now I wish I'd come out and put a stop to it."

Taking in the worried parties before him, Caleb realized just how deranged he was coming off. He put the sack down and pointed at Prentiss.

"Set to die for a crime he did not commit." Then he pointed at himself. "At blame. *At blame.* If he is to hang, then let me hang too. If he is to make it to freedom, then by God I will make that journey with him. Don't tell me neither of you ever wished to start again. I know what regret looks like. This is the better option. The *only* option."

253

His parents stared at each other, seized by the other's glance, apparently unwilling to put into words whatever was in their minds.

"I will make my own path," Caleb said. "And you owe it to Prentiss not to stand in the way of his."

His mother came forward, too choked up at first to offer any words. There was pride in her eyes along with the tears. She picked up the sack from the floor, her hands shaking.

"The brandied peaches were always your favorite," she said. "I canned them only a few days ago. But you should take the pears, too, and the apples. In the cellar there's some salted pork, and I have some sweetbread…"

His father, wearing a blank expression, hadn't stirred from his place in the dining room. What would he say? What might possibly come next?

His mother went to the cellar. She returned with a handful of goods and stuffed the sack to the breaking point. By now she was sniffling with every other word.

Caleb handed the sack to Prentiss and asked if he'd put it in the saddlebag.

Prentiss nodded. "Might as well pack up my things from the barn. Give y'all a moment." And he was gone.

His mother surveyed him, just as she'd done before he went out the door dressed for war. And just as she had then, she put a hand on his chin, felt the bristles—searching, he imagined, for the same softness she'd felt when holding him as a newborn, a softness that was alive only in her memories. She brought his head to her ear.

"You write me," she said. "More than one sentence at a time."

He laughed, and teared up a little.

"Whole letters," he promised. "Explaining everything. Telling all."

"*Yes*," she said, and it was all she could manage.

They broke their embrace and now his father was at his side, his back to him, hands joined behind his backside, staring out the window toward where Stage Road ran.

"I suppose I will take Ridley if I must," he said, as if a favor had been asked of him and this was the concession Caleb would have to accept.

"What?" Caleb asked, perplexed.

"There's not a place on earth I would deign to go without him."

"What are you saying, George?" his mother asked.

"I've traveled the woods of this county since I was a boy. I know them better than anyone. Your best chance at freedom is with me at your side."

"You *despise* travel," Caleb said. "You treat a trip to town as though you've journeyed to the gates of hell. You can't actually want to join us."

"*Want* is a strong word," his father said. "I'm needed, is all." He put a hand on Caleb's shoulder and walked by him.

Caleb thought to protest but knew it would be futile. His father was emboldened by his own stubbornness. There was a maddening insouciance to the way his eyebrows raised in moments like this, how the wrinkles of his face unwove themselves in total commitment to the finality of his conviction. There would be no changing his mind. Caleb wasn't sure his father could change his *own* mind once he'd come to a decision.

"I'll go only as far as the county line. Once I know you're off safely, I'll return home."

"To charges of assisting criminals," Caleb said.

His father waved him off as he began to head upstairs.

"Please. I'll tell them I was on a jaunt in the woods. I'd love to see them prove otherwise."

Caleb looked at his mother for assistance, but she had little to offer.

"I gave up some time ago with him," she said, laughing as she wiped her cheeks.

The sun had risen in full now, and the farm sparkled under its canopy of soft yellows, the barn no longer red but burnt orange, the fields brushed with gold. The effect would wear off as the day progressed, but it was a sight to behold when the morning light poured in. He would miss it dearly.

Just then, Prentiss reappeared. He turned to Caleb's mother—unsure, it seemed, whether it was polite to speak to her in such a condition. "Ma'am," he said.

She gave him another hug, then pulled away quickly. "Your *socks*," she said, heading for the stairs.

The muffled voices of his parents came from behind their bedroom door.

"We'll have a third on our journey," Caleb told Prentiss.

"George?" Prentiss nodded knowingly. "He looks out for his own. Best he can, at least."

His parents descended the stairs, his father dressed no different than he might be for any other day: ragged suspenders over a denim shirt, a sunhat for shade. His father instructed them to meet him out front after he'd fetched the donkey, then split off from his mother without a second look and went out the back door.

His mother approached them. The socks were blue and fine, just as Landry's had been. The white trim wavered a bit, but this only added to their charm.

"They're durable," she said. "Keep them clean, though. Don't go about in dirty socks, Prentiss."

"To commit an act so ugly against a pair of socks so nice—I would never, ma'am." He put a hand to her shoulder in the way a man might to another man, and she responded by placing her own hand on his. Then he pulled away and put the socks in his back pocket. "You take care, ma'am."

"You as well, Prentiss."

Caleb tipped his head toward the door. It was time.

Ridley slunk around the side of the house just as Caleb and Prentiss saddled the mare. His father appeared as calm as ever, yet Caleb couldn't deny the pang of fright in his chest, imagining what was to come. His mother was on the porch, the hem of her gown puddled about her feet. He collected the image and stored it away for moments just like these: when the fear overwhelmed him, and only she would do for relief.

CHAPTER 22

I sabelle napped on George's armchair, enveloped in his scent. When he'd left with Caleb and Prentiss only hours earlier, she was sure she would remain awake, that nothing could bring her back to sleep, yet the minute she curled her legs beneath her she was lost to a dream. She didn't recall the particulars, but it was not set in the cabin, and so it seemed a pleasant retreat from her splintered life. She was disappointed to awaken.

It was already midday, and the sun had brought the house to a low boil. She fried enough eggs for three, although it was less out of appetite than the amount she was used to seeing on the dining-room table. She was famished, yet there was more than half left when she was done, and she collected the pan and tossed the scraps out back for whatever scavenger might want its fill.

There was an almost catastrophic unease that followed breakfast. She felt the need to busy herself and thought she might clean Caleb's room, then remembered that this was unnecessary, seeing as she might never see him again if all things went to plan. This thought then met with the greater loneliness of George's absence, and the convergence of the similar yet distinct tracks of her loss was almost so great she had to sit on her hands just to keep them from trembling. She was there on George's chair again, feeling with her thighs the buttons protruding from the leather, each of them junction points for memories of her husband. He would sit and read so long it began

257

to feel like he was waiting for something to arrive that never came, and his melancholy when he took his glasses off and extinguished his lamp was matched only by the enthusiasm he showed in returning to that spot the very next night.

And the chair was where she'd found him after her attempt to visit Prentiss in jail. George, his glasses pushed to the end of his nose, had put his book down as she walked inside and asked her eagerly if she'd gotten past Hackstedde.

She hadn't known until that moment that she would choose not to disclose her meeting with Clementine. But Clementine's strenuous insistence on the innocence of George's visits forced her to look inward, at her own jealousy, and question why it had to be there at all. What was there to gain, in the sweeping landscape of her marriage, in meddling with the curious (and often mysterious) manners of George's charity? After all, wasn't that why he paid Clementine? The opportunity to give? She'd shaken her head and told George that she wasn't let in to see Prentiss, but that she had been to see Mildred and that the day, to her, still felt very productive.

The trembling that had overtaken her hands continued—it seemed to be reverberating from somewhere outside her—and she looked up and laid eyes on a team of horses trotting toward the cabin. She wasn't scared of whoever was approaching. If anything, she was relieved, knowing they were bound to come. She would rather get it over with.

She went outside and met a wind so frantic she had to steady herself against the porch railing. She recognized almost all of them: Wade Webler, the sheriff and his deputy, Gail Cooley from Morton's plantation. Two others: nondescript men of Caleb's age, though thoroughly hardened, their eyes fastened on her with disdain. One of them was upon a horse and the other had dismounted and was bringing up the rear with a hound.

"A posse?" she called out. "Really, Wade?"

"Check the barn," Wade said to the boy with the hound. "It's where they had him staying." He turned to Isabelle, his eyes sunken in exhaustion. "Where are they?" he asked bluntly.

"Of whom do you speak?"

"*Of whom do I speak.* Isabelle, trust me when I say this. You want no part of the stunt your son has pulled. It's best we get him to safety before he puts other lives beyond his own in harm's way."

"We both know the only person putting lives in danger is *you,* Wade Webler."

The boy with the hound was entering the barn and she hollered for him to stop. To no avail.

"This is *my* property," she said to Sheriff Hackstedde. "I have not given anyone permission to search that barn."

Yet the sheriff was statue-like.

"You're an officer of the law," she went on. "Do your duty."

Buried in his face was an anger that was missing the last time he'd visited her home. "I have suspicions you're harboring a fugitive," he said. "*Fugitives.* So don't you tell me about my duty."

"Bring George out here," Wade said. "I'd like to speak to him about his son."

"George is on a hike," she said, "and I still have no idea what any of you are speaking of. I deserve some answers."

The hound was baying. She could hear the boy talking to it, and she realized the men on horseback were simply waiting, now— enduring her presence as they must. With a few bellowing howls the hound reappeared and led the boy toward the main road.

"Sounds like we got a scent," Hackstedde said, perking up.

"Mrs. Walker," Wade said, "your son committed a foolhardy act last night, holding an officer of the law at gunpoint and freeing a prisoner from his cell. I also have reason to suspect that he's stolen a horse of mine. I'll have more proof once I see him on it. Which, I might add, is the only result that will come of this. He will be found, along with the prisoner, and I will see to it myself, considering the sheriff here has had some trouble managing on his own." Hackstedde looked away when Wade glanced in his direction. "I plan to keep that judge in Selby. And he is ready to act when those boys are brought before him."

The wind soughed again, and all the men were made to hold on to their hats. Isabelle let her hair fly free, whipping in the air about her face.

"You whine as if you're the victim of a crime when we both know quite well what August has done!" she yelled. "You disgust me. As for the rest of you, I can't imagine how you sleep a wink at night knowing you've been stupid enough to go along with this madness. I can't listen to another word of it."

This last part was enough to make Gail clear his throat and speak up.

"It's for the good of the town, Mrs. Walker. I think you might come around when you think about what your son has—"

"Mr. Cooley," Isabelle said, "you've worked those fields over there since I've lived in this cabin and not once have you said a single word I've paid any mind to. I don't plan to start today."

Gail shuddered. Wade's face looked as red as it had after he'd been spit on. The dog was barking maniacally as it headed farther toward the road and Isabelle hoped it would spook the horses enough to throw the men off their saddles.

"Your son is a blight," Wade said, "and the Negro is worse. It's as simple as that. There will be consequences for what your family has wrought. Let that be known here and now."

In classical Wade fashion he had gifted her a declaration so absurdly biblical, so unabashedly histrionic, she could only roll her eyes in disgust.

"If the world was just, Wade Webler, I would say the same about you and yours."

"I'm giving you one last chance to tell me where they've gone off to."

She crossed her arms resolutely and stared him down in stony silence.

"So be it," Wade said. He turned to the man with the dog. "Lead the way."

The men swung their horses round to leave.

"I don't ever want to see you here again," Isabelle said. "I've got a rifle in the cellar and I might not know how to use it, but I can learn."

With his back to her, Wade pulled off his hat to bid farewell.

George and the boys would have a half day's head start. She prayed it was enough.

———————

Two days and nights of peace followed. On the third night, sleeping again on George's chair, as she had since he'd left, she woke with a start at some tenebrous hour—the wind hissing furiously, the house creaking and moaning so loudly that it seemed fit to collapse under its own anguish. She wished to call out, as she often had during the past few days, yet there was no one to call out to. The most immediate humans she knew of were Ted Morton and his family, and if she had it her way it would be a lifetime before she saw any of them again. She considered going upstairs, if only for the change of position, but with George and Caleb and Prentiss still out in the elements, as far as she knew, it felt wrong to give in to a more pleasant sleep. There was no question in her mind that the three of them were dozing somewhere on a rough forest floor and she felt the ongoing urge to commiserate, as though she might thereby somehow lessen their burden.

She knew it was silly but misery felt appropriate under the circumstances. Perhaps she was simply lost to her fatigue—her wits slipping, leading her to odd conclusions and wild flights of fancy. Or maybe there was little practical difference between exhaustion and outright madness. In any case, to ponder it further only kept her motionless on the chair, captive to the darkness and the wind. Since the departure of her husband and son, her hearing had refined itself to an almost inconceivable perception. She could make out even the pecking of the chickens, so pronounced to her that it sounded like ice being chipped off a block. The grasshoppers were gathered in the forest, but their hum carried such that they seemed to be right outside the window, fighting to be let in.

Yet it was an unfamiliar sound that troubled her most. At first she attempted to ignore it, but when that failed, she rose to locate its source. Like twigs snapping, but louder—loud enough to break through the intermittent thrashings of the wind. She went out the back door and listened. It took some time to discern it, but yes, there it was, steady, like the quiet crackle of frying oil. And then a disturbance in the dark sky—a flickering ember disappearing into a cumulous fog of smoke stretching over the forest—told her what it was.

She began to run. She could not see the crops below the hill and she feared what she would find there, knowing already what had happened but still unwilling to believe it. Her breath came ragged and she coughed at the mere sight of the smoke. At the brow of the hill she halted, overtaken and overwhelmed, unable to process the sight before her. The entire peanut field was ablaze. The wind belted it with a fury and the long arms of fire that reached toward the sky waved back and forth in a frenzy and sent out giant plumes of smoke.

Two men on skittering horses patrolled the inferno, torches in hand, galloping about belligerently, then circling back to meet at a safe distance. The damage was so complete that Isabelle could feel her own insides, her very soul, burning up right along with the plants before her. She was both dazzled and horrified by the fanglike shadows of the flames groping toward the trees, claiming all in their path. The men had their faces hidden. They appeared to be arguing, gesturing wildly, and when the fire crept near them, they turned and disappeared into the night.

Her ankles were slick with sweat; her eyes watered from the smoke. *What have you done?* This was all she could say to herself, repeating the words like a refrain as she walked back toward the cabin, lost in a daze. *What have you done?* She was shaken but she wasn't afraid. Of course she was pained by her husband's work being ravaged, his land ruined, but no greater threat would befall her at the cabin. Those men would have needed to look no farther than her weather vane to determine that this was a punishing west wind. It would not bring the fire up the hill. No, it would march in the opposite direction unimpeded, feeding on everything it found. *What have you done?* It would barrel through the tree line along Stage Road itself, devouring first Ted Morton's home, then Henry Pershing's and all that came after. She hoped the riders had gone to warn the others, but judging by its size, and the wind, there would be no stopping their creation regardless. From the cabin it was a stampede of red streaked against the sky. The blaze would reach Old Ox by morning, and the town would have no means sufficient to prevent the coming devastation.

CHAPTER 23

They traveled through the day, then through the start of the night, and when George grew weary he took care to hide his suffering. With daylight things had been easier. They had passed the county line long before sundown, and although the forest there was similar to his own property, with the same animal life, the same trees, it still felt unexplored—another world for him to learn and memorize, each step forward tracked on the map he was drawing in his mind. The creek grew wider the farther north they ventured and the flora turned an exceptional shade of green, with leaves so thick he thought they belonged in a jungle. He'd known the land would grow into something of a bog—he'd heard tell of this from many other travelers who'd left the county this way—but he'd never seen the transformation himself. Caleb informed him that the creek would meet the river in another day's time, and that George had not seen anything so powerful as the water of the rapids. He believed his son, for already everywhere he looked there were unbelievable sights, nominations of splendor put forth by nature and presented with such grandeur he felt a tinge of regret that all he'd needed to do to find a new world of such beauty was to leave town, yet it had taken him a lifetime to make the journey.

When at last they made to rest, deep into the night, he was still juggling the images of the day in his mind and only that distraction was enough to keep him lucid as he rolled out his bedding.

"They'll be looking for a fire," Caleb said. "Best we stay in the dark."

George was already lying down as the boys began to eat.

"George," Prentiss said, and held out a jar of fruit.

George waved it away. "Perhaps when we're up," he said. "It's only a few hours."

For a time he thought of Isabelle—imagined her asleep beside him—but then his mind went blank and he dozed. He woke to a curtain of darkness and rose in a huff. Until his sight settled, the fresh smell of dirt and pine was the only sensation on offer. Then he made out Caleb in the roll next to his. The roll beside Caleb's was empty, and he had to squint to distinguish the silhouette of Prentiss, standing ramrod straight, embedded in the night. He was guarding their campsite with the same scrupulous focus he'd applied to his work back at the farm, and he seemed both perfectly comfortable and perfectly alert, two qualities George could hardly claim for himself in the present circumstance.

He walked over to Prentiss and asked if he'd seen anything.

"Nothing that big," Prentiss said. "I'd have woken you."

The forest was calm, silent save for the occasional dispatch from the dark: a trampled branch, the pitched squeal of a possum.

George pondered the comment for a moment. "That big... Wait, you don't mean the beast?"

"It could venture this far out," Prentiss said.

"You know, I haven't thought of it in days. Not once this trip."

Prentiss eyed him curiously.

"I must not have told you," George went on. "I saw Ezra last week."

With George there to share sentry duty, Prentiss finally relaxed, slumping against the closest tree.

"You know what he said?" George went on. "That I'm too curious. That I never should've been poking around in the woods in the first place the day I found you and Landry. To the contrary, I told him, it must've been some form of destiny, as I venture through those woods all the time and there's nothing to be found but all manners of solitude. Not that I believe in a higher being or what have you, but to come upon two fellows felt like a fitting meeting, bound up in something real, which is quite a foreign concept to me. So here is where we circle back, as I told Ezra then that the only other time I had that feeling was whenever I saw that beast from my bedroom window. I'm not one to share that story—least of all with Ezra—as it leads to a natural skepticism, but I was caught in the throes of sentiment, and it simply poured out of me."

Disregarding his embarrassment, George pressed on with the rest of the story for Prentiss. Ezra had stood before him, he said, listening intently as George related how the beast was exactly the way his father had described it: brooding, sturdy on two legs, ominous but graceful in its movement. Once he'd finished, Ezra had laughed uproariously, doubled over behind his desk, waving George off in seeming derision. Well, George told him, he wasn't the first to disbelieve him.

"It's not that," Ezra said between fits of laughter. And he explained to George, then. How George's father, Benjamin, would wait until night, dress himself up in layers, and put on a show for his son, a practice that he gleefully reported to Ezra, detailing George's reactions come morning, how shocked he appeared at the breakfast table, barely willing to eat.

"It was all in good fun," Ezra said. "He even had that colored girl dress up. I forget her name. The help. But she was nearly as tall as your father and he'd have her go out there when he wasn't up to it. Heavens. Benjamin could be a real comedian. I didn't know you still"—and here, George said, Ezra had to wipe away a tear of laughter—*"still believed it."*

George couldn't imagine his father having done such a thing to him. And to think that Taffy, his only friend, had been complicit made it that much worse. For her to have kept this conspiracy with his father felt like the ultimate betrayal. It wasn't funny at all. Just cruel.

Prentiss seemed embarrassed by the story himself, looking at George with pity, as if Prentiss, too, had been in on the joke all along. But his words indicated otherwise.

"There was a time," he said, "after my mama was gone, when I would sleep on the porch of our cabin waiting for her to come home. When the weather turned and I still wouldn't come in, Landry got so worried, so worked up, he'd try to pick me up and carry me inside. Had to kick and scream to keep him off. Sounds fool-headed, I know—I just couldn't give up hope. I knew her walk, knew her shape, knew the noise of her footsteps. Sometimes I could swear I felt her fingers grabbing my ear from behind, the way she used to when it was too late to be on the porch and I wouldn't listen."

He fidgeted and stared off into the woods.

"I s'pose I'm still looking for her. That's part of why I'm out here running, right? Even if it's a slim chance. I'm still looking, and I'ma keep looking. 'Cause if I ain't got that belief that she's out there somewhere, what's left?"

When George couldn't muster a response, Prentiss filled the silence for him.

"What I'm saying is I believed you all along. Even now. Ain't nobody got a right to say what lives in these woods—or anywhere else, far as that goes. We might not get a say in much, but we got a say in our faith."

"I still believe," George said in a low voice, grateful for the goodwill.

"That's two of us, then."

A thrashing wind swooped upon them and George began to shiver even as it calmed.

"You should go lay down," Prentiss said.

"Stop treating me like a fossil. I can rest on my own accord, thank you."

Prentiss put his hands up in defeat. "Just keeping an eye out for my own. We both know your bedtime. You gon' be good and grouchy come morning at this rate."

"I cannot wait to be rid of you," George said, laughing. "It will be my pleasure to see you off once and for all."

The hint of a smile formed on Prentiss's lips, though he quelled it. The wind sought them once more, unbearably loud this time, an aching susurration seemingly born from the shadows, provoking urgent declarations among the trees, as though there were specters howling from the void. For a while they were at its mercy, and then, just as suddenly, things calmed again.

"I'd like to ask you something," George said. He peered back at his son bundled in his blanket, resting peacefully. "It's a favor. You owe me nothing, of course. Let's make that clear. But perhaps you will grant it to me nonetheless." Fatigue had subdued his voice but he carried on. "My son is…fragile. There's nothing wrong with softness, but the world is a sharp place, if you will. Sometimes I fear for him. And I know there are wrongs, unforgivable wrongs, that you will always see when you look at him, but maybe you might find it in your heart to watch over him for me anyway."

"George—"

"I trust you, Prentiss. If I knew he had you watching over him, even from a distance —"

"You have my word. And you ain't gotta say nothing about it." His tone betrayed no emotion, but the assurance alone brought George great comfort.

"I thank you," he said.

"But I'll ask you one in return," Prentiss said.

"Anything."

"That you get on back to bed."

George met the request with a dismissive laugh yet obliged him.

"What about you?" he called back as he returned to his bedroll.

Prentiss told him he'd wake Caleb to cover the last hour. And then they'd be gone.

George wasn't sure he could sleep through the wind, but when he woke again the skies over the ridge were blue and the horses were making noise to start off. Both the boys were awake, scrubbing the site clean of any markings.

Caleb considered him cautiously. "We're past the county line," he said. "If you want to head home."

George had barely opened his eyes. "Why don't you hand me some of that jerky. I'm hungry."

It was the only answer he would give. They weren't to safety. He wasn't going anywhere until he had ushered them to it.

Strangely, as George grew more exhausted—his hip chafing at the labor of the ride, his hind end sore from sleeping on the ground— he thought less of his own woes and more of his son's. By the time they'd reached their third day of traveling it was as though he was no longer present within his own body but was rather a dim source of supervision. When he hurt he wondered if his son hurt and when he rested he often startled himself awake and wondered if his son's sleep was more peaceful than his own. It felt like the devotion of a mother, and notwithstanding a lifetime of finding such fawning behavior irrational on the part of Isabelle and other women, he was now attuned to it.

Meanwhile they'd ventured farther than he ever thought he would. The landscape continued to startle him, especially the river itself, which obliterated all his preconceived notions of nature's power. It was the breadth of many men and he stopped their caravan for a time just to stand in awe of the rapids, a sight that prompted a fulmination of humility the likes of which he had never known.

"Well, this is just..." But George was too overwhelmed for words and sat down.

They left him alone in his silence, perhaps aware that what he needed, above all else, was some rest. When at last he went to stand, it took both boys to bring him up and he knew then that his excursion was coming to an end. He wouldn't last much longer.

It was nearly night again. The ground grew soft and the heat wet. Limp tree branches hung low enough for their leaves to proffer even deeper shade. In the onrushing dusk he took special notice of a fallen log covered in so many ants that they moved like the current of an inky river, a great swell of black rolling on endlessly. He feared for their mounts upon the unsteady ground but both the mare and Ridley managed just fine, until they came to a deep swale that would call for wading through. They once again looked at George as though this might be the turning point for him.

"You don't have to," Caleb said.

George dismounted. "Lead them by the reins," he said. "Calmly now."

It took them fifteen minutes to work through the depression, waist-deep in mud, the gnats hovering but the animals unfazed and, if anything, happy to greet the intermission, and when they emerged on the other side they were greeted by the noise of another man not of their party. Caleb, already in his stirrups, swung around, rifle at the ready. George shuddered, then turned himself. A stallion stood on the other side of the swale, its tail swishing placidly. Hackstedde slouched upon it with indifference, yet he somehow appeared more vibrant in the wild—his skin golden, eyes alight.

Without a word he unstrapped his saddlebag, removed a pouch of tobacco, and placed it against his saddle horn.

"Boys," he said.

They were all consumed by silence. George stood stock-still as the sheriff unspooled a clod of tobacco, deliberate in his slowness. Then a hand was upon his shoulder. Prentiss helped him aboard Ridley and the three of them set out at a clip. The donkey could not keep pace with the mare but Caleb never let George fall far behind. He could still feel Hackstedde's presence at his back when he finally brought Ridley to a halt. Caleb and Prentiss rode some distance beyond him before they noticed that he'd stopped and were forced to circle back.

"We have to keep moving," Caleb said. "They'll be over that marsh in no time."

The crossing was what had done him in, and with the last light seeping out of the sky, George felt himself giving way to sleep, his body racked by the past few days—by a whole lifetime. He patted

Ridley once, this animal who had been as trustworthy as any man he'd known, then gave his son a faraway smile.

"I believe I am done," he said.

"There's no being *done*," Caleb said. "You saw Hackstedde just as well as I did."

"I'm tired, Caleb."

"You ain't thinking straight," Prentiss said. "Your boy is right. We can't stop this run now."

George dismounted. "I surmise they might make camp before they cross," he said. "They're in no rush. Their pace is steadier than ours, their mounts faster."

"And so you suggest we surrender here?" Caleb said.

George breathed in, paused, then let the breath out. "I believe I have a plan."

They stared at him with impatience. He was hardly unaware of the moment's urgency and yet both times he made to speak his voice failed him. The vicissitudes of the past few hours had been astounding. He knew what was required of him and still he did not possess the means to carry it out. He thought he had shed all of his fears some time ago but he now quivered in apprehension, unable to meet the gaze of his son, who would be either disappointed or relieved by his decision, neither reaction one he could bear.

When he spoke again his voice was thin, but he got the words out.

"You'll go on foot," he said. "And you will leave me here."

There were no stars that night. The forest seemed to observe him from every angle, shimmering eyes beaming from the cavity of a tree, shadows lurching violently in the distance. The whispers of the river and the insects built to a clamor whenever the wind dulled to a hush. He'd fastened a rope between the horse and Ridley and was making his way on his own, leading them both by the reins. The lightest canter was misery-inducing and he had resigned himself to walking.

They had left no trace except the trail of the animals' hooves, but having seen Hackstedde's eyes fixed on the ground at the swale, he knew that was what kept the sheriff on their heels. Out in the swamps the boys would have a day's lead, and without their mounts he felt confident that any hint of their progress would be concealed by the water. His only function now was that of a decoy, and he walked endlessly, his body burning up, his shirt soused in sweat.

He grew used to the voices rising over the noise of the night. Whether they were within his mind or without he couldn't tell, nor could he distinguish what they were attempting to tell him. He chose to believe they were no more than instructions to keep marching, empty babble to occupy his mind. He thought of the Indians who spoke to the trees and to the spirits and yet even as his senses offered evidence to the contrary, he could only protest it as superstition. His feet had gone numb and his tongue was thick with thirst. His son had insisted on giving him his pistol and he had the thought to pull it out now at some looming, unknowable danger, then changed his mind. A garish haze had invaded the night sky and the moon was branded red. Something was amiss yet what that might be was beyond him.

A labyrinth of ferns led him toward an obscure corridor of the forest and even at the resistance of the horse and donkey he followed the path. He could hardly see past his own body and when he reached his hand out to feel his way forward he touched coarse flesh of a certain size and make and it immediately registered as belonging to his own father. He stopped more out of anger than fear.

"You leave me be," he said.

The horse halted and yet the pressure came not through the reins but as a slight grip on his shoulder and once again he pulled away from it.

"I will go my own way," he said.

The ground became a soggy morass and he figured he'd somehow gotten himself turned around back in the direction of the swamps. He was ready to give up. His body was undone. He dropped the reins and fell to his knees in submission—and then a shadow moved, the kind of flicker in the corner of the eye that is gone once you look closer, and yet the thing before him was unmistakably there, unhidden. He could not rise, but had he tried he would have failed to meet its height; the beast, uncrushed by the density of the darkness, roused to stand, was double his size. Its chest was armored by a thick mane darker than the night itself and its milky eyes showed out from its skull like coins of moonlight reflected off a pond.

George thought his heart might burst in ecstasy. The beast stood motionlessly and stared at him with no aura of threat or danger between them and George suddenly had great confidence that the beast had laid eyes on him before—indeed (for he was certain now), it had been watching over him for years, and only now had he been privileged enough to glimpse its true nature, and what a rapturous joy it was, enough to bring a man to his knees were he not already there.

"Might you come closer?" he begged.

There was nothing he wanted more than to get a better look at the very thing that had eluded him for a lifetime, for in the presence of the beast his doubts washed away, his convictions grew in clarity, his spirits rose. So energizing was the sight that it brought him to his feet once more. His legs wobbled, and he wiped the mud from them. He stepped forward carefully. Never did the beast waver. It stood so still, in such peace, such stoic grace, that its face blended into the red gypsum haze that had overtaken the sky, and its chest began to fade into the cavernous blackness of the night; with panicked despair George reached out to touch the beast before it disappeared entirely, yet all he felt was an absence, and all that was visible before his eyes were his own hands. Never had he felt so confused, so unsure of his surroundings, and he began to spin in circles.

"Ridley!" he pleaded. "Do you hear my voice? Come find me. Ridley!"

The darkness was resolute in its stillness. Ridley was gone. He was accompanied by only the wind, which was so forceful now that it managed to transport him to the ground—and calm enough in its whispers to put him to sleep.

That night his mind cycled through the previous day with torturous repetition. He woke more than once, realizing where he was yet paralyzed by a passing dream, his body unable to rejoin the waking world. He felt cocooned within himself and the only thing that pulled him free from the grasp of sleep was the strong, reliable urge to urinate. He raised himself to a seated position, breathing calmly, happy to see the burgeoning daylight.

He felt fevered and removed his shirt, then pissed where he stood. A look around told him that he had (as he'd guessed) circled back to the swamps. The temperature was surprisingly cool, the heat from the night having sheared itself from the morning sky in a thick gray mist that ran on far enough to mask the distance beyond him.

The greatest relief was finding Ridley and the horse before him, still roped to each other, both of them idling quietly. It took no time to convince himself that the horse—young, restless, and excitable— had probably tried to run off, yet Ridley, dear Ridley, was too loyal to do so and had held the mare at bay, waiting for George to rise from his slumber. He was embarrassed by his conduct the night before and approached the animals with his head held low.

The sky was still concealed in smoke, the sun still glowing red, and he wondered what hell had descended upon the world. Once he was oriented, he took a jar of Isabelle's peaches from the horse's saddlebag. He was deathly tired, his skin pallid, his face gaunt, and he contemplated how much longer he could last. Would even the ride home be too much? He'd never missed a soul when he was on one of his jaunts in the woods but he missed his wife dearly now and could not shake the fear that Caleb and Prentiss had found harm somewhere—that his plan had failed them.

He could barely stomach the peaches.

"What will we do?" he said to Ridley.

Considering how little energy he had left, he didn't know if he should continue the plan to mislead Hackstedde or if he should instead begin home. But soon he was robbed of the choice altogether. He first thought the noise was his mind playing tricks upon him once more, but when the horse's ears flicked forward and Ridley turned toward the sound, he knew it was real.

There was a happiness that swept over him on a carnal level, the prospect of survival, the company of other humans after such a trying evening. Yet the relief was dashed when he spotted Wade Webler riding behind Hackstedde and Gail Cooley, along with the deputy and two young men, one with a hound. The six of them drifted leisurely into his ambit, and his only comfort was that they had found him and not the boys.

The sun bled a dark crimson at their backs. They halted before him and Wade came up to the front of the pack once he saw it was only one man alone.

"George," he said, "I must venture to ask how a man so old and so lazy as you managed to end up this far from Old Ox. With, I might add, one of my most prized horses."

George hobbled forward to meet them. It felt like he'd forgotten how to speak and he stood there in a trancelike silence.

Wade appeared downright triumphant. He sat stout on his horse, basking in the moment.

"Look at yourself," said Wade. "Absolutely beaten. With only three days' riding. The word *pathetic* comes to mind, but I'd hate to be so generous."

There was a time when the words would have rankled him, but he was no longer that same person, and whatever harm Wade wished to cause had already been self-imposed many times over by George himself. Besides, this man pontificating before his underlings like some cooing toddler was hardly the all-powerful potentate he imagined himself to be. It was probably the first time he'd ever looked upon Wade without even a hint of hatred, knowing how dire was his need for revenge compared with the insignificance of the trespass that had occasioned the man's entire expedition. George tried to listen as he went on—composing a metaphor about how he'd taken leave of work to come to the woods and bag a young buck, not a fat sow like George, insisting that he tell them where Prentiss and Caleb had gone off to—but he could think only of how petulant Wade had become. A father, a landowner, supposedly the town's most influential personage, capable of bringing even Union generals to heel, and yet at heart a scared little boy, too proud to shrug off a little spit to the face. George pitied him—thoroughly and totally—and he had no urge to argue, to play the role Wade needed him to fill.

"Speak up." It was Hackstedde now, who appeared as fed up with Wade's speech as George was. "Just tell us where the colored boy is so we can end this."

George gestured toward the horse—his eyes still on Wade—and found his voice.

"I have your property. What do we say you take back what's yours, charge me for any crimes done, and let this go?"

When his words met silence, he offered them once more, begging this time.

"*Let it go, Wade.* You want more land? Why don't I sign mine over to you. You want justice? Allow me to hang. You can even keep the bag off my head and watch me writhe, knowing it was you who brought about my agony. That's what you seek, is it not? Retribution? Consider it yours. Just let it go."

Everyone looked toward Webler for some concession, yet he merely shook his head.

"I've promised many good folks in the county a nigger to be hanged. I believe I'll have him."

So there would be no satisfying Wade without Prentiss. The chieftain of Old Ox had dreamed up some threat to his empire, to his people, and had placed the burden on Prentiss and Prentiss alone; he was a man in crisis, and reason had no place in the conversation. Words would not deter him. George could only sigh. Without any fuss he pulled his son's pistol from his waistband and held it out limply with both hands.

The men protested with a roar before drawing their own guns, all but Gail, who whirled his horse and cowered at the back, and the deputy, who screamed out that everyone needed to calm down, lest things spiral further, then joined Gail at the back himself. That left the two young men George didn't know, who had yet to speak a word, flanking Wade and the sheriff.

"Put it down," Wade said, holding forth his own pistol. "You don't even know how to shoot that damn thing."

There was some truth to this. The last time George had pulled a trigger he was a boy, hunting with his father, and even then he hadn't enjoyed the brutal tug of the hammer, or the way the cry of the scattergun obliterated the calm of the afternoon. But he would protect the boys' passage at all costs, and if Wade proved as unrelenting as his posturing suggested, George would take a shot at him. He had never been so sure of anything in his life.

"I want you to arrest me," George said. "Reclaim your horse, turn from here, and take me to Selby to be charged with whatever crimes you see fit."

Hackstedde had his gun perched upon his saddle horn, so lackadaisical it was as if he didn't have the energy to hold it steady himself.

"Listen to Wade," he said. "Consider this your only warning."

"*Put it down,*" Wade repeated. "I promised my son no harm would come to you or Caleb. I plan to honor that. Don't be difficult, George. Just this once."

"What if it was August?" George said. "You'd do the same. You would, Wade."

He felt no fear. In his mind he was a world away, back home on his porch with a glass of lemonade, the barn before him, the brothers sleeping there, and Caleb inside at the dining-room table, lost in conversation with his mother. Things were right again. So right.

A pistol spoke.

The men looked about at one another in confusion until the smoke floated off the end of Hackstedde's gun barrel.

"I gave the man his warning," he said casually. "That's how that works."

George inspected himself, as there was no pain, his body having gone numb. Finally, after a span of a few long seconds, a slow-burning heat spread through his leg, rising to a temperature so great that he thought the whole limb might be on fire. He crumpled to the ground and blood trickled and then poured from the wound and by the time the men had dismounted he was already resigning himself to a slow death at the hands of this corpulent sheriff.

"Goddamn it!" Wade said. He took off his hat and smacked Hackstedde with the brim repeatedly. "He wasn't going to shoot!"

"He was aiming like he was," Hackstedde said. "You all saw as much."

The others were horror-struck.

Only Wade had the nerve to approach George himself. He jogged over, still furious.

"Goddamn you too, George!"

He leaned down and repeated the same treatment he'd given Hackstedde, beating his hat against George's shoulder, though more lightly, whether in anger or sorrow or frustration or perhaps some combination of all three.

"Stop," George managed to croak. "Please."

The man was right upon him, a fear in his eyes—fear in the eyes of them both, George was sure—and they looked at each other as if with the realization of a misunderstanding that had gone too far and yet was now beyond fixing.

"I'm dying," George said.

"It's only your thigh," Wade said. "You'll be up and jabbering nonsense in no time." He turned to the others. "One of you cowards get off your ass and bring me something to tie off this leg. Now."

It felt to George as though the tendons in his leg had coiled like a wet rag twisted dry. He could sense nothing save the heat pouring off him in waves—the conviction, radiating through him, that this was the end. The sheer panic of his own death. And it was a true panic, like none he had ever met. He had no sense of comfort, no sense of closure. Only fear.

Wade was ripping off a piece of his own shirt and George reached out and clung to his forearm in terror. "What will you tell Isabelle?"

"George."

"Will you capture the boys? Tell me you won't. Tell me you'll leave them be."

"George, I'm busy saving your goddamn life! Quit it!"

Hackstedde loomed over them in shadow. He lit a cigarette.

"That's bleeding heavy."

"Wade," George said, his voice fading. "Tell me." His grip on Wade's arm loosened.

"Try to stay awake for me," Wade said. "Can you do that? George? Answer me."

His head sank into the ground, the soil soft and cool, a sensation that couldn't have been more welcome, for it brought him back home once more. Back to his own bed, swaddled under fresh sheets, with the night breaking over him as he descended toward sleep.

CHAPTER 24

I t would be described to Isabelle many times over, those first few hours when the fire ravaged Old Ox—told so often, by so many people—that she could piece together the entire event without having been present herself. A stable was the first to fall, after which the blaze stampeded through the square as though driven by the Four Horsemen themselves. Dirt wagons sat before each home and families who had been told repeatedly by the fire warden to be prepared with their water buckets shrugged off the instruction in favor of saving their possessions. There were the terrified cries of children and women, cries of glass shattering as storefronts fell, and cries of penned-up livestock that whirled about in a frenzy and died without mercy. The old and the sick who could not find their way to safety met the same fate as the animals, their lifeless arms hanging limply from the windows of burning buildings until the smoke clouded them from view. Braver men, leather buckets in hand, along with soldiers armed as though for battle, stood before the approaching flames with admirable intentions yet trembled in fear and eventually fled with all the rest.

Some said the whole town would have burned, with nary a soul left alive to see it fall, had it not been for a single person. Ray Bittle, on horseback, galloped through town with the alacrity of ten men, riding so fast he had to hold his hat down atop his head. He yelled at all who made to flee, making a great show of circling the men in particular.

"Cowards!" he screamed. "Vile cowards. Defend your home. Defend your town!"

Until the fire had made it to town, it was difficult to find a single individual who could remember seeing him awake, let alone speak, his spirit roused in the manner of a long-dormant geyser that had suddenly revived itself. He spewed forth vitriol with such animation that all who looked on could do nothing but stand in amazement, their flight arrested by the man's hysterics. In short order he energized them through the same passion with which he'd shamed them, and all who heard his pleas were unwilling to abandon the very place that had been left to burn so many times before.

Not that it worked. The bucket brigade was laughably futile, and the participants finally ran off, comforted by the attempt at bravery (at least they could tell the others they'd tried). The real hero, many claimed, was not Ray Bittle but the fire warden, who saved the latter portion of town with his decision to destroy Roth's Lumber Mill and Mr. Rainey's Meats and clear them out as a natural firebreak to arrest the spreading flames. With the fire stunted, the brigades from Selby and Campton arrived, making three hose carts in all. They fought the blaze for an hour and yet it still took the reinforcement of a dying wind to bring the chaos to a sudden halt. The town grew so silent as night turned to morning that the destruction felt absolute, but chatter resumed as citizens picked up the pieces and returned to their homes; oddly enough, a relief had already set in that, come what may, the sun would rise come dawn. The world would carry on and they would be there to see to it.

The next day, children ran the town. Families were so immersed in taking stock of their losses at home (with the council of the town penned up in the church discussing how to rebuild) that they had not the capacity to attend to their stores. Owners sent their children to watch for looters, and so the sight to any newcomer was that of young boys and girls, soot-colored and eager with energy, milling inside the shops and calling out to one another around the square, informing the others of what had been lost as though caught up in a competition.

Brigadier General Glass organized a cleanup crew of soldiers and yet no one would allow his men into the charred remains of their shops. The state of things was so dismal that he feared the sort of chaos that greets an apocalypse. There were whispers of revolt. He and his men braced against the possibility of looters overrunning the schoolhouse and stripping the soldiers of their weapons. He was holed up there, cowed by the total destruction of the town placed in his charge, and couldn't be roused from the stupor induced by his failure.

These were the conditions that met the federal agents sent by the military governor. They arrived with no fanfare and no warning, a cavalry of black and white men riding as one, in fresh blues and heavy boots, with a confident bounce to their gallop that verged on the arrogant. Behind them on a smaller pony rode a petite man wearing round glasses and a suit that was neither cheap nor fine. He dismounted first and asked a small girl what had become of the town and where he might find Glass. He walked the rest of the way to the schoolhouse, leading his cavalrymen, nodding to each child in his path, pleasant in every interaction. He was in the schoolhouse only a short while before he left it alone, composed as ever, and made his way to the church. There he and the cavalrymen were received with silence and dubiety, as all those seated craned their necks to watch him make his way to the altar, where he introduced himself to the councilmen as the Secretary of the Freedmen's Bureau, sent to assess the town in its conformity to the rule of law as enacted by the United States of America. There were gasps and groans—had they not endured enough?—but the cavalrymen, their rifles at their hips, ensured a climate of civility.

The councilmen demanded emergency assistance in such dire times, lamenting that Glass had let them down by never having enough stock to feed more than the poorest, the neediest, among whose ranks they would all find themselves in the wake of the fire. This demand then turned into passionate fulmination against the Union, which, according to everyone present, had forgotten a stitch in its fabric, a town that deserved more and had been left to smolder under the watch of an incompetent general. The Secretary smiled as these men went on, and when they were finished, he stepped up to speak. All citizens could claim rations that were only a day away, he said. They would receive the assistance they sought as well, as much as their country might give, much more in fact than Glass had been able to offer. All that was required of them was the reading out of an oath. Each citizen would have the opportunity to make the pledge. They would form a line and recite it in full:

I do solemnly swear, in presence of Almighty God, that I will faithfully support, protect and defend the Constitution of the United States and the Union of the States thereunder, and that I will, in like manner, abide by and faithfully support all Laws and Proclamations which have been made during the existing Rebellion with reference to the Emancipation of Slaves—So help me God.

One man threw a crumpled piece of paper at the Secretary (although it landed short). Another stood up screaming of traitors and scallywags before departing. Yet by then people were queuing, the women first, many of them holding their children, followed by their husbands. They went one by one, speaking clearly as the Secretary recorded their names and handed them a slip of paper to document their vow. Afterward they lingered outside. The sky was gray and dim and the fire was still fresh in their minds; the words they'd uttered moments before felt empty, part of the odd daze of everything. What did it matter if they said them? Were they not already under Union rule? It was just some words. Scribbles on parchment. Nothing. Nothing at all. And when they departed, even the memory itself began to fade away.

The first to see her, to share the story, was Mildred, who visited her that same afternoon, having attended the meeting at the church with her sons. Isabelle had never seen her so flustered—so red in the face she looked like she'd fought the fire herself. Thankfully, Mildred's home, which lay beyond the lumberyard, had never been in the line of danger. She'd done nothing more than sit on her veranda, anxious for it all to end.

Isabelle assured her anxious friend that she was perfectly fine.

"But your land is not," Mildred said. "And it could've been far worse. To have you out here all alone."

They were sitting at the dining-room table. The windows were closed to keep out the ash-strewn air and shuttered to conceal the destruction outside. She estimated the fire had consumed a good twenty acres. It had taken a straight line from George's crops and had scorched down the road, just as she'd imagined. All the trees along Stage Road (including her own) had been burnt naked, many of them having fallen altogether, nor had the conflagration spared the grand homes that flanked the road.

Neither of the women drank the tea in front of them. They seemed to have lost even the wherewithal to comfort each other, an ability that had never before eluded them.

"I'm healthy, Mildred. My house is intact. And you did the right thing by staying home. God forbid you rode out here and got caught in that wretched fire."

Mildred's eyes did not leave the saucer before her when she spoke.

"George will be back," she said. "I have no doubt of that."

Isabelle nodded vacantly. "Yes."

"I wish there was more I could do. I feel like a terrible friend."

"You're always looking to help but sometimes there's nothing to be done. Not here, at least. Perhaps in town. Bring me back another story. A bit of gossip. That will be sufficient."

"The boys are helping out in the square. I plan to help myself, however I can."

"Do that," Isabelle said. "They need individuals like you. People who know how to manage things."

"I'll come back more often. We'll clear those fields together, return them to life. Whatever needs to be done will be done. You won't be left alone out here."

Isabelle couldn't muster the energy to protest. The morning in her friend's company was the only respite she'd had from her own thoughts since George and Caleb's departure, and there was nothing more she might want than for her to return, whether she brought another story or not.

Mildred stood and put on her gloves, while Isabelle remained seated.

"Might you do me a small favor?" Isabelle asked. "I would be so grateful if you could send a telegram to my brother. Telling him I'm okay. That he might perhaps come visit." The younger sister in her recoiled at the weakness of needing Silas, but it didn't diminish her desire to see him.

"I'm not sure you understand," Mildred told her. "The post office is an ash heap."

"Right. Of course." Isabelle thought for a moment. "Then do me this much. See if Clementine and her daughter fared all right? That they are well."

Her friend evinced an air of suspicion about whatever this con-nection to Clementine might mean, but Isabelle knew she would not be denied the request in the present circumstances.

"As you wish," Mildred said.

Isabelle thanked her, shading her eyes as the door opened to dusty sunlight that swallowed Mildred on her way out.

———————

The body grew accustomed to touch, used to conversation, and when it was gone the loss manifested itself in what Isabelle could only register as a mounting pressure, an itching wound, located in no one location but rather across her entire person. Mildred's presence had helped, but the effects wore off like weak medication. Soon she returned to the same routines of isolation, knitting with no result in mind, taking stock of the cellar knowing it didn't matter what she found there. Sometimes she busied herself to the point of delirium, snapping out of it only to realize ten minutes had passed, or an hour. Other times she would sit still, an image in her mind of an infant reaching out from the cradle, a single plump hand searching for its creator, seeking comfort, and how different really was she from that child?

She napped, having been up all night for the second night in a row, and woke to find daylight still burdening the blinds. There was a knock on the door. She realized it was the sound that had woken her. How had she not heard someone coming up the lane? How could she have allowed herself to fall asleep? She sprang up and straightened her dress before approaching the door. There was no time to grow worried or frightened. When she opened the door, the air, thick with the accumulated heat of the day, hit her like an open palm.

"Isabelle…" Wade Webler had his hat in hand.

She'd never known him to fail in meeting someone else's gaze but he couldn't even put eyes on her. So few things could bring a man like him to look down at a woman's feet.

"Tell me," she said.

He hesitated further.

"I don't know what got into him. He just pulled that pistol out…"

She put her hand to her mouth, then to her chest, as if unsure which part of her might break first and need tending to.

Wade was clearly broken, too. Hackstedde, whom she had until now barely registered, moseyed up to his side, taking his time. He managed to tell her what had happened, with a measured steadiness she both resented and appreciated.

"He's not dead," Hackstedde reassured her, "although he seemed to think the end was inevitable. Can't blame him. It bled hard, but it was just a shot to the thigh. Made sure to get him back before things got too dire."

A surge of relief washed over her. She was looking at the man who'd shot her husband, and yet she had the urge to thank the sheriff for saving the very life he'd put in danger.

"We got him down there with Doctor Dover. You can see him when you please."

She was holding her breath now. "And the boys. What of the boys?"

"Right," Hackstedde said casually. "Those boys whose whereabouts you had no idea of. Well, a few of us turned back with Wade to get George home. The others who kept on ran into a man hunting hog. Told them Old Ox was on fire. They caught back up with us with the news and they were a bit more eager to see to their homes than to the fugitives. So we let that go."

He shrugged, and never had an act so minor meant so much.

"All I can tell you is that they're not in my possession. Now, if you'll excuse me, I best go see to the town's safety. People to protect and whatnot."

She watched him turn and go off, racked by the news, her body nothing more than a trembling collection of parts. Wade was still silent before her. His face was shaded by his hat, which he'd replaced on his head during Hackstedde's monologue, and eyed her from under its brim with great remorse.

"I'm sorry," he said. "I suppose I haven't said that. The situation seemed to escape my control. Lost a handle on things."

He looked out at the charred land then. The sky was a shade of mud and the ground beneath it burnt to a black crisp.

"And not only for George," he said. "I fear that everything is gone."

The smell of days of riding clung to the man, and the need to retch overwhelmed her. Her body was constricting under the challenge of tolerating his presence any longer—her fingers clenched, her throat latching shut against her will. A moment passed where she focused all her energy on calming herself, and then she managed to address him one last time.

"Go see to your family," she said. "And don't hide this pain, either. I want you to carry what you've done. But as far as I'm concerned, we're never to speak again." He made to utter another word, another sentence, but she wouldn't have it. "I told you to leave, Wade."

Finally, with this, he obeyed.

She stood stiffly on the porch, and when things settled, her eyes landed on Ridley, left in their wake without even a mention. The donkey was so bonded with her husband that her chest seized at the sight of the creature. She walked to greet him, grabbed him by the reins, and guided him to his stable.

"We'll go get him once I'm dressed," she said. "No need to worry. You just eat a bit."

She put a hand on his flank, and there in the privacy of the stable, in the confidence of only the donkey, she collapsed under the weight of her relief, which mingled with her sorrow to wreck her completely, until she sat in the hay with her head against her knees, soaking her dress with her tears. The donkey seemed not to notice and there was a comfort in his indifference, the way he carried on eating as though the world had not changed on them forever. She would get it out now. All of it. And then she would retrieve her husband.

———————

The leg was already gone when she arrived. He lay asleep before her, shapeless under the bedsheets. She sat beside him and took his hand and turned to ask Doctor Dover when George would wake.

"I'd give it an hour," the doctor said. He informed her that he'd finished up the amputation that morning. The leg had gotten infected in the woods, he told her. It could've killed him. Still might.

In sleep George's face lost its hardness and grew round, almost cherubic, and it seemed wrong somehow for this unguarded innocence to be on display in front of a doctor neither of them knew beyond his name.

"He fought with me," Dover said. "Said he'd rather die than lose it. Nothing I haven't heard from the soldiers, though, bless their hearts."

"What did you tell him?"

"That life carries on." The doctor was young, slim, his sleeves rolled to the elbow. "We'll have him on crutches shortly. We can get him fitted for a prosthetic. They send pamphlets all the time. Good models."

George was in private quarters now. At first he'd been placed in the general infirmary among the other sick, and Isabelle had decided to pay for this room. The privilege afforded them some peace and quiet, but only marginally. Even the hallways were full of bodies, those who'd been burnt the day before slumped against the walls and still awaiting treatment, pleading for the attention of harried nurses. Hearing their moans, Isabelle hoped it wasn't the money she'd paid that allowed the doctor to focus on George first, but she put the concern out of mind in the belief that the others would be attended to in due time.

"Well, I'll leave you two," the doctor said. "It's been a busy day. Call on me if he wakes."

She ran her hand through George's hair, watched his stomach rise as he breathed in and listened to him exhale, no differently from when he slept at home. Given all that had happened, that bit—that familiarity—troubled her as much as it soothed her. "We'll be fine," she said. "I'll let you know if anything changes."

———

He came to in fits. It took two days in all. He was not himself and lashed out at the strangeness of the hospital, at the foreign bed, the foreign doctor, the nurse who dared to see him unclothed as she changed his bandages.

When he was at last truly lucid, Isabelle sat up in her chair, impassioned by his waking, and looked upon him ardently. Yet there was only fear in his eyes, which searched the room for something unseen.

"Take me home," he said. "Please."

But the doctor was still concerned about the infection and wouldn't hear of it. So George stayed through the night, with Isabelle at his bedside, lending an ear to his moans of agony, though she could aid him with nothing more than words of comfort. At some late hour, when even the noisiest patients were asleep, she woke to the sound of his crying, and held his hand with such intensity that the firmness seemed to provide him the courage to quiet down.

A faucet, rusted crimson, was perched above them, extending down from the ceiling, dripping in rhythm with the passing seconds. The whitewashed walls carried a tint of yellow, which led Isabelle to believe that something noxious pervaded the building and took residence around them. Although the night had been difficult, she felt like it had forged her place as George's ward, his protector. Yet he wailed and beat the bed like a child when they wished to bathe him, demanding that Isabelle leave the room.

"George, how many times have I seen you bathe?"

"Get her out!" he commanded the attendant. "She won't see me like this!"

And so she stepped out of the room. When she returned, it was to more pleading that she take him home.

"I have asked so little of you," he said, which was of course untrue, but who was she to protest under the circumstances? "All I desire is my cabin. My own bed."

What he wanted was dignity, and she could not deliver it. As far as George was concerned, no one should see him compromised like this. Ezra had come to visit but George had refused him, same with Mildred.

The food was the final embarrassment. When he refused to eat, they tried to spoon-feed him porridge under the pretense that his stomach was sensitive, and yet after acceding to a bite, he spit it out upon his chin, oats sputtering onto the blankets. The attendant flinched and pulled back from the bed and Isabelle reached over to clean him.

"And now they feed me gruel! I won't stand for it."

"George, please."

"No more. I would rather die here and now than submit to this torture. I will end things myself."

She couldn't believe he had so much anger stored away. He was no longer her husband but a man possessed, and when he pointed at the attendant—demanding that she taste the food herself, humiliating her for not knowing the proper application of salt—Isabelle could stand no more.

"Please leave us," she said to the attendant. She was a young girl in training, who didn't deserve such treatment, and she happily excused herself, shutting the door as she left.

"George," Isabelle said.

He turned to her, his eyes frantic.

"I must return home."

"George."

"I can't *stand* these people, the smell of the alcohol and the cries of the children. I'm so tired, Isabelle…"

"It's only a hospital. We can manage this."

"It's hell. I will crawl if I must. I need only arms for that."

She was utterly exhausted, pained from sitting for so long, and she had hardly eaten in days. She took his hands. Now that he'd been bathed, the softness had returned, and it brought her great comfort, even as he conducted himself so terribly, to hold them in her own.

"You'll let them care for you?" she said. "If I was to bring in a nurse?"

"For what? You have done fine all these years on your own."

"And if I have to change you, George? And give you medicine, and turn you in bed?"

He stared ahead defiantly.

"I will have my own food," he said. "And my bed. When I am propped up I will see the walnut trees out the window, and at night you will fetch my books from the shelf. Won't you?"

She put her head on his chest, knowing, now, that what he truly sought were the comforts of home, during what might prove to be his last days.

"I will," she said. "If that's what you desire."

"It is," he pleaded. "It's all I want."

She told him she would return the next day, and promised to bring him home then.

CHAPTER 25

Ezra's shop had not survived the fire, but Isabelle found him at his home. He and his wife still lived in the same two-story cottage they had raised their boys in, although they were alone there, now. They met the standards of the neighborhood but there was no grandiosity to the place, and in choosing its dully brown exterior, the simplistic walkway with no place for a carriage, they had always seemed more determined to blend in than stand out.

She knocked and Ezra's wife, Alice, answered the door. They had spoken perhaps twice in Isabelle's whole life, yet she appeared not only to know Isabelle but to be expecting her.

"Come, come. Out of the smoke." She waved Isabelle in and offered her tea, which Isabelle declined. "A biscuit, then?"

Isabelle was ready to refuse this as well, but her hunger got the best of her and she accepted.

"He's in his study," Alice said, wandering toward the kitchen.

"Is he holding up?"

"We've been through many trials. A fire? Nothing. Nothing."

She returned with the tea that Isabelle had not wanted along with a biscuit besides and gestured for her to sit on the couch. The parlor was unlike her own, the cleanliness born not of upkeep but of a seeming lack of use. The cushion beneath her barely moved under her weight, and the fruit on the table looked so perfectly ripe it was fit to be painted in a still life.

"And you?" Alice asked. "I cannot imagine your pain."

Alice had the most durable features Isabelle had ever laid eyes on. There was a rustic element to them, skin like leather, a cauldron of energy underneath, hidden but ever present.

"It's difficult to discuss," Isabelle said.

"No need to confide in me. Why don't I let Ezra know you've finally arrived?"

"*Finally?* Was he expecting me?"

But Alice was already off toward the hallway, her dress trailing her. She returned promptly.

"He'll see you," she said.

Ezra's study was smaller than George's and less busy. There was no wallpaper, and the only print on the wall was a nautical map of some ancient city—something, Isabelle guessed, that had no connection to Ezra himself. An assistant was stacking documents into boxes and checking items off a list. Ezra, seated beside the window, was watching the boy with a focused intensity, and when Isabelle entered, he told the assistant to take a break and return later.

"Sit," he told Isabelle.

It had been only a day since she was at George's bedside, and thinking of those hours spent beside him, his constant pleading and endless anger, nearly made her shudder.

"I've been sitting so long," she said, "I believe I'd rather stand."

"Then stand. Whatever pleases you."

The room smelled of sweet perfume, and Ezra must have seen her nose pinch at the cloying aroma.

"It is my wife's fragrance," he said. "I could not stand the pungency of the smoke outside so I cloaked the place in other smells—though I have some regrets now, as it does linger."

She registered the lavender now. Probably a fine mix, if applied in small doses.

"Well, if your study smelled at all like George's, no doubt such a cleansing might improve things."

"Perhaps that will be the result. I will let you know when I return."

"And where are you off to, if it's not impertinent to ask?"

She glanced at the half-filled boxes, then back at Ezra.

He would be going on a bit of a tour, he said. Not an easy feat for a man of his age, but he needed to check in on his sons' shops to ensure they were maintaining his standards. With his own being rebuilt, there was no better time for it. Besides, they needed to make duplicate copies of their ledgers.

"If there's one thing the fire has reminded us of," he said, "it's how quickly records might be lost. How quickly *everything* might be lost."

They plunged into silence for a moment. Isabelle noticed upon Ezra's desk, almost hidden, a framed daguerreotype: his family, none of them happy, the boys stone-faced and their mother even more so.

"But you know that better than I do," Ezra said. "How is he?"

"They keep him plied with morphine and vapors. At night he cries. There's little for me to do but listen and hold his hand."

Ezra winced, then pulled his handkerchief from his pocket and rubbed his forehead dry.

"You are a godsend to him. And let us not forget his own heroics in the woods. Both of you make for quite the couple."

"He got himself shot, Ezra."

"Well, yes. But the boys are free, are they not? Hackstedde and the rest can say what they wish, but your son got that man out of jail and lived to speak of it. And George risked his life to see it through."

She did not dispute his claim, nor did she agree to it. Whether the man holed up in the hospital was a martyr was immaterial to her; he was her husband: frail, withered, beautiful in his way. Let him be a hero to others, but it was not their relation.

"He wants to go home," she said. "I don't believe he's taken his condition into account. But it's his only wish. I plan to honor it."

Ezra sat up, and, taking a hint—one she did not exactly mean to inspire—informed her that George had made all the necessary arrangements with him regarding his affairs going forward. Everything was set in stone. Everything that was his would be hers when the time came.

"I don't wish to speak of this," she said.

"And yet it is my duty to do so."

"Well, it ends there. My reason for coming here is simple, and yet I haven't been able to address it. I need some manner of conveyance for George. So I might get him home."

Her request seemed to energize Ezra, and she imagined him working through the contacts in his head, favors owed, deciding which to avail himself of. A carriage or coach would be easy enough, she went on, but George needed to be laid out and she feared the hospital wouldn't loan her an ambulance, considering his condition.

"Yes, yes," Ezra mumbled as if to himself before speaking up. "I'll tell you this. I am in the process of buying an entire catalog of goods, and a wagon or two will certainly be in the lot. I'm sure I can get use of one before the deal is finalized, as the owner is quite intent on selling as quickly as possible."

Ezra dabbed his forehead once more before finishing his proposition.

"There is one potential conflict," he said, "which I hope will not concern you, but the owner is Wade Webler himself."

She raised an eyebrow but did not say a word.

"As you can imagine, he is under quite a bit of…financial duress. Most of the blaze touched land and property under his ownership. I fear he had not considered such a sweeping loss as a possibility. And then there is August. Do you know his new bride of less than a week was a victim of the fire? Natasha Beddenfeld. So young. August made it out of the house first and did not even deign to go back in to retrieve her. Others saw him standing idly, calling her name but failing to run in after her. Shameful for a man of his supposed courage. I hear he is moving to Savannah, in want of a change of scenery. A new start."

He was waiting for her, now: waiting for an answer, an attack on the names he'd produced, on the family that had ruined her own, and yet she had nothing to give. No screed. No anger. She had seen the look on Wade's face. His pain was no better than her own, and it was his that would suppurate over time, eating away at his soul while she strove to let hers go.

"The wagon," she said. "You can have it to me today?"

"I'll have my assistant get word to Webler immediately."

Ezra called out to him with a severity that made her flinch. Once the boy was off, Ezra instructed Isabelle to fetch Ridley and return to the hospital, as though the deal was already done.

"The wagon will be there," he said. "That one or another. Take my word."

———

When she returned to the hospital, they had drained George's wound at the site of the amputation and he would not stop howling until he was loaded into the wagon, safe from the doctor's prodding. Mildred's sons had come at their mother's orders, and they hauled George into the wagon bed and sat beside him as Isabelle drove through town. Folks came to the side of the road, sensing a hidden curiosity, and even Ray Bittle gave her a nod as she came past the rubble of his home, knowing, perhaps, who lay in the wagon behind her.

Once George was home and in bed, she bade Mildred's sons farewell, and, after a slight break to get George comfortable, set to following the doctor's orders. She discovered immediately why they had shielded her from the wound, for the sight was ghastly. It took her entire being not to react at the foot of the bed. The sore upon his stump wept fluid the consistency of mucus, and the putrid scent punctured even the sharpness of the alcohol. Still she said nothing, offered George—still dazed, staring at the ceiling—a weak smile before she took off the gauze, applied a fresh wrap, and stood up beside him. She asked if there was anything she could do but he said nothing. Just stared off in endless silence, the last threads of his hair making wild patterns on his pillow.

She slept in Caleb's room and in the morning George was lucid again, his eyes welcoming when she came in and helped him sit up.

"You've been fevered," she said.

He looked at her quietly, as though he had no memory of the trials that had spanned the last few days.

"Well, I only needed to return home. I feel much better."

Still, she worried. He hardly needed his bedpan, ate nothing, drank only water, and passed the hours listening to her read the classics from his library downstairs (Shakespeare and Plutarch, the letters of Voltaire). She watched him from the corner of her eye, wondering what passed through his mind, if he was all there, or if this was still the version of her husband she'd been met with in the hospital, a man she hardly knew.

More than once he would clench the sides of the bed, his knuckles white, and she would calmly put the book down upon her lap. These moments were of great exasperation. He refused any medication, and she assumed full responsibility due to some action of her own— a tone of judgment that she could not control, or perhaps the suggestion of weakness shown before one's wife when offered relief—and she wished only to ask him to have some morphine in a manner so neutral, so discreet, that he might say yes. Yet he never did.

"I want to be awake," was all he would say to her. "Please. Continue."

The reading went on endlessly. When he fell asleep she would sit alone, staring blankly, waiting for him to wake again. When he failed to, she would head downstairs and tend to the home—or feed the chickens or Ridley or herself—then return to the bedroom, sick with boredom but unwilling to spend more time away from George than necessary. The second night home she made a beef stock, which the doctor had suggested, but George would have none of it. He simply took the bowl from her and set it down on the bedside table.

"You need to eat," she said.

298

"I believe that is the beauty of my predicament," he said. "I don't need to do a damn thing any longer that I don't wish to."

"George, I can't have you speak like that. I just can't."

The sun was dropping toward the horizon and he was still sitting up in the bed, looking ahead at the wall. She wasn't sure he'd even heard her. She'd already lost track of the times he'd spoken when she thought he was gone away in a dream, or ignored her when he'd appeared to be hanging on her every word.

"I saw them go," he said. "I watched them turn and run and I have no doubt, no doubt at all, that they passed through safely."

She knew the only way to urge him on was to maintain her silence and so she sat motionless, blending into the darkness now falling over the room.

"He held my hand. I was never so sure that he was my son as I was in that moment. Even in the hospital, when you held my hand yourself, I was certain it was his. Even now...yes. Even now I feel it. I can still hear him whispering in my ear. He said, 'Tell her I will write. Long letters this time.' And in the span it took for me to gather the words to say goodbye, they'd already gone into the night. He did not mention any sense of his love but I felt it."

And here he put his hand into her own.

"Don't you?"

She was caught up in the moment, in his account, so much so that she didn't realize that during its telling, without a word to note as much, George had wet himself. She could smell the sourness of the urine; only needed to place her fingertips upon the sheets to confirm the warmth spreading out from under him.

"Why don't we get you cleaned up," she said. "After that perhaps we can both get some rest."

In the failing light she saw the spray of yellow hair out the window, the build of his frame atop the horse, and recognized her brother.

She was in the kitchen eating the broth that George would not and dropped her bowl off in the sink to greet Silas outside. A dusty film still cloaked the darkening sky, a bitter vestige from the fire that she could taste at the back of her throat.

"Isabelle," he said.

"You've come," she said.

He looked pained to be there, at least that's what she gathered from his expression, until she realized he was dismayed by her own appearance.

"You don't look well," he said.

She hadn't faced her reflection in days.

"When you hear of what's happened, I'm sure you won't blame me."

She invited Silas in, and he went to the kitchen to fetch himself some water, then joined her on the couch in the big room.

"How did you—?" she started.

"Your friend sent a message for me."

"Mildred," Isabelle said. "But she told me the post office was gone. That no telegrams would send."

"She sent a messenger instead. I'm sure she paid dearly, too. The man must've traveled without interruption. He nearly fell off his horse in exhaustion. I wish I could've come faster, but work and whatnot…"

She eased his guilt, then told him the story, leaving nothing out. And when she came to George's wound, Silas immediately stood to go upstairs to see him. At this she protested.

"Don't even consider it. He won't have you there. Besides, he's asleep now. Rest will help more than anything."

Silas fell back onto the couch.

"At least let me stay for a time. I can help while you tend to him."

"What would you possibly do?"

"Whatever is needed. I've already told Lillian not to expect me back, and she assured me she'd keep the kids in line and the house in order. Do not even think of it as a favor. It's my wish to stay."

She tried to refuse the favor but he would not budge, and she couldn't deny how helpful it would be to have her brother at hand. Nonetheless, the nature of his presence continued to rankle her as the days passed, since seeing him around the house only reminded her of the last time he'd come, upon learning of Caleb's supposed death. But perhaps this was the role of a sibling: an overseer of tragedy, doling out gestures of sympathy when all else was lost. Though she was grateful, it seemed ghastly, an offense, and she began to mistreat him—sending him to clean Ridley's stable, or to wash George's sheets, but he never once showed the temper she'd known since their childhood. He was happy to absorb her anger, or pretended to be, and to accept whatever degrading task she assigned him. In idle moments he even sought out his own responsibilities, taking it upon himself to assess the land that had been scorched, coming back to dinner with figures in his head, work to be done, and the distraction was a great pleasure to Isabelle, although she did not show it.

All the while, George faded. Red spots tacked up his thigh like a spire lurching up from the wound to his waist and the fevers returned no matter how often she sponged him down. He would utter words in his delirium that she had no way to know the meaning of.

"I saw it," he would say with a hoarse whisper, a wry smile upon his face, so childlike she almost laughed at his own satisfaction. "It was real. Real. Real…"

"It was," she replied, encouraging him as she dabbed his forehead. "It was indeed."

Like this they conversed, neither one knowing the other's thoughts, empty words passing between them, and soon she fell asleep to his ramblings. When she woke she heard not just his voice but a full conversation in midstream, causing her to jump.

Silas stood with his hands in his pockets, his denim shirt half-buttoned, glancing blithely at George.

"It's just me," he told her. "You were still asleep when I peeked in; George invited me to stay."

"Not too long," George said. "I can only manage the man in fits."

George was so alert it nearly unnerved her. He had sweat through his fever, but there was no way she could delude herself into thinking the turn in his health might last.

"Thank you for helping with me," George said to Silas. "I can only imagine the strain."

"It's my pleasure. I must say with you locked up in here, that it's the best we've gotten along in ages."

"You two," Isabelle said. "Like old friends…"

"Hardly. I've asked Silas to go fetch Ezra. I know he wanted a word."

She was bewildered by his ability to recollect Ezra's attempted visit at the hospital, given his febrile ravings at the time.

"How nice," she stammered.

"I'll get on it," Silas said, and he put a hand on George's shoulder before turning to leave.

The smoke had finally cleared from the sky and the day was unseasonably mild; a shallow gust at the open window rippled the curtains.

George asked if there might be a way to bring the bed closer to the window.

"I'd like to see outside," he said. "It would mean the world."

She didn't know what to answer. For the first time since their reunion in the hospital, he was with her now, totally and fully, and knowing how short their time together might be, she felt it was paramount that they discuss the most prominent matters. But his needs overcame her own, and she swallowed her words.

"If I put pillows under the legs," she said, "it should move over without much issue."

"Oh, you must," he said.

She knew what he would find when he looked out, what had come to his land, and yet she would abide by his wishes. He had a right to see for himself what had happened, and besides, there was beauty amidst the destruction—in the forest beyond their own that remained intact, in the sky he'd observed from the porch for so many years.

"Wait here," she said.

"Isabelle," he said, "I don't think I'll be going far."

Once she'd wrestled the bed next to the window, George looked on without a word. His mind, she knew, was somewhere in the past. Even she could cobble together the memories in her own head—based around stories she'd heard endlessly—and imagine what George sensed taking place around them: his mother was in the guest room, tucking a sheet around the bed; his father outside, calling his name to join him on a tramp through the woods, the same woods where George would take his own son—the same woods where he'd find Prentiss and Landry.

She couldn't bear to sit idle, holding her peace, with the forest before them burned to cinders. Though the field wasn't visible from here, she was sure he was imagining what had happened to his crops over the hill.

"It was terrible, George," she burst out. "I'm so sorry for your land. For the crop. I thought of lying to you, but I could never do such a thing. It can be salvaged, though. I promise you that much. I'll do everything in my power to make it so."

He blinked once and studied her with a distant serenity.

"It's very persistent land. A few seasons, with your assistance." He shook his head knowingly. "It will be better than I might ever have made it myself."

Could the land he'd nursed and doted on be reduced to something as trivial as the calm of his demeanor suggested? The weight that was released from her—the bit of pain that was set free—made her want to believe it.

He offered her the faintest curl of a grin.

"Could you give me a moment alone with the view?"

"Of course."

"No need to keep anyone out. When Ezra arrives, send him in. And I was thinking of having some dinner. A chicken stew, perhaps? You know how I take to a stew."

"Can your stomach manage?"

"I believe it can."

"Then you will have it."

───────────────

The afternoon had nearly passed by the time Ezra made it to the farm. The chicken was already boiling, the vegetables lined up on the cutting board, and she asked her brother to deliver him to George so she didn't have to wash up. There could be no distractions. The recipe was a classic of George's, and its execution, although not the most difficult, would nevertheless take her total devotion.

When Ezra reemerged from the bedroom and came back down the stairs after only a short time, the mood of the house grew dire. Isabelle was convinced there was a darkness that followed the man, and when he appeared before her, checking his timepiece, she felt his presence loom over the cabin like a hex enchanted. The hallway was hardly lit and his shadow seemed quite larger than his being.

"He's...not well," Ezra said. "I believe I will delay my trip until his injuries are resolved. I can be called upon at any hour. Remember that."

"You're never far, are you, Ezra?"

"Not when I am needed."

She helped him to the front door, for he could hardly manage himself, and when he got there Silas rose from the couch and prepared to bring him home.

"Enjoy your dinner," Ezra said. "It smells delectable."

"Have a good evening yourself. Silas, get him home safe."

She thought when they were gone the home would be hers and George's alone, but before she could even get his stew ladled, hooves sounded on the lane once more, and she had to wash her hands and return to the door. The man was patient walking toward the cabin, and smaller than she'd estimated him atop his horse. She wouldn't have recognized him at all if not for the blue uniform and his shaggy mustache, which George had fixated on whenever he became so frustrated that only a violent monologue could bring him any peace.

"You are General Glass," she said.

"And you must be Isabelle," the man said.

His cheeks were rosy from the ride, his lips cracked, and she invited him inside and offered him water. He told her he'd been with Ezra earlier in the day and heard of George's worsening condition. That he'd wanted to give him time to see his friend, and perhaps, once he'd returned, make his way over himself.

"I can't fathom why," she said. "From what I've gathered you weren't my husband's biggest admirer."

Glass ran his hand over what little hair he had before answering. She reckoned he was much more imposing when surrounded by his soldiers, yet he retained his dignity alone, standing at attention in a stranger's home.

"My time posted in Old Ox has resulted in a number of regrets that I cannot make right. My treatment of your husband ranks high amongst them."

Having no interest in alleviating whatever discomfort or guilt he might feel, she held her tongue. Better to let him finish.

"My own aims occupied me so entirely that they became something of an obsession. Given as much, I did not find George's plight to be worth the trouble. Wade Webler assured me it would be handled in a manner that was fair, that would preserve a sense of calm..."

He seemed to need a moment, and he used it to look out the window—at the very land, she imagined, that George was just now staring at himself.

"He betrayed me in the exact manner George told me he would. And I have paid for it."

A smile spread across his face, yet it was false, and quickly curdled into a grimace of humility. Indeed, he said, he was being reassigned to go west, with only half as many men under his command as he was currently responsible for.

"I have no reason to wonder why," he said. "I have acted beneath my rank. And I believe George deserves to hear as much from me before I depart."

Isabelle had no words for this man, divorced as he was from whatever sense of certainty had once fueled him. She simply walked to the bottom of the stairs and indicated for him to follow.

"Don't take long," she said. "He really does need his rest."

Glass was upstairs no more than five or ten minutes and he soon appeared again, picking a loose hair from his jacket, taking a deep breath as he found her at the foot of the stairs.

"Were you well received?" she asked.

"He was certainly alert. He listened to me closely. When I finished he said not a word. It was strange. He simply patted me on the side. Like I was a boy, really…He then told me that we all must carry on. That he wished me well."

"Strange indeed," she said, considering the humor in her husband's attempt to show this man a little compassion, figuring George ached to be rid of him. Yet it appeared to have worked for Glass, and all the better. "I hope you keep those words close to your heart during your travels west, then."

Glass gazed into the kitchen as though it might offer access to a greater truth, then nodded and headed for the front door.

"Good luck, General," she said.

He turned and put his hand upon his breast.

"I wish the same to you and yours."

_____

The dark was total by the time the general was mounting his horse. Isabelle returned to the kitchen, finished preparing the stew, and brought the food tray upstairs. When she opened the bedroom door she was met with the smell of rotten meat, and the room grew dense in the thick air. She pulled a chair up next to George. The dew of sweat glistened on his forehead again and his hand trembled. All she wanted was another lucid hour with him, or even a moment, before she lost him to the fever once more.

"Where have you gone?" he asked.

"I was only making your dinner."

His brow arched but when he saw the food tray he nodded encouragingly. "What finer way to end the night than with a stew."

She was trembling herself now. Her only wish was for him to enjoy her creation, and her nerves clouded the tranquility brought on by the open window, by the dark mass of the trees in the distance. She scooped a dollop onto the spoon and he opened his lips to it, and she looked on, spellbound, as he swallowed.

He said nothing. She refused the idea that the stew wasn't to his taste and simply dipped the spoon into it once more. But when she invited him to open his mouth again, he turned his face away.

"George, you should eat."

He shook his head petulantly. "My stomach cannot manage."

"You *asked* for it."

"And now I am saying I don't want it!" He slammed the side of the bed. "It's no good!"

She could not look at him. Every few moments he whimpered in agony, the sweat pooling on his pillow now. There was no means to distinguish her sadness from her anger, for she was enraged that he'd given the last reserves of his energy to guests and left nothing for her but this undying bitterness; and yet, she also knew the pain that had racked him and desired only a moment of peace for her beloved. A resolution to his pain.

By the time she spoke, the steam had floated off into the night and the stew sat cold on her lap.

"I'm sorry," she said. "I'm sorry I cannot cook to your satisfaction. I'm sorry I was so cruel at times. That I grew so frustrated by your behavior when you were only acting naturally. I raged at you in a fever when you were too cold to understand my pain and I ran from you when you needed nothing more than my touch. And I blamed you. My God. I blamed you for so many things that weren't of your doing. Only someone like you could tolerate me, and perhaps you're an angel in that way. I am so grateful to have you. And I am sorry."

His face, hauntingly pale, had emptied itself of color altogether, and he lay still. Without warning he reached his hand out and took the stew from the tray. He gripped the spoon and took a sip. Then another.

"George, you don't need to—"

"It's excellent," he said.

He struggled with each swallow, his throat quivering as the food passed down.

"It is so excellent. All of it. Exquisite. Divine."

His eyelids began to twitch. The spoon slipped from his hand and fell to the ground. The bowl capsized on his chest. He was lost to convulsions, his leg skittering about as though it had acquired agency and wished to escape him; his fists clenched, his arms locked up at odd angles before his whole body abruptly went limp.

Isabelle ran for towels and returned to him; cleaning him carefully, slowly, returning to the parts that were already washed, selfish ministrations, for even though his pulse still beat, she knew, then, that her husband was gone to her.

———————

He lasted through the night. It was Silas who pulled the sheet over his face come morning. He put his hands gently upon her shoulders, telling her it would be all right—that he would stay with her however long her mourning might last.

Yet she would hear nothing of it.

"I've mourned enough in one lifetime for two women," she said. "I'll have no more of it."

Her only distraction was to keep herself busy. She collected a bin from the cellar and made her way to the bathroom, where she grabbed George's brush, his pomade, and all of his other possessions there, and stored them away. His scent was omnipresent, that sweaty musk she neither loved nor hated, a smell that was simply George, as familiar as the man himself. She was certain that once his body was removed and the house was scrubbed of him, she might have a moment to think of things other than the sound of his footsteps coming down the stairs, his oddly peaceful snoring, his delightful grin on returning from the woods. Perhaps she might even stop thinking of her son, who would have no news of his father's passing, lost as he was somewhere in the world with no way for his mother to reach him.

Silas appeared at the bathroom door to ask what she was doing.

She gestured to the towels on the rack beside the washtub.

"Grab those, please," she said. "Whenever I see them I can only picture George wrapped up in one, coming into the bedroom after a bath. Still wet. Always getting water on the floor. That won't do. I'll get new ones."

"Izzy, please. You aren't yourself."

He hadn't called her *Izzy* since she was a child. Surely her actions weren't that immature? When Silas didn't move to pick up the towels, she collected them herself and threw them into the bin. "If you won't get the towels," she said, "then you can begin with the pots and pans in the kitchen. His grip is worn into every handle. All I can see is him leaning over the skillet to smell his cooking. I can't have it. I'll get some new kitchenware in town tomorrow, too."

As she made to leave the room, Silas put his arms around her and held her tight, her cheek against his chest, and she dropped the bin to the ground.

"Isabelle," he whispered into her ear. "Give yourself a day. For God's sakes. Putting away his pan will not help things."

Without uttering another word, he walked her to the couch. They sat together in silence. There was nothing more to do about the house and the weight of the day finally caught up to her. After some time he told her he wished to roll a cigarette and wondered if she would be okay without him for a moment.

"I'd like to go outside myself," she said.

"Don't let me stop you."

So that was where she spent the rest of her day, and when night came, she watched the stars with a blanket in her lap. Surely there would be another sign of her husband, clustered in the constellations. But it was a nighttime sky like any other. Silas refused to sleep himself but kept his distance, staying inside but making a routine of coming out to ask if she was ready for bed. The final time he opened the door he was yawning himself, and she told him to leave her be.

"I suppose you won't be moved," he said.

"You cannot worry after me like this," she said. "I'm fine. I just wish to wait out the night."

"Wait it out for what?"

"For morning."

"And then?" he said.

"And then I will bury my husband. Let's not have it come too quick."

Silas remained in the doorway. It was plain he didn't understand his intrusion, and she wished he would grasp that there was nothing he could do but grant her this window of time where she could draw significance from the immensity of the countryside, and live one last night in a world that did not know or care that her husband was gone from her.

"Go to sleep," she said.

She didn't bother to see him off, but when she finally turned, a while later, the candles inside had been put out and the cabin was dark.

CHAPTER 26

It was Caleb who insisted they remain in the woods, claiming Hackstedde and Webler might still be after them—a fear that occupied Prentiss as well. They'd stopped a week into their flight, upon reaching a town he'd not heard of, and Caleb would go there for food, return to their campsite bearing bread and cans of meat, and after eating they would sleep surrounded by silence, awaiting daylight. Each evening Caleb would perk up, buzzing with an energy he'd stored away somewhere, and announce that another day had passed, his voice thick with pride, as though they'd accomplished something noble. *Eight days on,* he'd say. The following night it was nine. And each would lead to the next, all of them blending into one, until a few weeks had gone by and Prentiss had had more than enough nights in the woods to last a good long while, if not forever.

One morning they stood idle, cloaked in the shadows of the trees, looking out upon the road that led into that town. Convent, Caleb had told him upon his first trip there. The place was called Convent. Prentiss had yet to utter the word. Didn't feel right to tempt fate, to speak of it as an actuality, as the next step in his plan, only for it to be robbed from him when Hackstedde eased up to their camp, rope in hand, ready to shatter the very dreams of freedom Prentiss guarded in his mind's eye so zealously. But it was nigh on a month now, and Hackstedde was nowhere to be found. Seemed more and more likely it might remain that way.

"I bet they got beds in Convent," Prentiss said. "I can't be the only one of us who'd enjoy the feel of a real pillow under his head. No more bug bites, either. We ain't gotta be itching each other's backs all day. Imagine that."

Caleb offered him a noncommittal look and said nothing.

His unease made Prentiss try another tack. Hit the matter head-on. "I'd rather risk it than keep this up. Can't quite see the point of chasing freedom if you ain't gonna take it up once it's sitting right in front of you."

"I like it out here," Caleb said, his voice low and tinged with embarrassment. "I wish I could say why. I can't quite put my finger on it."

But it wasn't hard for Prentiss to understand. Out here, living with his guilt, the boy didn't have to worry about disappointing anyone. There was no one to see through his false confidence and call him out as so many others appeared to have done in the past, at least according to the stories he'd told Prentiss—about boys who were predators, boys who haunted his dreams. Prentiss saw some of himself in Caleb, for he and Landry had hidden on George's land in this same fashion. The reassurance, the blessedness, of being left alone was worth more than a thousand bug bites.

From their spot on the road, Prentiss could spy the start of the buildings at the edge of town, peeking out from chimney smoke and the occasional cloud. Already his imagination had mapped out the place—the cozy nook of the general store where Caleb had ventured for their food, the looming spire of the church where everyone gathered on Sundays. He even knew the homes of all the townsfolk—families he'd invented, going so far as to assign them hobbies and jobs, passions and secrets.

But Convent was not the place he wished to land for good. There was nowhere within journeying distance of Old Ox that he would ever call home. The very mention of it could make his mouth quiver. His feet go numb. And those old images of Majesty's Palace, of Landry's face as a boy, the brightness of his mother's smile (only on good days, when they had a rabbit roasting, when the night's work was done early and his mother tousled Landry's hair and his giggles bounced against the walls of their cabin), would penetrate him like a knife, only to be replaced by the emptiness of their cabin after his mother was sold, by the mangled gape of his brother's face in his coffin. Maybe with time there were parts of the past that could be forgotten, their sway over him toppled, but there would always be certain memories that survived the fall and stood amid the rubble. Monuments of loss.

"I'm not stopping you," Caleb said. "If you wish to go." He was tossing the last jar of his mother's canned fruit between his hands. He refused to eat it. That last connection with the woman he adored so much. It seemed he might well be content to stick right here in these woods for the rest of his life, holed away from society while the world carried on.

The wind was so violent it felt as though it might cut through flesh like a whip. It quit for a spell before it kicked up one last time and took off in the direction of town. Prentiss squinted again into the distance at the rooftops, shards of brick and wood, seducing him with the power of the unknown.

Yet for all his desire to take his chances in town, it was he whose heart began to gallop when a horse-drawn cart appeared on the road bearing a man who looked to be asleep, chin against chest. He shielded himself behind a tree, while Caleb, unconcerned, only gazed in the other direction, still playing with that jar. Prentiss scolded himself silently, brushing bark off his shirt, which only brought him to think of how badly he longed to bathe. But it wasn't just the man in his cart—something in the daylight menaced him: a steady drum, growing louder, the sound of a threat creeping near, the same sound that followed Gail's horse in the fields of Majesty's Palace, or Hackstedde's horse in the forest, and although the noise was not as real as Caleb made it out to be, it did not make it less persistent, less tangible in the sight of every stranger that came down the road before them. To his great shame, he was scared.

"What is it?" Caleb asked.

Nothing, Prentiss told him. He had no interest in alarming the boy, who worried enough as it was about what had happened to his father. The trek alone had provided ample concern. He didn't need to add to Caleb wondering, every night, if some distant rattle was George coming to reunite with them. Having returned from the war in one piece, Caleb apparently didn't realize how these situations so often ended. No reunion. No resolution. Instead, the spark of life that connects you to the other you cherish simply dims and then goes black entirely. The present thunders on while the past is a wound untended, unstitched, felt but never healed.

"I think we should both stay awhile in town," Prentiss said. "Get up to something. Work a little. It's possible, I think—to just live normal—even if it ain't for long."

Time, he'd found, was different in the woods. Without a man like Gail—or George, in his milder way—keeping him attuned to its passing, he had learned to tell it by bearing witness to the emotions of the sun: its fury showing orange in the afternoon; its loss of interest in pockets of time, when it let the wind take flight and cool things down; its violet at sundown like a wink, a flourish, before turning in altogether, teasing the world with what it might have in store come morning. It might bring out your passions one minute but it could lull you in the next, and he was not surprised to find Caleb in a trance. He pondered how long he'd been standing there in silence; how far down the road the man with his chin to his chest had ridden since he'd last put eyes on him.

What he would give to be so careless! To not look over his shoulder. To miss a signpost and find himself two towns over, drinking ale on a stranger's porch and speaking with him of the last stranger who had made the same mistake. He wished to do *wrong*, too. That was what George, what Caleb, what no one quite got. They underestimated his passion for living. The freedom to steal a glance at a taken woman, one who reminded him of Delpha, or Clementine, and sneak in a word one day when her man was off at work—who she belonged to be damned, for every woman was her own woman, and he was his own man.

Or what of the freedom to learn? There were so many things that Prentiss yearned to know, subjects he wished to be educated on in the coming years. Not all of it was pure speculation. They'd had so much free time that Caleb had begun to teach him letters, even. Caleb would often test him with words all morning, each more advanced than the last, and he'd begun to crave the smile that crossed the boy's face whenever he meant to trip Prentiss up and failed.

His success seemed to energize Caleb as well. He would tell Prentiss how he never wished to work with crops again, that there was so much else to do in a world so vast. A printing press would be pleasant work, he said, and although Prentiss knew little of it, the thought sounded just as fine to him, too. He'd need to know numbers, perhaps, know how to make a transaction with a customer, or calculate stock on hand, but Caleb assured him that this could be learned in due time. Up north there were teachers, eager to work with freedmen just like him. If this was true, the borders of the possible and impossible were not entirely clear. A job like that, with a bit of education—Prentiss saw himself becoming no different than any white man. He'd walk through a city with the sort of pride that fuels a whole brigade of soldiers on their way to battle.

This was when his mind would return to Clementine. To his mother, even. If he could spell their names, and pay the cost to the right man, the imaginary was suddenly *true*. Of course they could be found. How ignorant to have thought otherwise, to have shrugged off the potential, the great rewards, that might come in the cultured life which could follow this one. He could see himself already, leaving work early to get home, his mother playing with Elsy, and Clementine in the kitchen, pregnant, cooking up a meal from a recipe that his mother had passed on to her new daughter.

Good money. A family. A house of his own. It wasn't just that he could be free, he realized. He could be *happy*.

CHAPTER 27

One hand. That was all she'd felt of George's body after he passed. His wrist was smooth as hardened wax—so cold, so foreign, that she convinced herself it wasn't her husband at all. They buried him the morning after he'd passed (a walnut coffin, identical to Landry's), Isabelle and Silas alone, for she did not wish to see anyone else on the occasion. His death was hers—she claimed it, and the others could mourn on their own time if they pleased.

When the burial was over, Silas told her she should come with him. There was room at the homestead in Chambersville. She could be closer to her nephews.

They were before the cabin. Silas had already retrieved his horse from the stable. He stood ready to leave, his saddlebag stuffed with worn clothes, his hat on, his hand upon the horse's flank, calming the animal in anticipation of their ride.

"Bring the boys here," she said. "To me. I'd like to get to know them better. But I won't be leaving Old Ox."

He raised one of her hands to his face and kissed it briskly, then let it fall to her side.

"Remember," she said. "I told you once I might have need to call on you. That hasn't changed."

"It'd be foolish to think I won't be back to check in of my own accord," he said. "I predict you'll soon be calling on me to leave your home rather than come to it."

"It will never be so," she said.

He mounted his horse and gave her a wink.

"Just wait until you have my boys here raising hell."

He reached back and patted the horse's rear, then dug his boot heels into its side. Dust kicked up like smoke and he was gone before the cloud even fell back to the ground.

Alone now, she had no one to answer to but herself. Still, she was prepared to take on the task George had spoken of. She walked to town the following morning. The place continued to recover. It was odd, the spectacle of men and horses tramping over the ashen floor of what had once been the lumber mill, the abattoir, cleaning out everything that had been razed only weeks ago. The scene felt distant from her, like someone else's dream, but Isabelle did not allow the sight to threaten her mood. An energy coursed through her, clamoring for her to take action. She carried signs she'd written in George's study, ten in all, and she put them up proudly about town: a board against the furniture depot; a utility pole before the schoolhouse. She was determined that they be prominent— the words bold and the letters large—so that all who passed would take notice.

HELP NEEDED ON THE WALKER FARM.
ALL RACES, CREEDS, AND COLORS. FAIR PAY. EQUAL PAY.

When she'd run out of signs—her hands empty, her feet tired— she returned home. The only thing left to do now was wait.

The first man appeared several days later like an apparition formed from the morning light. A hunched fellow, hobbling with each step, not unlike George. Isabelle saw him out the bedroom window, coming up the lane, and she dressed and hurried downstairs.

When she opened the door she was met by a colored man wearing a cotton shirt jumbled at the collar and a blue suit jacket. A small yellow flower, already wilting but still bright against the jacket, spilled from his breast pocket. He was older than she was, perhaps sixty, and seemingly so wary that even after she greeted him he seemed reluctant to speak.

"Ma'am," he said, finally. "I'm looking for the owner of the Walker estate."

She told him that was her.

"There's no mister?"

"Not any longer, no."

Although reticent, he was not afraid to look her in the eyes. His own were largely hidden within the deep creases of his skin and yet they revealed themselves when he spoke, deep beds of hazel, each expression given gravity by their sudden emergence from beneath his furrowed brows.

"I've seen that sign in town," he said. "If you're still offering."

She joined him on the porch and walked to the railing, thinking of the burnt land and all that lay beyond it down the hill. He followed her, still wary, keeping his distance. She told him what had happened. Then asked if had a skill with farming.

By way of an answer he held out his hands, so weathered that Isabelle could hardly make out the lines on his palms—whittled by years of toil.

"Tell me your name," she said.

"Elliot."

"Elliot, I own many acres beyond these ruined ones. More than I could ever manage myself. I don't plan to sell any of them. What I will do is give you a proposal. I will allow you your own slip of land to farm. I won't ask for any of your harvest, or any money. It's yours to keep for a year, perhaps two—enough time for you to get on your feet before I give someone else the same opportunity. But in return, I want you to help me with that ruined land down the hill, that same land my husband tilled. I want you to give me a few days a week of your service. I'll be out there, and I'd like you to join me, and together we'll do everything in our power to make it not just beautiful again, but prosperous."

Elliot was silent. His hair was one great tuft, and he ran his hand through it as he pondered her proposition.

"You gonna give me my own land to work and all you want is some help. And there ain't no more to it?"

"That's it," she affirmed.

"But why?"

She looked upon Elliot squarely and minced no words.

"I mean to do as my late husband did," she said. "Even if only to avenge him. To restore his land."

She surveyed her rose bushes, the petals shriveled and drooping, ready to be snipped, and pictured the display come winter if she put in the proper work.

"That's a very pretty flower, by the way," she said, nodding to Elliot's breast pocket. "Where did you pick it?"

"My wife. She said I should look my best."

"You've managed well on that front."

He laced his hands together, cleared his throat.

"I don't mean to say too much, and you tell me if I have, ma'am, 'cause I got nothing but respect for you, but there's a bunch of men in town who seen that sign, and they too afraid to come up here. We heard about those brothers. Heard what happened to the big one. Nobody wants trouble, is what I'm saying."

A chill coursed through her.

"His name was Landry," she said. With a hand, she guided Elliot's sight to the forest. "And he is buried there, right beside my husband."

"Ma'am, I—"

"Allow me to finish. I've lost more than I ever imagined, but they're the reason I've brought you here, and will bring as many others as I can. Why I intend to make this the most gorgeous and bountiful bit of land in the county. There's a risk, yes, but there are more soldiers in town than ever before, ones who look like you, and have your interests in mind. The Freedmen's Bureau sends them around every week to assure that things are safe. Still. Anything might happen, it's true. And I would understand if that prospect frightens you too much to accept."

His face was closed to her, and she thought of what lay under the surface—how his eyes might grow wide at the telling of a joke, or the pleasure he might show as he danced to a tune with his wife. The blossoming of his personality under the proper circumstances.

"I'll take the land," he said, finally. "However much you offerin'."

"Fifteen acres," she said.

"That's a deal," he said, his voice registering surprise.

"And you'll help me fix up that land down the hill?"

"That's my promise."

They did not shake hands. He simply nodded and shuffled over to the stairs.

"Ma'am," he said. "Expect me back next week."

"Until then, Elliot."

As he walked off, she called out that he should tell the others they could have the same deal. Space was limited—she had only so much land to go around—but all were welcome, just as the signs proclaimed.

CHAPTER 28

Autumn was brilliant. The sun became tolerable and the walnut trees so yellow they looked like enormous dandelions just flowered. Others were vibrant tones of pumpkin orange. Isabelle made her rounds in the morning on the back of Ridley, surrounded by the gorgeousness, checking in on the handful of men who'd arrived these past few months after Elliot. Many of them still lived in the camps beyond town, but some had taken up residence on the farm, setting up makeshift tents wherever pleased them on the plots that were theirs.

On any given day the acreage was so extensive that if Isabelle wished to, she could avoid seeing them at all, but she enjoyed watching them work the land, knowing their own visions were being met, their goals attained. They were all freedmen and most had brought their families in to aid them. Often she was met with skepticism, as though she were simply the latest incarnation of an overseer, but in time they were eased to her presence by the nature of routine, the comfort built through her questions on how to tend the land, and eventually by their toiling beside one another on George's plot. She had help from at least one of them every day, and already the reseeding efforts—with nothing more than hoes, along with some manure being spread with an eye toward healthy growth—had begun to heal the damage done by the fire. There was little optimism that the produce would be plentiful that initial season, she was told; it would be a year at least for it to return to its former condition. But a year seemed not far off.

Her last stop after working was always the forest. She would see Landry's grave first: the blue of the sock upon the cross, a beacon bright in the pending darkness. She would sit in the space between his grave and George's and speak as though they were there with her—catch them up on her work, promise to return with roses once they came in. George had never liked them but if he could tolerate them in life he could tolerate them in death. Landry loved all things pretty, all things holy. He would be happy for the gift.

Sometimes she'd try to speak out loud to Caleb, to tell him of her life, just as she did with George, but it was never the same. To speak to Caleb carried an unsettling sense of finality. Hardly anyone asked of him in town, knowing what had transpired, but when they did she could only give a glazed smile, wish them well, and excuse herself. The memories of her son and of Prentiss were preserved for things far more valued than casual conversation: a prayer late at night when the loneliness crept over her, when she would pull her knees to her chest and ask God to keep them from harm, wherever they may be. Or sometimes she'd bring them to mind in the morning when she needed that extra push to keep going, to get dressed for the day, to go forth with the pride she demanded of herself and meet whoever was waiting in the field to help with the work there. The boys would want her to carry on living, she thought. So she aimed, by every means, to do just that.

Indeed, she'd had herself a typical day and was exhausted when she returned home one evening to find Mildred on her porch, pacing ceaselessly. She was in her riding wear, black trousers and white gloves, and she faced Isabelle with a fervency much in contrast to the slow pace of the past hour in the forest.

"You are quite dirty, aren't you," Mildred said.

"Had to fix the water pump in the morning. I've been in the fields ever since."

"Of course you have. A man dropped by with some turnips and said they were for you."

Isabelle came up the stairs and Mildred pulled her in for a kiss on the cheek. She could smell Mildred's sweat and was sure Mildred could smell the soil on her, though neither shirked from the other. The turnips in question were beside the door. Isabelle picked them up.

"It must have been Matthew. He hardly has his own crops in but he told me he'd give me a bit of what his mother was growing over in Campton. A taste of what's to come on his own land. I didn't think he'd follow through but he's kept his word. Will you come in?" Isabelle asked. "I don't have much to offer but company, unless you want a turnip of course."

Mildred was already following her through the door.

"You must take better care of yourself," she said. "You look slight."

"Without George, I live on not much more than the plants in my own backyard and a few eggs here and there."

The big room had many of George's planting books laid out on the table in front of the couch. On a large piece of parchment on the floor she had drawn a map of the land, with names representing the plot she'd given to each person who'd agreed to take it.

"Good Lord, Isabelle, it gets worse by the day." Mildred shuddered. "We'll need to get you a maid."

"I suppose I won't show you my bedroom, then."

"Joke all you want, but you'll come screaming for assistance when vermin are tramping around the place."

Isabelle lit a candle on the dining-room table, then went to the kitchen and washed her hands and her face before removing her sun hat and returning to the table. She sat down and unlaced her boots and Mildred took a chair beside her. Since George's death her friend had visited quite a few times, and always they talked late into the night, invigorated by their own private musings, with neither having anywhere to be come morning. Recently Mildred had announced that her son Charlie was getting wed, and it had come as both a shock and a delight, although Isabelle got the distinct sense that Mildred was taking it as a loss—a gesture of abandonment—and so didn't ask any more about it.

"It's going well?" Mildred asked, taking her gloves off.

"I'd say so. They need nothing of me and it's comforting to know I'm not alone out here. Elliot is a friend. I believe we get on. He introduced me to his wife and children. And I'm friendly with Matthew, too."

"Yet you *are* alone in your house, miles from town. I don't like it. What if someone has ill intentions? You don't even lock the door."

Isabelle nearly laughed. "Please. I sleep more peacefully than ever."

"Better than with George?"

"Oh, George is here," Isabelle said, sighing. "He's everywhere. He's in the fields, in the forest. I can't get rid of him. But much as I begrudge him, I can't wait to see him each day. No different in that way from when he was alive."

Mildred stood to resume the pacing that had occupied her on the porch.

"You no longer need to dote on him, you know. You could retire from here. We would be wise to move to Europe, start anew. That was a thought I had. The Italian countryside would welcome us, I'm sure."

"Two American widows."

"See? We already share a title."

Isabelle leaned over the table, her chin on her knuckles, as Mildred ventured into the big room.

"I'm perfectly content," she told her friend. "I do what I do because it brings me happiness. If we could just figure out the same for you, we'd be in a very fortunate place, the two of us."

The candle's light carried toward the big room, where Mildred stood tall beside the couch, peering down at the cluttered table before it.

"You should at least allow me to draw a proper map for you," she said. "It would be disgraceful if your poor drawing muddled up your land. One man might believe he has one area to work, and then another the same, and God knows what could result. What a mess you might make! And your kitchen."

She wheeled about and marched toward the kitchen.

"It's filthy, Isabelle. I could clean this. And if your house is in order and you have a place to return to that is even remotely unsoiled... Well then I would feel better about all of this."

"Mildred," Isabelle said, and put a hand out toward Mildred's seat. "You really must relax. Sit down."

Mildred quieted and her breathing slowed—the white lace ruffling her blouse had been heaving—and took a seat.

"It's just—I've just been thinking of what comes next. You continue to forge this path, while I do nothing but tarry about my home—"

"*Mildred,*" Isabelle said firmly. Her friend looked up from the table, the lambent flame of the candle revealing the tremble of her jaw. "I would *love* your help. More than anyone else's. You would be indispensable to me. You *are* indispensable to me."

To Isabelle's surprise, the statement seemed to come as a great and necessary relief to Mildred. Immediately her friend calmed and Isabelle put a hand on her shoulder.

"Whatever I'm doing, I want you a part of it. We could start to-morrow. I'd love for you to begin that map. If you're free, that is."

Mildred's composure settled further—a deep swallow, a long breath, her eyes hardening once more to their usual piercing cast.

"I believe I will have some time tomorrow," Mildred said, with her old confidence.

Little did Isabelle know that the following day would turn into every day thereafter as well.

———————

Mildred's map carried the name of every freed person who took up residence on the Walker estate. By the cusp of winter there were seven lots divided up and, with the forest, nearly no more room left to plant. There were two women, Clarinda and Jane, who took up a small plot beside Matthew's. They purported to be sisters yet looked wildly dissimilar. Clarinda was heavyset and boasted a voice so deep she often seemed to be on the verge of breaking into a somber hymn. Jane was lithe, half the size of Clarinda, and spoke in a tone so high that Isabelle sometimes clenched her teeth at the sound of it. They both wore the same outfit, which consisted of a white bonnet and a homespun dress patterned with petaled flowers. They were garrulous, often seeking out Isabelle to disclose knowledge of their family—cousins a few states away they had never met or known; other erstwhile slaves they now viewed as kin who had moved a county over—and Isabelle grew curious as to when they managed to get their work done, for their garden was indeed quite lively with carrots and onions that seemed on track for a spring harvest. A visit to their plot one afternoon provided no answers, as neither sister was there. Only when Isabelle was returning from George's grave at the end of one day did she find them walking past the cabin, describing to her how they worked at a weaving mill and often weren't able to return until dusk. Whatever they earned from their yield come harvest would supplement their earnings. Enough to launch them in search of the family they'd described to her.

There were others, like Godfrey, who hadn't spoken to her since he'd arrived a month earlier. She'd given him a plot far east, on the outskirts of the property, and on both visits she made he did not deign to say a word. Something had happened to the man. He used little of the land, planting enough to feed himself alone. She wasn't surprised to hear from the others that he never made an effort to converse with them either, or that he hardly left his land.

He was harassed once by a few teenage boys from town looking for trouble. He wasn't beaten but they woke him and pushed him around, and after word got back to her and Mildred, Isabelle was surprised to find a bouquet of flowers on her porch the next week from one of the offenders. Apparently Mildred had told her sons about the incident, and they'd dealt with it their own way, tracking down the assailants and doling out punishment. Isabelle informed her they should tell the authorities next time, yet neither could quite argue with the outcome.

Isabelle delivered the flowers to Godfrey's plot of land, but he was nowhere to be found. Upon her next visit, his tent had been taken down and removed, and with his tools gone as well, she realized he'd abandoned the land altogether. In time, another freedman took up residence. Nonetheless a message had been sent, and between the reputation of the Foster boys, the threat of federal law, and the fallout from the fire, few dared to set foot on the Walker estate again without an invitation.

Most days, Mildred would arrive early for breakfast and while Isabelle was out making her rounds would clean and serve in the role of administrator, taking note of anyone who came to the house with a request for help or in want of land. The signs in town had been removed, but some folks still arrived having heard rumors that there was free land to be had. With room for only so many, and with all the plots already spoken for, they had to be turned away, in a manner for which Mildred had the heart and Isabelle did not. But there were also a few of the freedmen, like Elliot, deep into the winter season, who were happy to have the assistance and share the proceeds from their harvest.

At night Isabelle and Mildred ate together, discussing their day, their lives, what was to come in the future. Afterward they sat on the couch and read, or knitted, or continued the conversation from the dinner table. They were inseparable in their way, and Isabelle wasn't afraid to hold Mildred's hand, or place her head upon her friend's shoulder when fatigue came over her. Yet they did not share a bed. What was between them was unphysical, an entanglement of the spirit that transcended any act of passion. To see each other in the morning and the evening was enough, and when Mildred rode home to see her boys and to sleep, the distance only gave more emphasis to their reunion the following day. Whenever the front door opened,

Isabelle barely said hello, but both the newfound routine and her friend's presence were like treats to be savored.

Occasionally they argued. Isabelle felt strongly that those working her land should have a place to stay on it. Already many of them camped out and she saw no reason not to allow them something more comfortable. If they were to build some housing it would not be permanent—they would still leave when their time had run out and they had money in their pockets. But Mildred believed that a family with a home would never give it up, and the question consumed their conversation for some time.

On Sundays they rested and talked of lighter topics. It was the last week of December now—just after Christmas, Isabelle's first without George—and they sat on the porch, tea in hand, each cloaked in her own quilt. A bird landed on the railing, cocked its head, then took off again. The tea warmed them, though only briefly and still the heat swiftly dissipated against the chill of the morning. They would go inside soon and make a fire, but no day was spent without a little fresh air, the spot adjacent to the hearth their reward for the outing.

Mildred was in her most persuasive mode, trying to convince Isabelle that she should take up riding. There was an auction approaching and Mildred knew there was a filly from an unheralded stable that would be priced cheap. She could train it, and soon the two of them would be riding through the country together without a care to their name.

Isabelle stopped listening when a carriage, its canvas top littered with holes, appeared up the lane. It was led by a single horse, and as it grew near she could see it was piled high with boxes, but the mystery of the driver, under wrap against the cold, wasn't revealed until she noticed the slight body beside the one holding the reins, swaddled in blankets and resting against her mother.

Isabelle put her teacup down and grabbed her wool coat from the back of her chair. "Is it you?" she called out, and stepped down the stairs as the carriage came to a halt.

"What part of me has withstood through the cold!" Clementine said. She eased her way from the carriage and grabbed her daughter as she dismounted.

They had survived the fire intact but had lost their home, as Mildred had reported to Isabelle. Clementine had come to the farm once since then for dinner, visiting George's grave after the meal, but it appeared from the carriage, which was packed with belongings, that it was unlikely there would be such gatherings in the future.

Elsy's hair was as bountiful as her mother's, and her tangles eclipsed Clementine's face as she carried her daughter toward the porch.

"But I want to see the horse! The horse!" the child said.

Clementine put her down but gripped her hand.

"The horse will pick you up with its teeth and toss you like a ragdoll. Is that what you want?"

The child laughed, nodding her head.

"Really?" Clementine said. "We'll see how you feel when you're face-first in the mud."

"I like the mud!" the child exclaimed.

To this her mother had no response, and could only resort to holding her still as Isabelle walked to greet them. Clementine was dressed in a wool gown beneath an overcoat long enough for a man, a graceful red scarf snaked around her neck. Formless yet beautiful. Isabelle embraced her and said hello to Elsy, then inspected the carriage.

"It's quite ragged, I know," Clementine said. "I dread its failure. But it was the only one I could manage to acquire for the price I had in mind."

"You made it up the lane just fine," Isabelle said. "What does appearance matter?"

Clementine eyed the carriage suspiciously.

"Might I ask what you plan to do with it?" Isabelle asked.

"Well, I'm afraid we don't have a great deal of choice but to move on. The hotel isn't exactly suitable lodging. There were complaints of Elsy being noisy, of me returning late. It wouldn't do."

"And now?" Isabelle said.

Just then she felt the cool shock of a hand upon her shoulder, and Mildred, who had joined them, stepped toward Elsy.

"How about I take the child to visit the chickens?" she said. "They could use some food, if this one is brave enough to feed them."

"I am brave!" Elsy was quick to tell her.

"We shall see about that," Mildred said, looking at Clementine, who only nodded—happy, it seemed, for a break from the child. Mildred and Elsy wandered off toward the coop.

"When she wakes from her naps," Clementine said, "there are no bounds to her energy."

"It's a lifetime ago for me," Isabelle said, "but I can recall what that's like."

She turned to Clementine.

"Why don't you come to the porch? We can at least have some tea."

They went on together. Clementine sat in Mildred's seat and Isabelle poured another cup from the tray.

"Do you know where you'll go?" she asked.

"Not precisely. I simply wish for a quieter existence somewhere, is all. And a climate more fit for my services. The men here are more involved in building back their lives than visiting with women like myself. The money has dried up."

"I see…"

"I have always done what I must to survive," Clementine said. "And although I've made a decent life here, things will only be better up North. Amongst a more welcoming audience. Perhaps a wealthier audience."

"I have no doubt you'll succeed in whatever you set out for. What of Elsy?"

"I plan to get her in school, shortly. However that may be done."

"You have quite the journey in store!" Isabelle said. "I wager there will be a good number of trials."

"Don't think I feel any different. I'm terrified, truth be told, but it's better to make the break while she's young. At least that's what I tell myself."

A shrill wind picked up dust from the ground, and both women took a sip of their tea in defense of the weather.

"I wonder," Clementine said, her voice low, "if you've heard from them."

Isabelle took a second sip for good measure. Perhaps it was the comfort of Clementine's stolidity, or the way she asked with so little judgment behind the words, but for the first time in a long time, Isabelle felt capable to answer the question.

"No." she said. "Not yet."

"Oh, Isabelle."

"Now don't even begin down that road. I need no sympathy. I'm sure they're both fine. It's only Caleb's way."

Clementine pulled the scarf from her neck and stared at Isabelle with obvious concern, waiting for more; waiting, perhaps, with the same exasperation that punished Isabelle's heart on a nightly basis. But Isabelle had nothing more to share. Nothing in the realm of the known.

"The letter will come," said Isabelle, and her tone lurched toward the optimism she'd been forcing herself to practice. "I often imagine opening it. The childlike loop of the letters, the sentences that slant off diagonally as they carry on. That laziness with words he has…"

Isabelle looked down the lane, relishing the working of her mind—the oft-constructed scenario she conjured during her darkest moments. The content of a letter that did not exist.

"It will say so much more than any of his paltry letters during the war. He'll tell me they're well. It's either Philadelphia or New York they've landed in, I haven't decided which. They're employed at a hotel. A remarkable one. One of fashionable society. Caleb serves dinner to the patrons, roasts with champagne sauce and jelly, kidneys stewed in wine, and all through the night an orchestra plays classical music that keeps everyone's spirits light. Prentiss, well, he works in one of the smoking rooms. There's smoke in the air, of course, and you can hear the clack of balls from the billiards table. The place is populated by the greatest minds visiting the city and they talk of new inventions, of what the future might hold, and after months of quiet in the woods, Prentiss basks in the atmosphere, the invigorating intelligence, storing it all away in his mind for safekeeping. The boys have beds just like the patrons. Spring beds, not straw. Even the help deserves more than a straw bed in New York City. They're allowed to eat whatever is left over from the extravagant dinners, and late, when everyone else is asleep, they might sneak into the smoking room with Prentiss's key and play a game of billiards...

"I don't know, Clementine. This is what comes to mind. I do wish there was more. Perhaps my imagination is limited, but with such a picture in place, who needs the words to make it all true?"

Clementine stirred, rapping her seat with the palm of her hand in delight. "Truly magnificent. I have no question it's accurate. A mother has a sense of such things, and those boys have the determination and cunning to make it true."

"Thank you," Isabelle said. "That makes two of us, then."

"I bet Landry would be ecstatic for his brother," Clementine added. "For Prentiss to have made it so far in the world..."

Hearing the name was enough to make Isabelle seize. They had spoken of Landry once before, at the graves, that time Clementine came for dinner, but as with Caleb, he was never discussed with Mildred, and so Isabelle hadn't talked of him with anyone since.

"I'm sorry," she said. "I wasn't expecting to hear his name."

Clementine leaned forward in her chair, the dank smell of her overcoat reaching Isabelle as she drew near.

"I didn't mean to upset you," she said. "It's just that from what Prentiss told me, he had a strong tie to his brother, and I can only assume Landry would be happy for him to be gone from the madness of this place."

"Prentiss told you of Landry?"

"In his cell," Clementine said. "I envy you for knowing him. How curious he came off. Prentiss told me about his fascination with water."

This was news to Isabelle, for neither brother had shared such a thing with her, and she said as much. Then Clementine told her all. How Landry would gaze upon the fountain at Majesty's Palace, seeking it out whenever he could. The way Prentiss had described him, it was as though it was a part of his build, this connection to its beauty, its inner workings. How something mysterious and fine lay under the ground and caused it to operate endlessly. On and on, just like life.

Perhaps Clementine noticed the pain on Isabelle's face, the realization of an intimacy kept from her. Her tone shifted, her enthusiasm cooled.

"Of course, this is based on what little Prentiss told me under duress," she said. "Between his words and the impressions you've given me, I've probably made something of a myth out of him."

The wind returned, a frenzied, bitter gust, and even within her wool coat Isabelle wished she had a shawl. Her skin would be blotched by the end of the day.

"I'm not sure what to say."

"Then say nothing," Clementine said. "My interruption has been long enough already. If I can just find that girl of mine running about."

As if on cue, a sharp cry of joy erupted behind the cabin. Isabelle called Mildred's name, and although her friend didn't respond, the door of the chicken coop shut with a thud.

Clementine was already standing. Her hair was buffeted by the wind, waving like the branches of a tree caught up in a storm. She gave Isabelle a hug and stepped down the stairs.

"Perhaps one day soon, somewhere along my travels, I will run into our two young men walking down the street as a pair, dressed to the nines as attendants for the greatest hotel around. Their day done, their ties loosened, perhaps. Hats in hand. Readying for a night on the town."

Isabelle smiled, warmed by the idea. "There have certainly been greater coincidences."

"I can promise you I'd let them know that someone back home

is waiting to hear from them. That they should write promptly. With an address where they can be reached."

"It would be the greatest gift," Isabelle said.

How was it she was choking up at such a playful comment by her friend?

"Tell them I'm well. That I get on. And tell that boy he must not only write, but write with *detail*. Long letters. Just as he promised."

When Clementine opened her mouth to speak, Elsy ran up beside her, screaming of the chickens, and the moment was gone. Mildred climbed the stairs to the porch and there was a world between these two pairs—Clementine and Elsy near the carriage, their clothes rattled by the wind as they huddled together, and Isabelle and Mildred by their chairs, mere feet from the door that would lead them inside to the hearth.

"Just be well," Isabelle called out.

Mildred waved, and Clementine, obscured behind her scarf, waved back. Elsy was reaching for the horse. Clementine called her to attention, raised the child's hand, and made her wave as well. When they climbed into the carriage Isabelle was still watching them, as though there would be more to the interaction—one last farewell. Yet the horse circled the roundabout, and it seemed that no sooner had Clementine arrived than she was gone.

CHAPTER 29

There was a well-dressed man of squat stature who, at day-break, rang a bell as he walked through the quiet town of Convent. There were mornings in the winter when the sun had yet to clamber through the darkness of the previous night, and on those occasions, in his other hand, he carried a lantern that drew men toward him in the same manner that light lures passing insects. The doors of houses would open and shut without a sound, footsteps would patter, and soon the man with the bell and lantern had formed a silent flock about his person. The whole lot would venture forward as one, never stopping, growing ever larger as they carried on. They were a pack of ghosts floating toward the fog and the woods beyond.

"Prentiss," Caleb called out in the dark of their room, watching the men go. He was accustomed to receiving no answer in return at this early hour, but he tried again. "Prentiss, they're out front now."

He did not know how long the two of them had been in Convent. Enough time to lose track of it. Four months? Five? The town was the first they came across after they'd stopped fleeing in earnest, the inn the first one that would house them. The woman in charge, with her peculiar hospitality, reminded him of his mother, and her domestic duties seemed one with her insistence on keeping a strictly harmonious home. If the door between the kitchen and the parlor was left ajar, Mrs. Benson would issue no qualms, but one would find it properly shut the next instant. At a loud noise from upstairs she

335

would call up to ask if a guest was in need—a way of asking for quiet. To let the house rest.

She had stowed them in the cobwebbed attic, two beds alone across the room from each other, and although there were spiders so enormous as to seem more beast than bug, and a dampness that turned the floorboards the color of rotted teeth, Caleb felt blessed to have a space all their own.

Caleb said Prentiss's name once more, and the body across the room began to stir. Prentiss had never once risen before Caleb since they'd arrived. Each morning, as though he were pinned to his bed by the cold, it appeared that Prentiss might give up altogether and sleep all the way through the dregs of winter like an animal. But then he would wake suddenly, spurred on not by Caleb (for Caleb recognized that he had little effect on the man, who was mostly silent, a world away), but seemingly by some wellspring of diligence that demanded he put himself to the task and see it through to a completion so devastatingly assured that no employer could ever have even a whisper of grievance. For it was work they were waking to. Work that occupied their days.

"Let's get gone, then," Prentiss said, the sleep still clinging to his voice. Such was his way that he was dressed before Caleb's eyes had adjusted to see the figure drawing near him in the shadows.

———————

The morning was still cold and the men hugged their coats tight to their bodies. All of them carried burdens. One man spoke often of a wife to whom he sent his earnings, a woman who failed to return his letters and might no longer be his wife at all. But given that he was an escaped convict, the return home that would satisfy him on the status of his marriage would also end with his hanging, and so he'd learned to bear the mystery as it presently stood. The other men were quieter, although in their darting glances, their fear of a spooked horse or a squawking crow, it was clear that some darkness from their past loomed with the ominous power to arrive at any moment and deliver a fate worthy of flight.

The man with the lantern quit his ringing as they exited town. The ground they trod was swampy marshland, although folks had still managed to build farms here and there along the winding webs of water. Each home had a lantern out front glowing faintly like a minor star in the morning dark. To Caleb the lanterns felt like guideposts urging him on, but to what exactly was unclear, and the gang of men always turned off the road before ever drawing near enough for him to contemplate their meaning further.

"Mr. Whitney wants his usual lot," the man with the lantern said.

There were those landowners who wanted the same men day after day, the ones they were happy with. Caleb and Prentiss had fallen in with Mr. Whitney in their early days in Convent and had never gone elsewhere. They stepped forward with the others, eight in all, and the man with the lantern told them to get on.

The road led to a sugar mill, a wooden structure with no roof and no walls. Whitney greeted the men with a single piece of fried bread each. Their chewing was so loud it snuffed out the sounds of the river down the way.

"Five minutes," Whitney said.

In the biting cold the men huddled as one, eating like wolves in a pack. The temperature would rise once the kettles got boiling.

"I been chopping wood all morning," Whitney said, as if to suggest the morning had passed them by, when it had yet to come at all. "'Spect three of you to take that over. The rest of you man them kettles like yesterday. Caleb, get yourself on them barrels."

He knew Caleb by name, for he was the only white man on a crew that otherwise comprised Indians and Negroes, and he was often singled out for the job of least labor. He had once tried to switch roles and hand it off to another man, and it was one of the few times he'd drawn Prentiss's ire; he'd left his kettle and confronted him with a face covered in sweat.

"You gonna fill those hogsheads," Prentiss told him. "Heed that man's words now. Acting up 'cause you got it easy. Too much of your father in you." That was that. Caleb never made the same mistake.

The routine rarely wavered, and this day was like the others. The men not chopping wood lit the flames beneath their kettles. There were four in all, lined up in a train. When the water boiled off from the first, the syrup was ladled to the next, and the process of refinement finished with Caleb, who stood by the hogsheads, watching the syrup flow in, and when a barrel was full he'd install the lid, store it in the corner as it cooled, and bring the next one out to fill.

The heat built upon itself unabated, and their coughing was incessant, long barks that began to carry the signature of each man's toil. At day's end they'd rush down to the freezing water, jumping in like animals, shedding the grime of the day and floating still-like so their limbs might have a moment's reprieve from the endless stirring, the endless standing.

Caleb recalled his first week of work, when a young man, no older than himself, had dropped his ladle. The syrup oozed like lava, and they watched the man's silent calamity, his eyes overtaking his face, his hands crinkling together into balls of pain. It was a fascinating interaction, so much so that no one moved for a moment: the syrup seeping through the man's boot, the grim realization, when pulling it from his foot, that the leather had latched itself to his skin. He later described the pain of the doctor finally removing the boot: like his tongue being ripped from his mouth. Caleb hadn't forgotten that. He doubted any of them had.

He did his job carefully, and often watched Prentiss from the nearest kettle; Prentiss had a beard now, having grown it out of some fear that he and Caleb might be sought out early on, that he might need some disguise. He had never cut it, and while in the intervening months he had managed only a small clump at the chin and a middling mustache, he looked older these days, though Caleb knew the younger version was still in there somewhere, waiting for the proper time to return. At least that was his hope.

Mr. Whitney was seventy and nearly toothless. He walked among them with one hand in his pants and the other holding his chrono-graph. The sugar boiled off at precise intervals, and it was strange that he kept the time at all, considering how regularly he spoke of his instinct for knowing when to end the process based on sight alone. Over time, his actions—the fondling of his groin, the incessant clicking of his watch—began to seem less involved with their work and more a symptom of his mania, a means to calm his nerves.

It was midday before Whitney called for a break. The men walked out in single file. A bucket of water sat beneath a tree beside the mill, and they each took a swig, sitting among themselves, their bodies beaded with sweat in the cold, all of them silent. Whitney took a moment to expound, once more, on his intent to purchase an evaporator, which would make them all expendable, for the boiling would be exact to the machine's standards, but the talk had been repeated so many times that no one paid him any mind.

Prentiss stood away by himself, his shirt tied off at his waist, rubbing a leaf against his forehead, staring into the woods.

"Where are you today?" Caleb asked, joining him.

"Nowhere but here," Prentiss told him.

No one flogged himself with work quite like Prentiss: no one consumed less water, complained so little, sweat so much. Punish-ment, Caleb knew. For wrongs he had not done. For losses that would never be recouped. And despite his profession early on that Convent wasn't far enough away from Old Ox for him ever to call it home, it was Prentiss who wished to stay. Although they'd spent some money, they had enough to be gone, but the work was good, and Prentiss was content in a place where he wasn't known and wasn't asked questions. A place where he could distract himself with his ceaseless stirring of the kettle, his eyes full of some torment that doubled as pleasure, the heat expunging the demons that plagued him.

"Mrs. Benson said we can have some of those rabbit leftovers for supper," Caleb said.

"Think she's got more of that milk?" Prentiss asked.

"That goat's milk?"

"It's like sipping on butter. Cows don't compare."

"If she doesn't, we can go back there and milk one ourselves, I imagine."

"I ain't touching a goat's teat. That's where I draw the line."

"I, for one, am not above milking a goat's teat," Caleb said. "It'd be an honor, really. I'm sure there are some men in the world who don't consider a day complete until they've milked a goat's teat."

He picked up a leaf himself, dabbed his forehead, and let it fall to the ground. He didn't look over, for if he caught Prentiss in a smile, he would only try to hide it, and so they simply waited there together for the rest of the break, chilled by their drying sweat.

There would be no rabbit that night. No milk. When the boiling was done, Whitney set them to fashioning staves for the hogsheads that would be filled the following day, and by the time they made it home, Mrs. Benson had retired, the house so dark they had to feel their way upstairs. They had an apple each, and Caleb feared that the sound of their eating might wake the old woman. A little ham they'd bought the previous day was dessert. Some evenings, with a free hour, Prentiss would swipe at a piece of wood with a razor, making something, or nothing, for Caleb couldn't tell and didn't wish to interrupt him. But this night Prentiss turned in quickly, and Caleb was left to his own restlessness, which found him every night: thoughts of his mother, his father, his old bedroom. That donkey, Ridley. Images that cycled through his mind, feeding on the guilt he kept stored up, the filial duties he had failed to uphold, until the thoughts and scenes became a story, a dream, such that his sleeping world was populated by the very people and circumstances he had tried so hard to flee.

Some hours later, then, awaking from just such a nightmare, he felt as though he'd hallucinated into being the discernible figure from his past looming outside the window, as though that man had been waiting for him to take note of his presence all along. The man lingered ominously beside a hitched horse, inspecting the home, and removed his gloves with a quick stroke.

Caleb lunged out of bed. It was not yet morning, and perhaps owing to the creaking, so odd at the hour, Prentiss poked his head up from his pillow to seek out the noise.

"What you doin'?" he muttered.

"It's him," Caleb said. His head throbbed, as though the nightmare had manifested a physical affliction. He reached under the bed—the wooden floorboards cold against his hand—his razor blade revealing itself against one of the legs.

"What you mean *him*?" Prentiss said, propped up on his elbows now.

"You know who. And I'm going to kill him." Caleb flicked the blade open and clattered down the stairs two at a time.

"Caleb!" Prentiss called out.

By the time he was out the door there was nothing between Caleb and August but the cold of the night, the leaden silence of the sleeping town. If August spoke even a word, if that familiar voice reached him, Caleb knew he would falter—that his old friend's hold upon him was simply too strong to resist. So he wouldn't give him the chance. He stalked forward with the blade ready, and for a moment, a slip of time that fell away as he drew near, it seemed that his nightmares had intertwined with reality—that to end his friend's life might abolish the pain of the past and afford his mind the freedom to wander the landscape of his dreams in peace. Such was the temptation of his revenge that it felt like a single night of true rest would make every day spent languishing in a prison cell—or even a walk to the gallows—more than worth the crime.

But when the man lit a cigar, Caleb wavered and the blade fell from his grip, striking the ground with a ring that echoed in the quiet street.

"Good evening," the man called out, more in threat than in greeting. He was tall and lanky with auburn hair—not blond, as Caleb had seen it from the window. His two front teeth burst from his mouth. It was a wonder he could close the thing at all.

"I'm sorry—" Caleb was stuck in place. "I mistook you for someone else. An intruder."

"An intruder!" the man said, chewing his cigar like a teething infant takes to a toy. "I nearly drew my pistol, but I don't draw unless I'm shooting, and I don't shoot unless I'm killing, and so you might glean your luck in this instance."

Caleb's teeth began to chatter, the frozen air cutting through the vacant part of him that had, just a moment ago, been overcome by anger—by the swelling need for retribution.

"Might I ask who you are?" the man said.

Caleb gave his name and said that he was lodging at the inn.

"I'm Arthur Benson. My aunt owns this place. I had no idea she was taking guests these days. Is he with you?" And Arthur pointed at the house.

Caleb turned to find Prentiss hugging himself in the cold. "It's the two of us," he said.

"I see," Arthur said, and though he had only just begun smoking the cigar, he reached down and put it out against the side of his boot, then brushed the ash away.

"I'm sorry about the fright," Caleb said. "I was acting out of sorts."

"Oh, I wasn't frightened in the slightest. Auntie, Auntie."

Mrs. Benson, disappearing inside an enormous frock coat pulled on over her night dress, pushed Prentiss aside at the front door. "I received your telegram just yesterday," she called out, "but I expected you at a more regular hour. Do come in."

Caleb had never seen her move so quick, and he retreated backward as she hugged the man. Was his presence an intrusion now, or would it be rude to leave at such a moment?

"You have guests," Arthur said.

"They're paid up until the end of the month," she said. "But there is always room for you, Arthur. Always room for family."

————————

An hour later they were back in the attic, both silent, but neither sleeping. Caleb could hear the quickness of Prentiss's breathing, the way he shifted restlessly.

"I was certain it was him," Caleb whispered. "You must believe me."

"Get some rest."

"You think I'm crazy."

"Didn't say that. Said to get some rest."

"I know. But I—"

"Caleb."

"You must listen—"

"*What,* you think I ain't see 'em like you do?"

Caleb felt a jolt, as though a snake had hissed at him from the foot of his bed.

"What you think I be looking out at all day? In the woods. I see my brother every which way I turn, beaten and bruised, blood running down his face. I been seeing my mama ever since she been sold. I see Mrs. Etty standing right beside me like we back in those fields, like she ain't never run off. Half the time you wake me up I think it's Gail rousing me for lazying up a proper workday. I s'pose that boy August gon' be outside your window for the rest of your days. That's how them demons work. How them ghosts follow you around. Be proud you gone out and faced him straight on. Ain't everyone brave enough for that. But you should know it ain't gonna change nothing. You still gotta get up each morning. Still gotta settle down each night. So if you ain't gonna get some rest for yourself, at least let me get mine."

There was a rustling downstairs, born of who knew what, the quiet of the home acknowledging the noise.

"I'm sorry, Prentiss."

"Don't be sorry. Just sleep."

From a distance, the men at the kettles appeared to be warlocks stirring cauldrons, sorcerers conducting rituals in a forgotten remove of the forest where no man was meant to wander. Caleb was relieving himself on a tree beyond the mill, looking back at them. The day was almost over. The boys cutting wood slowed at the height of each swing of the ax, and each man at the kettles had found a calm rhythm to his stirring. The final hour passed quickly and the men were standing out in the cold for a rest when Mr. Whitney motioned for Caleb to come with him. Caleb tapped Prentiss on the shoulder, and the three of them walked to a clearing that opened onto Whitney's house and the farmland behind it that bore his crop.

The river ran between the two at a steady clip and Whitney pointed at it, telling Caleb that the water was seeping into his home. He had dug a levee a good ten years back but now he needed to reinforce it. It had to be deeper, with some ditches so it would drain right. It would be a few months of work, once the sugar was sold off. "I could use the help of a boy like you," he said. "I gather you're learned. Know numbers and whatnot. You'd be a mighty help."

Caleb put his hands in his pockets, spied the land suspiciously, wondering what trouble, or fortune, lay in the proposal: the choice between the ease of acquiescing to another man's desires over his own and the difficulty of chasing something beyond the horizon, the cradle of the unknown and the intangible, the possibility that he might follow his own path, as he had done when he rescued Prentiss, with a result, whether right or wrong, never to be undone. When he looked back at Prentiss for guidance, he was scratching the scruff of his beard, staring at the ground, abstaining from the decision.

"I think you might have the wrong man," Caleb said, more weakly than he'd intended to. "Perhaps you've misjudged my condition. I don't have the heart to lead others. Never have."

Whitney ran his thick tongue across his gums, what few teeth he had left.

"That's a learned skill. And anyway you ain't leading no one. I'd be out there with my pant legs rolled up just like you, and I'd keep them boys in line. I just need a fellow with some brains at my side."

Caleb imagined the life: waking each morning in the cold of the attic, and outside the window that lantern, a floating orb cutting through the fog. Then the muddied shores of the river, reinforcing this levee. Then the heat of the mill when the season returned.

"I plan to be gone from here," he said, and the certainty of his voice surprised even him. "I might change my mind tomorrow, as I'm prone to indecision, but that is my want. To find a spot of my own somewhere. I'd like this man behind me to come along, but I can't say that he will. He seems content these days, and I can't blame him for wanting a little contentment. If he stays, I'd recommend him for your job. He's double the worker I am, with double the smarts. I should be getting on for the evening now. Though I thank you for the opportunity."

Caleb tipped his head in respect, although Whitney failed to acknowledge it.

"There be more like you," he said. "Reckon I'll manage."

"I am sure you will," Caleb said. When he turned, Prentiss uncrossed his arms and sidled up next to him. They walked together with the whoosh of the river in their ears.

Prentiss spoke only once they'd gone past the mill and landed on the road.

"Bet she made that nephew of hers some dessert."

"What'd you have in mind?" Caleb asked.

"Chocolate cake. That's what I'm seeing."

"You can do better than that. I see six layers. Chocolate and vanilla, one on the other."

"Got my mouth watering. Think she'll set aside a slice for us?"

"Her nephew's a twig. And he seems like the sort that's too proud for sweets. Thinks they're just for children."

"We'll get our fill, then," Prentiss said.

"I'll say," Caleb told him, rubbing his hands together. "We'll eat till sunup."

"Till our stomachs burst."

Caleb's muscles ached, but the chill of the day was like pinpricks on his skin, distracting him from the pain. They would be back in Convent shortly and would sleep until dinner. Get some tinned meat at the general store, eat in the attic before falling asleep once more. And then, in the predawn, he would be woken by the bell. The lantern outside the window.

The sound of a clanging, an announcement of metal, woke Caleb in the night. Yet it wasn't the bell he'd expected. Out the window he found only darkness. Beyond him, gripped in layers of shadow, a shirtless Prentiss sat in the lone chair of the attic, leant over, holding his straight razor, with the bowl on the ground beneath him.

"Prentiss?"

Prentiss reached down, then stood up, a blanket in hand. He folded it to the size of a cloth and opened the window, the cold flooding in.

"What are you doing?"

He unfolded the blanket, giving it a shake, closing the window once more and turning to face Caleb's bed. Even in the dark he could see the nakedness of his face. Back at the chair—the bowl on the ground.

"A little late for a shave," Caleb said.

Prentiss moved toward him with soft steps, and Caleb sat up. Perched above him, uncharacteristically tall against the arching beams of the low attic ceiling, Prentiss offered a hand.

"What you say," he began. "What you say we get gone from here?"

The sleep drained from him in an instant. He did not need to respond for Prentiss to know his answer. Caleb rose and grabbed for his belongings under the bed. There was little to bundle up. His own razor. The extra shirt he'd bought at the general store and the few other clothes he had. The last jar of his mother's canned peaches, which he'd kept sealed and uneaten all this time, if only to remember her by.

"You never liked to walk the woods in the dark," Caleb said. "We can wait till morning."

"I don't want to hear that bell. Not once more. I want to be gone."

Prentiss's clothes were already laid out on his bed. He'd been ready, Caleb realized. At least for some time that night.

"No reason to be in the woods anyway," Prentiss said. "Ain't nobody after us. We'll stick to the roads. Be two towns over by sunrise."

"Catch a train. North in no time."

Under the bed, beside his mother's peaches, was where Caleb kept the rolled-up piece of parchment that Mrs. Benson had given him. He had meant to use it yet never had, all these months, having convinced himself that his current life—the grinding work, the freezing attic—was not what his mother would hope to hear. But he had kept it beneath his bed all along, knowing the day would come when he would put words to page. The conditions had to be right. Now he knew that full well. He would compose it from a desk, his own desk, in a sunny house that belonged to no stranger. Some place of safety, and beauty, and peace. A place where he would feel himself set free. A place worth writing home from. He would be there soon, he knew, Far from Convent. Far, far from Old Ox.

CHAPTER 30

The ground had nearly frosted over and a gloomy mist fell upon Isabelle as she walked down Stage Road. She had given Elliot use of the donkey early that morning. There was little need for her on the farm this deep into winter and she did not feel like helping the others with their land. Not today.

All these months later the trees were still bare from the fire and for some distance there was startling clarity, the grandeur and mystery of the forest having been betrayed by this newfound nakedness. Not so much as a rabbit or a fox could be spotted. Just unending stillness. Which would be the better part of the country for some time, she thought, with no means to change it but to wait for another season.

Ted Morton's land had fared no better, and she hesitated at the gate to his property. The fountain was where it had always sat, right before the road. It was no longer running, the lower basin lined with rust. The cherubs on the second tier continued to pose, shooting their arrows and pointing at one another with mawkish looks of adoration. At its top stood a goddess, slender yet muscled, holding a vase from which the water would typically flow, staring upward with astonishment; now she was left to look only at the sky, and it took on a sorrier note, as though the goddess were praying, desperately, for the stream to return to her.

Morton's land had been so disfigured by the fire that there was still hardly a shrub to speak of. The mansion had been scorched to

a skeleton of its former self. Even the stone pillars failed to hold—
the heat cracked them and when one fell, the second-story veranda
followed, collapsing such that a heap of stone and rubble covered the
front entrance. The family somehow managed to survive, although
all of their furniture, not to mention their land, was consumed by
the fire. All that had been left of the manse was the foundation—an
absence so odd it had given Isabelle the shivers when she'd first laid
eyes upon it some months ago. A raft of Negroes now worked about
the place and the first floor had been built back with an eye toward
mimicking its original design. Wooden beams lay in enormous stacks
and a few men passed her by with wheelbarrows of stone. A gang
of mired, barefoot women carried small bundles of bricks to a pile
before the home.

Isabelle finally spotted Ted beside the trail to the back of his
property, standing idly with his young son, looking over some papers
and smoking a pipe. As she approached, the sheaf of papers slowly
descended from his eyes, and once she was upon him, he handed it
to his son.

"Go find Gail and tell him what we've discussed," Ted said. "If he
must go to the mill once more, so be it."

Seemingly content with his errand, the boy ran off. Ted regarded
her suspiciously, sucking on his pipe until his cheeks caved, smoke
trailing out the side of his mouth. His suspenders hung limply at his
side. Dust had collected in all the fissures of his face—the pocket of
his chin, the lines of his brow—as though an ancient rug, long stowed
away, had been unfurled right before his face.

"Hello, Ted," she said.

"I see you found your way onto my property," Ted said.

"I don't wish to be a bother."

"Once you let me know why you're standing here, I'll make a
judgment on that myself."

There was a crease upon the thigh of Ted's pants, a small fold,
where his child had clutched at him. She watched the boy running
off, looked back toward Ted.

"I bear no ill intent," she said. "Just a proposal. I wonder if you would indulge me in a short walk? It will not take long."

"I don't know how my wife would feel about me going on a walk with another woman."

"Is she here?" Isabelle looked about. "Or do you fear her oversight from afar?"

The mouth of Ted's pipe was a fine goose quill, and smoke funneled through it and entered his mouth as he considered her words. He exhaled once more, and said, "Way I feel about you Walkers, I doubt she'd have much concern."

"All the better."

Isabelle began to walk back down the trail toward Stage Road and Ted stalked a few feet behind her.

"She is well, I trust?"

"Staying with my sister over in Savannah while we get this house redone."

"That must be difficult."

"She ain't the sort to complain. Besides, quite a few folks headed that way after the fire. They got themselves a little society, keep each other company. You know, Webler's boy got some properties over there. Hear he's been loaning them out to the others for a fair price."

Isabelle decided that silence was the best response.

"Sound of it," Ted continued, "he's something of a recluse these days. Just keeps his head down, collects those checks, and stays to himself. Hardly utters a peep. I estimate he was one of the most popular young fellows in town. Wasn't a bad word said against his name. To have his wife meet an end like that. And after all your boy put him through. Well, I hope God grants him some peace."

Such comments had once harmed her grievously, yet she'd developed a resistance to such attacks; from the stares in town and the words uttered behind her back. A hollow pit, somewhere within her, where she stored such viciousness away, let it die, then released it to the air to float off forever. She sensed it, somewhere beside her heart, a compartment at her core—her hand felt the spot, let it rest for a moment, before her anger settled and she closed the door to the cruelty of his words.

"I wouldn't have taken you for a gossip, Ted. That's best saved for the social butterflies nattering on in their parlors, don't you think? Let's stick to matters of importance."

Ted raised an eyebrow and let her admonition go unremarked.

"And what important matter have you brought me?"

They had reached the fountain and she stopped and placed a hand on the basin.

"Your fountain," she said. "I'd like to purchase it from you."

He did not take it as an odd request, but demurred.

"I got that made for my wife."

"I'm sure the money might be of use in hard times such as these."

"It quit some time ago."

"Well, when it is mine it will be none of your concern."

"Why would you want the damn thing in the first place?" He threw his hands up in exasperation, the straps of his overalls jangling as he gesticulated. "Folks tell me you've gone crazier than George since that fire, and my God, this fits in line with that. Coming all this way about a busted fountain. It ain't for sale. If it was, you ain't who I'd turn to."

She looked at Ted, then beyond him. She wondered how Landry had spotted the fountain from the fields. She knew where the house lay—knew where the cotton rows he'd picked were stationed. Yet she could not determine how one could catch sight of the fountain from such a distance, for even those rows that hugged the sides of Majesty's Palace were some distance away, the ones at its rear even farther. And even if he had, perhaps the fountain he imagined, the fountain that preoccupied him, was one he drew himself on those long days at work, stored in his mind, a possession all his own. Yes, perhaps Ted's was only a surrogate. A gaudy, cheap one at that.

"Might I ask who constructed it?" Isabelle said.

Ted's anger lifted.

"Oh!" he said. "Now *that's* a yarn. Had a nigger I sent to town to learn how to work stones, and what'd he do but pick up and leave when he got the first chance. And now I hired myself a mason back in town who ain't worth half as much as that boy but wants double a normal man's wage while doing a quarter the work. Ain't that somethin'? I know I shouldn't be talking business with no woman but I can't believe the way that boy—"

"That's very good, Ted."

The embers had died in the bowl of Ted's pipe. He turned it upside down and tipped the tobacco out, then gave the backside another thump of his hand. He was pondering something. It took him a moment to gather the words.

"You know," he said quietly, "I ain't have nothing to do with that fire. Gail neither. Wade put out that call but we ain't answered it. No, we ain't."

She'd lived through that night once. No part of her wished to do so again.

"It's over and done with, I suppose."

"I s'pose. I just knew it wouldn't change nothin'. Thought it silly, really. Things'll carry on. Them Yankees with their little uniforms and swords won't be here forever. They'll go back where they belong. Them Negroes will keep working as we see fit. And whatever that hubbub you got goin' on back at your property, well, folks'll see to ending that, too. Just like it's always been done before. We got ways about us. Ways that don't need no fixing."

She looked upon his face once more, drubbed by time, scored and pitted by the elements.

"Ted," she said, picking a bit of dirt from her nail. "Let's end this here."

He snorted back phlegm and nodded his head, though it was more of a craning—a thorough investigation of just what it was that stood before him. This being. This woman.

"I'll get on," he said.

"And I will do the same. Send my regards to your wife."

The road was empty once more as she returned home. She thought of Ezra, of all people, and the last time she'd seen him before he went off to visit his sons. *A squandering. Total dissipation.* That was how he'd referred to her plan: the farming, the cause, as she considered it to be, and she could only face him then and confess that this was possibly true, but if her life was to stagnate, or begin its descent toward the inevitable final act, she would take pride in knowing that George's land, her land now, would continue to prosper after she was gone. Others would carry on in her stead. And she felt quite certain that, for all his talk, no one as foolish as Ted Morton was going to do anything to stop it.

When she walked up the lane, the cabin was cloaked in the shadowy mist of the winter afternoon; the upturned V of the roof was like a flag announcing her safe passage. Mildred's carriage sat in the roundabout. Smoke from the chimney relinquished itself to the mist, disappearing as it emerged. A stooped man was leaving the stables, his hat crooked atop his head, his boots soft against the ground—Elliot returning Ridley. Perhaps he had knocked and Mildred had told him she was out, or perhaps he'd thought he would be a bother. His body rocked as he took each step, and Isabelle imagined how much like George he was, joint grinding against bone, bone against joint, a solemn dignity in the way he hid his weariness. Someone like Elliot had taken thousands more steps in his life than she ever might. If there was a set allotment for each person before surrendering to time, he would run out of them far quicker than she ever could. There was nothing right about it. It just was. Before long he had vanished into the mist, like the smoke, rejoining his family, his crop, his day.

She thought of Caleb—the cruelty of his absence. How on days like this in his boyhood, rife with silence, they had once huddled together on the couch, suspending all else in store for the day in favor of each other's company. Before long coffee would be brewed, and the house would find heat as though created purely by the words they shared, the laughter between them, and the day would draw to a close without either noticing. The fact that her only son was somewhere unknown in the world, somewhere lost to her, felt like the ultimate defeat. A defeat no mother could ever conquer. No matter how much purpose, how much meaning, the world might offer her otherwise.

Perhaps the only saving grace was his letter, which had finally arrived. It was months late, by her estimation, and of course far shorter than she would have liked, but he had kept his word. He had sat down to write his mother and in doing so had delivered to her the greatest gift she could possibly have asked for. She had read the note so often, inspected it so closely, that she worried the parchment might crumble to bits. Still, even with the closest reading of each sentence, each word, it never revealed the information she wished for most. They had arrived in a Northern city, but he would not reveal its name, lest the authorities catch wind of where he and Prentiss were located (and how like Caleb, to imagine the sheriff still waiting eagerly to intercept his mail, to punish him for a crime forgotten and put to rest). There was no note of his feelings, no note even of whether he was happy. But there was routine to his day, he had written, a feeling of gratification. They had money to feed themselves, to dress themselves.

What few particulars he had given left her eager for more. Prentiss smelled like fish each day from his work at the dock loading cargo (what dock? what cargo?), and multiple evenings a week he was learning to read, to write, at a local church that aided many other freedmen who were eager to gobble up an education after a life where it had been withheld. Caleb, meanwhile, kept to himself and found a job that suited him perfectly well. He washed each night at startling length, for the ink stains from the shop were impossible to rid himself of. (What shop was this? Was he good at what he did?) Without any more information, she would begin to think of George, the stains on his hands from the walnut trees that would blot her dress when he arrived home from a jaunt. What she would do for a hug from her son, to hold him close, to have the chance to tell him of the bravery of his father and the fact that he was gone from them now. So many questions were left unanswered, and so much was left unsaid. But they were alive. Until he wrote again, she would keep worrying a mother's worry, but at least it would be with the knowledge he was out there somewhere, safe and sound, making do.

In the end, only distraction could save her, and even that was temporary. At the barn she ran her hand along its splintered side, then drifted back toward the cabin. This was where it could be erected, she thought. Before the barn. She could hire someone from town. A freedman. A proper mason who could build her fountain. It would be at once grander and less extravagant than Ted's. No cherubs or goddesses. A commemorative note upon its front to honor the memory of a man who had deserved his own fountain in time. He would have it at last.

"And where have you been off to?" said Mildred, standing in the doorway, her cheeks rosy from the fire.

Isabelle didn't wish to say, for she knew the story would unpack itself quickly and her excitement over the fountain would then spill out of her and lead to Mildred's critiques, mostly detailed in the general idea that her mind was full of ideas but that she was scant on execution. Right now she simply wanted the peace that had gathered in her imagination—the thoughts of what might come to be.

"Mildred," she said, her voice unsure, "this is a life, isn't it?"

Mildred looked at her in confusion, her fingers gripping the door as though, with a proper squeeze, it might provide the answer Isabelle sought.

"I suppose it is," she finally said. "If that helps you."

"It does. It does."

"Might you come in?"

"I'll be in shortly," Isabelle said. "Just let me be for now."

Mildred appeared ready to burst out and carry her friend inside herself. But she relented.

"Don't be too long," she said, and closed the door.

Isabelle returned to her thoughts. The fountain would go in the center of the roundabout, she decided, where all who came would see it first, before the cabin, before the barn. It would not quit. This was important. That it run without ceasing in all weather, in all seasons, and that it endure. The dream preoccupied her for so long that she was surprised to find the daylight slipping away from her, and the thoughts followed her into the night, once Mildred had gone home, washing over her as she sat in the dining room staring out the window into the darkness, toward the forest, her imagination venturing further than ever before.

It crossed her mind to have some brandy, a treat she rarely afforded herself. She drank and thought of George, for hadn't he long said the forest was full of magic, strange beasts, great mysteries? She thought of sights unseen, shadows skittering across the landscape—reifying into something more: George himself and Landry, enmeshed in the surroundings, part and parcel with the fluted leaves of the walnut trees, their whispered breath riding on the wind that shook the cabin on long nights.

Or perhaps it would be Caleb and Prentiss who would appear from the hidden depths of the forest, two figures wandering out from the trees as though sprouting from nothing, returning from a journey that had, in time, led them back home. She relished the thought of them observing the farm anew, each plot of land teeming with life—and then, then, they would stop before the fountain, shocked that such beauty might take root in their absence, the water cresting heavenward, forever on, toward parts unknown.

These were just inventions, of course, and she lived knowing, quite well, that such things were not promised to her. She might hope for more but had long ago learned to live with whatever came to pass. Yet sometimes—just sometimes—hope was enough.

ACKNOWLEDGMENTS

———————

To those whom I am eternally grateful to have in my corner:

Emily; Ben; Lena; Bret; Elizabeth; Jason; Mason; Jony; Stevie; Sara; Sarah B.C.; Jane; Billy & Holly; The Michener Center; Evan and Michael; everyone at Little, Brown; Susan; Aaron; Adam; and Jacob.

Mom & Dad. For everything.